LUCIENNE DIVER

QUOTES

"*Bad Blood* is a wonderful read. The mystery keeps the reader engaged, the action makes the reader want to roll with the punches, and the romance makes the senses tingle. This is a great book to coil up with on a lazy Sunday afternoon."
—*Fresh Fiction*

"*Bad Blood* is a delightful urban fantasy, a clever mix of Janet Evanovich and Rick Riordan, and a true Lucienne Diver original."
—*Long and Short Reviews*

Crazy in the Blood

"A smart, sassy heroine, gods and monsters aplenty, a couple of sexy might-be-love interests and knotty mystery to unravel—what more could you want? Lucienne Diver's writing is sharp and funny, making Crazy in the Blood a must-read from start to finish and a more than worthy successor to Bad Blood."
—Christina Henry, author of *Alice* and *Red Queen*

"This is a novel that anyone seeking a terrifically fun novel will enjoy, and just quirky enough that it will attract lots of other readers as well.... One heck of a rollicking good read."
—*Night Owl Reviews*

"The second book in this series is like a mashup of Greek mythology and a Janet Evanovich mystery, with snappy dialogue, romantic entanglements and bodies dropping everywhere."
—*Romantic Times Book Reviews*

Rise of the Blood

"There's a lot going on in this story. It's really pretty much non-stop action of one type or another from beginning to end. Along with it you get a smooth plot flow, nice imagery, a unique locale, lots of interesting characters and great bantering dialogue."
—*Literary Nymphs Reviews*

Battle for the Blood
by Lucienne Diver

ISBN: 978-1-61475-612-5
Cover design by Janet McDonald
Cover artwork images by Kanaxa
Kevin J. Anderson, Art Director
Published by
WordFire Press, an imprint of
WordFire, LLC
PO Box 1840
Monument CO 80132
Kevin J. Anderson & Rebecca Moesta, Publishers
WordFire Press Trade Paperback Edition 2018
Printed in the USA
Join our WordFire Press Readers Group and get free books,
sneak previews, updates on new projects, and other giveaways.
Sign up for free at wordfirepress.com.

❀ Created with Vellum

DEDICATION

*To my fans, who keep me writing, and to Pete and Abby for abso-
lutely everything.*

1

———

Dear Penthouse Forum, I never thought it would happen to me ..."

I stretched invitingly as hands skimmed over my backside, spreading my legs for better access to ... whatever. I wasn't thinking yet. I was barely awake. But feeling, I had that down cold.

In contrast, the hands were warm, almost a furnace against my skin, and that somehow made it all hotter. Slowly, memories of last night came back to me—Apollo's hands cupping my breasts, his thumbs playing with my nipples while I sank down on top of him, my wings flaring out for balance ...

Wings. My eyes shot open, and I tried to roll, but those same wings got in my way, keeping me on my stomach ... or at least half on my side. Those lovely hot hands were gone, but the eyes staring into mine more than made up for the heat. They were, in fact, blazing like the sun.

Apollo. Bed. Gargoyle-like wings. Wrong. All of it.

The fact that it felt right showed just how messed up I was. Yesterday I'd been a bridesmaid at my cousin's wedding, fought off a mother goddess who wanted to reenact *Clash of the Titans,* with me as one of her shiny new avatars, and broken up with my boyfriend ... or, anyway, he'd broken up with me.

Today I woke up in bed with a god. It wasn't as though we hadn't been dancing around our attraction for some time now. Or that I wasn't free to do what I wanted. Or that as rebound sex went, it hadn't been ... amazing didn't even begin to cover it. Earth-shattering, mind-bending, insert-compound-word-here, because one single solitary descriptor just won't do.

The problem was that I wasn't sure it *was* rebound sex. I was terribly afraid that whatever was brewing between Apollo and me was something much more, and I didn't know if I could survive it. The problem with a public figure—god or film star, and he was both—was that a) you knew too much about their past loves and b) you had to live it all out loud. I didn't want to become a tabloid headline or a cautionary tale, like the prophetess Cassandra. I'd already been there and done that and wasn't looking to repeat the experience. Although, the other experiences ... Apollo's hand was now moving over my hip, the one I wasn't lying on, and my body was coming alive, reminding me that there were other experiences I'd practically kill to repeat. My eyes rolled back into my head as his hand slid down to the juncture between my thighs, which started to move farther apart all on their own like he had some kind of power over my body.

"Look at me," he commanded.

I did, but I didn't look him right in the eyes. Not at first. Too intimate. Too revealing. First I wanted to see what this was doing to him. I got an eyeful. A naked Apollo was a glorious thing. His golden mane of hair was wild and tousled from the night before. Bedroom hair to go with his bedroom eyes, rain swept turquoise right now, darker than their usual color of sun-kissed Mediterranean waters. His chest and shoulders were impressive, his washboard abs begging to be touched, tapering to hips that were made for skintight jeans ... or nothing at all.

Like now. But none of that was what held my gaze. His shaft was standing at attention and twitched as my gaze swept over it, as though I'd given it a caress. I felt an answering twinge between my legs and wanted Apollo to bury himself there. Last night, because of my new appendages, I'd had to be on top— not that I'd minded—but I was starting to get other ideas as well, and I wanted to try them out one by one.

Apollo practically purred at that. While he couldn't read my mind, our mental link meant that he could sense strong emotions and right now they were creating a feedback loop with Apollo's own lustful thoughts that were about to reduce me to instinct and incoherency.

Before that could happen, I put a hand to his chest, resisting the urge to stroke and then taste it. "Stop," I said. It came out a lot breathier than I wanted it to. "What are we doing?"

"I'd rather show than tell," Apollo said, his own voice ragged and his hand now exactly where he wanted it, doing exactly what he knew would send me over the edge.

I put my hand over his. "I mean, this can't happen."

Apollo's lips quirked up, and his hand squirmed under mine. "I hate to tell you this, but it already did. If you'll stop overthinking, it can happen again. I'd like that."

He leaned in to kiss my neck, his breath hot against it. My eyes closed against their will and my breath hitched.

"I think you'd like it too," he murmured. Then he bit down on my neck, just a little. Hard enough to feel but not hard enough to mark, and all my objections and any restraint went right out the window.

An hour or two later—because, *dayum*, gods and whatever I was becoming had stamina—we were sweat soaked and waiting for our breathing and our heart rates to come back within doctor recommended parameters.

I was curled up against Apollo's chest, my wings furled tightly against my back, still unable to form coherent thoughts beyond *ohmygod ohmygod ohmygod*. Literally. God. Apollo. Mine. At least, mine for the moment. And *ohmygod* the things he'd done and we'd done and ...

"I think we need to see the Grey Sisters," he said out of the blue. Just like that.

It stabbed me through the heart that he was already back to coherency. But then, he was a god, and I was a mere ... something ... I didn't know anymore. Maybe his mind hadn't been blown like mine had. It was a reminder of why I hadn't gotten involved with him before. Why I couldn't now. He'd own me lock, stock and barrel. I was already half in the bag, the receipt in his hand, complete with return policy.

He must have felt my recoil, because he squeezed me tighter where his hand rested against my hip. "Tori, what's wrong?"

I didn't answer him, but I did rise, needing space. I couldn't look at him, so instead I looked around the hotel room for my clothes. I didn't find them and couldn't remember what I'd done with them the night before. Shredded them, for all I knew. Before I could search, Apollo was out of bed and holding my shoulders in his hands, staring down at me and demanding that I meet his eyes.

I did, reluctantly.

"Don't do this," he said.

"Do what?" I asked nonchalantly, like he couldn't feel me pulling back, no matter how much I pretended otherwise.

"Shut me out. I wasn't thinking about the Grey Sisters while we were ... you know. I mean, I was thinking about your wings, and how I'd like to take you up against the wall if they wouldn't get in the way, but it wasn't until we were lying together that I had a eureka moment that if anyone would know what to do about your wings, it would be them. I was thinking about the next time and how much more I'd like to do." He grabbed my chin as I would have looked aside and held me so I wouldn't break away. "I promise you, there will be a next time. And a next. And a next. You're not getting rid of me now."

I could have kneed him in the nuts or done a million other maneuvers to get free, but that would only give me physical distance. Emotional was another thing.

"I'm rebounding," I told him.

Apollo eyed me, his lips pressed firmly together. "You tell yourself whatever you have to, but from the moment we met, we were inevitable."

"The *sex* was inevitable, maybe," I admitted. Because, why deny it? That ship had sailed. "But the rest? We all know how this ends."

"So now you're omniscient?"

"Maybe. I was yesterday. Or anyway, the mother goddess riding me seemed to know all. Today I have wings. Who knows what tomorrow will bring. Maybe the ability to cloud men's minds. Or read them. I don't imagine that's terribly time consuming. Probably more of a bathroom book than the Great American Novel."

"Now you're babbling. And making sweeping generalizations about my gender. That's like me assuming that all you're interested in is the size of my wallet—"

"It's not your wallet I'm sizing," I cut in.

Apollo growled. It was a little bit sexy, dammit. "You're getting me off point."

"Then make it already."

"You and I can work. There, I said it. You're worried about some inequity of power. I get that, but, Tori, you're not just another mortal. I don't know just what you *are*, but it's neither mortal nor pliable. You challenge me. You surprise and intrigue me. And despite everything you've done to push me away and my best efforts to let you, I have feelings for you that won't seem to be squashed."

The hope in my heart was just a tease, and I knew it. I couldn't even hold a mortal lover.

How was I going to hold a god?

But he'd made one really valid point. I could feel the force of those feelings through our link, and the worst part was, they echoed mine. I'd tried not to want Apollo, which had worked only as long as the very appealing wedge of Detective Nick Armani was between us. Now …

"Fine," I said, finally looking at him again. "I'm not saying we're giving this a shot, but I won't kick you out of bed for eating crackers."

His brows lowered over his eyes, clouding those crystalline waters. "Why would I eat crackers in bed?"

"It's an expression."

"A damn silly one. I'd rather eat—"

"Never mind about that. You were saying about the Grey Sisters?"

"They know all … or can see it with that one crazy eye of theirs. If anyone can tell us what's happening with you, it's them."

"If they don't eat us first."

"Well, there is that."

The Graeae, or Grey Sisters, were a trio of women who shared between them one eye and one tooth. Given the latter, it had never made sense to me that they were also purported to be cannibalistic. What were they going to do, gum people to death? But that was how the tales were told. Rumor had it that knowledge seekers desperate enough to go to them for help, more often found themselves in the Grey Sisters' cookpot. Perseus had tricked them out of the answers he needed to slay my ancestress Medusa only by virtue of stealing their single eye and holding it ransom for the information. But then, Apollo and I had faced down much worse already than three nearly blind, toothless old women.

"Don't you have filming to do? What about your movie?"

"It's on hold right now while our permissions are reevaluated in the wake of the Delphi disaster."

"Which wasn't our fault!" I said.

Sure, there was some major league reconstruction needed on the Pythian field, but that had had nothing to do with the film and everything to do with a titanic mother goddess with a mad-on for the latter-day Olympians.

"Which the authorities might absolutely believe if it hadn't also been for the church."

An earthquake coupled with the open flame of hundreds of tea lights. Come to think of it, the fire hazard aspect of the whole thing might have been a teeny bit our fault.

"So, the long and short of it is that you're a free man."

"At the moment," Apollo said.

"And you know where to find the Graeae?"

"They haven't moved in about a thousand years."

"And you'll order us breakfast?" I asked, hoping to slip that in. It was *his* hotel room, after all. He'd have to authorize the charges.

"What will you be doing?"

"Trying to figure out how to shower with these wings."

"I could wash your back."

A wave of need seemed to crash over me, but I fought it back. "I'm not even sure *I'll* fit in the shower. I think two's a crowd."

He eyed me like he knew there was something more to it. Which there was. "What do you want to eat?"

You, I thought. "Everything," I answered.

"One of everything, coming up."

I disappeared into the bathroom and closed the door behind me, leaning against it for support. My legs were jelly, either from our exertions or in reaction to the events of the past week. Plus, I couldn't shower with Apollo. And not just because of the wings. The last time I'd showered with anyone, it had been Nick in *our* hotel room, just days ago. Nick, the man I thought I'd end up with, who'd ditched me when the crazy world I'd dragged him into had beaten him down. When he'd stepped between me and trouble and gotten a blast of fiery dragon breath in the face. Third-degree burns. He didn't blame me for them. Or at least he hadn't said as much. What he did tell me was that I was walking a path he couldn't walk with me. He was a police detective. He had responsibilities. Nothing about my dangerous don't-ask, don't-tell life fit in with that. Now he was out of commission, flying back to the States for further treatment.

And what was the first thing I'd done? Fallen into bed with his competition, Apollo Demas—Greek god of stage, screen, prophecy, the sun and, apparently, the bedroom. The fact that Nick had taken himself out of the running didn't make me feel any better.

I started the water, as if it would keep Apollo from hearing me think ... or sensing my conflict or whatever. It turned out that by pulling my wings in tightly to me, I could fit them through the door into the shower, and I was able to more or less soap up around them and sluice myself down, but long term something would have to be done with them. Everything was going to be tricky otherwise, from riding in a car to flying in an airplane—or even getting through security. Stakeouts and surveillance would be a special challenge. Hard to blend in when you looked like John Travolta in the movie *Michael*.

Gah, too much to think about. One thing at a time. Surviving the Grey Sisters with all my flesh still on my bones. I let the water wash away everything else.

It was amazing how much a shower could change your mood. I felt clean and fresh. I couldn't quite wrap the towel around myself properly since the wings were in the way, so I looped it around my waist and left my chest bare while I brushed my teeth and hair and generally made myself presentable. I felt nearly alert as I stepped out of the muggy bathroom into the less humid air of the room. The scent of coffee and bacon greeted me, almost better than ambrosia.

"That was fast," I commented to Apollo, who was staring hungrily not at the food, but at me.

"You look like an angel," he said. I gave him a dubious look. "Fallen angel?" he tried.

"Angel of death if you decide to get handsy before I've had copious quantities of caffeine. And bacon. And maybe a croissant."

He laughed and pushed the breakfast tray fractionally in my direction. "Please, help yourself. I don't want to pull back a stump."

The man—god—*guy*—learned fast. But his evening had been every bit as strenuous as mine, so I only took half the bacon and left him the pancakes, though I did fall on the scrambled eggs and chocolate croissant. When we finished I was feeling almost human, despite the fact that I was most assuredly not anymore, not entirely.

Apollo went off to take his shower, and about two seconds later, as I was trying to figure out how to cover up sufficiently to get back to my room for clothes that weren't covered in blood and gore, my cell phone rang.

I had to dig under a pile of discarded clothes to find it, and answered probably an instant before it went over to voicemail. I hadn't even had the chance to see who might be calling. The voice that answered my *hello* was like a slap in the face.

"Tori?" Detective Helen Lau said sharply. "What the hell is going on?"

Detective Lau was Nick's partner ... or had been before she'd flown off on the back of the dragon that had awoken from his sleep beneath the pinnacle of Mount Lee in LA, knocking the *H* off the Hollywood sign.

"Can you be more specific?" I asked.

"Did I not tell you to take care of him? What's this I hear about Nick in a hospital in New York recovering from extensive burns? Needing skin grafts? What did you do to him?" My heart clenched, and all my self-recriminations came back to tackle me to the ground.

"Nick stepped between me and trouble and got burned for it. I'm so sorry. If I could go back ..." I'd still have been possessed by a psychotic mother goddess and unable to change the outcome.

"You make this right. You know people. Gods and ... whatever. You heal him."

"He doesn't want my kind of help, Helen. He flew off without even a goodbye."

"So your feelings are hurt. Boo hoo. You'll heal. He won't. Not without your help. I'm on my way back. When I get there, you'd better have come up with something or I swear I will hunt you down."

She'd do it too. Detective Lau was nothing if not serious. "You're flying back?" I asked.

"Not a commercial flight. No one stamps your passport when you fly off on the back of a dragon. With food and rest stops, it'll take me probably a day and a half, but I'll be there and then we'll have a reckoning."

"Helen, I'm not in New York."

"I don't care where you are. You get help to him. Pronto."

She hung up, and I was still staring at the phone when a very naked Apollo stepped out of the bathroom moments later.

"Who was that?" he asked at the look on my face.

"Detective Lau."

"The Dragon Lady?"

Accurate on so many levels. "The same. She's ordered us to fix Nick. Or else."

"Or else what?"

"I didn't get specifics."

"First we fix you. Then we worry about Nick."

"So you think I need fixing?" I asked, wings fanning out as my hands went to my hips, as if my feathers were ruffled. Only, I didn't have feathers. I had black, membranous wings like those of a bat … or like some images of gorgons on ancient shields and pottery shards.

Apollo came over and kissed me. It was weird how normal it seemed, and how quickly. I stepped back and gave him a dirty look, letting him know he still had to answer. "No," he said with a slow smile. "I think you're perfect just the way you are."

"You have a 'but' face."

He looked like he was about to ask, and then I could see him get it. *"But,"* he added, "you might be a little hard to explain to the paparazzi."

A jolt hit my heart. Despite facing killer gods and goddesses, gargantuan Titans and multi-headed serpents, it was the thought of featuring in the tabloids that sent me running for the hills. "No paparazzi," I told him, like he had control of such things. "None."

Crap, how were we ever going to get out of the hotel without being swarmed? The press had arrived in force. With all the recent insanity, the police had their hands full with crime scenes and damage control. No one had time to body-guard or babysit a Hollywood heartthrob. Apollo could have hired his own bodyguard, of course, but that would only have cramped his style and potentially exposed secrets he'd guarded thus far, like his godhood.

"Don't worry," he said, "I've got it all worked out."

Telling me not to worry or obsess was like telling water not to be wet, but I did my best. "What am I going to wear?"

Apollo took care of that with a phone call and an excessive tip to the maid when she appeared with a bundle of clothes from my room, tucked into a pile of towels she'd brought in case anyone was watching. My pants fit. My shoes from yesterday were badly abused but still wearable, but shirts were out, and bra bands chafed my wings. Luckily, I was not of the size where a bra was an absolute necessity. Certainly not at the level of the stunning starlets Apollo was used to …

I shut that down. I was not an insecure person or one who obsessed about my appearance, and Apollo wasn't going to make me that way. He wanted me or he didn't. After last night, I couldn't doubt that he wanted me, but for how long?

I whooped my mental ass, stole one of Apollo's shirts—blessing him for his broad shoulders—and disappeared into the bathroom with a borrowed brush to do what I could about the wild mass of hair I blamed on the gorgon part of my bloodline. At least my serpentine locks didn't actually have minds of their own. Apollo had some kind of hair gel that I decided to try despite the distinctly masculine scent, and for a wonder my curls practically transformed into ringlets on the spot and played nice. I vowed to buy stock in the product.

I was without makeup, but I never wore much in any case, and if I looked somewhat scary, maybe the Grey Sisters would think twice before eating my face.

Apollo was up next. There was a knock at the door a minute after he stepped out of the bathroom, looking amazing, as always. Upon answering it, we found a doorman ready to conduct us down the service elevator to the dock entrance through which supplies and laundry came in and out. And, apparently, special guests trying to avoid a media frenzy. Just outside the dock doors a car waited. I didn't recognize the car itself, but the driver …

"Viggo!" I cried.

Apollo opened the back door and hurried me inside before I could draw attention. "Ms. Karacis!" our driver answered. "I am so glad to see you okay. But your back … You are carrying yourself with difficulty. You are all right?"

The wings flapped under Apollo's shirt, fighting for space I didn't have to give them. I just hoped Viggo wouldn't notice. "Just a little stiff still," I told him. "But what are you doing here? I thought you worked for Uncle Hector."

"I have him on loan," Apollo said.

"With a bonus!" Viggo agreed. "Hazard pay."

I laughed. "Glad to have you aboard."

Viggo took off as soon as Apollo was in beside me with the door closed, before we'd even had the chance to snap our seat belts.

"Where to?" I asked, realizing I still didn't know.

"Oh, didn't I tell you? We're on to Metéora. The Grey Sisters' cave is halfway up the side of one of the cliffs."

I groaned. No wonder he'd waited to tell me until I was a captive audience. Viggo drove only slightly slower on the switchbacks down the side of Mount Parnassus than he did changing lanes in Athens, and my heart was entirely in my throat. I hated heights. And now I had to contemplate scaling the cliffs of Metéora to meet three carnivorous crones. My life, I thought, could not possibly get any crazier.

I was wrong.

2

If Delphi was the navel of the world (so said myth), then Metéora was Gaia's hand flipping mankind the bird. Great projections of rock shot up out of the ground like Mother Earth giving us all the finger several times over. The rocks rose straight skyward to the height of mountains but without a single gentle incline. It was cliffs everywhere you looked. Metéora was a spot so unique, so stunning, so inhospitable as to be absolutely one of the most compelling places in the world. Even we Greeks, who liked to build on the tippy-top of mountains, had left it alone for ages and ages ... until hermit monks determined to withdraw from the ever-encroaching world, scaled the heights and eventually built atop the unlikely peaks.

I couldn't even imagine how that had been accomplished. There'd been no roads, no gentle gradients to allow for the transport of materials. No airlifts or giant cranes or any modern conveniences, which nonetheless would have been difficult if not impossible to maneuver on the rocky surfaces. Legend had it that the founder of the first monastery, Athanasios, had been carried to the heights by an eagle. Now monasteries stood atop the various cliffs of Metéora like fairy tale castles.

But before there were structures, there were the caves. The cliffs were peppered with them. A few were highlighted with ancient symbols or more modern graffiti. One or two were decorated with brightly colored flags, candles and kitsch like a memorial wall. But most were unobtrusive, difficult to see with the naked eye, at least from the base of the cliffs or from the stone steps or few roads that had finally been carved out of the rock. I was guessing the Grey Sisters' cave would be off the beaten path. Otherwise, there'd have been scads of tales about tourists or supplicants going missing over the years. As for the hermits, well, they'd kept to themselves. Who was going to report them missing?

With family in the nearby town of Kalambaka, I kept up somewhat with local news. I knew the cliffs claimed a few casualties each year, disappearances chalked up to tragic accidents or becoming lost in the crazy thick fogs that would sometimes roll in, making the monasteries look like castles in the clouds. I wondered now whether the cliffs were truly to blame.

Viggo had parked in a little visitors' area, alongside tour buses and a few rental cars. Apollo and I stood outside the vehicle now, contemplating the massive stone formations.

"We go the rest of the way on foot," Apollo said. "Their cave is on one of the deserted pillars. There's a monastery up top, but long since abandoned. There never were steps built for this one. In the olden days, pilgrims and visitors were lifted in a net to the top."

My heart nearly stopped just at the thought. "That sounds ... safe."

"It's all about faith. Anyway, I'd never let you fall."

My wings flared in indignation at the thought that it was his business to *let* me do anything, but the shirt kept them contained. "I think you've got that backwards. I might let *you* fall, but good luck with the vice versa."

The thought should have been more comforting, but I'd lived with the fear of heights a lot longer than the wings, and it wasn't going to give way quite so easily.

Apollo led the way to a path that seemed to wind among the pillars, and I followed, wondering how on earth my life could get any weirder. It wasn't a healthy thought, I knew that. The universe tended to answer such rhetorical questions with a big, hearty belly laugh and an avalanche of irony.

We stopped before one particular pillar that jutted straight toward the sky. There were small rocks at our feet, indicating some erosion, but at a glance I couldn't see any decent hand- or footholds.

"I don't suppose you grabbed Spiro's climbing gear?" My brother's ropes and anchors had come in handy when we'd descended into the underworld, but we hadn't exactly come out the way we'd gone in, and for all I knew, the gear was still in place.

"No. We wouldn't be allowed to use it here anyway. It's a sacred site."

"Well, I can bust out my wings, but someone might notice."

Apollo was shaking his head before the words were even out of my mouth. "No, we have to free-climb."

I stared. "Come again."

"You know, one hand over the other, feet tucked into toeholds."

I eyed the sheer cliff in front of us. "What toeholds?"

"Follow me."

Yeah, because I wouldn't be distracted at all by his fine backside in his tight jeans. On the other hand, hanging on to a slab of rock for dear life might have a way of focusing my attention. I wondered momentarily if having wings was really so bad. I'd get used to them. If the PI business failed, I could always go back to the circus as a sideshow act, assuming the Rialto Bros. hadn't blacklisted me throughout the circus world ... a story in and of itself.

"You're not afraid, are you?" Apollo asked.

He knew very well that I was, but also that I was too stubborn to ever admit it. "Whatever, just go. I'll be right behind you," I snapped.

"That's my girl."

It gave me a pang. Armani ... Nick ... had said the same thing, and where was he now? Apollo hoisted himself up, using nothing but the strength of his arms and legs, which, as I knew, was pretty impressive. The muscles in his arms bulged, straining the fabric of his heather-gray Henley, but I forced my gaze away, made myself focus on where exactly he stuck his hands and what tiny divots he found for his feet. Then I tried to mimic him. With my fear of heights, I'd never been a climber, and now with the weight of my wings on my back, my balance was all off. I was down before I was even up. I landed on my feet, like a cat, my wings beating against my borrowed shirt, trying desperately to give me the lift I needed.

Apollo looked down at me, concern written all over his face.

I tried again, this time not straining to hold my wings tightly to my body, but letting them adjust as they felt they needed to, but the shirt kept stopping them and the whole thing was just awkward.

I looked back up at Apollo. "You know, a real god would be able to just snap his fingers and get us to the top."

"A real god, huh? Do I have to remind you whose name you were calling out last night?" I blushed. I *never* blushed. Not since I was about fifteen and walked in on my brother, Spiro, with one of his many conquests.

"A reminder would be good," I said. It certainly beat out scaling a mountain. "You'll have to catch me first."

He was off like a rocket. He climbed like a spider ... or like the rays of the sun as it rose in the sky. Smooth, effortless. I could have watched him all day. I was tempted to do just that. But then I'd never hear the end of it ... or see the end of my extra appendages. What good were wings if you couldn't use them for fear of being seen? And what then? It wasn't like Nick Fury was going to descend and insist that I join the Avengers or anything, which was good, because I'd totally have to kick Tony Stark's irresponsible ass, and I wasn't entirely sure I could take him.

My brain tended to babble when faced with fear.

I grabbed a handhold, psyched myself up, and heaved. Two feet off the ground, points for me. I shoved one of those feet into a teeny-tiny crevice and felt along with my free hand for a protruding rock or something else to hang on to. And so it went, inch by grueling inch, Apollo calling out encouragement from above.

"Now to the right," he said after a while. My arms were shaking, and I could feel one of my calf muscles starting to twerk. "There's a little ledge. It will give you some relief."

I was beyond ready for relief.

Going sideways, as it turned out, wasn't any easier than going upward, especially not with muscle fatigue setting in, but as soon as my big toe touched that ledge, the sense of relative safety that washed over me was immense. And dangerous. My muscles wanted to relax, and I couldn't let that happen. I pulled myself fully onto the small ledge from which Apollo had watched my ascent and glanced over at him, my face still pressed against the rock and my hands holding me there. The ledge wasn't large enough to let go.

"Good girl," he said.

"Should I bark? Wag my tail? Are you going to pet me behind the ears?"

"Is that where you want me to pet you?"

"Down, boy. We're halfway up a mountain."

He leered. "I didn't say it had to be *now*."

"Later then, if we live."

"Incentive. I love it."

I smiled. Halfway up a mountain, hanging on for dear life, and I smiled. A sure sign of insanity.

"Come on, it's not much farther," he said.

I groaned, but followed. He was right. Five minutes that felt like fifteen later, we hit another ledge, this one much broader. As soon as my weight rested on it fully, I wanted to collapse. My legs wanted to give out. But I knew that would be a bad idea. I might not get up again, and I'd be a sitting duck for the sinister sisters.

Apollo handed me one of the bottles of water Viggo had provided, and I drank it down in two gulps.

"Don't make yourself sick," Apollo said.

I eyed him over the rim of my water bottle.

"Oh right," he added.

Whether it was the ambrosia, the nectar, the possession by a pissed off mother goddess or Apollo's breath of life, something had recently kickstarted some of my dormant gorgon genes. It had rebuilt me—better, stronger, faster ... and with wings. I was still waiting for the tusks and serpents to sprout. I wasn't sure I *could* get sick anymore, not naturally. I could probably still die of thirst ... probably ... but it would likely take a helluva lot longer than it used to. I wasn't planning to test my limits.

"So where's the cave?" I asked.

Apollo got a funny look on his face. "You haven't noticed the trail?"

"What trail?" I looked around. All I saw were rocks, rocks, sheer rock face and some scree. Our ledge did go on for several feet, at the end of which there was a wrinkle in the stone that might possibly be the entrance to a cave.

Apollo reached out a hand, and for a moment I thought he

was going to wipe sweat off my brow, but instead he tapped my forehead, directly above and between my brows. The something chakra or ... The world blurred and returned, like a lens had dropped away, and I looked down at the rocks around us ... or what I'd assumed were rocks.

What I saw now were bones of every kind, some with ends broken or gnawed, bearing deep gouges like toothy track marks. Most disturbing of all were the skulls, some clearly animal and some clearly ... not. I was no forensic expert, but even I knew a human mandible when I saw one. A complete cranium would have been creepy enough, but skulls had become commercialized, used to decorate tables and T-shirts. Bracelets and barrettes and purses, oh my! But mandibles, long bones, fragments that defied identification were much creepier, especially because there were so many of them. We were walking the crime scene of multiple murders.

"Why didn't I see it?" I asked, focusing on the mundane, doing my best to breathe through my rising tension.

"Glamour. Anyone with human blood is susceptible."

"Can they glamour me again or will whatever you did hold?"

"I don't know. I dropped your blinders, but this was a blanket glamour. If the sisters try something targeted to you directly, I might not know it but for your reaction."

"But our connection ..."

"Whatever you see or think or feel will seem perfectly normal to you, so you won't radiate any alarm. Unless, of course, they make you see *me* as a flesh-eating monster."

"Good, let's hope for that."

"Yes, let's," he said with a wry smile.

We made our way toward the cave entrance, which I could now see for what it was. The parade of bones got thicker as we approached, as if the bones had just spilled out like fast food wrappers from a junker car. Three steps and we were no longer able to sweep the bones aside or step between them. There were just too many. We were walking on arms and legs and worse. The bones rattled and shifted and grated against each other like a cheap alarm system, pots and pans under the windows. My only consolation was that nothing squelched. The slaying sisters, to their credit, did seem to make the most of their meals, leaving nothing behind for scavengers. Or maybe the scavengers had already been and gone ... or become dessert.

The entrance itself was nothing special. Or wouldn't have been, if not for the bones piled knee-high and higher against the walls.

"Do we slog or blast our way through?" I asked. "It's not as if the sisters could have missed the fact that we're here."

Apollo did his best to step over the bones piled in the entryway and reached a hand back to help me do the same. Blasting through would have been my preference, but, then, he knew that. I didn't really see a point in being all polite with mass murderers. They never showed the same consideration when serving you up with fava beans and a nice Chianti.

Sighing, I took his hand and played the lady for once. My foot came down badly on something that rolled beneath my foot, and I knew that I'd found a skull. My ankle twisted, and I was actually glad to have Apollo's hand holding me up.

"Strange how this wasn't on any tourist map," I quipped. "It's a gothic paradise."

"So it is, dearie," came a high, sweet voice from within the cave. "Come, come, let us get a good look at you. It's been so long since we've had willing visitors."

Three cackles greeted the statement, and it sent a shiver from the base of my spine straight up to my hairline, raising the little hairs there and all across my arms.

My eyes adjusted slowly to the darkness within the cave, but there was nothing immediate to see but more skulls. Apollo and I stepped carefully, testing our footing with every step. I wondered what a caver or some other unwary visitor would see and feel. Would the ground seem not to shift under their feet? Would it appear to be a cave-in with an abundance of detritus?

After about fifteen feet, the cave opened from a fairly narrow tunnel entrance—the better to limit and trip up escape—to a full-blown chamber with high ceilings and enough space for three sinister sisters, a large stone cooking pit with a tripod cauldron in the middle and a hole in the ceiling to draw away smoke. Their gothic version of home decorating. Oh, there were chairs (made of bone), a long table (also bone), and sleeping mats against one wall that seemed to have been woven from hair. I didn't want it to be human and hoped I wouldn't get close enough to find out. I debated seriously whether we needed the Graeae enough for me not to end them. My wings were nothing compared to the murder of innocents.

"Just wait," Apollo said, gripping my hand harder. "Information first. Remember, many have tried to take them down. You're probably walking on some of their bones."

It didn't make me feel any better. My wings ruffled, met the resistance of the shirt and reluctantly settled. I shook with the effort to restrain myself and gripped Apollo's hand even harder in return, as if punishing him for my restraint. He could take it.

We got close enough for a good look at the sinister sisters, and I almost regretted the glamour having fallen away. Without it, the three women were cadaverous, looking more like Gollum from *Lord of the Rings* than anything semi-human. Their clothes hung on them like rags, blood and possibly other fluids dried onto them. I couldn't see their ribs beneath the rags, but the sisters' arms stuck out, bones visible beneath their paper-thin skin. Their faces looked half-mummified, dried-out husks with sunken cheeks. Their eye sockets were eerie for their emptiness. Only one sister held an eye to the center of her forehead, right where Apollo had tapped me to make me see. The eye was milky, like an opal without the fire, and rolled as she held it, looking from one of us to the other. The water in my stomach wanted to come up again, and I realized I *could* still be sick.

She laughed wickedly at the sight of us. One of her sisters sniffed the air like a canine, a lascivious smile spreading across her face. "I smell godling. Godlet? Godget? Hard to tell. The scent is strong with this one, but overlaying it. Human. Female human." Her mouth curled in on itself as she talked, toothless, her words sibilant like a serpent's hiss. She sniffed again. "Or, somewhat human. Hmm, something I have not scented in a long, long time." She stepped out from near the cookpot and toward me. It was all I could do not to retreat from her. Apollo stepped between us, shielding me, and she snorted wetly, wiping away the snot with the back of her hand. "Musty ... like gorgon."

"Gorgon!" hissed the other sister without the eye, and I noticed that *she* bore the tooth. Not pointed and fanglike as ancient art portrayed, but one long, freakish protuberance, curved inward slightly like a shovel and serrated like a saw blade. Like a beaver's front two teeth had been fused and sharpened to points, the better to rip flesh off bones.

"Part gorgon," Apollo admitted while I was still worrying about whether they considered gorgon a delicacy. "And, thus, family."

I stared at him now. The gorgons and the Graeae were related? My family tree kept getting weirder and weirder. If I looked closely, their ropy hair, like long-neglected dreadlocks, might possibly resemble sluggish serpents.

"Family," the one with the tooth hissed. "They don't call, they don't write."

"Ah, but it seems they send care packages," the eyeless, toothless one said slyly, coming closer to me.

It was all I could do not to give ground and show weakness as she leaned in to sniff me like a bloodhound. I planted my feet instead, ready to fly into a frenzy if she tried anything more. My wings flared, wanting to stretch and prep for launch, and she fell back, searching the vicinity blindly. "What's that? Wings? Who do you have with you? Not the trickster. He is forbidden."

The one with the eye had held back, taking it all in. When she started cackling, my head wanted to split open right down the center. It was as sharp as a hatchet to the skull. The other sisters joined in, cackling with her, sharing a joke they hadn't even heard. Unless they had ... unless they shared some kind of unspoken communication, which was creepy on a strategic level. Between Apollo and me, we could take them, no problem. Even at two against three, they were frankly outnumbered. But three who thought as one, forming an unholy trinity ... It was a concept that occurred one way or another throughout mythology. Numbers didn't have any meaning we didn't assign them, but there were certain numbers—3, 12, and 666 just to name a few—that held untold eons of belief to reinforce their strength. I wouldn't say I trembled, but my certainty fled.

"This is the one!" the sighted sister crowed. "She will fight the Bringer of Plagues."

"Ah, but will she win?" queried one of her sisters. I didn't look to see which one. I didn't take my eyes away from the single opalescent eye staring at me with a mix of glee and avarice I didn't understand.

"I'll do what?" I asked, feeling queasy. Bringer of Plagues didn't sound at all promising. "Apollo, what do you know about this?"

He was still next to me, but also not. His gaze had unfocused, and it was clear he was miles away, maybe entire continents. "Prophecy," he said, largely to himself, caught up in suddenly inspired foreseeing.

"Give me the eye," the toothless sister insisted. "I want to see her. Does she look good enough to eat?"

I stared at Apollo and debated slapping sense into him or just grabbing him and running, but settled for shaking him by the shoulder. I met no resistance. He wobbled but didn't go down.

The toothless one plucked the eye right from the forehead of the other, and a fight ensued. The third chomped on the arm of the one now holding the eye, blood gushing out as she shrieked and dropped the orb, which splatted on the ground and rolled in the blood, taking on a rose-red cast.

My wings were desperate to unfurl, and this time I gave them free reign, tearing my shirt off so that they could reach their full extension and facing the sisters bare-chested as a harpy. I gathered my legs and leapt up into the air, making a beeline for the bouncing eye, the demented little deejay in my brain playing "On Top of Spaghetti," imagining the eye as the lost meatball. *That's all it is*, I told myself, diving for it and trying to ignore the gory, gooshy feel of it in my hand as I flew with it back to Apollo. Two of the sisters were scrabbling about on the floor, trying to find the eye by feel. The third was listening to the wing beats, sniffing the air, figuring it out.

"She's stolen the eye!" she wailed to her sisters. "Stop her."

She lurched my way blindly, driven by her other senses, and I knocked her aside with a wing as she came close, sending her nosediving into the bones of her previous meals. The second sister fell over her feet, and the third mystically veered around them, heading straight for me. The eye in my hand rolled, and I shrieked but held tightly. Could she still be connected to the eye? Seeing through it? I wanted to be sick, but later. No time now.

The Grey Sister still standing leapt as if the rolling bones were springboards and flew in my direction. I instantly rose into the air, winging my way to the top of the cave, leaving Apollo behind, still locked in his vision. I dove as she would have hit him, knocking her to the ground in a literal flying tackle. We went down in a daze of brittle bones snapping beneath us. She fought like a rabid dog, kicking, screaming, snapping at me as if she would bite, but, luckily, she wasn't the one with the tooth. I wondered, though, if her nails might be toxic enough to do me in all on their own. They were ragged and filthy, and she herself smelled of vermin droppings and decay, the sweet-sour scent of death and body odor. I choked on the cloud of stench and pulled back the hand fisted around the eye to let it fly hard at her jaw. She went limp beneath me as my fist connected, her arms falling to her sides.

I breathed out a deep sigh of relief. I didn't dare take a corresponding breath in, not until I got some distance from her.

Apollo snapped back to himself suddenly and flashed a gaze around to catch himself up on what he'd missed. A look of amusement crossed his face. "Chick fight? And I missed it?"

I had a sharp retort ready, but the other two sisters were collecting themselves and skittering toward us on hands and feet.

I fixed them with my gorgon glare and debated hitting them with it, stopping them in their tracks, but I needed information. Silence and stillness were all well and good, but they couldn't solve everything. Instead, I held the eye above my head and threatened with all of my body language to smash it to the ground.

"I have the eye," I told them, realizing that while I held it they couldn't appreciate the full effect of my posturing. "All I want is information. If you tell me what I need to know, you get the eye back in one piece. If you hold back or you make one wrong move, I'll stomp it to paste."

"It's ours," the toothy one protested.

"Yes, it is, just like the flesh you want to rip from my body is mine. I'd prefer to keep it, thank you very much. I'll do the same with your eye unless you tell me how I can control my wings. Is there a way to banish them until I need them? Get rid of them entirely?" Though I wasn't actually sure I wanted to do that last. As annoying as they could be, especially for my wardrobe, they were proving very handy.

"You're naked," Apollo said with amusement, but quietly so as not to ruin my moment.

"Only from the waist up," I countered.

"I like it."

"Later," I told him.

"Is that all?" asked the sister who'd originally worn the eye. She cackled. "No world peace? No end to strife? Riches beyond your wildest imaginings?"

"The wings," I repeated. "I have no confidence in world peace. The only true peace lies in death, isn't that right?"

The other two sisters joined in the cackling now. "Oh, she's good. Wise beyond her years. Medusa was like that...."

Great, Medusa and me ... just like two peas in a pod. But where she could turn men ... or women ... to stone, all I could do was stop them in their tracks. And only temporarily. Hell, Hollywood starlets could stop traffic without even the gorgon glare.

"Enough with the laugh track," I snapped. "Tell me about the wings."

The sisters turned blindly toward each other, seeming to communicate without words. I was certain they made up for a lack of the usual senses with others of an extrasensory sort. "There is a way," the toothy one admitted finally, "but it must be taught. There is no snapping of fingers, no potion."

"Then teach me."

"For a price."

"The eye—" I began.

"Make no mistake," said the toothy one, "we will get the eye if we have to rip your arm off with it." The other two licked their lips at the very thought. "But the teaching comes at a cost. It takes time you don't have ... that the world might not have."

The eye rolled again, and it was all I could do to hold on to it. When I turned my hand over and opened the palm to see what it was up to, the disembodied orb stared back at me. No, not *stared* ... glared. If it could shoot lasers, I'd be toast.

"So dramatic," another sister cackled. "Death, destruction. Sickness, sadness, chaos, killings ... It sounds divine."

"And when the hunger comes for us?" another sister asked. "When there is nothing left of the world but the bones?"

The first hissed. "We will eat like queens."

"For a time," she agreed.

"What is this about death and destruction?" I demanded. "What about this price and the world running out of time? Stop speaking in riddles."

The toothy one stared at me. Or rather the eye stared and she seemed to look right through it. "Namtar, God of Plagues, has risen. Even now he calls his followers to him—the nosoi, the demons, the djinn. Already they converge. The apocalypse has begun."

"Apocalypse?" I asked, not happy when it came out semi-strangled.

"That is the cost," agreed the so-far-silent sister. "You defeat Namtar and we will teach you. Otherwise, none of this will matter."

I looked to Apollo, hoping he'd tell me that they were pulling my leg, that they did this to everybody, but he met my gaze gravely. "It's true," he said. "I've seen it."

"Your vision?" I asked.

"Cities laid waste. Billions dead. The Black Death, the Spanish Flu, cancer, AIDS ... they are nothing by comparison. It has to be stopped."

"And *I'm* supposed to stop this thing?" I asked, horrified.

"*We* are," he said, taking the hand not holding the bloody eye.

I stared at the sisters. "So, basically, I save the world and you'll teach me how to control my wings? It hardly seems like a fair trade."

"There is one more thing," the toothy one told me, ignoring my protest. "You will need Perseus's famed sword, forged by Hephaestus and coated with Medusa's venomous blood when the hero severed her head from her body. It is the only chance you have against Namtar."

"And where am I supposed to find this legendary sword?" I asked, torn between stunned disbelief and abject fear. I'd been through so much already. Karma seriously owed me some downtime before saddling me with an apocalypse.

"You'll have to pry it from his cold, dead hands, of course," one of the other sisters said with glee.

"Now," hissed the other toothless sister. "The eye!"

She said it with such longing, such desperation, that I felt mean for what I was about to do, but only for a second. Only until I thought about the fact that we were standing in a cave loaded up not with treasure but with the remains of their kills. Then I felt much better about lobbing the eye between the sisters and watching it disappear into the pile of bones. They screeched and dove, scrabbling with hands and feet, pulling each other's hair when it got in their way or gouging flesh.

Apollo and I fled. We didn't run, not with bones sliding beneath our feet with every step, but we hit the ledge as quickly as possible.

"Can they be trusted to teach me?" I asked. "Once I've defeated Namtar—*if* I defeat him—can I trust them not to go back on their word?"

"If you defeat Namtar, do you really think they'd dare get all up in your grill?"

That put a feeble grin on my face. Apollo's slang was years out of date. It was cute that he tried.

"Besides, bargains are sacred. There's no saying they won't try to eat you afterward, but, by gods, you'll know how to use your wings when they go in for the kill."

"That's comforting," I said. "Isn't it?"

3

———————

"Buttons aren't rocket science."
   —Tori Karacis

I realized as soon as we got out into the sunlight that I'd left my shirt behind. I was full frontal with wings unfurling out of my back. Anyone looking up at that moment would either see me for an angel or a flasher, depending on the strength of their faith and their eyesight.

"Shirt!" I demanded of Apollo.

He didn't take his eyes off me until he absolutely had to in order to pull his shirt over his head, but at least he didn't dawdle. Undressing wasn't exactly rocket science. It didn't require his full attention. Apparently, my near nudity was another matter.

Thankfully, it didn't last. As soon as he handed me his shirt, I slipped it on, wrestling with my wings and finally accepting his help. *He* was now naked from the waist up and I totally understood his distraction. I might have breasts, but he had washboard abs and pecs to die for, not to mention broad shoulders and strong arms ... I had to look away before I tore the rest of his clothes off and gave Metéora's tourists and pilgrims some destination photos that would never make the family album.

"So, up was fun," I said, looking pointedly to the left of him. "How about down?"

"Same way we came."

"I was afraid you were going to say that."

If I wasn't afraid of exposing myself to the world, I'd have tried out those wings again. As it was, our descent was slow going, and I slid the last ten feet or so, but I managed to make it to the bottom with more than half the skin I'd started with, which I counted a victory.

Finally at the car, Viggo looked us over, Apollo in particular, because how could you not, and asked, "It's good we find a hotel close by?"

It hadn't even occurred to me that we'd need a hotel, but, of course, there was no way we were driving hours back to Delphi now. For one, I was pretty sure we'd be violating some kind of labor law with Viggo, and for another we needed to figure out our next move before we went anywhere. No sense going backward to go forward, and I had no idea where to even start looking for Perseus's cold, dead body.

And so we drove into Kalambaka, a place dimly remembered from my childhood and occasional trips back for family. If I'd thought ahead, I could have called someone and found us a place to stay, but then I'd have had to explain why I brought one date to my cousin's wedding and was there with another. And a visit was never just a visit. It was a reunion, an excuse for a gathering that turned into a party, with much drinking and more storytelling, most of it likely at my expense.

I was tired and still shaken from the heights and the homicidal sisters. I vowed that after Namtar, after I learned to control my wings, I would do something about the Graeae.

No more tourists were going to go missing on my watch. It had killed me to walk away from them. No, bad choice of words. It hadn't killed me. That would have been noble, going down fighting. Instead, I'd run and lived to fight another day.

We got two rooms. Viggo took one, and Apollo and I the other. Shacking up, and so soon. I pushed the thought aside. We had way bigger things to worry about than whether I should be ashamed of myself. (I was.)

As soon as we got into our room—nice but not large, with a town view rather than one facing the stunning vistas of Metéora—I grabbed the remote and turned on the TV, looking for news. If the grand high poobah of plagues had risen, surely there was news. There was always something—swine flu, Ebola, E. coli outbreaks, hepatitis, brain-eating bacteria. It wasn't like Namtar's hench-demons had taken time off in his absence. But I was looking for something bigger. I had a feeling I'd know it when I saw it.

I found a news station, but it was on the financial segment, so I flipped around again, finding mostly commercials before going back to the program, determined to wait it out.

In the meantime, I commanded Apollo, "Tell me about this Namtar."

He eyed me, as if he could see my breasts *through* his shirt, which maybe he could since I was braless. I crossed my arms over my chest so he could focus. His gaze rose to mine, disappointment in his eyes. "Like the sisters said, he's an ancient bringer of plagues. Babylonian originally, I think, though he certainly didn't confine himself. Ugly as sin, slothful by nature, hence diseases that self-perpetuate. All he has to do is start up an infection, then sit back and watch the carnage. I hear he's partial to popcorn." He and Hermes had that in common. Chaos and properly popped kernels of corn.

"You're acting calm now, but I saw your face back at the

cave," I said. "Even the Grey Sisters were afraid, not savoring the death and destruction. What did you see?"

Apollo looked away, like maybe that would help him hide the truth. "Madness," he said. "Madness and ugly, violent death. People ripping each other to shreds. Blood, so much blood. Rivers of blood."

His words had a tremor to them, which made them that much more powerful. If Apollo was worried ...

On the television, the news anchors were back, and something they'd said swung my attention back to the set, where they were showing an external shot of a hospital in a city setting. It was big, brick and blocky with lots of small windows ... and cordoned off by police vehicles. I turned up the sound. Apollo came to sit beside me on the bed and took my hand. "... in front of Lenox Hill Hospital in Manhattan, where both perpetrators and victims from yesterday's so called 'zombie attack' have been brought for treatment. We're being told that all involved are being kept in an isolated area of the ICU until the cause of the incident and any possible contagions are evaluated. While the police have said only that they won't comment on an ongoing investigation, and the hospital has yet to release any statement, witnesses have made reference to the 'Causeway Cannibal' case a few years ago in Florida, where a Miami man attacked and ate the face off another man before police were forced to shoot him dead. Drugs were blamed for that incident, though official toxicology reports didn't find drugs in his system that would have explained such extreme and irrational behavior."

The scene in the inset window behind the anchor changed to that of a park and a grainy stop-motion picture of a man and a child, looking wild and unfocused. "This was the scene yesterday in Riverside Park." The obviously amateur video began to animate, and the figures jerked in a disturbing fashion, as if their brains and bodies weren't communicating with each other. The child, a girl, had long, lank hair. As she shambled along, the videographer made a comment for the camera, speculating about whether this was a zombie crawl or promo for another upcoming show. The girl suddenly raised her head and lurched in his direction with an inhuman sound that made all the hair on my body stand on end. Then she jumped as though someone had shot her out of a sling, and the camera spun and landed face up at the trees while howls of shock and horror echoed off to the side. Not a millisecond later, it caught the other figure in midair, the herky-jerky man launching himself right over the camera to join the attack.

The scene stopped, and even the news anchor, who must have seen it time and again already, was stunned to silence for half a second. When she started up again, the horror lingered in her voice. "The man taking the video was rushed to the emergency room, but unfortunately died of shock and blood loss on the way there, his throat apparently ripped out. His girl-friend, who was with him at the time of the attack, is listed in critical condition."

The camera pulled back to show a male co-anchor at her side and then panned entirely to him. "Since then, other reports have come in of a woman, a tourist from the Nether-lands visiting the United States, discovered perched over her husband's bloody body when the maid came in to service the room, his throat reportedly torn out. Trouble on the L Line when a commuter, apparently covered in blood, dropped a heart rolled up in his morning paper and people fled in panic, one falling between cars.

"No official link has yet been made between the cases, but according to our affiliates in New York—"

There was a knock on the door, and I nearly jumped out of my skin. "Are you expecting anyone?" Apollo asked me.

I shook my head and reached into my bag for my pepper

spray, tossing it to him. He caught it one-handed on his way to the door and looked out the peephole.

"Who is it?" I asked.

"Trouble."

Apollo opened the door and stepped out of the way so that I could see. There stood Hades. Not the flaming-haired, James Woods, Disney-fied version of him from *Hercules*, where Hera is a wispy little blonde and Megaera is the heroine rather than a crazed killer. But the real deal. Dark hair, eyes as black as kohl, overtall and unmistakable in light-wash jeans, a sunny orange Pirana Joe T-shirt and a white blazer with rolled-up sleeves. His aboveground wear. Possibly he would have blended in back in the original Don Johnson *Miami Vice* days, but in the twenty-second century he was an anachronism.

Behind him walked Hecate, all in black leather—pants, biker jacket, knee high stiletto boots. Even her hair was jet black, twisted and uncontrollable, sticking out like live wires around her head. She looked like a badass biker/dominatrix. Strangely, it worked for her.

Hecate slid down her sunglasses—black, of course—as she entered the room. Light seemed to disappear into her eyes with no escape. My brain dithered, as it sometimes did, wondering how she'd fare as a manga character with no little white wedge of light for her oversized eyes. My mind worked in mysterious ways.

Apollo closed the doors behind them. With everyone else standing, I felt at a disadvantage as the only one sitting, but I wasn't about to reveal my discomfort. Hades stopped by the desk and leaned casually against it, studying Apollo and me. There was no missing that I was in one of Apollo's shirts or that Apollo ... wasn't.

"Don't you two look cozy," Hades began.

"We are," I said. "Not that it's any of your business. I suppose you're here about this." I gestured with the remote toward the television, but already they'd moved on to some trouble in the Middle East, face eating forgotten.

"You've got to do something," Hades said. But it wasn't me he was looking at.

"About?" Apollo asked, crossing his arms over his chest. Hecate clicked her tongue in disappointment.

"Look, I was about to call in that favor you owe me, have you turf-sit the underworld while I go on a well-deserved vacation. I'm thinking maybe an active volcano somewhere, get a front row seat for the panic and destruction. Reconnect with an old flame."

Hades and Pele? The mind boggled.

"But there are rumblings. Your blood woke Rhea. She woke the Titans. Whatever fallout exists, it's *your* job to fix it," Hades continued, giving Apollo his best stare-down.

"First of all, it was *Zeus's* priests who spilled my blood and performed the ritual, so if you're looking for someone to blame, I'd start there. Second of all, *what rumblings*? For Olympus's sake, you sound like one of my Oracles. Can't you talk in a straight line?"

Hades's dark brows raised, and I thought I saw the hellfire spark in his eyes. "Be glad I don't strike you down where you stand."

"Hit me with your best shot," Apollo fired back. I tried not to laugh as I heard Pat Benatar in my head singing backup. Death threats from the god of the dead were no laughing matter. But still.

"Boys," Hecate said, stepping between them, drawing all eyes. "Apocalypse first, grudge match later."

I latched on to the important part of all that. "What do you know about the apocalypse?"

Hades looked from Hecate to me to Apollo again. Yes, there was definite hellfire in his eyes. "Souls started arriving yesterday. Well, souls are always arriving, but these ... these were mad.

Stark, raving mad. No humanity left, just appetite. Hunger, thirst. We have a place for damaged souls like this, of course. It is a dark place, howling and unhappy. Dante would have called it the seventh circle of hell, although his *Inferno* is about as accurate as the *National Informer*. If he'd ever had a tour, he'd never have lived to tell about it. But now, the lost souls batter against their barrier, ravenous, hungering. Our boundaries wear thin as it is, with the damage of the Titans rising and all of our energies going to repairs. With the world's population explosion, the various underworlds are stretched to their breaking points."

"Wait," I cut in, "*various* underworlds? You're not just talking about the Elysian Fields versus Tartarus, are you?"

Hades's eyes blazed as he turned them on me, twin infernos that looked about to explode. He was *not* happy about what he had to say. He was not happy that he had to say it to *me*, a mere mortal ... or something. In fact, if looks could kill ...

"No," he growled. "I am sure you're aware by now or have been told ..." he shot a glare at Apollo, "... that belief and worship fuel our power? They also shape reality. There are many different beliefs and many different afterlives, with divinities for all. Sometimes there are turf wars as one faith is lost and another rises or is usurped or stamped out. Holy wars, plagues, 'missionary work'—all change the landscape of not only your world, but ours. You have overcrowding on Earth because of all those who live. Imagine the overpopulation in the underworlds due to all those who have died."

"But—but I've been to the underworld, the caves. There's room for expansion," I protested.

"Ever closer to your living world and discovery. Remember, much like the Hotel California, you can check into the underworld anytime you like, but you can never leave. Even as it is, a few of the living find their way every year. There are some missing persons cases that will never be solved. If we keep expanding at this rate, there will soon be no barrier, no boundary between the living and the dead."

"I'm not sure I understand what that means," I said, "or why souls take up space."

"Then you understand nothing. Remember, *belief* fuels reality. So much of the human imagination or religious teachings have focused on what comes after death. Except for the atheists, for whom there is nothing, all involve elaborate setups. Pearly gates, harps and wings, scales and a great book in which deeds are weighed or recorded, servants or grave goods, beloved pets or virgins aplenty. Belief takes *shape*."

My wings ruffled at that, and I wasn't sure why. Was that some kind of key? My wings existed because I remained aware of them? It made much more sense that I was aware of them because they were there. I put that aside for later, when I wasn't facing down the god of the dead and the dominatrix of the damned. Okay, not quite fair. Hecate was the dominatrix of the undamned as well and the mother of witches. She'd once brought Apollo back from the brink of death ... or the godly equivalent.

"So what do you want us to do?" Apollo asked, cutting to the chase.

"There are rumblings that Namtar has risen again, the bringer of plagues, purveyor of death and destruction, and that the apocalypse has begun. If this is true, we are all doomed. Cassandra has come to me—"

Pain rippled across Apollo's face, and his eyes closed, as if what went on behind the windows to his soul was just too raw and private. Was Hades talking about *the* Cassandra? The prophetess of Troy, whom Apollo had granted the gift of prophecy, then cursed to be powerless in the face of her visions when she spurned his advances. It was one of the tales that had kept me from giving in to my attraction to him for so long. I kept a watch on his face. Hades and Hecate watched just as avidly.

When Apollo opened his eyes again and saw all us staring, he tried to glare back, but the pain was still too present. "How is Cassandra?" he asked.

Hades ignored that. "She said that you—you two—are to fight. And win. Or die. Apparently, the future is unclear. Also, she says to tell you that you'll find what you need at Mycenae."

"Of course, Mycenae," Apollo said.

"Why of course?" I asked.

"The founding was attributed to Perseus. It makes sense he'd be buried there with his sword."

I'd always wanted to see Mycenae, which I knew best for the legendary Agamemnon and Clytemnestra, the brother-in-law and sister of the notorious Helen of Troy, with the face that launched a thousand (battle)ships when she ran off to Troy with Paris. As usual, the whole trouble was started by the gods and paid for by humanity. Well, started by goddesses, anyway— some petty squabble between Hera, Athena, and Aphrodite over who was the fairest of them all. Poor Paris had been roped into judging, as if there were any *right* answer, and let himself be bribed by Aphrodite with the hand of the most beautiful woman on earth. Never mind that she was already married. Schoolchildren learned of Aphrodite as the goddess of love. Lust was a lot closer to the truth. Physical slaking of thirsts, maybe, but Aphrodite had never contributed to *anyone's* happily-ever-after.

But I digressed. Again.

"Hecate will stay with you to make sure the job is done," Hades said. "Don't fail me in this."

I started to protest that we didn't answer to Hades and *certainly* didn't need a babysitter, but Apollo got to Hades first, putting a hand to his arm to stop him as he turned for the door.

Hades stilled, making the stop-motion somehow threatening, like he'd had to leash all kinds of potential energy that might not be a ton of fun if *un*leashed.

Apollo was undaunted. "Tell Cassandra ..." he began, then seemed at a loss. "Just tell her that I'm sorry."

Hades took his arm back and glowered at Apollo. "She knows. She's had centuries to get over it. Probably time for you to do the same."

And with that oh-so-helpful pronouncement, Hades was out the door, and we were left with Hecate, who stared at Apollo's chest while we stared at her. "Well, this is fun," she said wryly. "Where do we start?"

"First, we get you your own room," I said. "Three might be a crowd."

"Done," she said. A room key appeared in her hand as if she were a magician producing a bouquet of flowers. "Now what?"

"Asclepius?" Apollo started. "I know he's deceased—Zeus lightning-bolted him for raising Hippolytus from the dead," he said as an aside to me, "but surely you have access. The god of medicine seems the perfect ally for countering supernatural plagues."

Hecate averted her gaze, studying her nails, which made *me* study her nails, which led me to discover that they were sharpened to points. Note to self: Avoid catfights with Hecate ... or invest in a nail file of my own. "He's, um ... indisposed," she said without looking up.

"Indisposed?" I asked.

"Gone, okay? When the Titans busted out of Tartarus, they weren't alone. We've rounded up most of the escapees, but Asclepius ... we're still tracking him. If stopping the plagues were that easy, why would I even be here? Anyway, what about your granddaughter Panacea?" Hecate asked. "This sounds right up her alley."

Panacea! I nearly smacked myself upside the head. "That's perfect!"

I ignored the twinge about Apollo being a grandfather. *A grandfather!* Hell, he was probably a many-times great-grandfather thousands of times over by now. Which made us, what—a January-December romance.

"Disappeared," he said sadly, "into Africa. The AIDS epidemic."

"But—" so much I didn't understand, "—if she's there, why is it still raging?"

"At the height of our power maybe she could have controlled it, but almost no one believes in miracles anymore. Everyone is suspicious, even of modern medicine. And why not? Medical disclaimers are longer than the ads themselves— touch this and you'll go blind. Take that and risk depression, thoughts of suicide ... impotence. Unlike germs, her cure doesn't spread. She needs to heal individually, and she's only one woman. But, still, it's something. She's still a miracle for some."

"So even if we find the epicenter of the problem and take her to it, she can't magically save the day?"

"We'd only be stealing her from one epidemic to face another."

"Well, damn," I said eloquently. "So, the Sword of Perseus."

"Tonight?" Apollo asked. "First, we have to reconnoiter, eat, and rest. Mycenae is many hours from here."

"Does the great god fall with the sun?" Hecate taunted.

"Does the mother of witches fail to realize that the sun never falls, the Earth simply turns away, unable to stare too long at its glory?" Apollo fired back.

Hecate snorted.

"All right, children," I said, both annoyed to have Hecate foisted upon us and amused to be the mature one in the group, at least temporarily. "We reconnoiter, eat, and sleep. It's not like we need a lot of sleep anyway. Five hours enough?"

Apollo and Hecate both gave me a surprised look, maybe

expecting me, reasonably enough, to be the weakest link. "You're enough changed now that you no longer need sleep?" Apollo asked.

"I didn't need much last night."

A look passed between us, and Hecate groaned. "Oh, get a room."

"We've got one," Apollo answered. "Unfortunately, you're in it."

"So no threesome then?"

4

———

ut Hecate didn't push it. She and Apollo sat down at the desk in the room and pored over the Mycenae maps she'd produced out of thin air, talking about ancient burial sites and the most likely spots for Perseus's grave. After Cassandra's pronouncement, Hades had questioned Perseus himself about the whereabouts of the sword, but, unfortunately, he had no recollection of those events. He'd been alive and then he was dead—or so he'd figured out when he appeared on the bank of the River Styx with a coin for the ferryman.

Apparently, the underworld was spelled against swords and other weapons, as the newly dead were sometimes known to take exception to their sorry state and attempt to fight their way out of it. Hades stockpiled the only weapons allowed in his realm and kept them under lock and key. And while Cassandra could point to Mycenae, she couldn't pinpoint the tomb more exactly, as it seemed to be protected by some kind of concealment. I hoped it wasn't any stronger than the illusion used by the Grey Sisters, but if Perseus's final resting place hadn't been

found in all this time, I suspected I was destined for disappointment on that score.

In the meantime, I had minions. Well, *a minion*. My
assistant, Jesus (pronounced *Hey-Zeus*), but he was worth his
weight in gold. We'd left him back at the hotel in Delphi, probably sleeping, probably with my brother. I didn't want to think
about that. Luckily, it was only seven in the evening. I likely
wouldn't be interrupting anything. Probably. Maybe. With
Spiro's libido and the way those two looked at each other ...
avert, avert, avert ... the alarm sirens in my brain went off,
popping up pictures of LOLCats and red pandas pouncing on
pumpkins and other cutesy Internet memes like a shiny, happy
firewall. Things that had nothing to do with sex and my sibling.

In deep denial, I called Jesus. He picked up on the first ring,
talking a mile a minute before I could even get a word out.

"Boss lady, where are you? The police and press are having
a field day. They say you've disappeared, just like that. Poof." I
could hear him snap, as if that were the sound that went with
poof instead of, you know, the word itself. Onomatopoeia and
all that. The nymph herself would be so disappointed. "Where
are you?"

"We're on a case. I'm sorry I didn't have time to tell you. But I
need you on the clock. Code red, got that? I need you to get me
everything you can find on the zombie virus or whatever it is and
see if you can figure out where it struck first. Find out if the experts
have narrowed it down to any sort of epicenter or patient zero. I
don't want links or crazy conjecture. Just pull together whatever
you can find right from the sources—police and rescue, medical
personnel, specialists. Also, I want you to find anything you can on
Namtar. He's an ancient Sumerian or Babylonian god of plagues."

"Boss lady?" he asked. The *are you crazy* behind it coming
through loud and clear.

Zombie viruses and plague demons. Yeah, sounded crazy

even to me. "Just do it. You know that bonus you've been campaigning for?"

"Yes," he said, drawing the word out dramatically, as he did everything.

"If we live through this, it's yours."

"Live through this?" he asked, but I hung up before he could expect an answer. I had one more call to make, and it wasn't going to be pretty.

I hit the speed dial button for Yiayia and took a deep breath to prepare myself for what was to come. Such a stream of profanity, all in Greek, hit me as she answered that I let the breath out again. I wasn't going to need it until she wound down. I wasn't going to get a word in edgewise until then.

Finally, my grandmother took a breath, used it instantly for questions and demands. "What are you thinking, running off with Apollo? Didn't I warn you against him? He hasn't kidnapped you, has he? Turned you into some kind of sex slave? If not, you're in big trouble, young lady, for worrying everybody like this. Your mother is beside herself."

My head was swimming from her abrupt turnabouts. Which was worse—the sex slave thing or the running off of my own volition? I wasn't sure. Anyway, there was no recourse but the truth.

"Yiayia, I didn't run off with Apollo. That's not what this is all about." Although it sounded a whole lot better than the reality. I debated how much to tell her about that. As a career, my grandmother was the bearded lady in the Rialto Brothers' sideshow. As an avocation, she ran the Goddities website, like a hot sheet on contemporary Greek gods. She knew everything there was to know about the latter-day Olympians, especially the more salacious parts of their histories ... which meant she knew better than I about Apollo and the dangers of becoming too attached.

"So, what is it about then?" she asked. "What is so important that you would leave your family, who you haven't seen in far too long?"

I wasn't going to debate that. They could have come to see me at any time, far more easily than I could have gone back to the circus to see them, especially with Lenny Rialto still hot for my blood.

"Yiayia, forget that you're my grandmother for a minute. I need your expertise."

There was silence on the other end of the phone and then. "Something is up? Tell me all."

"Not for your website," I said immediately. "Completely off the record. We don't need to cause a panic."

"A panic?" she asked, more delighted than concerned.

"What do you know about the Nosoi?" I asked. Of all the things the Grey Sisters had said, that was the one word I hadn't quite grasped.

"The Nosoi? Pfft," she said. Just like that, as though it was a word and not just a sound. "They're like the wind. Nowhere and everywhere. I can't keep track."

"I haven't even gotten to current whereabouts. I'm still on *what* are *they*?"

"What are they teaching children in school these days?" she asked. I'd been homeschooled, as she well knew, so any gaps in my education ...

"The Nosoi are the demons of plague and pestilence that escaped Pandora's Box. But if you don't know, why are you asking about—" She stopped, and the silence had weight, as though she'd just come up with the answer to her own question. "Are they stirring? Do we have to worry about the plague?"

Damn, she was far too perceptive. I didn't dare ask her now about Namtar, probably not a great loss, since ancient Babylonian wasn't exactly her bailiwick, but still.

"Tell me," she insisted. "You know something."

"I don't *know*. But I fear. Listen, if you hear of any strange movement from the gods you track or you're able to trace the Nosoi doing whatever voodoo you do, would you let me know?"

"Just tell me," she begged, "are we safe? Is your family safe here in Delphi?" Her fear practically vibrated through the phone. "Is there somewhere—"

"I don't know," I said, hating it. "But it's a tourist spot, which means people converging from all over the world, having ridden together on public transport—planes, trains, buses. I don't know a helluva lot about these things, but I'd say that increases the chance of contagion. It might be best ..." To what? Barricade themselves in their rooms? Bug out? And go where? Using what means? "Either we stop this thing or I'm not sure there is a 'safe.'"

"So we are up schist creek?"

I loved the way Yiayia always got slang twisted up. For a moment, I missed her so fiercely I could cry.

"Not if I have anything to say about it. I'm on it. And Apollo ... and Hecate."

"Hecate?" I braced myself for an earful. "Say hello to the old bat. We raised some hell in our youth. Well, *my* youth. Helpful hint, do *not* gamble with that woman. She could teach that Lady Yiayia a thing or two about the 'Poker Face.'"

"Lady Gaga," I said automatically, the main part of my brain struggling to banish visions of Hecate and Yiayia raising hell and what exactly that might have entailed. I wondered if Yiayia's beard was shorter then. Or if she'd waxed.

"Tori, are you still with me?"

I snapped out of the reverie. "One more thing—I don't suppose you know where Panacea might be keeping herself these days?"

Despite what Apollo had said, I thought there had to be a way she could help. If nothing else, an epidemic sounded like an all-hands-on-deck situation. Maybe Yiayia knew something more specific than "Africa."

"She's not one I track," Yiayia answered regretfully.

"Too tame?"

"Yes," she said without embarrassment. "But I'll see what I can find out."

"Thank you. And, Yiayia?"

"Yes, *Egona*?"

"Stay safe."

"You too. You and Apollo, you are using the protection?"

My heart stuttered in my chest. *"Yiayia ..."*

"Don't tell me it's none of my business. If you won't protect your heart, at least protect your body. You don't know where that thing has been."

I held the phone away from my head to stare as though it were her face and she could actually see the reproach. I realized how silly that was. "I'm hanging up now."

"Egona—"

But I was as good as my word. I loved Yiayia, but she should have been one of the Fates the way she liked to meddle in peoples' lives.

Apollo caught my gaze as I put the phone away. "She loves and approves of me, yes?" he asked with a twist of his lips to let me know he was being ironic, at least in the Alanis Morissette way.

"She sends her love. The gift basket of puppies and rainbows is on the way."

"Oh good," Hecate said, "breakfast."

"And Yiayia says *hello*," I told Hecate, ignoring her attempt to get a rise out of me.

"Ah, how is the old bat?"

"Funny, she asked me the same about you."

"Speaking of dinner," Apollo cut in.

Right, we hadn't eaten since ... I didn't remember the last time we'd eaten. "I know just the place."

Normally, I'd have taken visitors to Thea Marya's little hole in the wall restaurant, which had the best moussaka in all the world. I might have been biased, but I didn't think so.

Instead, I took them to Galina's. It was well off the touristy beaten path and into the section of Kalambaka where people actually lived. It was a hole in the wall as well, a white door in the side of a whitewashed building with only a discreet sign beside it as advertising. Galina's didn't need it. Just like booze in a Prohibition world, which in Greece would have been called the apocalypse, locals would and could have sniffed out this place without any signage whatsoever. But here I never got the moussaka. Here I got the braised lamb, which melted in your mouth. I tried never to think of the cute, innocent animals that gave their lives for my meals. Maybe the Grey Sisters did the same. The very thought turned my stomach and right there I vowed to stick with the spinach-based spanakopita.

The young woman who seated us didn't recognize me, but Kosmo descended on us the second we were seated. I prepared for fuss and introductions, but instantly realized that he hadn't seen me at all. He had eyes only for Apollo.

"Lord in Heaven," he said, clapping his hands together. "Apollo Demas, gracing my humble eatery. I can hardly believe it, and yet it must be. There can be no one like you! I heard you were in Greece for a movie, but I thought ... Ah, but perhaps you are filming at Metéora as well? But where are my manners, you must have our best table!"

There weren't that many, not inside, anyway, but following the old ways, just about every building still had an atrium or a courtyard, and I knew that Kosmo's was beautiful—a little grotto with a small fountain made of cement and stone with a statue of the Blessed Mother set into an alcove. Greenery and creeping vines always threatened to overtake the little fountain and never quite managed it, I suspected through careful maintenance. The vines' pink flowers that opened up at dawn would be closing with the setting sun, but the tiny white lights strung about the grotto would be winking on like fireflies. The candles on every table would be lit. It would be completely romantic for two, but three was a crowd.

"Please, don't fuss," Apollo said, opening his napkin and setting it in his lap as a sign that he was staying where he was. "I'm happy here."

And, really, he should have known better. We Greeks will kill you with kindness, whether you like it or not.

Kosmo snapped his fingers, and in less than a second, the woman who'd seated us and his one other server were at our table, taking the napkin from Apollo's lap, pulling out his chair and bustling about.

Hecate shot me a look of amusement and Apollo sent one of apology. I didn't care about the fuss, but Thea Marya was going to kill me. If word spread, and Kosmo would be sure of it, that the famous Apollo Demas had visited his restaurant and not hers ... and if Marya spoke to Yiayia ... well, everyone would know who to blame. Again. Why always me?

In no time flat, we were at a grotto table, as I'd suspected we would be. The other occupied tables stared at the fuss and whispered among themselves. I wanted to disappear into the vegetation, just like the fountain.

"Nice?" Kosmo asked.

"Nice," Apollo agreed with a sigh. *"Sas efcharistó."* Thank you.

My phone began buzzing up a storm as soon as we were settled again, allowing me to ignore the curious stares. I studied the files that had arrived from Jesus and hid behind my phone when Kosmo came to take a picture for his wall. Me in Kosmo's in a photo with Apollo would just cement my guilt. I was lucky enough not to be disowned already with everything I had to answer for.

I took the quick respite after the picture to share Jesus's findings with the others. "According to Jesus, Namtar is married to an underworld goddess, Hušbišag." The last came out as *Who-bi-sag*. I had no idea how it was actually pronounced. I looked up at Hecate. "Maybe you know her?"

She eyed me back. "Sure, we have mimosas every Wednesday and play Mah-Jongg once a month. All us underworld goddesses do."

"So you don't know her?"

"Now, I didn't say that. I know *of* her. Back at the beginning, she more or less had the market cornered on the afterlife. But her heyday came and went pretty quickly, partially, if you ask me, because they made their afterlife so damned hard to get into. You know Dante's nine circles of hell? Well, theirs was something like that, but you had to pay the guardian at every level. If you were too poor or your gift was unacceptable, poof, no entrance. It worked out okay when the empire was on the rise, but not so well on the fall. Haven't heard from her in a dog's age. I don't even know if she and Namtar are still an item. I mean, thousands of years is a long time and those celebrity marriages never last."

She looked at Apollo beneath her lashes. "I mean, how many women did *you* marry over the years?"

Apollo looked steadily back at her. "At least *I* don't have commitment issues."

"Oh, I am wounded," Hecate said, miming plunging her fork into her heart.

"Children," I cut in. "Am I going to have to separate you two?"

"No," Hecate said, at the same time Apollo came out with, "Yes, please."

"Anything you can tell us about her or about Namtar?" I asked to get us back on track.

"She was a beautiful woman, back in the day. Beautiful like a snake with the bright colors and gleaming venom. Namtar was ... Namtar. Dark like the color of dried blood, fever hot, eyes a miasma that would draw you in and with a cutting, biting, poisonous wit. And that tail ..." She sounded wistful.

"Weaknesses?"

"Lack of faith, the same malaise that affects us all."

"But he's back. Any guesses why?"

"Could be that Rhea woke him when she rose. Could be the modern zeitgeist—dystopian fiction, the zombie craze. Hell, just think about that one for a minute. You have zombie runs, zombie pub crawls, television shows, movies, comics ... even the CDC with their zombie-preparedness guidelines to educate people about what to do to prevent an infectious outbreak. Then you have those people on the news we heard about, the ones eating each other's faces ... Hell, we could have woken him ourselves with all the insanity. People might not know Namtar by name, but they believe in what he does. They have *faith*."

"Holy crap."

"You have such a flare for language," Hecate said.

Our food arrived, and we dug into it. I was glad I'd opted for the vegetarian dish. Even with that, it was hard to eat past the lump in my throat. What was it Hades had said? *Belief forms reality?* If so, we might have done this, mankind as a whole. America alone had become a nation of germaphobes—hand sanitizer on every desk and every key chain, whole tubs of it at the grocery store to wipe down carts. How on earth did we pacify an entire populace and calm people's worst fears even as they were coming true?

First thing in the early, early morning, we had a grave and a legendary sword to dig up.

MYCENAE WAS ... epic, even in the dark of night with only the moon and a few security lights shining on it. No, epic was too small a word, a four-letter word even. Mycenae was—

grandiose, splendiferous. To quote *Pinky and the Brain*, "fantastically amazing." It was the textbook example of Cyclopean construction, meaning that the stones used were so monstrous and massive that latecomers could only conceive that they were placed there by the Cyclopes, legendary one-eyed giants. For all I knew, they had been. Looking at the incredible Lion Gate, with the huge stone monoliths several times my height standing to either side of the entrance and the multi-ton lintel above them holding up the slab of rearing lions carved into it, all I could say was "wow"—even with the lions currently missing their heads.

"You've never seen Mycenae before?" Apollo asked.

"Wow," I said again. It seemed all I was capable of. It was on a loop in my brain. "Wow."

"You said that," Hecate pointed out helpfully.

"It bears repeating," I answered with a glare, but it was a short one, because it took my gaze away from the majesty all around me. Like all other ancient sites in Greece, Mycenae had been built on a mountaintop. The scenery was amazing, and normally I found it hard to believe that man (or Cyclops) could create anything as beautiful as nature, but Mycenae was enough to shift my whole worldview.

"Where to now?" Apollo asked. "Did Jesus's research give any indication of where Perseus's grave might be?"

"Well, if it *is* here, the earliest graves found were to the west of the acropolis near the cistern."

"In or outside of the walls?"

"Both, the walls were built overtop of them."

"But if Perseus founded the city ..." Apollo began.

"Then *his* grave is likely inside the walls," Hecate finished.

Which complicated things about twofold, since there'd likely be security measures to prevent people vandalizing the site.

"Can you get us inside?" I asked her.

It would be great if the witch was good for more than finishing Apollo's sentences. I knew the thought wasn't fair. I'd seen her heal. Him in particular. But I was surprised to find myself a little bit jealous of Hecate. She was striking and gorgeous in a way I'd never be, and clearly, she and Apollo had history. They knew all the same gods, had probably even been to some of the same orgies. *Yes, and they'd had thousands of years to get together and hadn't. What does that tell you?* my saner, more sensible side asked.

"Piece of cake," Hecate said.

She squatted to the ground, a centimeter or two shy of kneeling and scraped together with her fingers a pile of dry dirt and rocky soil. Once it was nearly to sandcastle size, she began to swirl her right index finger around and around in the dirt, muttering something darkly beneath her breath. As her volume rose, so did the pile of dirt, becoming a tiny tornado. Hecate rose along with it, her hands coming up to her sides and then rising to shoulder level and above. The cloud of dust, dirt, and pebbles rose with her, drawing more debris to itself until it was a cyclonic sandstorm. I had to avert my eyes as the grit and winds grew more severe, and clench my lips against asking what she was up to lest I get a mouthful of dirt.

The cyclone moved toward us, enveloping but not flaying us somehow, and as Hecate's hands reached their pinnacle above her head, the cone rose up off the ground, taking us all with it. I made a sound I was sure Hecate would taunt me for later and clutched to my side one of the shovels we'd bought along. With my other hand, I reached out instinctively for Apollo. He was reaching for me as well, and we met in the middle, holding each other as the cloud lifted, taking us over the closed gates, and releasing us inches above the ground inside so that we had to stumble to keep our feet. Hecate kept chanting and lowered her hands slowly, letting the cyclone lose force and materials at a steady rate until it was no more.

I wondered what she would do for an encore.

"Cool," I had to admit. It occurred to me then that the mother of witches was probably one deity who'd never had to worry about losing her worship or her power.

"Thank you," she said, turning an almost-feral smile on me. Her eyes had gone darker than ever, black holes with the brown of the cyclone still swirling like an afterimage. She had to blink a few times before they got back to somewhat normal.

That was when I remembered that I could fly and could probably have brought the others in one by one, but it wouldn't have been nearly as flashy. Damn, I had to get used to these wings and start thinking in terms of probabilities rather than liabilities.

"This way," I said, retaking, if not leadership then, at least, an active role. I knew from the map Jesus had sent that the cistern was on the far side of the complex from the Lion Gate, and so I started off in the right direction, figuring that when paths diverged, I could consult the file to orient myself again.

It was cool up here at the top of the mountain without any buildings to block the wind—at least, none still standing in near totality—and no modern conveniences to blow hot air. In fact, it was as though the modern world had dropped away entirely, leaving us in another time.

We had to be careful with our footing once we got beyond the pressed-earth walkway at the entrance. Everywhere we looked there were roped-off excavation pits with oversized stones, some still stacked on top of each other, forming the foundation of what would have been buildings at some point in the past, and some laying by themselves with grass growing all around. In the near dark, it was tricky to navigate. My wings wanted to flap every time my balance got iffy, until I was half tempted to rip out the back of my shirt and let them loose. Apollo's shirt. Whatever. It was too bad there wasn't any ancient god of tailoring I could go to for a custom wardrobe. Wait, was there? I'd ask, not that it would matter ultimately. Either I'd save the world and the Grey Sisters would keep their end of the bargain, or I wouldn't and wings would be the least of my problems.

There were stones to the left of us, stones to the right ... the demented little deejay in my head sing-songed in a parody of Steve Miller Band's "Stuck in the Middle with You." Just to be certain of our bearings, I took out my phone to study the map, but the complex wasn't as big as I'd have expected, given how huge it looked in myth and legend, and it wasn't very long before we hit the steps down to the "secret cistern," according to my map.

"You know, in Mayan times, cisterns were a place of sacrifice," Hecate said casually. "People would be cast into the very same cisterns from which people drew their water."

I turned to stare at her, "Are you trying to tell us something about *these* cisterns ..."

"I'm just making conversation. Sheesh, chill. She always like this?" Hecate asked Apollo.

"She hasn't had caffeine in hours," he said, in poor defense of my honor.

It was true, I hadn't. Come to think of it, I also hadn't had any ambrosia since the great battle where I'd gotten my wings and nearly lost my life. And yet I'd healed anyway. It would be cause for celebration, if it meant what I thought it did—that my addiction was gone, but with my metamorphosis and my supernatural healing, I knew there was something more to it. I was becoming ... something other. I just hoped I still matched the picture on my passport when all was said and done. Otherwise, I was going to have a helluva time getting home.

The water in the cistern was blacker than the tail end of night. Those same chunky stones that were all around the site formed a wall surrounding the well. They were bleached nearly white—or so it looked in the moonlight—like bones scoured clean by scavengers. The conservators of the site had roped off the approach to the cistern, both to keep people from falling in and from defacing the site. While we could easily access the pool by stepping over the rope "barrier," the moonlight couldn't penetrate the pool so easily. All this talk of watery sacrifices had me imagining stinking, waterlogged bodies pulling themselves up out of the cistern and coming for us, skin sloughing off, bellies bloated ... I'd had nightmares like that.

Of course, we probably had more to fear from some kind of site security than from supernatural forces.

Famous last words.

"Where do we even start?" I asked, looking at Hecate. "Any chance you have some kind of grave sense?"

"That would be nice, wouldn't it? Some kind of locator spell? But it doesn't work like that. Once the soul is gone from a thing, the connection is severed. I couldn't trace Perseus back to his body, and if he ever knew where he was buried, he's forgotten in the thousands of years since. It's amazing how much memories can fade over time."

Hell, witnesses had trouble remembering what they saw on the same day they saw it, I could well imagine spiritual senility.

My precog kicked me in the gut, whipping my head around just as Apollo said, "Um, girls, maybe we can start there."

It didn't seem like the time to take him to task over calling us "girls"—not when the stuff of nightmares was ripping itself out of the ground farther west of the cistern.

5

———

By nightmares, I meant a live Halloween set with the skeletons clawing their way out of the earth. Already, bones—sheer bones that should no way, no how have been able to animate—were scrabbling and arm bones were straining to use muscles no longer attached to pull the rest of the body up out of the ground.

We weren't exactly loaded down with weaponry, prepared to dig but not take on whatever the hell we were about to face. But Apollo gave a war cry and heaved his shovel up over his shoulder. He ran forward, poised to cut the arms off at the elbows before they could raise the rest of the creature, but another pair of hands suddenly erupted out of the earth, wrapping around his ankles with preternatural accuracy, and he started to go down. My wings flapped and I tore at the back of my shirt, ripping it in half so that it clung together just at the yolk and my wings burst free, lifting me off the ground. I swooped toward Apollo, hands out to grab him up out of the fray, but the skeletal hands were unnaturally strong, and they weren't letting go so easily. There were more now, gripping and binding him to the earth, and I feared my tug of war would tear him in half. Hecate launched herself at the ground, hacking at brittle bones with the trowel she'd brought for excavation, but it was torn almost immediately from her hands.

She began to mutter a spell. Something rose up behind her, a full skeleton, wearing a sagging clay necklace with more than half the beads missing and the flapping remains of what might once have been a dress ... or a sack. Dried patches of hair still clung to the scalp, dark like rot. I opened my mouth to call out a warning as the thing reached for her, but the cry was knocked out of me as arms suddenly banded around my chest, squeezing me from behind like an anaconda and rooting me to the ground.

Desperately, I fought the grip, kicking and thrashing, clawing at the arms, but with no flesh to rip into, all I hit was bone and the only blood spilled was mine when my nails tore away. My wings flared futilely, panicked at the constriction, but the grip on me only tightened, and my vision started to blacken with every breath I failed to draw.

This was *not* going to happen. We weren't going out like this, at the top of the world, at the hands of mindless monsters.

The one that held me in its iron grip hissed in my ear. Speech—I knew it even if I couldn't understand. There was a cadence to it ... and a scent. The breath was fetid with long-ago death, the kind that had fertilized new and poisonous life, like whatever motes had sickened archaeologists who'd opened ancient tombs without proper care, giving rise to lingering death and legends of mummy's curses.

As I struggled for breath, Apollo began to sink into the ground, pulled by the innumerable hands clawing at him. I fought all the harder. I had to get free before I blacked out. I had to get to him.

I launched back with my heel, hammering away at the brittle shinbone of my captor. I heard a crack, but the arms around me didn't even loosen, and so I didn't stop, battering at the same spot again and again until the entire leg buckled and the skeleton canted to the side. I took swift advantage, hurling my weight in the same direction. I began to slip, and my wings flapped outward, throwing off the grasping arms trying for a new hold. Grabbing and missing threw the thing even farther off-balance, and the skeleton staggered forward ... right into the roundhouse kick I launched at chest level. The sternum was right there, a relatively fragile bone for protecting such important infrastructure, all of which was long gone. But something moved behind those dark eye sockets, a flash of intelligence or at least cunning, and it grabbed at my foot as it would have connected, twisting hard. I had to flip fast, knowing I'd go down but lashing out with my other foot for the head, hoping to take the thing with me. It connected, and the skull jerked to the side, but didn't go flying off or anything wonderfully cinematic.

I fell to the ground and the thing fell on top of me, mandible gnashing, going for my throat, even though the human mouth was so not meant for ripping out jugulars. It also wasn't made to animate without muscle or brain or nerves to send messages back and forth between the two. I struck out at those eerily alive eyes, carving fingers into the sockets and fighting down bile as they met something wet and suctiony deep inside. Whatever they struck seemed to pull at my fingers like tentacles, as if they'd yank me in and make me part of them. Horrified, I pulled back, but the skull came with me, mandibles still chomping together. I shook my hands so hard I nearly dislocated my wrists and finally the skull came free, sailing through the air. My fingers were still gunked, and starting to lose feeling, as if necrosis was setting in. But I couldn't think about that now. I had to get to the others. I kicked the rest of the skeleton out of my way and rose to find Hecate stabbing her trowel up through the nose and into the cranial cavity of a skeleton that had her similarly pinned. Apollo's shovel lay abandoned a foot from the god-shaped indentation in the ground where I'd last seen him. I was afraid to stab the blade into the ground to dig for him for fear that I'd hit him somewhere vital, so I knelt beside the disturbed earth and thrust in with my arms. They didn't go far. Whatever I was becoming, it was clearly not the *X-Men*'s Wolverine. No adamantium for me. Just flesh and blood.

"Hecate!" I called. "A little help here?"

She snarled, but came to kneel as well. She held out a hand to the dirt, muttering a spell that whipped out of her in a gust of power as she made contact. The dirt suddenly seemed to shift more like sand than hard-packed dirt. We both reached in, arms buried up to our chests, searching for Apollo, but to no avail.

"Cover your eyes," Hecate warned, and without waiting to make sure I obeyed, she started to swirl her finger around in the sand as she had the grit at the front gate, and another cyclone started, ready to raise sand out of the pit.

I yanked my arms from the grave and covered my face with them as the first of the sand lashed out, scouring me as though it would whip the skin from my body and leave me like the skeletons we'd fought. The wind continued to whip, gaining force, and then there was a great sound, like a gasping breath, and I had to risk my eyesight to look.

I peeked over my concealing arms to see Apollo rise up out of the pit, gasping and filthy and grasping a sword. He flailed it around him like he was blind—which maybe he was from the sand—and still expected to be fighting enemies. Hecate let the wind die and called out to him, telling him to stand down. The tension drained out of Apollo and the sword fell to his side as he let her help him out, coughing up dirt and wheezing with the haste to take in the air he'd been lacking.

My precog kicked up again, louder this time, flooding me with adrenaline.

"We have to get out of here," I told them. I didn't know if it was site security or more skeletons, but *something* was coming. Something ...

I tried to reach for Apollo to help him up, but while I saw my hands connect with his arm, I couldn't feel it, and they didn't have the strength to grasp. Whatever had reached for me from the eye sockets of that skull still had hold of me, and once again my body wasn't my own. Not all if it. I was damn sick of the arrangement.

He didn't seem to notice, still sand-blind. Hecate helped him to his feet and reached a hand for his eyes, theoretically to quick-heal them, when a voice stopped her, as rough and cracked as a desert grave.

"Good, you have found it. I knew you would with the proper motivation ... Now, hand it over."

Hecate whirled, my wings flared and I turned, half-levitating as I did so and instinctively moving closer to Apollo, standing between him and the threat, because there was no mistaking that's what it was. For his part, he grabbed the fallen sword and held it at the ready.

The figure we faced looked like something out of a sci-fi flick. Not *The Mummy*, because we were in the wrong place geographically for that, but close enough. Her clothes—a tunic or chiton or something—hung off of her like a sack, in contrast to the skin that seemed to be baked onto her bones without the meat or fat or muscle to separate them. Her elaborate jewelry sat hard on her deflated chest. She looked like well-tanned leather. Her eyes weren't dark pools like the others, but glittered in the darkness like the moonlight striking black water. Whether her nose would have been hawklike before her cheeks and all had sunken was a moot point, because it certainly was now. In one clawlike hand, she held a sinew-wrapped spear—obsidian tipped, it appeared. She was, in a word, intimidating, all seven plus feet of her.

"Hušbišag," Hecate said, sounding as though she were choking on the name. "You're looking ... well."

Hušbišag made a dry coughing sound I took to be a laugh. "I am flattered that you bother to lie, however I won't be distracted. Hand over the sword."

"What do you want with it?" I asked.

Bones rattled behind us, and I took my gaze off her long enough to see the skeletons rearticulating. One had a half-bashed-in skull, glaring at us from its one good eye; another's leg was bent at a ludicrous angle; yet another was missing arms. None that I could see were whole, but I didn't have time for a full study.

"To foil you, of course," said the seven-foot skeleton, snapping her fingers together with a crack like a wishbone breaking.

The skeletons fell on us, grabbing for the sword, reaching for shoulders, heads, necks ... I beat my wings hard, knocking them away from me before they could latch on. Apollo lashed about him with the sword as I rose up into the air. If Airbag, or whatever her name was, went down, so would they all, I was sure of it. I launched myself straight at her, and she braced the spear she held, ready to impale me. She was staring right at me, her target, and I glared back into those eerie eyes and yelled, *"Freeze!"*

She thrust forward with the spear, and I was so shocked at her movement that I faltered in flight, but wasn't able to dart out of the way. The spear tip pierced the membrane of one of my wings, and she ripped downward with it, tearing a gaping hole all the way through. I plummeted to the ground. My feet hit hard and off-balance. I lunged forward, straight into her. She couldn't get the spear in place again quickly enough to pierce me, but improvised by whipping the shaft against my back, cracking across my shoulder blades. I arched in pain and reached for the haft of the spear to wrestle her for it, but I couldn't even feel it when my hands hit. They were still dead, numb, unable to grasp. For the first time since I'd seen Apollo disappear into the ground, I had a spike of fear, and my precog amped it up tenfold, not that I needed it to know that things were going horribly wrong.

She had me trapped between her spear and her desiccated chest. My heart was beating hard enough to hurt, but not cartoonishly hard enough to pound right out of my chest, knocking her away.

Hecate cried out something behind me, but I couldn't understand a word of it.

I thrashed in Hubashag's grip, trying to fight my way out, but she started to constrict her embrace, crushing the life and the air out of me. I stomped desperately down on the fragile bones of her feet, protected only by flimsy sandals that looked as dried out as she was, but while I heard bones crack, her only response was to squeeze tighter.

I didn't know how much longer I had. For the second time, black spots crept into my vision, which was flickering out. I craned my head to look into the goddess's wild eyes and saw a sudden shadow flash across the moonlit depths. I didn't know what it was, whether it was something for us or against, until I heard the growl, eerie and awful ... the kind that made every hair on your body stand up and made your heart go cold as, well I'd say a witch's tit, but I was sure Hecate would take exception to that. I knew what I'd see next would be glowing eyes, sleek, powerful bodies with jaws dripping death.

Hellhounds. Hecate had called for backup.

The ghastly goddess let me go suddenly to fling her arms up as one of the hounds launched himself right over me to get to her. I dropped, gasping for breath, and the beast's hind claws scratched at my back and wings, trying to find purchase to keep up its attack as she tried to bat it away. I pivoted, still on the ground, but with my vision clearing now that I was able to breathe. I thrust my hands up to knock away her spear. My hands still weren't clasping, but I struck with enough force that, distracted as she was, it fell to the ground.

I kicked it away and rolled in the opposite direction before rising up to get a better look at the battlefield. A second hound launched itself at Hubistank or whatever the hell her name was. Then a third. She howled and fought like the wind, like a dervish, but there were so many claws and teeth going for her. Now the black spots in my vision resolved into hellhounds, all as excited as any dog with a bone.

Apollo was swinging about with the Sword of Perseus, cutting down skeletons left and right, slashing through bone like it was butter. Hecate was doing her whirlwind trick again, but instead of swirling dirt, the sun-whitened stone all around was flying, mostly at skulls, which came tumbling off and rolling on the ground.

"Enough!" Hubistank yelled. "We fight another day!"

She got her fingers free of the hellhounds and snapped them hard, again the sound of bones breaking, and then suddenly all was silence. The ghastly goddess and her posse were gone as though they'd never been. Even the bones some of the hellhounds had been chewing disappeared straight out of their jaws, and they made an almost comical sound of doggy disappointment, somewhere between a yelp and a whine. Hecate took pity on them and materialized a few bones, possibly even from the Grey Sisters' stash, and sent them away happy.

"Wow, she's really let herself go," Hecate said when the hellhounds had dashed off back to Hades.

I stared at her like she was crazy ... the same way people often looked at me. "Seriously, we were almost wiped out and *that's* all you have to say?" I asked.

"Well, maybe not *all*," she admitted.

"What's with the skeleton army?" Apollo cut in, getting us back on track.

Hecate eyeballed him, and there was nothing like a witchy moon goddess to make that expression seem absolutely accurate. "You don't know about Irkalla?" she asked, waiting for one of us to say it wasn't so. When we didn't, she *tsk*ed as though she expected better. "Well, I told you about all the levels of their afterlife. Here's the crazy thing—once you get through them all, paying your bribes every step of the way, your soul gets to live on, but you keep decomposing, just like your body. Some eternity, right? So after a few thousand years or so, bones are all you have left. I'm surprised she was able to pull anyone together to fight. I ask you, is it any wonder their worship died out?"

It sounded like a pretty lousy afterlife to me, but also like we were getting off topic. None of this explained how Hubistank—I really was going to have to learn her actual name—knew where to find us and what she wanted with the sword.

Before I could voice any of that, a voice called out, "Stop right there!"

It was almost full daylight now, and I whirled right into a blast of the rays from the rising sun. "Drop the sword," the voice continued.

"Officer, I'm sure we can work this out," Apollo said.

Officer. Oh, thank the gods. Then there was hope. Maybe not of escaping an arrest record, but ...

My eyes started to clear, and I blinked away the last of the sunspots, making an abrupt movement the second I could see to draw the officer's attention. As soon as it riveted on me, I commanded, *"Freeze!"*

Unlike with the skeletal goddess, this time it worked, and the newcomer went as still as a statue. I shouldn't have been caught flat-footed back in the battle. I *knew* my mojo didn't work on the really old gods ... and they didn't get much older than Hubistank, but I'd become so used to relying on my gorgon glare to get me out of trouble. Next time I'd know better.

"Let's go!" I said. "I'm not sure how long it'll last."

We ran back toward the Lion Gate and Hecate did her whirlwind trick again. I would have flown us out, but my wings were gashed, my hands still weren't working, and I was afraid I'd drop them.

"What's wrong with your hands?" Hecate asked as we ran for the car.

They were hanging like dead weight, flopping as I ran. "I don't know, I can't feel them!"

"Then I'm driving," she said, like I was going to fight her for it. We'd given Viggo the night off rather than involve him in grave robbing and defacing a historical site.

"*I'll* drive," Apollo cut in. "You heal."

Hecate grumbled at that, but when we hit the car, she opened the back door to let me in and slid next to me.

Apollo leaned the sword up against the passenger seat and took off. "Let me see," Hecate ordered.

I raised my hands to show her, but it was getting difficult, as if the feeling ... or lack thereof ... was creeping up my arms. It seemed to take an inordinate amount of time to get things into place, which made my forearms and hands seem longer than they were, but finally I flopped them into Hecate's lap, where she and I both noticed at the same time the blackening of the flesh. My hands were becoming clawlike, constricting and hardening ... dying.

"Necrosis," she said. "Shit."

It seemed so funny coming out of her mouth. I didn't know why. Gallows humor, maybe. I needed something to laugh at or I'd cry. I couldn't feel my cells dying. I had a vague sense that it should be horribly painful, but it was as though they'd already winked out, switched off like a light.

"Can you save them?" I asked.

"Shhh, I'm concentrating." Even with her eyes closed it looked like they rolled back into her head. I didn't dare say another word, but I feared. Necrosis ... dying cell by cell ... it was about the most horrifying thing I could think of.

"Pull over," she called out suddenly.

"What? Is everything okay?" Apollo asked, worry coming across loud and clear.

"Just do it. The creeping death hungers. I can't stop it, but I can redirect. Right there, that olive tree."

The car stopped, and Hecate dragged me out of it, toward a tree, beautiful in its contortions. Old, gnarled, laden with leaves and fruit.

"But," I said as she reached out for it.

"It's you or the tree."

She thrust the hand she held against the trunk of the tree and then grabbed my other as it flapped uselessly at my side. She held both in place with one hand over both of mine and put her other palm directly to the bark of the tree beside them, which had her leaning intimately against me. She muttered low and constantly, emphasizing certain words and nearly dropping others.

The air around us became charged, and my hands started to tingle and then to come alive with pain, nerves suddenly raw and screaming as if someone were holding them to a fire. I cried out, and she held my hands tighter to keep me from drawing back. The pain raged through me, rippling from my upper arms on down, washing the numbness and the death before it, pushing it out toward that poor olive tree, which I could practically see sagging with the onslaught.

Leaves dropped around us, browned, dried, dead. Fruit fell heavily to the ground, exploding with the sickly-sweet smell of decay. Smaller branches cracked as the weight of the dying fruit suddenly became too much for their brittle state.

And then I sagged to the ground, residual pain and tingling still strobing through me, like limbs that had been slept on wrong just waking up. But the relief of feeling anything at all, of commanding my fingers to move and having them obey, was immense. I let my forehead rest on the trunk of the now-dying tree, saying a prayer to Ceres to apologize and beg for the tree's renewal. I hoped there was no truth to the legends of dryads and such. Poseidon and his minions—the water divinities— were already against me. Adding earth, or at least an aspect of it, would really ice my cake.

"Thank you," I said to Hecate, my voice creaky and weak. "I think you saved my life."

"Damned straight."

"I owe you," I said, dreading it, but failing to acknowledge the debt wouldn't make it go away.

"I know."

6

I turned my phone back on as we got into the car and it lit up with buzzes and bleeps like a carnival game. My heart nearly stopped when I saw that one of the texts was from Nick. I stared at it a minute and then over at Apollo, then back down at the phone, afraid to open the message, but knowing I would anyway.

"What?" Apollo asked, alerted to my emotions through our weird empathic link.

"Nick," I said, voice strangled.

"What does he say?" Apollo's voice was carefully neutral.

"I don't know yet."

He didn't say anything to that, and I swallowed down a panic attack. Last I'd heard from Nick had been when he said goodbye. In a message left for me at my hotel. Not even a text, something I could have gotten quickly enough to rush to the hospital and try to change his mind. He was going back to the States, he'd said, to get treatment for his extensive burns and to heal. He'd already ended things between us, told me that I was walking a path he couldn't walk, but I'd hoped that it was the pain talking or the drugs ... or anything but the truth. But leaving me with no chance to say goodbye—that seemed pretty final.

But what if it wasn't? What if I'd rushed into Apollo's arms too soon, trying to deal with the pain while also giving in to whatever had been growing between us? Nick had reason enough to hate me. What if—?

I opened the text. Nick deserved the chance to beat me up himself and here I was doing the job for him.

But it wasn't Nick.

Of course it wasn't. He couldn't text. He could barely move without massive amounts of pain. If my common sense had overridden my guilt for half a second I'd have realized.

Tori? This is Amanda, Nick's sister. Nick's doing ... as well as can be expected. He wanted me to tell you that weird things are going on here. The hospital's under a quarantine and ... he said to say it's not natural. I guess that means some-thing to you? Anyway, you won't be able to visit. I'm not supposed to be using the cell phone even, so I'm not sure how well messages will get in and out, but, well, he seemed insistent.

I stared at the message, horror creeping throughout my entire body. I didn't know if it was my danger sensors or just natural-born fear, but ...

Where are you? I texted back.

Five seconds later came the response: *Lenox Hill Hospital in New York, but you can't get to us.*

Fear flooded my system with toxic chemicals. Cold, so cold. My heart threatened to ice over.

"He's in New York," I said out loud. "Right where the first victims were discovered ... or at least the first we know of."

"But he's okay?"

"For now. That was his sister writing. Nick wanted us to know what's going on. The hospital's been quarantined."

"I think we knew that already."

"Yes, but *Nick's there*," I said, since he was missing the obvious.

Apollo slid a glance at me in the rearview mirror, and I realized that if the horror and fear didn't kill me, the guilt would. I could sense his pain through our link. He didn't know if I felt responsible for Nick because he was Nick or because I loved him and would go back to him in a heartbeat. I didn't know myself. Apollo and I had something powerful, something primal and undeniable, but ... was there a *but*? Nick was normalcy and sanity and ... And he'd made his feelings clear. Nick couldn't walk my path with me and I couldn't walk any other. That didn't mean I could just shut off my feelings for him. So, I was torn, and there was no hiding it from Apollo.

"You two are giving me a headache," Hecate sniped, as if she could sense the undercurrents. "So what's the big deal? You were already planning to save the world. What's the movie quote? 'This time it's personal.' Very motivational."

I glared. She was right and she'd saved my life, but she was also really, really wrong. This changed everything. Now I didn't only have to worry about an epidemic, I had to worry about Detective Lau. She was going to kill me.

"We've got to get to New York." There, I'd mastered the obvious. "But we're never going to get the sword on a plane, not to mention my wings. What are we going to do?"

"Hermes?" Apollo suggested. "He's got that private jet."

"Even with that, we have to go through security, don't we?" Although, maybe not.

Money could grease a lot of wheels. "One way to find out," he said.

Lord, I could only imagine what Hermes would extract in payment. Last time it had been my best friend's phone number and now they were dating. *Hermes*, the trickster god, and my BFF. The trickster god who was apparently at the center of the illicit ambrosia trade and had been starting up a little something else on the side when I'd shut him down. I didn't want to make the call, but I couldn't see that we had a lot of options.

I dialed the phone. After two rings, a strange voice picked up.

"Hello?" he said. It was gruff and deep, and I got a strange tingle at the sound of it.

Something was going on here.

"Hello, is ..." Crap, what name was Hermes going by these days? I knew him alternately as Thom Foolery, the humor columnist, and as head of a worldwide messenger service, but under what name?

"Herman," Apollo whispered in my ear, "Molyvos."

"... is Herman Molyvos available?" I asked.

There was the briefest pause on the other end of the line before the response. "May I ask who's calling?"

My eyes met Apollo's. He could hear everything through the line and feel my spike of panic, but he didn't have any better answer than I did about what to do. I'd called Hermes's cell phone, so whoever was on the line would have my number and could easily find my name, even if I didn't give it. Anyway, I didn't have anything to hide ... exactly. Beyond defacing ancient graves and making off with a priceless artifact.

"Tori Karacis," I said, "PI. Who's this?"

"Carsten Bremmer," he answered. "Interpol."

"Is Mr. Molyvos in some sort of trouble?"

"He's helping us with some inquiries. Might I ask how you know Mr. Molyvos?"

I had a feeling that was a loaded question. Interpol was an international police force. They'd have access to all kinds of records, I thought. But while Hermes had played a part in every case I'd recently been part of, none of it had ever been official. I was pretty sure his name had stayed out of the reports, just like he'd managed to vanish when it came down to any real conflict ... except for that last time when Rhea had risen and it was all-hands on deck.

"He's dating my friend," I said innocuously.

"That would be Ms. Christie Farris?"

"Listen, what's going on here? They've only just started dating, so whatever he's in to, she wouldn't know anything about it."

"Why do you assume he's involved in anything?"

My blood pressure was rising. "You're freakin' Interpol. My keen PI powers tell me he's either a suspect or a witness and either can spell trouble."

"You're quite perceptive, Ms. Karacis. Perhaps we should be calling you in to help with our inquiries."

I hung up on Agent Bremmer. Special Agent Bremmer? I had no idea how Interpol worked and no desire to find out.

"*Skata!*" I said, looking from Apollo to Hecate. "I think Hermes is grounded for the time being. Interpol is with him."

"Why?" Hecate asked.

"They wouldn't say, but I think we can count him out. Even if he shakes loose, we don't want to be under that kind of scrutiny, not with a stolen sword, a ransacked historical site, and no plausible deniability."

"My winds won't take us that far," Hecate said. "They're strictly ground based."

I snapped my fingers. "Lau!"

Before she could ask who, what or where, I was punching her name into my phone and summoning up her number.

I was prepared for it to go to voicemail, when she finally picked up on the fourth ring. The whooshing sound of wind, like she was driving in a car with all the windows down, nearly drowned out her greeting, but I knew it was a lot cooler than a car ride. She was on dragonback. Soon, I hoped, we would be too.

"Helen, we need a ride," I said loudly, assuming she'd have as much trouble hearing me as I had hearing her.

"You ... what?"

"We're in Greece. Mycenae, to be exact, though we should probably get the hell out of here as soon as possible. We're headed to the same place you are, and we have ... something ..." cagey, just in case Interpol or someone had already found a way to listen in, "... that should help, but we can't get a flight."

I hoped she'd read between the lines.

"We're somewhere over the Middle East right now. It's going to take us another day to get to you. I don't exactly know when. There's no GPS on this thing. Where can we meet that a dragon landing would go unnoticed?"

So much for circumspection. And that was a damned good question.

"I'll get back to you. Right now, veer toward Greece. I'll call or text you coordinates."

"Fine," she snapped. "But, Tori, you save my partner or you and I will have a reckoning."

"No less than I'd expect," I told her.

She hung up on me. I couldn't blame her.

Once again, everyone was looking at me.

"First step, we blow out of here before anyone connects us to Mycenae. Second step, find a place to land a dragon."

"Dragons," Hecate said with a shake of her head. "You've been holding out on me."

Apollo didn't see the headshake ... or anything else. He had his eyes closed and looked almost as though he was meditating, murmuring something under his breath like a mantra. "What are you doing?" I asked. If it were Hecate, I would have worried about interrupting a spell, but Apollo didn't roll that way.

He opened those eyes, the stunning blue of Mediterranean waters. I wasn't clear on how a Greek god had ended up with such crazy eyes or that mane of blonde hair, but then there were so many rumors of his origins it was hard to know truth from fiction, and I'd never asked. He'd been many things in many cultures and pantheons, some of which must have decided that the sun god should have hair that caught fire in the sun ... figuratively speaking. "I'm communing with the winds," he said. "You asked for a place to land a dragon. I've found one."

"Well, don't keep us in suspense."

"Not far from here, a mountaintop near Olympia."

"*The* Olympia?" The origin of the Olympic Games, which, interestingly, were originally played in the nude. I could only imagine what kind of viewing audience that would get today.

"The same. There's a summit that has not been settled."

"There's actually a peak we haven't built on?" I asked. As previously noted, we Greeks were sort of obsessive-compulsive about such things.

"Building was abandoned. The winds don't know why."

"Sounds ominous," Hecate said. "I like it."

"Well, I don't. How about a nice field somewhere? What about the one at Olympia?"

"You want to defile *another* heritage site?" Apollo asked, eyebrows raised as if they too doubted my sanity.

"We're just talking about landing a dragon."

"Do you ever listen to yourself?" Hecate asked.

"Frequently. Sometimes I even make sense."

She snorted dryly.

I sighed. "Fine, lead on." I wasn't crazy about scaling yet another summit, but Olympia or a private peak, I guessed it didn't really matter where I had my panic attack over impending doom.

7

Houses dotted the landscape on the approach to the summit we were aiming for. Not a town so much as isolated houses popping up here or there. It was near twilight as we approached the top, still light enough to see the abandoned construction there. The boxy white building shone pink in the setting sun. The first floor was only three-fourths the size of the second with the last quarter taken up with columns supporting the rest of the structure, creating an open carport area beneath.

The second floor looked like it was meant to support a floor-to-ceiling bank of windows, but instead of glass, tattered black tarps flapped in the breeze. There was something ominous about it, like the tarps were really shrouds, billowing out to reveal glimpses of the dead.

My imagination was in overdrive. There was nothing to suggest there *were* any dead or ever had been. It was common enough, unfortunately, for builders to go bankrupt or halt construction in the face of cash flow issues. There was no reason to think this had been anything else ...

Except for my inner alarm system, which stood up and took

notice, not going off, which meant nothing was going to lurch out at us, but aware, it seemed, that something *could* at any moment. The hairs on my neck and arms stood up. I couldn't tear my gaze away, and was glad not to be the one driving so that I didn't have to.

That was how I came to see the hand reach out from inside and grab the edge of one tarp to hold it down, keep it from flapping in the breeze and exposing secrets.

"Did you see that?" I asked Apollo, who *was* driving.

"See what?" Hecate asked.

I knew it wasn't a hallucination. I hadn't so much as craved ambrosia since the battlefield transformation that had given me wings and let me withstand things that would have killed a mere mortal. There hadn't been any withdrawal symptoms. No cramps, sweats, shakes, weakness, hallucinations or death. Even so, I was comforted when Apollo verified my vision. Or not so much when I considered what it might mean.

"There's someone in there," Apollo said.

"A squatter, maybe?" Hecate ventured.

"But what kind of squatter?" I wondered.

The road petered out not far beyond the house since there was nothing else on the mountaintop. No other construction. No ruins ... or at least none significant enough to be known. The place was, as the winds had said, deserted ... except for whatever hidden horror we were leaving at our backs as we continued on up.

I knew Apollo's and my precognition would warn us of danger, but it wasn't exactly very instructional. It didn't, for instance, give us anything like "vampires on the rise, bring garlic"—not that I'd ever met an actual vampire or even knew that they truly existed. With belief fueling reality, it was entirely possible they now sparkled in the sunlight and I'd see them coming a mile away.

Still, I didn't like it.

"We'd better watch our backs," I said, just in case they'd missed my message.

The hilltop was hyperalive with growth. Huge weeds and determined clumps of grass grew between the rocks that hadn't yet eroded to the point of soil. Some grew up to our knees. A hearty few struck at chest and even shoulder level. There were only a handful of trees, not much higher than some of the weeds. I hoped Lau would be able to find us.

I checked my phone. I had one bar with which to find out. "How close?" I asked when she answered.

"Do you know how hard it is to talk while traveling by dragon?" Lau asked. I assumed it was rhetorical. "I kind of need my hands for other things. We'll be coming in around full dark. You setting off flares?"

"We're going to have to clear a little ground cover first, but, yes, you won't be able to miss us."

"Good. Then I'll see you when I see you." She hung up on me.

We didn't have too long to wait until full dark. Already, the sun was dropping in the sky. Flares on the deserted hillside risked calling unwanted attention, but except for Lau and our creepy squatter, there shouldn't be anyone around to take notice.

Still, I felt weird ... like we were already being watched.

And there could have been anything in the high weeds. Anything. Spiders, snakes, scorpions ... I didn't know that any of those actually got up this high. But I didn't know they *didn't*.

Suddenly, every brush of every leaf was the creep of furry spider legs. I whirled the first time, swiping at it frantically, only to catch Hecate doing the same. She gave me a rueful smile when our eyes met.

"Would you two stop being so girly and help me out here?" Apollo asked, his hand squeezing the tall weeds in his hand so tightly it looked like he had them by the throat.

For a second he was menacing. His broad shoulders massive, his hands meat hooks. I took a step back, and the look on his face changed from cantankerous to ... I couldn't tell, and that scared me.

"Something's going on," he said. "You're afraid of me."

I shook my head too hard in denial, not wanting to provoke him. With the weeds so high—high enough to trip and choke, like strangler vines—and the stones ready to slide from beneath my feet—sending me shooting down the mountainside—I wasn't sure I could get away from him in time if he came for me. I shot a look at Hecate, to see if she was thinking of flight as well. I wondered if I could outrun a goddess.

I couldn't tell. I couldn't tell anything. Her eyes were darker than the night, and she was looking from me to Apollo and muttering something beneath her breath. I didn't understand a word of it, but my inner alarms were blaring.

"Duck!" a voice called out, sharp and unknown in the onrushing dark.

I dropped to the ground without thought, just as Hecate let loose a hellfire blast straight from her fingertips. It caught the high grass behind me on fire in an instant, and I rolled away instinctively, trying to put distance between me and the goddess, me and the fire, but my wings got in the way.

Apollo's voice, raised in shock and awe, stopped me. "Lyssa? Is that really you?"

Lyssa? Who the hell was Lyssa? It was Hecate he had to be worried about....

I opened my mouth to tell him so when it occurred to me that he might be talking about the person behind the warning to duck. My ire rose. Who was she? Some blast from his past? A nymph or demigoddess or prophetess or any of the hundreds of thousands who must have shared his bed over the eons?

I flipped to my feet, wings flashing out in agitation, and whirled toward the person behind the voice. A woman stood there, cloaked in red, her hair crackling at the edges, her eyes all madness, swirling like a maelstrom that made you feel that if you stared long enough, you could catch sight of your doom. From them leaked blood tears.

My blood ran cold.

"You weren't supposed to come," she said, her voice quiet now, pained. "No one was supposed to come."

"What is this?" Hecate asked sharply, her eyes reflecting the crazy, hellfire forming once more between her hands. "An ambush?"

"You came to *me*," the ... woman Apollo had named Lyssa said sadly. "You can't stay. The madness ... it burns."

Madness. Yes, I felt mad. Paranoid and panicked and more. More than I'd felt before, even in the midst of ambrosia withdrawal. I felt like the world was out to get me. Like Hecate and Apollo and this whole setup had been to lure me to the top of a mountain. To kill me where I'd always known I'd die.

"What do you mean?" Hecate snapped. "Who are you?"

"Maniai," Apollo said softly. "The demon who drove Hercules to his doom ... or to Megara's doom anyway and ..."

"Stop!" Lyssa said, the blood tears flowing faster now, thicker, like in a killer virus movie when the heroine bleeds out. My wings flared again, desperate to fly me out of there, out of danger.

I didn't know how much longer reason would hold sway.

"That's why the place is deserted. You drove everyone out," Apollo said.

"No," she said, but not as if she was certain herself. "I've slept. Slept for so long, but the call ... don't you hear it? The call to arms. The call to act. It pulls me. It ... I can't hold on. You have to go too. Now, before—"

A cry split the night, sharp and chilling. Something deep inside me recognized it, wanted me to react like a mouse in the shadow of a hawk. I wanted to dive into the tall grass, regardless of what might be there, knowing it was still safer than what flew overhead.

Dragon.

How had that ever seemed like a good idea? "Run!" Lyssa said. "Run or die."

My legs were already moving, but I crashed into a wall of sheer muscle. Arms like steel bands came around me to hold me in place. "Tori, no. This is what we came for."

"This is madness."

Hecate was regrowing her hellfire orb. The air crackled and burned between her hands, the heat reaching me even at a distance. I didn't know how she didn't burn. I didn't know how to feel. The dragon was death. I knew it deep in my bones. But it was also life ... somehow. I couldn't remember why. And I didn't know that it mattered. If the dragon caught Lyssa's insanity ... I knew the story Apollo was talking about—Hercules driven crazy, crazy enough to kill his wife and children, his whole family in a murderous rage. It had destroyed him. I'd thought the Maniai were a myth, a personification mankind used to make sense of murder, but if Lyssa was one of them ... and if they were being called ... But called by whom?

No time for that now.

"Hecate, no!" Apollo shouted, releasing me to tackle her to the ground.

She whipped out of his way and aimed the full force of her hellfire straight for his chest, seeing him as a threat.

"No!" I cried. I ran to get between them, but there was no time. He was too close, and the orb struck him right at the heart. His eyes went wide and he flew back with the force of it, his shirt catching on fire and his skin seeming to go translucent with the glow of the hellfire burning its way inside. And then, to my shock, it burrowed inside. For an instant, he looked like a jack-o-lantern, all lit up, his ribs showing like sharpened teeth, and then the fire seemed to race through his veins and he roared, his whole body crackling with energy. The sun god, absorbing a fireball.

I was still trying to process this when a powerful wind blasted us and I rocked on my feet. Wing beats blew cool mountain air over us, and Lau yelled from the back of the dragon.

"Get back, she's out of control!"

Her voice was lost over another primal cry from the dragon that turned my blood to ice.

Lau! If the dragon went berserk, what could we do? Fighting the dragon put Lau in danger. Yet everything inside me screamed that it was kill or be killed. The madness pounded at me, stronger than the winds now whipping us like a hurricane.

"The sword," I yelled to Apollo. It was carefully wrapped and tucked away in an army duffle we'd found in a secondhand store. But if he could get to it in time ...

Something was pinging away at the back of my mind, beating at the madness like a dragonfly trying desperately to get at the heat of a lamp. I tried to focus on it, to tune out the ice in my veins and the deafening sound of my internal alarms going off. Then I caught it by the wing and stopped the fluttering long enough to get a glimpse of the thought ... There was more to the Hercules story ... How had his rampage been stopped? A blow to the head, wasn't it? From a stone? Like David and Goliath.

I wasn't willing to brain Apollo or Hecate, and I certainly had no chance at the dragon.

Lau, well, she was another matter. But I thought I had a better idea.

I crouched down while all eyes were on the sky. We could see the dragon now, too close. Time was running out. It circled like it was about to dive, talons the size of steak knives out and aimed. I felt around frantically for a stone of sufficient size, almost sobbing in relief when I found one. I grasped it tightly in my right hand, rose and aimed in a single motion, letting it fly with all my strength straight for Lyssa's head.

It struck her right between the eyes, which rolled back in their bloody sockets, sending her crashing to the ground.

Immediately, the constriction around my heart and the fog around my brain started to recede. The dragon cut off in the middle of another blood-chilling cry, sounding confused and not happy about it.

Apollo stared down at the stunned demon, who now looked like a girl to be pitied rather than someone to be feared. "This isn't good," he said, apparently trying to take my title as Master of the Obvious.

"Well, that's new," Hecate added.

"What?" I was totally lost.

"Lyssa ... in the past, she's had some control over her powers. She's been more like a targeted missile, not a nuclear weapon. The fact that she affected us all, even reaching out to Lau's beast, and that she clearly didn't want to ... It goes beyond disturbing."

The winds whipped her words away. My hair lashed my face, slashing across my eyes, flying into my mouth. The very air seemed to displace, and then with a few more great flaps, the air stilled, and there was a dragon before us and a severely pissed off former detective Lau. I didn't know which was scarier.

I *did* know which held my attention. I'd only gotten a glimpse of the dragon when he'd busted out of Mount Lee. He'd been a whirl of motion then and I'd been too far away for a good look, in any case. Now ... he—she?—was massive. I couldn't tell in the moonlight whether it was gold or bronze, but it was something in that family, with lighter, almost luminescent scales beneath the wings where a cockatiel might have bright yellow. In fact, cockatiel was a pretty good comparison, with the dragon's massive crest and ridges down its back like ruffled feathers. Its maw was somewhat beaklike as well, but instead of cracking nuts, it seemed designed to crack bones … big ones. It had six legs rather than the four of the classic European dragon, and its tail was a whipcord, lashing in agitation. I jumped back as it smashed to the ground a foot from me. Too close for comfort.

"What the *hell* do you think you're doing?" Lau asked, sliding down off her perch near the dragon's neck. If she could have breathed fire, I imagined she'd have been doing so. "What did you do to get her so riled?"

Okay, so the dragon was a *her* then, I thought, focusing on the least relevant portion. "*We* did nothing," Apollo said, striding over to put himself between me and the dragon.

Chivalrous, but totally unnecessary. At night, with my wings and his lack of access to the sun, the source of his power, I was probably better equipped to take care of *him*. Still, it was heartwarming, and I needed all the warmth I could get after the night we'd had. "She did," he continued, nodding at the unconscious woman.

Lau spotted her for the first time. Her eyes widened and even in the dark flashed with something like interest. Her inner homicide hunter coming to the fore.

"What happened to her?" she started to approach, but stopped halfway there, eying the blood leaking from Lyssa's eyes distrustfully. "Ebola?" her voice rose on that.

"Demon," he responded. "Part of her fearsome aspect, all the better to incite madness."

"Is she part of this?"

Apollo, Hecate and I all exchanged looks. Time to say what we were all thinking. "She said she'd been called, asked if we could hear it. Do you think it has anything to do with Namtar? With what's happening in New York? They've got sickness. Panic and rage would be icing on the cake."

I hated the very thought. Lyssa had nearly brought us to

violence on each other in the time it took for our ride to arrive. I could only imagine what she could do in a powder keg like New York, especially on a subway at rush hour or in the endless lines at the DMV.

Lau looked at me in horror.

"After all, Namtar is the god of demons and plagues, right?" I said. Apollo and Hecate nodded silently.

"I think we'd better take her with us," Hecate said into the silence. We all stared at her like she'd lost her mind.

"What? I can set her to sleep. She should be safe enough. But if she's being called, maybe we can follow her to the source. Do you have a better idea for finding him?"

I sure didn't, but I didn't like it. Based on the looks of horror on the other faces gathered around, they didn't either.

Not waiting for permission, Hecate squatted beside the downed demon, weaving her magic, which seemed to settle on Lyssa like a net. I wanted to go prod her with my toe, make sure she was really out, but thought it best to let sleeping demons lie.

"Really?" Lau asked Apollo, clearly deciding that he, at least, had the potential for sanity.

He shrugged. "I don't see what else we can do. We can't leave her here for someone else to stumble on."

She turned from him without a word and went to the dragon, who'd watched the whole scene as if she understood. When Lau got close, she lowered her head, her sharp beak at Lau's chest, centimeters from her heart, and they went forehead to forehead. Lau stroked the smooth, serpentine neck as they communed, and when she turned from the dragon, the fire was back in her eyes.

"Eu-meh will carry us, but if the demon starts trouble, I swear I will push her off myself." I goggled at Detective Lau. Just Lau, now. I had to get used to that. Everything had changed if she would not only condone but commit murder. Of course, maybe she didn't consider it murder for a demon. Maybe she was even right. I didn't know what kind of abuse they could survive.

"But *you* hold her," she added to Apollo. "She's your responsibility. Now, why don't you introduce me to your dominatrix friend?"

Hecate laughed.

My shoulders untensed fractionally, my wings drooping to an at-ease posture. We'd gotten the Sword of Perseus. We had a demonic dowsing rod to get us to the source of the trouble ... or so we suspected. All we had to do now was get to the epicenter of an epidemic ... on the back of a dragon.

My fear of heights kicked in with the force of an *Alien* from the original sci-fi horror flick bursting through my chest.

8

______

I was at the rearguard of our little puppy pile on the dragon, because my wings wanted to flare out every time we hit turbulence or made a course correction, as if I could help it fly. My nerves were shot. Apollo had rigged a harness with his shirt to help him hold Lyssa while he held on to Hecate, who held on to Lau, who held to the dragon, leaning closely over its neck as if it were a racehorse and she was urging it on. I clung to Apollo with all my might, thankful that my transformation hadn't come with claws, because there was no way I'd have kept them sheathed. His shoulders would have been shredded. Riding a dragon was much like riding a giant kite. A giant, living, breathing kite that might get a sudden itch and forget you were there.

There was no talking. The wind whipped any words away, and froze us in place, literally and figuratively. By the time we landed—a lifetime later at least—I felt like an ice sculpture.

"Wh-wh-wh-where are we?" I asked through chattering teeth.

Lau climbed down and grinned fiercely at me. I was sure that ice must run through her veins. She looked in her element.

"Not sure exactly. Scotland? Ireland? Eu-meh had to rest, and so we found a good spot." My legs felt like soggy noodles with all the starch boiled out. I hadn't realized until then how hard I'd been gripping with them, until they threatened to give out on me. I sat down rather than fall, so that I could control my descent. It was a graceful collapse, if unceremonious.

"I think we all need to rest," Apollo said, looking down at me.

He looked drawn as well. It had to have been twice as hard for him, keeping Lyssa's dead weight on board.

"And sleep," Hecate said, trying to finger brush her hair out, which I could tell her was a lost cause. I could feel my tangles without even touching my hair and figured there was no point using a finger comb where only a rake would do. And failing that, a buzz cut. "I don't know if you're aware, but all this beauty comes at a cost."

Her hair crackled with static electricity and she actually yanked back a hand as if shocked.

Lau stifled a yawn herself. "Yes, sleep. Eu-meh and I have been going nearly nonstop for days. I think I'd have buns of steel if the turbulence didn't keep tenderizing them."

I so didn't want to think about Lau's buns it was ridiculous. "Where should we sleep?" Apollo asked. "Right out in the open?"

"No caves!" I said quickly. Not after the Grey Sisters. Not after our prior descent into the underworld where the literal clash of the Titans nearly brought the ceiling down on us.

"Open it is," Lau said decisively. "Easier to see danger coming, easier to escape and much easier to fit a dragon."

"Also easier to *spot* a dragon," Hecate put in.

"Oh, is it?" Lau asked.

I looked over to Eu-meh then, squinting into the night ... and squinting ... If I hadn't known where she was, I'd have mistaken her for a hillock or a fairy mound. Gone was her gorgeous copper color and almost luminescent underwings. She'd blended right into the earth like a chameleon. It was only by looking really closely that I could tell that her head was on her front claws and her tail curled around her like a cat's, her eyes already closed. I wondered if dragons snored and if any of us would get any sleep if they did.

"Huh," Hecate said, unwilling to be impressed. "I need to check in with Hades. If you'll all excuse me."

She started to walk off, when Apollo asked, "Private call? Now is not the time for secrets and plots."

He'd lowered Lyssa to the ground now, beside the dragon, who, strangely, lashed her tail out to encompass the sleeping demon. It made me think of Tauntauns and *Star Wars* and sharing body heat ... only without so much blood and guts. I blamed exhaustion for the odd imagery.

She blew out a breath in irritation. "Fine."

I expected an arcane spell, some chanting, a window to the underworld opening in midair. I *didn't* expect her to pull an electronic device out of her tight leather jacket and jab her fingers at it like you'd dial any other ...

"I thought there were no cell towers in hell," I said.

She shot me a darkly amused look. "You're thinking cell phone. What I have is a *hell* phone. Way more powerful."

I looked at Apollo to see whether it was a joke, but from his blank look, I wasn't sure he knew. "You're pulling my leg," I told her.

She shrugged. "Why? If I rip it off, does candy come pouring out?"

My eyes probably goggled, and when she opened her mouth to laugh, her teeth gleamed in the moonlight. She turned her back on me then, though, and held the phone in front of her face.

I heard the connection when it came through, but it was

like Hades was at the other end of the tunnel ... or like Hecate was on speakerphone.

"No time right now!" Hades yelled into the phone. "Unless you have something earth-shattering to report, like an end to this madness...."

There were cries in the background, inhuman, pained cries, like westerners would expect to hear in their conception of hell, only these weren't the cries of the damned. Those would be thin and weak from eternal torment. These were surprised, cut off in fiercely final ways. Prayers rose up on some lips, *Hades, help us.* Hellhounds snarled and yelped and died....

"What's going on down there?" Hecate asked in a panic.

"Don't come!" Hades grunted and breathed at the same time, fending off an attacker while he held on. "You won't turn the tide. Souls are arriving, but with no body tethers. No meta-physical form, which means no way to hold them. They're mad, ravenous. They're destroying ... Oh, Olympus!"

He cut off then and we heard flailing, thrashing, more cries. A chant and then an explosion. When his voice came back, it echoed, like he was now inside a bubble.

"Fix this!" he demanded.

The connection cut out, and Hecate turned to stare back at us, torment plain on her face, along with an expression she didn't wear well ... fear. She looked like Helena Bonham Carter staring down the barrel of a bald cap.

I was already fiddling with my own phone. If there were so many souls without bodies below, there had to be that many bodies sans souls above, which meant that things had escalated quickly. There had to be news coverage.

But first, there were a dozen texts and messages from Jesus.

Boss lady, where are you?

Boss lady, this zombie virus you asked me to look in to ... it's spreading. People are making a run on stores for iodine [?] and that drug they mentioned in World War Z, *like it's for real. There's already been some looting. Your cousin and her new husband left for their honeymoon, but no one can reach them. Have you heard?*

Listen, chica, call me. I'm worried. Your brother is beside himself.

One from Yiayia interrupted the flow. I didn't even know she knew how to text. *Egona, you call, you hear me? I know this isn't your doing.* Which was more than she'd known when Rhea rose and brought the Titans with her. *But if you're out there doing something crazy ... just call.*

"Look at this," Apollo called out. He was fiddling with his own phone, and turned the screen out to face us. Lau, Hecate and I watched in stunned silence at the scenes from New York City. Hospitals overflowing, barricades set up and police phalanxes to protect them. Schools shut down, houses boarded up, the subways at a standstill. There were shots of supermarkets, corner stores and bodegas busted and broken or with their metal curtains locked down tight with taped-on signs that they'd run out of everything and that there was no cash kept on premises.

"All nonessential personnel are being told to telecommute. Stay at home, stay indoors, avoid gathering where there are large numbers of people. Mass transit has been shut down. The airports and bridges have been closed ..."

It was like the news coverage in every zombie or outbreak movie ever ... only this was real. This was happening. And Nick was there, right at the epicenter.

A sob escaped me, and I turned away, speed-dialing Nick's line, hoping to get his sister or, even better, him, but I got a blaring double-bleep message almost immediately, like a busy signal. I'd never heard that before.

I hung up and dialed again, to the same response.

"I can't get through to New York!" I said, horrified. Surely, all communications weren't down as well. There was news footage getting out, so ...

"Probably all lines are jammed with too many people trying

to call in or out, checking on loved ones, panicking. It was the same way on September 11," Apollo said, gravely, clearly remembering.

"You were there?" I asked.

"Filming. We ... I ... I still can't talk about it."

"We've got to get moving," Hecate cut in. "We can't just stay here. Hades is under siege."

Lau gave her the evil eye. It was refreshing to see it used on someone else. If only I were in the mood to appreciate it. "You want to move on, help yourself, but Eu-meh needs a rest. A few hours at least. We're not going anywhere until then."

Hecate looked murderous. Her hair crackled and smoked. Hellfire lit in her eyes, but it was quickly extinguished when Lyssa moaned and shifted in her sleep. "Fine," she spat. "I'll renew the sleep spell and take first watch. I can't sleep right now, anyway."

Lau softened at her capitulation and reached out like she'd put a consoling hand on Hecate's arm, but stopped short of actually touching her. Probably scared of electrocution. "It'll be okay," she said.

But the fire had gone out of her eyes, leaving behind black holes. "Really? Are you a seer?"

Lau drew her hand back. "No. But now that I've found Eu-meh, now that I've seen the hidden world, I know that all things are possible."

"Including the world's end."

No one had anything to say to that.

Hecate renewed the spell. Lau grabbed a thin blanket out of her pack and tossed it to me, shooting a glance at Apollo. "I've seen the body language. I assume you two can share?"

The censure in her voice was powerful, and I felt another pang for how quickly I'd fallen into Apollo's arms after Nick ... He'd broken up with me, dammit. I had nothing to be guilty for ... Except for the circumstances and the fact that it was our relationship that had put him in harm's way to begin with. My fault he was suffering with third-degree burns. Me he'd been trying to protect at the time. This ... this might kill him.

"No," I said, handing the blanket off to Apollo. "I'll stay up with Hecate. There's no way I can sleep anyway. Not now. You two ..."

I turned away before I broke down completely, and stalked off. Hecate had gone left, walking a perimeter, so I went right. Eventually we'd meet in the middle, but first I'd have time to collect myself. I didn't look to Apollo as I did. I didn't want to see whatever was on his face. I could feel it already through our link. Pain. Understanding. A hollow ache. I wish I knew how to shut down, keep myself to myself.

Out of the corner of my eye, I saw him and Lau move off, back toward the sleeping dragon and unconscious demon, as I stalked the night.

THE MUSIC WOKE ME UP.

Oh, not at first. First it worked its way into my dreams.

I'd turned over my watch to Lau, but, unlike her, I couldn't bring myself to lie down at the dragon's side, scared she'd roll over in her sleep and crush me or knock me straight down the mountain. Lau's assurances that dragons were protectors and that Eu-meh would do no such thing fell on deaf ears. Hecate, though, had no such qualms and lay down by the dragon's belly, the fiery warmth of a stoked furnace reminding her of home.

Apollo laid the blanket Lau had given us over me. It was toasty from his body heat, but still I shivered in the breeze atop the mountain. When I finally shook myself to sleep, some variation of *Werewolves of London* made its way into my night-mares—maybe the idea of being caught out at night on the

Scottish Highlands. Maybe my recent personal experience with unwanted transformation, but in my dream something stalked.

When the music started, it seemed perfectly natural—a soundtrack to the horror film playing out in my head. When my mental alarms started going off, they were so perfectly in line with the growling, prowling menace in my dreams that I didn't register them as anything else.

It wasn't until the torrent of lust and hunger shot through me that I realized something was wrong. Really wrong. I snapped awake, my wings momentarily tangling in the blanket before I flapped it off, frantic in my dream-fogged confusion and treating it like a threat.

I realized immediately that that wasn't it, though, and looked frantically around. There was no sign at all of Apollo or Lau, our two lookouts. But off in the distance, that music played. That strange, haunting, mesmerizing music that had invaded my dream. Before I'd even consciously decided to investigate, my feet were carrying me in that direction, moving me in time to the music. A foot came down with every beat, and as it sped up, so did I. I'd been controlled before, by one of the grand high mother goddesses of them all. I hadn't liked it then and I didn't like it now. The harmony of the music called to me, spoke to my soul. It hurt not to give in, but still I fought against the music and managed to struggle out of the rhythm, but it was like forcing my heart to beat out of time. Against the natural order of things. The world seemed discordant and the night to swirl around me, ever so slightly unclear, like a mirror image in a lake someone had skimmed a stone across. Wavering.

I nearly fell as I broke away, and the step after that fell naturally back into the pattern. I forced it out, spotting something up ahead that had me faltering again ... the Sword of Perseus, lying on the ground, abandoned. My heart rate kicked up, way too fast for the music now, even as it took on a faster pace and more urgency.

I quickened my steps along with it, still trying to stay offbeat, and grabbed up the sword, swinging it twice experimentally before hurrying on. It was a brute weapon and took more muscles and probably more mass than mine to use it effectively. My wings extended with each swing to counterbalance me so I didn't fall on my face, but it was a close thing. If it came down to a battle ... I'd make it work. I had to.

I crested the hill and spotted the source of the music, freezing at the strangeness of the scene.

Apollo dancing.

Lau dancing with wild abandon.

Three bewitching women in emerald gowns with long, golden hair that flowed like waterfalls down to their teeny-tiny dancers' waists, writhing with them ... no, leading the dance. A fourth woman stood apart from them, stomping a foot and playing a mouth harp, creating such music it was almost unreal. Enchanting. Her eyes speared mine as she spotted me, and they flashed a pale green, as if reflecting the moon. My feet started to move of their own volition, in time to the music. The sword felt heavy. Clumsy. Ugly. An artifact of war, rather than peace and harmony. Not joyous like the dance.

I felt Apollo's joy, his lust, his want. The dance was wonderful, but the promise of more, a deeper dance, a joining ...

I'd heard about fairy circles, about people whisked away to the land of the sidhe where time moved differently and the world went on without them. The women were certainly fair enough to be of the Fair Folk, but I thought there was something more sinister to the equation. *My* inner green-eyed monster—jealousy—had all but come alive, shredding the fog that wanted to draw me into the dance.

The sword in my hand snapped up. The music maker's eyes widened at the sight, and she hit a discordant note.

The other three women whirled instantly toward me, the threat. Cold iron, I realized. If myth and legend had it right, if these witchy women *were* related to the Fair Folk, the sword was a very powerful weapon, even in my hands. As soon as they spotted it, they hissed and grabbed Apollo and Lau to use as human shields. The women no longer looked beautiful, only feral and somehow sticklike ... and then I realized it was their fingers. Their nails had grown and sharpened like stakes that pricked into Apollo's and Lau's skin. Both stiffened on contact, their eyes rolling up into their heads. Their faces seemed to go slack, and then ... and then the women's nails turned blood red, as if ...

I launched into the air, my healing wings at first beating frantically to get me aloft. I swept in, waving the sword in front of me, hoping that the fear and the iron would knock the demons back. Because surely they were demons, riled up in the same way as our captive Maniai. Oh, they might be called something else here—Unseelie, perhaps, part of the dark fairy court—but if their actions were any indication, that was just semantics.

I fell on the first wicked wench, swinging quickly, but ready to check my blow in an instant. She threw Apollo at me, and I had to pound my wings hard to rise up rather than let him crash into me. He fell to the ground, but I had to let him go. It left the one woman unguarded. A second aborted her attack on Lau to face me as well. That one leapt for my legs and managed to grab on. I kicked and flapped and tried to dislodge her, but she held on like a leech, her pinprick nails piercing my calves. The pain sliced through before lassitude started to overtake me. My wing beats slowed and I began to sink down to the ground. The sword again grew heavy in my hand, which relaxed around the hilt.

A second demon woman grabbed me from the side as I reached the ground, startling me into bringing the sword up reflexively. She hissed and fell back, and I whirled at the sound, striking the other woman a blow upside the head with the cold iron before she even registered my movement. The smell of burning flesh woke me from my daze. Or maybe it was the feel of those needlelike nails sliding out of my skin.

Lau cried out softly and sank to the ground as the woman who had hold of her released her. The demon and her two attacking sisters retreated to the side of the fourth, whose music had stopped. I had to decide between checking on Lau and Apollo, and making a run at the women going in for the kill, ensuring they could never attack anyone ever again.

A red haze fell across my vision, rage coming on with it. The demons had to die. It was the only way.

I went for them, slashing about me like a Fury, empowered by my rage. The sword no longer felt heavy in my hands, but as light as a feather. I brought it back like a baseball bat, ready to put everything I had behind my swing. The women's flashing eyes widened, one brought her hands up in a defensive posture, looking helpless and afraid. A second of doubt pierced me, but it was too late. I was in full swing.

Just as I would have connected, there as a *pop* in the air, and the four women were gone. I was overbalanced with my swing and managed not to fall on my face, only by burying the sword tip in the ground and using the rest like a prop.

I stood there for a minute, breathing through the red haze, trying to banish my bloodlust and disappointment that it wouldn't be satisfied. I should have taken yoga instead of kickboxing. I needed the meditation techniques.

But I didn't have time now to slip into some kind of Zen state. I had to check on Apollo and Lau.

Lau was closest, and she was breathing, but not strongly. She looked denuded, skeletal, like the demon wench had looked as she began to drain her. I wondered how the wench looked now, flush with stolen lifeblood. I hadn't noticed as I tried to murder her.

I patted both of Lau's cheeks, trying to wake her up, and debated giving her a harder slap. It worked in the movies. In reality … well, if she did wake, she'd slap me back, and given the red haze still teasing at the edges of my vision, I didn't want to risk the fallout. I didn't know if our Maniai had awakened or whether the mania she inspired could reach out even in her dream state.

For now, I gave up on her and went to Apollo, who was waking already and rolling to his hands and knees, shaking his head as if to clear it. He looked drunk. Or drugged.

He looked up at me as I approached, his eyes widening, and he got clumsily to his feet, coming into a wary, squared-off stance.

"Tori," he said, wariness making his voice deeper than usual, colder than usual too, "you're glowing."

"What?"

I looked down at myself, saw nothing.

"Your eyes. They've gone golden and feral. You're … you don't look entirely … sane."

I stopped where I was, fear suddenly taking root and blooming like it had found overly fertile ground. First my wings, now my eyes. What would be next?

"Is it … just my eyes?" I asked.

Apollo picked up on my fear through our link, and he figured out exactly what I was getting at.

"I'm not sure."

I started to panic, and he tried to head me off. "I mean, it's just the eyes right now, but, Tori, things aren't adding up. If I couldn't resist the lure of the *baobhan sidhe*, being a god and all, you shouldn't have been able to either. Coupled with your new wings and now your eyes … something's going on."

"Tell me something I don't know," I said sourly. "And the *who what*?"

"The *baobhan sidhe*." It sounded like *ban-she*, but I knew that couldn't be right. Banshees were supposed to be ghastly, ghostly women who floated outside of old castles warning occupants of imminent death. So said Scooby-Doo. "Just about every culture has its version of the vampire," he said, "and this is it for the Scots. They're related to Lamia, strigoi, Lilitu, Mandurugo, Penanggal ..."

"I can see the family resemblance," I said ironically. If I had it right, Penanggal were supposed to have detachable heads that flew through the air, dangling their entrails behind. "But what does any of it have to do with what's going on with me?"

Apollo looked away. "We should check on your friend." I snorted.

"She's fine. Answer me."

"She's lost a lot of blood."

"Answer me," I roared. My voice deepened and took on its own reverb, scaring even me. I took a step back, clasped my hands at my back, beneath my flared wings, holding on tightly for fear of what I might do. They wanted to clutch at his chest, lift him into the air and demand answers. It wasn't me. And yet, it was instinctive, impulsive ... and weren't those things that came from the very deepest levels of our being, beyond even conscious thought? The things that said what we really were, caged only by culture and control? I was afraid of myself, and I knew Apollo could feel it. If he had any sense, he'd be afraid for himself.

But when he looked back at me, his eyes held mostly pain, liberally mixed with sorrow. "Think, Tori, when did all this start ... your physical transformation?"

I forced down my impatience. If he knew, why didn't he just *say*. "On the battlefield," I growled. "With Rhea and the Titans, after I'd been ... after I nearly died."

"*You* didn't die, but it's like the weaker parts of you did. Maybe. Only the strong survived. And those parts are rising to the fore. Now with Namtar, the god of demons, rising ..." He stopped, swallowed. "No, best if I let you come to it on your own."

I was in his personal space faster than even I could register, my teeth bared like *I* was some kind of vampire. Like they might actually constitute a threat. The shock of it was all that kept me from actually laying hands on Apollo. I needed them to check for tusks or any other crazy features the gorgons seemed to sport in ancient art.

"Tell me," I demanded, trying for quiet but hearing the rumble in my voice. "You said I don't look sane. I don't feel it at the moment. I need to know what's going on." My voice rose as I went on, but I fought to keep it under control.

"Tori, I don't know if the gorgons are related somehow to demons or if demon blood slipped into your family line somewhere else along the way, but what I'm saying ... I'm afraid that side of you may have awakened on that battlefield. Nothing works with you the way it should. When I gave you prophecy it opened up other pathways of your brain; it gave us our link. When I gave you the breath of life ... I don't know. Maybe I shouldn't have done it, but it was the only way to save you. The point is that if you do have demon blood, and if Namtar is stirring things up, amplifying things, as Lyssa implied, as the *baobhan sidhe* hunt would seem to indicate ... there might be worse to come."

I looked at him blankly. My anger had ebbed, but left behind a void where I knew I should be feeling something, but I just couldn't. If I thought too deeply right now or let my emotions loose there might be no coming back from gibbering insanity. If I looked into the abyss right now, it was going to look back. I wasn't going to win that staring contest.

"Let's get Lau back to the others," I said.

He nodded, understanding that we were not going to talk about this. Not right now, anyway.

Instead, we dropped beside Lau. She moaned as we lifted her. Her eyelids fluttered open; she smiled sleepily and closed them again, laying her head on my shoulder as we got her upright. Awake, she'd have been horrified at the very thought. I considered having Apollo take a picture with his phone for posterity ... or the Internet, but I let maturity win a rare battle. Since Lau wasn't inclined to wake and walk by herself, Apollo scooped her up in a fireman's hold and carried her back to camp. I remembered being held that way PW—pre-wings— back when Apollo had rescued me from an oceanic attacker, back when I was a mere mortal as opposed to ... whatever I was now.

Time to worry about that later, when people weren't dying and trying to eat each other's faces off.

Eu-meh was awake when we got back to camp, staring at us as we crested the rise, as though she'd heard us before she saw us. Not just staring ... staring *intently* at Apollo and the limp Lau he held in his arms. I had a feeling that either Lau moved soon or she would. I didn't get the sense that would go well for Apollo.

"She's okay," I said to Eu-meh, hoping she'd understand. "She's just ... weak."

Eu-meh squawked and started to rise. The tremors rippled out like she was at the epicenter of a quake. Lyssa slept on, but Hecate bolted upright, eyes as wild as her hair. Lau moaned right then, and Eu-meh skip-jumped over the prone and nearly prone forms on the ground to get to her side. She stuck her long neck out and nudged gently at Lau's arm with her beaklike muzzle. Lau smiled and tried to roll in Apollo's arms and he had to adjust his stance to hold her. Eu-meh's head shot up to Apollo's level, staring at him eye to eye, as if trying to communicate something like *if you broke her, I break you.*

"What happened?" Hecate asked, on her feet now.

I explained and the gaze Hecate fixed on me was nearly as intent as Eu-meh's. "You met the *baobhan sidhe* and you didn't wake me?"

"I didn't know you were a fan," I said wryly.

"Let's just say that I admire their work."

I shivered, glad that she was on our side. *Note to self: Never agree to meet Hecate in a dark alley. Find recipes that feature garlic and chili peppers.* I didn't know if the garlic would work on Hecate or any of the bloodsucking super-gnats she admired, but I figured if I couldn't ward them off, at least I could give them heartburn.

"Whatever," I said aloud. "We'd better get going. It's too dangerous to stay here."

"It's too dangerous to stay anywhere until we get this whole situation under control. Haven't you been paying attention?" Hecate asked.

Oh, she was *so* not going on my Christmas list. "We'll have to sleep sometime," I snapped back.

"Take it from me, you can sleep when you're dead."

Apollo cut in before I could make the scathing retort I hadn't yet thought up. "How are we going to fly with *two* unconscious women?"

Eu-meh nudged Lau again. This time she moaned and opened her eyes, focusing on the dragon with a sleepy smile.

"Mornin' already?" she mumbled.

Then she seemed to realize she was being held. "Hey, waz goin' on?" She turned her head toward me. "Wha' dija do?"

Why was everyone always asking me that? "Sucked your blood out through my fingertips. Only it wasn't me. I'm the one who saved your ass. You're welcome, by the way." Eu-meh's head whipped around to me, and I was afraid she was reacting to my tone rather than my words, but then she blew hot air in my face and bumped me softly under the chin with her head like a cat might nuzzle her human. I stood there a little stunned.

"Don' expect a ticker-tape parade," Lau said, waking up a little more. "It's your fault I'm in this mess."

I stared at her dumbfounded.

"You were on your way to see Nick yourself," I reminded her. "You were headed for the epicenter of the trouble, and you're blaming *me*? It's not like I put out an APB—*Calling all demons. Be on the lookout for an ungrateful ex-cop wearing her cranky pants and riding a dragon. Tasty blood, all you can eat.*"

Hecate snarfed at that.

"Uh-huh, and why is Nick in New York to start with?" Lau asked.

Recovering ... from burns he'd gotten while with me. I'd never asked for that either. I'd never have put out *that* call —*Wanted, multi-headed dragon-lizard. Fire breathing a plus.*

"Fine," I said. "It's all my fault then. Death, taxes, Donald Trump's hair, the Kennedy assassination. Cellulite, *Star Wars Episode 3*—"

"Airline baggage fees?" Hecate asked.

"Those too. All my fault. We good now? Can we move along?"

"I'm all for moving on," Lau said. She swiveled her head to look up at Apollo. "And you can put me down now. I think I can stand on my own two feet."

She swayed as he set her down, but looked like he'd pull back a bloody stump if he touched her with the hand he reached out to help steady her. He checked himself and after a second, she seemed steadier.

"Can you hold on?" I asked. "Eu-meh, can you fly?" I didn't want to be rude by talking around her as if she weren't there. I suspected that she understood quite a bit.

Eu-meh hopped and extended her wings, as if to show that she was ready to go. Rocks skittered away down the mountainside as she landed, making me very aware of how easy it would be for us to do the same. With everything we'd been through in the past week or so, my fear of heights had gotten some pretty intensive exposure therapy, but even so I wanted to drop to the ground and hug the earth.

Apollo looked at me in sympathy.

"Okay then, let's go," Lau said, which I guessed was all the answer we were going to get about whether she could hold on. "But I think you might want to let someone else hold that sword. I heard something about demon blood."

Hecate snapped a look at me, her eyes narrowing. "Demon blood?"

I refused to look away. "Maybe. We don't know. I might have gotten a little carried away back there."

"Damn, girl, I like you better all the time ... except for that whole thing about the airline baggage fees. Not your finest moment."

"Yeah, well, wings ... grow a pair."

I flapped mine in emphasis and Hecate's laugh split the night.

"*I'll* hold the sword," Apollo cut in, before anyone else could suggest it.

Eu-meh squatted on her six legs, like a lizard hunkered belly to ground to suck up the last of the heat on a desert night. We all climbed on, adjusted, readjusted. I held Lyssa this time, way too intimately close to the demoness who, according to Apollo, had driven Hercules out of his head. Had driven him to murder. It was a comforting thought in the midst of all my other comforting thoughts. Luckily, they were too busy crowding each other and fighting for ascendance for me to focus on any one freak-out.

The trip passed in a haze of near insanity. Not exactly a new experience for me.

I remembered reading Tolkien when I was a kid and

thought now that a special kind of madness must have possessed him to take forty-some pages to describe a trip in which nothing major happened. All I could say about our trip was that it was long. It was dark; it was night. There were stars. For a little while there were city lights, but for the most part we were soaring over the Atlantic with the ocean below darker than the sky above. It was windy; it was cold; it was fairly miserable. And to top it all off, Lyssa snored like a camel with sinus issues.

But we knew when we were getting close long before we actually reached the outskirts of the city. The lights themselves were bright enough to be seen from far off, but on top of that, boats and floodlights in the harbor practically made night into day, and powerful lights swept the city from the skies—air support. Helicopters. We'd heard that the city was shut down, cut off from the outside world. Seeing it was a completely different matter.

We were facing martial law.

Somehow we had to land a dragon in a city on lockdown without getting shot out of the sky.

9

———————

Hecate cursed fluently—or so I assumed from the tone. The wind whipped away her words, reducing them to angry energy.

"What do we do now?" she shouted. That much I got.

"Hold on!" Lau shouted back. She was pressed low over Eumeh's neck, riding her like a jockey, and suddenly the dragon dipped, headed at about a forty-five-degree angle straight for the choppy waters of the Atlantic. I squawked and squeezed Lyssa tightly in the effort to get a better grip on Apollo in front of us. I suddenly wished my arms were long enough to wrap around him and back on themselves like Velcro straps. But there was a demon between us. My legs were trembling with how hard I'd been holding on already and for how long. I was terrified they'd give out at some strategic moment, like when we suddenly banked to avoid unfriendly fire.

"What the hell!" Hecate yelled.

"Going in low," Lau shouted, the wind shearing off her words, "beneath the radar."

"So we get shot down from the ground rather than the air?" I asked. My heart was pounding hard enough to break ribs.

But either no one heard me or they didn't find it worth a response.

The wind chill was ridiculous now, and my muscles were trembling from more than exertion. We leveled out as we neared the water, growing ever closer to the city lights. I wondered where on earth one landed a dragon in the Big Apple and how long it would take panic to set in. Oh right, we were already there. Zombie plagues tended to have that effect. Maybe it would even help us if everyone obeyed the warnings and stayed inside, away from possible contagions.

"There," Lau shouted into the wind, daringly lifting a hand to point.

I tried to follow her gaze, squinting into the stinging air, but she clearly saw some kind of pattern or lack thereof in the lights that I didn't.

As we got closer, I thought I might be seeing what she was seeing, A big rectangular area of blackout in the sea of lights ... or near blackout. There was a smaller illuminated spot in the center and paler areas of light here and there, but a definite break in the pattern nonetheless. Central Park? I could think of nothing else beyond maybe the Chrysler and Empire State buildings that would make such an impression from far off. But as we got closer, I saw something that made no sense, something I couldn't reconcile with the concrete and neon of the city that never sleeps. It looked like ... it couldn't be—a castle atop a rocky hill. Did they even *have* hills in Manhattan? Or castles?

"Where are we?" I yelled to Apollo, hoping he could hear over the rushing wind.

My precog kicked in right then, sending voltage through my heart, and whipping my head around to locate the danger. Apollo was doing the same, and I knew he felt it too. Beneath us, Victorian-looking streetlamps provided pools of illumination. Everything looked okay on the ground, as far as we could see from our height, but ...

I registered the thwapping of helicopter blades a split second before a blinding light hit me full in the face. A searchlight, sweeping us from Eu-meh's tip to tail. I hadn't heard the beating of the blades over the wind whipping past my ears, but now that I was aware, I wondered how we could have missed it. The light passed for just a second, but I blinked after it, knowing it would be back.

"Dive!" I shouted.

"Dive? Are you nuts?" Lau responded. "You can't just drop a two-ton dragon. We need a runway, space to slow and land."

The sound of the helicopter was getting closer. Eu-meh rolled to the right as the light swept us a second time. The sudden movement knocked me half-loose from my seat and Lyssa started to slip from my grip. My legs tightened on Eu-meh's sides and I grabbed for Lyssa, my hands closing on her like clamps, feeling the adrenaline rush of panic give me superhuman strength. But I didn't have the leverage to compensate for the overbalancing of bodies, and her weight whipped me out of my seat.

Fear kicked me like a mule in my chest. I was already kissing my ass goodbye, my life passing before my eyes—Mom, Yiayia, Spiro, Nick and Apollo—my life measured in people, when I remembered my wings. Or rather, they remembered themselves, beating furiously, trying to slow our descent, but I was at such an awkward angle, Lyssa pulling us down, already plummeting.

Some kind of warning issued from a loudspeaker on the helicopter, nearly drowning out my name as someone, probably Apollo, called it out. I couldn't respond anyway. Every breath, every ounce of strength I had I put into my wings, into beating back the ground before it could flatten us like pancakes.

Lyssa jerked suddenly in my grasp, choosing that moment to come awake. I had an instant to hope she was just twitching in her sleep before the screaming began, amplified by madness and fear.

I felt something flood through me, like adrenaline on speed, like ... a crazy cocktail of energy, anger, and denial. *This was not happening.* If I had to bitch-slap reality to get it to fall in line, I was not going out like this. Power pushed out to my wings. I flapped harder, gripped Lyssa more tightly to contain her struggles.

The ground was only a few man heights below us when our descent stopped and I was able to hold us aloft. The searchlight hit me full in the face as I searched the sky for the others, but it passed quickly by, leaving me momentarily blind. Before it could find us again, I brought us to the ground at the base of the castle's promontory. Lyssa's feet hit first, of course, and I had to let her go rather than unbalance. She immediately scrambled to keep her feet and backed away from me, her eyes black holes of madness.

I landed close by and without thinking swung open-handed to slap her face. Maybe I'd seen too many movies, but it always worked there to bring the hysterical woman around ... and it was almost always a woman. (Damned sexist filmmakers.) She hauled back on contact, staring at me in shock, but the madness pulled back from her eyes like the tar pits letting go of a sunken prize—still clinging to the outskirts, ready to suck it back in. Anger boiled in the depths of those eyes.

"You nearly killed us!" she shrieked. "You crazy ... whatever you are."

"Saved you, you mean. And you're welcome," I countered.

Eu-meh's cry pulled my gaze back to the sky, where she banked and wheeled, clearly headed to hide behind the castle. With a flash, something shot out of the copter, and Eu-meh suddenly arched, her wings faltering. Her cry changed to one of pain rather than defiance. I ran toward where it looked like she'd go down, hoping that the copter would hold fire, those inside tasked to capture and question rather than annihilate.

My wings created drag, wanting to act like parachutes behind me. I was awkward on my feet, something I hated, especially now when it counted. I launched myself into the air again—not high, but high enough that I could clear the ground and eat up the distance between me and my friends. I hoped Lyssa would follow. I didn't want to think of unleashing her on an unsuspecting city or working her madness on those already on the attack, but I couldn't babysit her while my friends fell to their deaths.

Eu-meh was flapping frantically now, panicked instead of purposeful. One wing wasn't working the way it should, and while she was slowing their descent, she was still going down hard and at an angle. The way she was canted now, she was going to land on her shoulder, tearing up her damaged wing, if not the bone and muscle that went with it.

I flew around to her other side, yelling, "This way. Everyone lean this way. She needs the ballast!"

For once, not even Lau argued with me. Hecate, Apollo, and Lau all leaned their weight over the side of the good wing, but it wasn't enough and there was no time for anything else. They'd strike in a flash.

"Bail!" I shouted. "You're going to have to bail. I'll catch you."

"All at once?" Lau yelled back.

"I'll do my best."

It wasn't possible. I knew that. She did too, clearly. There was no time to explain that what I couldn't prevent, Hecate could heal. There'd still be the pain and the danger of something they couldn't come back from.

With faith that humbled me, Apollo made the leap first, falling into me and knocking me back. I caught him in a way that would have made my family of trapeze artists proud. If only they could see me now ... The thought flashed even though I didn't have time for it.

I pounded my wings hard to keep us aloft. The loss of Apollo's weight had barely registered on Eu-meh, pain or panic making her flap with greater urgency and less effect.

"Next!" I yelled.

Hecate glanced at Lau, who shook her head adamantly. Hecate didn't waste breath convincing her, but slid off, reaching for my neck and hanging on for dear life. That was all the weight I could take. We sank to the ground, and Hecate slid down my body as soon as she could touch. Apollo right after.

Eu-meh struck as he did, the whole area quaking from the impact. Hecate, Apollo, and I ran for the stone cliffs of the castle that had stopped Eu-meh's flight. She was crumpled against the base of it now, a tangle of legs, wings, and neck. There was no sign of Lau.

The helicopter was looking for them as well, the searchlight sweeping the ground. It would find us at any second. Panic squeezed my heart in my chest.

"Can't you do anything?" I yelled at Hecate.

"Do you want me to hide us or do you want me to heal?" she snapped back, looking poisonous at the idea that she was asking rather than telling me what to do. I knew there was a reckoning ahead.

"Hide now, heal later." If there was a later.

I expected her to stop dead in her tracks and begin muttering a spell, but instead she ran even faster for the castle cliff, dodging the downed dragon to put her hand flat against the stone wall, holding the other out toward the oncoming helicopter. Her eyes rolled up into her head and came back black as night, flashing as her chant grew in power and volume. I was torn between watching her and the air rippling in front of her, and crawling over Eu-meh in search of Lau.

The dragon let out a piteous sound, and I went to her head,

looking to calm and quiet her. Her eyes were glazed with pain, but they were aware, alert. One of her wings moved and Lau pushed out from beneath it, looking shaky but alive.

"We have to get out of here," she said, sliding down Eumeh's body toward her head, taking her muzzle between her hands to gaze into the dragon's pain-filled eyes. "Are you okay, baby? Can you move?"

I looked away; it seemed like a private moment.

"We're okay for now," Hecate said. "I've cast an illusion to make the cliff appear to extend out farther than it does. We're 'behind' it, so they can't see us, but they're bound to land and explore. If they hear us or if they spread out to search ... I don't know how much time I've bought us."

Lyssa ran up then, possibly having decided she was better with us than with men shooting out of helicopters. The madness still licked at the corners of her eyes.

"What the hells was that?" she asked. "What have you dragged me into?"

"You ever see the movie *Escape from New York*?" Apollo asked. "In this case they're trying to contain a contagion and not criminals, but it's the same idea. They don't want anyone getting in with the power to get anyone out."

"But the news reports—the virus isn't limited to the city anymore," I protested.

"You want logic or you want reality? The reality is our dragon was just shot down. The city is quarantined. Maybe the plague has broken free, but it seems to have started here. Whether they're thinking about containment and slowing the spread, or still trying to isolate patient zero, we've entered a no-fly zone. We might be wingless right now, but the guys—or girls," he jumped in before I could protest, "—in that copter are not going to forget what they saw."

"But they will rationalize," I said.

Because there was no way they were going to report an

unidentified dragon-shaped flying object.

"Focus, people," Lau snapped, looking from Eu-meh to us. "Where are we? What do we do?"

"Belvedere Castle," Apollo said. "I was here once for a shoot. It's a weather station in the center of Central Park. Impressive as hell from the outside, but not much to it on the inside. No place to hide a dragon, even if it wouldn't be the first place they'd look since we landed practically on top of it."

"Great, any suggestions?" she said wryly.

My phone chose that moment to ring—"Chalk Outline" by Three Days Grace, a song that always made me think of Hermes ... or possibly the way I'd like to see him. I reserved it just for him. Of course the trickster god *would* call at the worst possible moment. But the tingle that ran through me as my hand closed around the phone said that this was a call I should take.

"What," I growled into the phone as low as I could. "Now is not a good time."

"Is it ever? Where are you?"

"Where are *you*?" I countered, wondering if he was calling for bail money or a character witness. Last I knew, he was stuck with Interpol.

"Certainly not right behind you," he said.

I whirled around, phone still pressed to my ear, to see Hermes in his Iemisch form—body of a fox, tail of a serpent. The fox face seemed to laugh at the look I wore, and the tail lashed happily, like a cat who'd gotten into the cream.

"What the—" The shaken look cleared from Lau's face as she dropped into a warrior stance, ready to take him on.

Hermes barked out a laugh, and in the blink of an eye went from semi-serpent to man. I didn't know how he ended up with clothes on. Maybe it was all illusion, but I was pretty happy for at least the appearance of those khakis and the open-necked white shirt.

Lau went from shaken to stunned. "But—how—"

"You ride a dragon and *that* impresses you?" Hermes said. "If you like that, I have some magic beans and a bridge you could buy. The latter has a troll under it, but he works for tips." He was in full-on charm mode, even showing a dimple in his right cheek I didn't remember seeing before.

"Keep it down," I spat. Because in the distance, the sound of the copter blades was winding down and a drill sergeant voice was issuing orders for the crew to fan out and search the grounds.

"You need a diversion," Hermes said, more quietly at least.

"You have some kind of trick up your sleeve?" Hecate asked sourly.

The look he gave her would have withered a mere mortal. "Think who you're asking."

"More importantly, what will it cost us?" I asked.

He turned his look on me. "*Agape*, I'm hurt."

"You will be," I said. "Cost?"

"Fine, I may be in a bit of trouble. I thought we could arrange tit for tat." His gaze fell to my chest and Apollo glared and took a step forward. Hermes raised his gaze again, the dimple back full force. "Relax, big guy. I meant metaphorical tits. Well, maybe not entirely metaphorical."

He held up a finger to signal that we should give him a minute and walked off toward Eu-meh's far side, like her body could shelter the sound of his voice from our searchers. He spoke into his phone and waited for the result.

A second later, someone must have picked up, and he said as quietly as he could and still be heard, "Mel? Yeah, it's on. They're at Belvedere Castle. I think if I can get them to the Central Park stables, we'll be in the clear. Think you can handle it?" He grinned a salacious grin at whatever he ... she? ... said next and responded, "How could I forget?"

Then he hung up the phone and turned to all of us, who

were watching him expectantly. "Give her five minutes," he said, cutting off as voices came closer, orders given to go left and right, two by two, and to move out. The voices were far too close for comfort, and I said a prayer to whatever gods still had the power to answer pleas that the corresponding people would trust their eyes and not get any closer. Most had no idea about magic and wouldn't have any reason to doubt their senses ... as long as we didn't give them one.

We waited in anxious silence. Lau went back to Eu-meh, stroking her neck and keeping her calm. Apollo held Perseus's sword at the ready. My prayers became more fervent. I didn't want to see bloodshed, especially not that of someone who was only doing his or her job, just protecting and defending ... exactly what we were trying to do.

Hecate's illusion was like a one-way mirror. They couldn't see in, but we could see out, though it was like looking through a film. We saw one soldier jog past, then another ... Something told me he was higher up on the chain of command. I didn't know anything about insignia, and anyway he was in field dress, but he had an air of authority. He didn't walk, he stalked, and right now he was headed straight toward us, his brow furrowed like he sensed something. He stopped just before the wall, staring as if he could almost see through it, as if he knew someone was there. His gaze practically locked with Hecate's and I could see her lips moving, even though no sound came out. Performing a spell? Getting one ready?

My precog kicked me with the force of a bucking bronco, and I knew that whatever she had in mind, it wouldn't go well for him should he pierce her veil. I readied myself to jump between them and take whatever she was preparing to throw, all while stunning him with the gorgon glare.

He took a step forward, reaching out a hand toward the illusion. My muscles tensed, my wings wanted to flare out and I held them to me only with an effort of will.

Lyssa gasped and I flinched toward her for a split second, ready to shut her up, but Apollo already had a hand over her mouth and another wrapped around her body, holding her still. Her eyes blazed red, the color of madness and blood.

The soldier lunged—

And a scream tore across the night. High-pitched, throat-tearing … the sound of someone who knows that if help doesn't come in that next second, there will be no tomorrow to worry about vocal cords or eardrums or anything else ever again.

He whirled toward the sound and was off like a shot. My wings flapped, ready to take off after him, thinking zombie or demon attack, thinking that Lyssa's bleeding insanity had reached out and touched someone, but Hermes grabbed my wrist and held me there.

"Distraction," he said, "let's go."

"But—"

"Wait, could Mel be … Melpomene?" Apollo asked incredulously.

"One and the same. Now, let's go!" He looked to Lau. "Can you get your dragon up?"

"She's not *my* dragon."

"Fine, she's her own dragon. Can you get her up? Can she walk?"

Lau glared at him, but not even for half a second before turning back to Eu-meh. "Baby, can you stand?"

"Here, let me help," Hecate said, dropping her illusion. The rocky illusion fell like a sarong at the beach, and she swiftly laid hands on the dragon. A blue light, much like that from a breath mint commercial denoting magically fresh breath, flowed over Eu-meh. Immediately, her muscles seemed to relax, giving up the tension of pain. "That'll help, but I can't do any in-depth healing until we're out of here."

Eu-meh struggled to her feet, as if she understood it all.

There was a second scream, so full of panic and fear that all the hair on my body and my precog stood up and took notice at the same time.

"She's not faking!" I said.

Apollo cursed, feeling it too. "Hecate, you get Lau and the dragon to safety."

He didn't have to tell the rest of us what to do; we were already off in an instant. Even Hermes, who was not usually a headfirst into danger sort, was chewing up the ground. His winged sandals would have come in handy. I wondered if they'd been confiscated by Interpol. But I didn't spend a lot of brainpower on it. I was airborne already and racing toward the danger, leaving the other two in my dust.

I saw the gunfire before anything else, and a soldier going down in a hail of it, his final burst going wild, cutting one of his fellow soldiers down under the burst of friendly fire. He was immediately swarmed by the human-shaped horrors he'd been trying to fight. They fell on him, tearing, ripping ... His clothes, my mind tried to supply, but I knew from the wet gleam of their hands as they raised them dripping toward their mouths that that wasn't the case. They were after flesh and blood.

"Sword!" I yelled to Apollo, circling back for it. I was going to get there first. It made sense for me to have it and to cut a swath through the horrors.

"They're people!" Apollo said, trying to impress it on me with his look, afraid, I thought, of the bloodlust that had come upon me before.

"What do you want me to do? Let them kill and infect others?"

"No ..." He said it reluctantly. Right, Apollo, god of medicine, among all those other things. He'd think about a cure. He'd want to preserve life.

"I'll aim to brain and not behead. That's my best offer," I said, wanting to mean it, willing to say anything to gain the weapon and join the fight. "Now give me the damned sword!"

I looked back momentarily and saw the second soldier struggle to his knees. He made it to one knee, the other leg bloody and useless. I prayed his brother-in-arms hadn't struck an artery with his wild shooting. I had to hurry.

The sword hilt hit my hand, which instinctively closed around it, and I was off, flying furiously for the scene of the carnage. As I closed in, the soldier took out one of the horrors chowing down on his friend with a headshot, but I didn't think he was going to get them all. "Hold your fire!" I yelled as I flew between him and the body, swinging the sword with all my strength, blade first. I wanted to see the stolen blood fly. I wanted to stop any chance of another man going down to be rent to death.

Apollo shouted my name, seeing my intent. I howled in frustration as I let his voice be my conscience, turning my swing at the last possible second so that it hit with the flat of the blade. The head of the zombie thing caved beneath it. I could feel it like an unripe melon ... hard, but not hard enough. It fell away, but others grabbed at my legs, pulling me down. I slashed the sword around me, unable with multiple targets to keep to the flat of the blade. It sliced through flesh like some kind of Ginsu commercial.

Out of the corner of my eye, I saw Apollo and Hermes come up on the scene and grab the downed soldier from under the melee that had forgotten him in the wake of my attack. I couldn't tell if we'd been in time to save him, whether it was any kind of rescue at all or whether he'd become one of the zombie things in short order.

My attention snapped back to my own situation as something latched on to my leg, and I looked down to see a head. *Teeth* ... Teeth were latched on to my leg. In the adrenaline rush of battle, I couldn't feel any pain. I could only hope that they hadn't broken the skin or penetrated my pant leg or ... I swung the sword once again, using the flat of the blade. It was a bad angle, but I was highly motivated. On impact, the head jerked to the side, tearing my pants and bringing a piece of them along with it. I struck again, now at a better angle, and the zombie fell to the ground, still twitching.

Nothing new reached for me, and I flew up to survey the scene. Nothing but twitching bodies directly below. Apollo, Hermes and the two soldiers off to one side. To another, a body lay as still as death. Female, if the flared hair and the gown were any indication.

I flew to her and landed at her side. Her neck … her neck was gone, nothing but some stringy, bloody goop holding it together on one side. And her stomach had been ripped open, turning her once white dress to scarlet. Her eyes and mouth were still open, staring, the terror still in the set of them, even if there was no glimmer of life left. Her skin was pale and perfect, almost porcelain. Her eyes and lashes as dark as her hair, not needing any enhancement. The blood had drained from her cheeks and lips, like it had from the rest of her. She didn't look real, but like someone staged for film. So beautiful and yet so dead.

"Is she alive?" Hermes called.

I looked toward him, but we were too far away for my eyes to tell the tale. "No. Yours?" He glanced at the soldier at his feet, the one they'd pulled from the melee. "He's unconscious but hanging in there. I'm not sure if he'll consider that a win, given …" He stopped, because the soldier with the shot-up leg had leveled his gun at Hermes and Apollo, trying to keep his eyes on both.

"Don't anyone move. I've called for backup. It should be here anytime. You're going to have to explain … everything." His gaze flicked toward my wings, and Hermes lashed out with lightning, trickster-god reflexes to snag the gun during the millisecond of distraction, turning it back on the solider.

"I don't want to use this," he said. "But you need to be quiet and let the grownups talk." He looked to me. "We can't leave her here. And we can't stay."

"I can take her, but we can't leave the others alone and defenseless," I said, nodding toward the soldiers on the ground.

"That *is* a dilemma," Hermes agreed. He shifted his grip on the gun and removed the magazine, holding it in one hand and the gun in the other and fixing the conscious soldier with a blood-chilling gaze.

"If I give this back to you, you can probably fire on us before we can get away. But that would be a grave mistake. For one, we might be the only ones who can stop this whole mess. For another, you might want to conserve your ammunition in case more of these things arrive before your backup. You've got to consider one question: *Do you feel lucky, punk?*" Hermes's grin ruined the moment. "I've always wanted to say that."

The soldier looked at him like he was crazy. "What do I tell my superiors?"

"Tell them you were bested by a winged woman wielding a sword and two unarmed guys. I bet that will go over real well."

"I think I'm delirious," he said, swaying on his knees. "Yeah, best to go with that."

I lifted Melpomene in my arms, her hair and tattered ends of her dress falling dramatically toward the ground so that she looked every bit the tragic heroine she inspired as one of the Muses. A broken doll, barely articulated. I hadn't even known her and I could feel the sadness pulling at me, stronger than gravity. My wings seemed to beat more slowly with the weight of it, but I got us airborne. Hermes and Apollo backed away from the soldiers. Hermes still held the gun until he decided he was far enough from the soldier to toss it and run ... which he did.

The three of us raced off the way we'd come, with Hermes calling directions to the stables as we went. No gunfire followed us. No more zombies stumbled out from behind.

10

Red sky at night, sailors' delight.

Red sky at morning, sailors take warning.

—an old proverb, often spouted by Pappous to predict travel conditions

---

We were almost there when Melpomene spasmed in my arms. I almost dropped her in shock and primal fear. She was dead. I *knew* she was dead. Which meant ...

I glanced down at her and met eyes staring up into mine. They were still filmed over, but somehow no longer sightless. Her head wobbled, like she was trying to get the few strands of muscle still attaching it to her neck to work. If that happened, she'd attack. I knew it by the intensity of her glazed eyes and the sudden tension in her body.

Hecate ran out to meet us as we came upon the stables, appearing seemingly out of nowhere. I landed beside her, Hermes and Apollo, on foot, trailing behind. As I started to set

Melpomene on her feet, she lunged toward Hecate. It was more a falling forward than a targeted strike, but still she hit home.

Hecate yelled in shock and reached defensively for the falling Muse, grabbing her by the upper arms and holding her gnashing teeth away from any sensitive spots. Melpomene's head lolled forward, her neck unable to support it, but still straining with the rest of her body toward Hecate.

"What the hell?" Hecate asked. "Is this—?"

"Melpomene. We didn't get to her in time." I stated the obvious for the record. "We have to get her inside. And keep her away from the others."

"Duh," Hecate responded.

Hecate risked taking a hand off one of Mel's arms to tap her firmly on the head. "Sleep," she commanded in ancient Greek.

Melpomene slumped forward into Hecate's embrace, but Hecate pushed her back into my arms, brushing disgustedly at her clothes to swipe away any bodily fluids that had transferred. I wondered how well blood came out of leather and whether she had a decent dry cleaner in hell. My brain was once again going off on tangents to avoid what was right before it. Our side consisted of a zombified Muse, a witch goddess, a trickster, a sun god, a garden-variety human (former) detective, a not-so-human PI, a wounded dragon, and a mistress of madness. *This* was our army. We'd barely begun to fight, hadn't even come face-to-face with the actual enemy, and already we'd fallen back to lick our wounds.

Unacceptable.

But Hermes knew more than he'd said so far. I was sure of it, and as soon as we had a quiet moment, I was going to beat it out of him. Or maybe he'd volunteer the information, but the edge hadn't yet come off my bloodlust, and I was sort of hoping to do things the hard way.

Then there he was—Hermes, with Apollo right on his heels. Hecate motioned for us to follow her, and we did, disappearing through a door that still looked to be gated and bolted but clearly wasn't. Inside, the snoring was enough to rattle walls. Eu-meh, recovering. She was in a stall down on the far end of the building we were in, but it wasn't a huge building, and the sound echoed through the place, reinforcing itself.

"Where's Lyssa?" I asked.

"Sleeping. Stall across from the dragon," Hecate said. "You can put your Muse next door."

Melpomene couldn't have weighed much over a hundred pounds, some of which had been lost to the zombie bloodlust, so it was easy to hoist her up with one arm and open the stall door Hecate had indicated with the other. I laid her down gently on the bare earth inside, even though I knew she was beyond feeling anything.

I closed and locked the stall behind me and looked in on the others. Lau had abandoned her stall and was spooned with Eu-meh, her back pressed up against the dragon's chest between the first and second set of feet, one hand beneath her head and the other resting on one of Eu-meh's huge front paws. It was kind of adorable. If I'd been in another kind of mood, I'd have snapped a picture. But that wasn't what I wanted to snap. A neck, now that was a different matter. One neck in particular.

I turned back toward the gods and goddess still conscious and fixed my gaze on Hermes. "Talk. Whatever's going on, you tell us now. No riddles. No cryptic crap. Just lay it out."

Hermes looked sad. I'd seen mischievous, pissed, teasing, intense ... so many other emotions from him in the past, but sadness was a new one. It looked sincere, but I didn't trust it.

"Fine, but can we sit? This may take a while and I've had a rough few days. Even gods need a rest sometimes."

To demonstrate, he collapsed where he was standing, falling cross-legged to the ground. It was the first sign of weakness I'd ever seen from him, and considering that he was one of our few allies, it was less than comforting. I sat with more purpose, as did Apollo. Hecate decided to stand. And pace.

"How much do you know about Javier Kontis?" he asked.

Holy non-sequitur, Batman.

"Who?" I said.

"Exactly," he answered, as if that made all the sense in the world. "Javier is an eccentric collector. Reclusive, yet controversial in certain circles for outbidding museums and cultural consortiums for artifacts that interest him, particularly with occult or end-times significance."

A chill ran up my spine. "Okay, creepy, but he can hardly be alone in that, with all the false prophets, doomsday preppers, prognosticators, and collectors out there."

"Yes, but I wasn't shipping for any of them when my cargo got hijacked or flew off on its own or whatever ..."

"Come again?" Apollo asked.

Hermes glared. "I don't know how much clearer I can make it. I was over in Greece to check out my movie, yes. To crash your cousin's wedding, yes. To sweep your friend Christie off her feet and maybe rub your face in it just a little," he admitted, gaze flashing to mine, the mischief temporarily animating his face. "But also because I was asked to personally transport a precious cargo, a very ancient artifact. Babylonian, Sumerian, something like that. I'm no kind of scholar, but even I've been to a museum or two—mostly interested in portrayals of me, of course, but all so static and *boring*. My god, I think if I see one more statue with the tightly coiled hair, one leg out in front of the other and my arms raised holding something or other, I'll scream. *Seriously?* They call that art?"

Hecate growled and paused in her pacing right behind Hermes, as if she might knock him upside the head to get the story moving again.

He looked up from his seated position and winked. "I can

see straight up your nostrils from this angle, especially when they're flaring like that. Sex-y."

She raised a fist and Hermes caught it in both his hands, kissing her knuckles like a courtier. She wrenched her fist back out of his hand and would have beaten him with it if Apollo hadn't cut in. "Children! Apocalypse now, grudge match later, okay? Hecate, if we live through this, I'll arrange for the cage match myself. Hell, I'll sell tickets. We'll rent out the Coliseum." He turned on Hermes. "For now, have we forgotten that Melpomene is dead? And probably that soldier as well. How many more? I think they've earned your undivided attention."

The light went out of Hermes's eyes and he looked almost as dead as the Muse we had locked away in a stall. Hermes's face was not built for sorrow or seriousness.

"Fine," he said, defeated. "Point is, we've all seen artifacts from that time. Fairly crude, badly eroded, culturally significant, but hardly aesthetic."

"Yeah," I encouraged, before Hecate could threaten him again to get him to the point.

"This was a work of art. Truly. Not just sculptural, but like a being fossilized and frozen in time. I'd call it a gargoyle, but I'm fairly sure the Greeks invented them, if not the actual word. Plus, I'm talking a relief of tendons and muscle, struts in the wings, veining. It would have taken a master craftsman with tools a lot more modern than they had at the time. Either Javier was getting scammed—hard to believe for a collector of his caliber—or ... this was something else."

"And it was hijacked?"

Hermes shook his head. "No. I mean, that's what the police think—some kind of air pirates, but there's just no way. First of all, how on earth? Second, we'd have noticed we'd been boarded, unless you believe someone successfully tricked the trickster. Which I don't."

"So what do you think happened?" I asked.

"There was a horrendous noise, a cracking, a clanging from the cargo hold, and then a rending, a loss of air pressure, a great dip like something massive had pushed off, and then we leveled. When my steward ran back to check the window into the cargo hold, the crate had burst open and the side of the plane had been punched out. Not in, not cut open, *busted outward*."

All of us stared, thinking over the implications. "Where does Interpol come in?" I asked.

"I guess they'd been tipped off about the artifact, which maybe wasn't technically supposed to leave the country. They were waiting for us when we landed, but the cargo was gone. Try as they might, they couldn't prove we'd ever had it. Oh, clearly there'd been *something* in the crate, but without evidence ..."

"And you think this has something to do with what's going on?" I prompted.

"I don't believe in coincidence, do you?" he asked, going on without waiting for an answer. "An end-times artifact comes alive and breaks out of captivity as we near the East Coast and then all hell breaks loose? I think it's worth investigating. And Javier seems a likely place to start."

"You mentioned he's reclusive," Apollo cut in. "Can you get to him?"

"Not so far. He's had his people call my people. It's all been through intermediaries. With the loss of the cargo, there's, uh, even been the threat of a lawsuit. I can't get close. But you, Apollo ... that's another matter, especially with that tasty trinket you all are lugging around."

He looked to the sword in my lap I hadn't even realized I was still holding. And stroking.

Like a cat.

I stopped midstroke and glared back defensively. "We can't sell him the sword!"

"We don't have to. We only need it as bait to lure him into a meeting."

"Great, so we have tea and play twenty questions. What about action?"

"Are you so anxious to act without intel? Who are you striking out against? Where do you even start?"

The adrenaline still rushing my system didn't like his logic. Not one bit.

"Hecate," I said, maybe snapped. "You've met Namtar. Does Hermes's description sound like him?"

"Tail?" she asked him.

"Curved, wicked looking, like the tail of a manticore or a scorpion," he responded.

"And wings, you said, but basically human looking?"

"In that over-muscled, bulges in funny places kind of way," he agreed.

"Sounds like him," she said. "I can't be sure, of course, but how many can there be who match his description? But we already knew he was here. I don't see that knowing how he got that way helps us a whole helluva a lot. We still have to find him, and we're not going to do that hiding out in these stables."

"I wasn't expecting we would," Hermes answered. "I transported Namtar. Unknowing as I was, I feel responsible. I know, not a word you generally associate with me, but there it is. I was planning to take you to Mel's but, as it is ... Let me make a call." He didn't sound happy about the idea. In fact, he sounded a lot like a messenger who fully expected to be shot for delivering his news.

Hermes was already dialing before we could ask any more questions. My senses were sharp enough to pick up a sleep-cranky voice on the other end of the phone. Feminine.

"Cori?" Hermes asked, voice as serious as a preacher's. "It's Herman. I ... I have some news. You're not going to like it. Are you sitting down?" He waited for a response. "Laying down?

Good, good, listen ... Mel ..." he looked at Apollo and me, as though we could help him get the words out, "... Mel's been bitten. She's in bad shape. Really bad."

There were a string of slurred words all run together and then Hermes cut in. "Worse than that. We had no idea. I thought ... I only meant her to be a distraction, but ... No, no, we'll bring her to you. It's not safe for you to come here or to go out at all. You just stay put." There was sobbing coming through the phone now with a few words mixed in, but I couldn't listen. All I could hold in my head was the image of Melpomene with her throat gone, still trying to attack.

"Cori?" Apollo said as Hermes hung up. "Not Terpsichore, by any chance?" Terpsichore ... another of the Muses?

"The same," Hermes answered, and I realized it was in response to Apollo's out loud question and not the one I'd left unspoken. "As you might expect, she's really torn up about Mel and ... well, I wouldn't be surprised if she tries to take off my head when she sees me. She might even aim considerably lower, but we can't hang around these stables indefinitely. For one thing, my cell battery isn't going to last forever, and we need contact with the outside world. We need to know what's going on."

"You think she's going to let us *stay*?" I asked. "After what we let happen to her roommate? What about Eu-meh? I doubt she's going to fit into a New York apartment. Or any apartment, for that matter."

"I'm saying we need provisions, electricity, and weapons. None of that is going to just drop into our laps. I'm saying we split up. You and Hecate go for provisions—weapons, food, batteries, water. Think siege, just in case. Think long-term. Apollo and I will get Mel back to Cori and make some phone calls, see what we can learn. See what she knows."

"And leave Lau here with Lyssa? How is that a good idea?"

"We'll have Hecate reset the sleep spell before she goes. It should be perfectly safe."

Hecate made a hacking noise, something like a cat choking on a hairball. "Are you asking me or telling me, trickster? One will get you a lot farther."

Hermes rose to one knee, like a knight at the behest of his lady. He tried to take Hecate's hand, but it was crossed over her chest with the other as she stared sourly down at him. "My most gracious and beauteous lady," he began, "I grovel at your feet, lowering myself to beg of you, oh Queen of Cats, oh Moonlit Lady, oh most amazing and fearsome of visage, who puts the bella in belladonna—please aid these poor *avótoi* in their noble quest, without which we are sure to fail."

From where she stood, she couldn't see the glint in his downcast eyes, but he caught me looking and gave me a wink.

Even without it, Hecate was unfooled. "Idiot god. I'll help because it amuses me to do so and because my realm is overrun. But don't mistake me for one of your minions to whom you can lash out orders and expect them to be obeyed."

Hermes sat back on his butt and smiled up at Hecate. "Fine, fine, but if you ever want to do a bit of role playing ..."

She swatted at him, and he fell back just enough for her to miss, but she let it be. "What if *I'm* not on board with the plan?" Apollo asked. We all turned to look at him in surprise. "Tori, can I talk to you?"

I kept my smart-assery to myself, though I wanted to point out that he'd just demonstrated his absolute ability to do so. Instead, I stood, presuming that he really meant in private. The intensity in his gaze sent a blaze of heat through me. I'd never entertained any fantasies about doing it in a dusty stable, but if we were alone I'd have been more than willing to give it a try, especially if ... But, no, I was not going to think about Apollo pushing me up against the stable wall and taking me hard. Even not thinking about it stirred my libido, which flared, much like my bloodlust earlier, and I wondered if it was all part of the same thing. My primal instincts so close to the surface that they wanted to push right through my skin. Apollo, connected to me as he was through our link, grabbed one of my upper arms, firmly but not painfully, and hurried me toward a stall at the far end of the stable. It wasn't big enough that I thought it would give us much privacy, especially if we … if we did exactly what I wanted to do. I didn't suspect I'd have enough control to be quiet or that we were in the kind of company that might not notice. And in Hermes's case, maybe even take video.

Apollo got me into the stall and shut the door behind us, even though it wasn't floor to ceiling and hardly offered sound-proofing. It gave the illusion of privacy, anyway. He put me gently up against the wall, my wings taking the brunt of it. I was torn between elation and disappointment. I didn't want gentle, but he was headed in the right direction.

"Stop," Apollo said softly through gritted teeth.

"Stop what?" I asked, rubbing against him.

"That," he said. His lips moved. His teeth didn't, still clamped down hard as he fought his reaction. I could feel it like a tsunami, surging to meet my shoreline.

I knew he was right. Now was not the time, but still. I could feel his response, physically and through our connection, and it was all I could do not to rip his clothes off. But to stop rubbing … that was beyond me.

He pulled away from me, letting me go. I'd been pressing so hard into him that I nearly fell with his sudden absence. He held a hand back toward me, like a traffic cop, clearly a sign for stop. He faced the other way, breathing. Getting himself under control. It felt like failure on my part. Rejection. Even though I knew …

I was tougher than this. I closed my eyes so that I couldn't see those ridiculously broad shoulders tapering to that narrow waist and that perfect butt, so that I couldn't so easily imagine the powerful thighs under those jeans and the incredible everything that would be revealed if he'd just turn. If the clothes would drop away. If we were alone ...

I thought instead of those horrors out there in Central Park. I remembered glistening hands rising to twisted lips, the squelching and wet sounds of ... I gagged. The lust receded, but the bile didn't. I fought down the need to toss up the acid that had just burned its way up my throat.

"I'm okay now," I told Apollo when I could speak. It came out hoarse, but it came.

"Lords of Olympus, Tori, what the hell?" Apollo sounded out of breath and not in the good way.

"I don't know. It's like all my hormones are raging. I'll ... I'm trying to keep it under control."

"Maybe it's a good thing that we separate for a little bit, but sending you off with Hecate ... That's what I wanted to talk to you about. I don't trust her."

"She's on our side for now," I protested, though I knew exactly where he was coming from.

"Is she? What if Hades 'commanded' her? What if she responds to his commands as well as she did to Hermes's?"

"What are you saying?"

"I'm saying you take the sword and you be on guard."

I stared at him. "I have wings," I said. They flapped as if in demonstration. "If she tries anything, I can fly circles around her. Same with any zombies we might encounter. You're the ones who will be hampered by a zombified Muse and no weapons to speak of. Not to mention, Hermes."

"You're taking the sword, that's all there is to it."

"Why, 'cause I'm a girl?"

"No, 'cause *I'm* a god." He had me there. "Look, the sun is coming up. I'll be in my element. I'll be fine, but you ..." He looked away. "Just come back in once piece, okay? For me?"

I wondered what he'd been about to say. But I, what? I wouldn't be okay? Had he seen something? Sensed something? Had his gift for prophecy flared?

No, that couldn't be it. If he knew something, he'd never let me go. And my own precognition would surely have kicked up as well, wouldn't it?

"Okay, for you I'll come back in one piece. Mostly because, well, there's this one position I want to try ..."

I visualized it, not because he could read my mind, which he couldn't, but because I couldn't help myself.

"Tori, you're killing me."

"Shakespeare's 'little deaths,' right?"

Apollo turned suddenly, grabbed me by the back of the neck and pulled me in to him. Our lips met and that heat that had been licking at me blazed up until I thought I'd spontaneously combust. I grabbed him back, holding him tightly, in case he was tempted to pull away. Our lower bodies pressed so firmly against each other I could hope the heat would singe our clothes away and leave us exposed and ready. I was anyway. The moisture gathering down below was not nearly enough to put out the fire. That would take everything we had. Maybe twice.

"Get a room," Hecate yelled from outside the stall.

Apollo broke away, looking dazed, and I snapped, "Had one. You crashed that party."

"I'm crashing it again. Let's get a move on."

I made a rude noise and gazed back at Apollo. "Rain check?" I asked.

"Rain. Shine. I'm not particular."

"Good, then it's on."

He'd let me go ... physically. Mentally, I could still feel our bond, still feel the fire that we hadn't quenched. I hoped that the farther away we got, the more it would fade, because right now it was distracting as hell, and that could get me killed. Or him killed. I'd finally gotten used to having him around. I couldn't lose him now.

The very thought was like an ice bath. *This* was what I'd worried about all along. That I'd become this attached. Even in the Romeo and Juliet couldn't-go-on-without-him kind of way. But that was just stupid. I was made of sterner stuff, and, anyway, he wasn't going to die. I wasn't going to die. *No one* was going to die. Except maybe ...

Bah, I didn't have time for this. I was *not* going to become some lovelorn waif out of a Greek tragedy, turning into a flower or a tree or a deer shot through the heart by a stray arrow.

"Let's go," I said to Hecate, sweeping back into the main part of the stable. "You," I added, pointing at Hermes, "you keep him safe. If anything goes wrong, I'm holding you personally responsible."

"Same goes for you," Apollo said from behind me, talking, I presumed, to Hecate.

"I'm quaking in my boots," she answered. "I've renewed the sleep spell, and filled Lau in on the plan, so we're good to go."

Lau was awake, standing just outside where Eu-meh slept. She had to be feeling the rumble of that snore all the way through the soles of her feet, but she didn't show it. "We're going to need *a lot* of water," she said, voice still groggy from sleep. "And snowballs, if you happen across them."

"Snowballs?" I asked.

"You know those pink balls of coconut and cake you find in the junk food aisle? Eu-meh loves them, and after all she's been through, she deserves a treat, don't you think?"

Hecate and I exchanged a glance. "Sure, why not," she answered for us. "If we see them, they're yours."

Lau emptied the pack in which she carried all of her supplies and offered it to us, along with the use of her spare clothes for Hermes to rig a harness for carrying the unconscious Muse to keep his hands free in case of attack. Still, they were going to be at a huge disadvantage.

"Isn't there anything you can do for them?" I asked Hecate as she eyed the arrangements. "Maybe," she said. "I can't mask them while they're moving and making noise, especially not at a distance, but I can hit them with a kind of apathy field. If anyone notices them, they won't really care. But I don't know if it works on the zombies."

"It's worth a try."

"No," Apollo said, firmly. "If you can enchant an object or something, that's great. But no enchantments on us. If Hermes or I need to create some sort of ruckus or lead people away, say if Cori's building is under attack, I want to be able to drop the field."

Hecate looked annoyed. "More work for me. The one way draws on your own energies, the other on mine. But don't worry. As always, I live to serve." She gave Apollo a mock bow and ordered, "Give me something you can spare."

He reached for his wallet and took a quarter out of it, handing it to Hecate. She took it in one hand and closed the other over it, muttering something beneath her breath. Her hair lifted, as if static electricity filled the air. Her eyes had gone black and rich with the feel of a starscape behind them, of galaxies dying and being born. And then she blinked and it was over. She removed her upper hand, and the quarter looked just like a quarter. No glow, no shine, nothing to tell it from any other coin, but when she handed it back to Apollo, he seemed to get a brief shock as he took it. His fingers jumped, and a look of surprise rushed his face, but he held on and tucked the quarter away in a front pocket, away from his wallet and any mistaking it for ordinary coinage.

Nothing changed. Apollo was still there. I knew he was still there. But I was no longer worried about him or Hermes or …

whoever else they had with them. I focused back on Hecate. "Shall we go?"

"After you," she said.

She and I went first, making sure the coast was clear. Outside, the morning was crisp but not cold. The sky was pinky-red, where we could see the sunrise off to the east, creeping over the skyline. Pappous used to have a saying about that—*Red sky at night, sailors' delight. Red sky at morning, sailors take warning.*

If only I'd listened.

11

———————

Hecate and I were just about to set foot out of the park when I felt Apollo's sudden alarm and I knew they were in trouble. My precog yowled like a tortured cat nearly instantaneously, and for a second I thought it was warning me about Apollo, but that didn't make any sense. Usually it was imminent danger. I whipped around to tell Hecate that we had to go back for them and met her sharply pointed boot with my jaw.

Pain shot through my head, which torqued to the side like my neck would break. I brought the sword up, slashing blindly where she'd been, as my wings beat the air, trying to keep me upright. I caught something with the flat of my blade. Hecate *oof*ed, and I caught a flash of motion as I was bringing my head back around. The next thing I knew, my hand holding the sword went numb and started to open. Stunned by Hecate's betrayal, I was slow to respond, but as the tip of the blade dipped to the ground, I had an idea. I played up my weakness, falling forward onto the pommel of the sword and using it as a pivot point for my body. My wings flared, and I swung both feet for her, aiming for a mule kick to the chest.

She fell back with a cry, her eyes blazing black fire, muttering under her breath. If she got off a spell, I was dead meat. But why the sudden attack? What the hell—My precog had me dodging to the left, taking the sword with me as I launched myself into the air. A molten ball of hellfire blew past me, singeing my calf as it flew by ... too close.

My one hand was still numb, clutching but not with any surety, and the other was my off hand. I had no choice but to transfer the sword to it. I tried to catch Hecate's gaze for the gorgon glare, but there was no chance to lock on before she was hurling another ball of fire at me. I used the sword like a bat, sending it back at her, but all she did was catch it again, whirling to relaunch right at my core.

But I wasn't there anymore. I could fall faster than I could rise, and I crashed back to the ground, immediately ducking and rolling. More awkward with a sword and wings than I would have been without, but I did come up under her guard.

I swung the sword at her for all I was worth, hoping that what I'd lack in finesse with my bad hand, I'd make up for in ferocity. The bloodlust bubbled up through me again, demanding that I cut deep. I wanted to see the blood, wanted to fell her. But suddenly she wasn't there.

I'd no sooner registered it than Hecate landed a blow right between my wings with the force of a sledgehammer, sending me falling forward. Uncontrolled, the pommel of the sword caught and bruised my breastbone but kept me from hitting the ground. It also held me in place, a perfect target for another blow, hard enough to knock me aside from the sword. It stayed quivering in the ground, close enough to grab again if only I had the strength and speed.

"Surrender the sword," Hecate said, pausing in her attack long enough for me to focus on the growing ball of hellfire in her hands.

"Why do you want it?" I coughed the words out, my chest

dented and my breathing painful. "And why now? I thought you were on our side."

"Why? Because I was ordered to be? Because I seem so docile and sheeplike? I *was* on your side, until you gathered the information I wanted and got me where I needed to go. Now I'm on *my* side."

"*What* side? There's the apocalypse or saving the world. There are no sides."

Hecate looked at me pityingly. "That's where you're wrong. You're a smart woman—smart-ass, anyway—I shouldn't have to explain it to you."

"Pretend I'm stupid," I said, feeling it at the moment. "Make me understand and maybe I'll give you the sword."

She snorted. So elegant. "You want to stop the apocalypse. You're thinking too small. I want to control it. Think of it like demolition or like the immolation of the phoenix—destruction so that something new can rise from the ashes. A new world order ... mine. But I can't do it alone. I'll kill you if I have to, but I'd rather you join us."

"Who's us?"

"Come with me and find out."

The bundle of hellfire in her hands was practically the size of my head, hissing and spitting like it couldn't wait to burn something to the ground. Me, to be exact.

I'd learned all she was going to tell me. It was now do or die. The longer I put it off, the longer Apollo and Hermes went without reinforcements. I had to end this.

"Go to hell," I told her, rolling for the sword.

She roared and instantly let the fireball go. I had to flinch away to avoid it, the fire singeing my back, charring my wings and starting the remains of my shirt smoldering. I turned the flinch into a roll and came up in a crouch, facing both witch and sword.

We both reached for the pommel at the same time, and my

hand came down on top of hers. My nails, ragged from all the recent battles, scraped her skin, but failed to tear her hand away. Her gaze met mine, and I yelled, *"Freeze!"*

At the same instant she threw open the palm of her other hand and a field shot from it, something I'd seen before when she was fighting alongside Hades, feeding power to the shields of Tartarus. This time the shield spell bounced my gorgon glare back at me. It struck me between the eyes, stunning me just long enough for her to grab the sword from under my grasp and vanish with it.

I shook myself out of the paralysis, but by then both the bitch and the blade were gone. The ground still smoldered from the hellfire that had strafed it, but there wasn't enough smoke to conceal anything. Hecate and the sword had disappeared as if they never were.

Inside I raged. I wanted to shout uselessly at the sky or beat at the ground or, better yet, at myself for failing, but instead I did something very strange. Instinctively, I lifted my hands to my lips, where Hecate's blood stained my nails, and I licked at the leavings. The voluntary part of my brain shuddered in horror, but involuntarily ... something shifted inside. I felt the blood rush through my system, signals flying fast and furious to some newly awakened part of my brain. My head hurt like I was having an aneurysm and my eyes flew open wide as some revelation seized me. First, that I liked the blood. It was salty and spicy and ... distinct. Second, that I could track her now. I knew it like I knew my name or that I needed caffeine to live. I'd remember the taste of her blood and I could use it.

Apollo screamed in my brain, not for himself, I sensed, but for ... something. Something had gone horribly wrong. But Hecate had given them that charm ... Hecate, who had betrayed us all. Who knew what that charm might actually do.

As much as I wanted vengeance, as much as I wanted to hunt the witch down right then, Apollo's urgency came first. My precog pushed me to my feet and sent me launching into the air, flying across the park in his direction, straight into danger. I blew past Belvedere Castle and the green turtle pond at its base. Not far beyond, shambling figures ignored my flight, stumbling toward others in the distance as if drawn to them. One or two did look to the sky, as if some instinct remained, some sense of self-preservation, as a mouse might watch the sky for a hawk. But I ignored them, intent only on Apollo and the others.

———————

I SAW THE BODY FIRST, lying in the grass like a puppet whose strings had been cut and another beyond that, charred and smoking. Beyond that ... a mob, gathered thick like the crowds on Black Friday awaiting the doorbusters. In the midst of it, I knew, were Hermes and Apollo.

I prayed to the gods I wasn't too late. As I hit the outskirts of the mob, there was a flash of light, like a solar flare or a burst of heat lightning, and suddenly there was fire in the mob's midst. I expected screaming, peeling away, some move to save themselves, but there was none. My wing beats fanned the flames, and in an instant, it seemed, the whole mob was aflame. It didn't change a thing. The bodies pushed against each other, teeth gnashing, some so close together there was barely enough air getting through to feed the flames. I started at the back, tearing bodies aside, throwing them to the ground, meeting faces, grasping hands and anything else that lashed out at me with powerful kicks meant to break bones. Not because I wanted to hurt, but because there was no other way. Pain wouldn't stop these creatures. Immobilization was all I had.

In the air, I didn't have the leverage I'd have on the ground, and while my blows set them back, they didn't keep the horde down. I fought two and three at a time, with others turning toward the commotion, grabbing for me, some even latching on.

I flapped hard to rise. One or two came off the ground with me, attached like leeches. I kicked like a maniac to loosen them, but the blows had no effect.

"Tori!" Apollo called.

I managed to catch one of the clingers just right, and he spiraled down into the smoldering crowd, taking one of the other zombies down with him as he crashed, but more just closed over them, still coming.

Still aimed like arrows straight for Apollo and beside him ... a giant spider? It had to be one of Hermes's other forms. He could take on Spider or Monkey or Coyote or the shape of any of the other trickster gods that existed in every culture. I'd never seen this form before and had to fight my freak-out, even as its—his—mandibles snapped, gripping one of the plagued and throwing him aside. The horde swarmed around him, still oncoming. There were too many of them and not enough of us. I didn't see any sign of Melpomene and feared that she must be one of the bodies scattered about.

"Apollo, what can I do?" I yelled to him.

"The sword!"

My heart dropped to my stomach, sliding right past my compressed ribs. "Gone," I said, but it came out strangled and possibly unintelligible. "Hecate."

I didn't give him the chance to ask. I flew over the crowd that Hermes was barely fending off and that Apollo had already blasted with concentrated sunlight. He was slightly behind Hermes, concentrating not on me, but on the sky, readying another solar flare, I thought. But the first hadn't had much effect beyond setting the rabid horde on fire. I didn't think the second blast would be any more effective. But I had another idea. I just hoped it would work.

"Hold up," I told Apollo. "Hermes, give me the floor."

Compound eyes met mine and creeped me out, even though I knew who was behind them, but I didn't have time to dwell. I got in front of him and let out the most shrill, most annoying sound I could think of that didn't involve Pan pipes or yodeling. It involved sticking my thumb and forefinger into my mouth and blowing for all I was worth.

A dozen or so eyes rose to me, the wolf whistle breaking through their fog, getting their attention. I met their gazes, refilled the bellows of my lungs, and yelled *"Freeze!"* at top volume.

They froze, and I nearly fell to the ground in relief that I was good for *something* after letting Hecate get the drop on me and steal the sword.

Hermes, maybe testing the waters, lashed out a leg at the crowd, the front man fell like a domino into the one behind, but the thickness of the horde held them more or less upright.

Still, the front of the line was neutralized ... for now. If we could just get to the rest ..."

"Hurry," I told the others. "Before they unfreeze. I have no idea how long the gorgon glare will hold. Plague minds could be more or less susceptible."

"We can't go without Melpomene!" Apollo said.

"Where?" I asked.

"Back the way you came."

I flew back and discovered her on her stomach at the back of the pack, trying to crawl toward the others, head lolling toward the ground, horrifying in the way her neck barely held together. Her entrails had to be dragging on the ground beneath her ... I had to stop thinking or my stomach would rebel.

I landed and grabbed her up, cradling her like a baby so that the crook of my elbow supported her head while my arms supported the rest of her body. I nearly gagged at the smell. There wasn't just blood and guts. There was the scent of everything the body released at the point of death and that was ... whew. It wasn't any better for being a day old. She tried to claw me as I got her settled, so I looked down at those filmy eyes and told her the same thing I'd told the others. *"Freeze!"* She stopped, hand reaching for me, mouth gaping, lacking the muscles to close. As a zombie, she was going to starve to death. My brain refused to consider how to deal with that.

I flew back with her toward the others and found that Hermes was himself again. I made my noise a second time and froze a whole new bunch of zombies.

"Let's go!" I yelled, and we took off across the park, me still in flight with Mel in hand and the others on foot. We ran away from the stables and shelter.

"You can't possibly think it's safe still to head for Terpsichore," I said, out of breath. "You'll lead them right to her."

"No choice," Hermes said. "We still need supplies and information, now more than ever."

"But if Hecate betrayed me and you—which she must have, because those things were far from ignoring you as they should have—anything could be happening back at the stable. Lyssa—"

"Skata!" Hermes cursed.

"Okay, look, you move faster than the rest of us with those wings. Give me Melpomene and head for the stables. We'll grab weapons and provisions as quickly as we can and rush back to you," Apollo said.

"I'm going to skin Hecate alive," Hermes cut in.

"Fine, good," Apollo said, "we'll make that our endgame. You can wear her skin like the Nemean lion pelt. Let's just hurry."

I bent my knees, poised to launch myself into the air when Apollo grabbed me suddenly for a kiss. It was brief and bruising, and when he let me go, I could feel his roiling emotions. If

I'd been a girly girl, I would have stopped to sort through them, but I didn't have the time.

It was a lucky thing, though, that the kiss made me pause. It suddenly occurred to me that if the zombies had risen just as they'd died, one of the walking undead was bound to be carrying a concealed weapon. If not a gun, then a flip knife, a pocketknife or *something*. This was New York City, after all.

I did a quick search, patting out flames, and feeling up frozen corpses. It was not my finest moment. I found an empty belt sheath for a gun that was now gone, maybe lost in the battle with the zombie who'd turned the guy, but I found pocketknives on just about all of the men and some of the women. I stopped when I found a flip knife several inches long. It would do. It would have to. I couldn't take any more time, and the milky eyes of the guy I'd taken it from were starting to track me. He was beginning to unfreeze. In a moment, I'd be lunch.

I tossed the other knives to Hermes and Apollo, who'd put off their quest long enough to see what I was up to. I was airborne the second they caught the bounty, speeding back toward Lau and Eu-meh, worried for Lyssa too, nearly as much as I feared her.

I wasn't even to the stables when I heard Eu-meh's furious cry. My wings couldn't beat any faster, but I tried anyway. My breath stuttered and caught. At times, it felt I could either breathe or beat my wings, but not both. I was near enough now to hear the second cry—less piercing and a lot more human. I landed in what had been a staging area outside the stables and rushed to the door we'd previously broken open.

I bumped it hard with my shoulder, expecting it to just swing open but it didn't give an inch. I bounced back, shoulder now as bruised as my breastbone. "Lau!" I yelled. "Let me in. What's happening?"

There was another furious dragon cry and something hit a wall hard enough to shake the building.

"Lau!" I yelled, voice pitched with panic.

I backed up quickly and took a running start at the immovable door. It gave just a little. My shoulder gave more. Something was barricading the door shut. My arm was already hanging, in screaming pain at the shoulder and numb below. Another run at the door couldn't cost me any more.

I did it, hurling myself at the door with everything I had. It burst in a bit ... just enough for me to fit myself between it and the jam, which I did. My sudden appearance distracted Lau, who was out in the aisle, facing down Eu-meh, who stood, head bent against the low ceiling in the remains of the stall she'd busted down. The dragon noted her distraction and took advantage, her tail lashing like a whip, catching Lau in the chest and hurling her backward toward me. We both went sailing against the barricade and I hit it wings first, hearing something crack as I did. I wanted it to be the door, but knew otherwise.

"No," a woman yelled as Eu-meh advanced. "No, stop." It was Lyssa, as tortured as she'd been on that Greek hillside, but unable to stop her mania from afflicting everyone around her. Her power totally out of control.

No time to think. Eu-meh's tail lashed again. I pushed Lau one way as I dove the other.

One of my wings didn't tuck properly as I rolled, and the pain was immense.

Eu-meh drew her head back then, her belly rumbling. "Fire!" Lau yelled. "Run!"

There was nowhere to run. Not ultimately. No way to outpace a dragon. I had to take down the demoness.

"You run," I said. "Make sure she follows. And misses. I don't want to explain to Nick ..."

She probably glared, but I didn't look her way as she lunged for the gap I'd left in the barricade.

Eu-meh bellowed, her breath hot enough to scorch all by

itself, the scent alone bringing tears to my eyes ... like an over-filled dumpster stewing in the sun.

I ducked into the nearest stall, thinking *out of sight, out of mind* ... just in time. I heard a massive *whoosh* a millisecond later and peeked out when it subsided to see the barricade completely set ablaze. Even at a distance, the heat scorched my face. The flames superheated the very air, it seemed. Particles of hay or chaff or whatever highly flammable crap had been left behind went up in a flash. In the time it took to blink, that whole half of the stable was ablaze with tongues of flame licking the ceiling and chasing fault lines in the walls.

Eu-meh bellowed again, in fear this time as the fat fingers of flame reached for her. She backed away and backed away until she pushed right through the back wall opposite the barricade, bringing it mostly down with her. The sudden influx of air caused the conflagration to flare to ludicrous levels. I was burning. And choking, unable to draw in enough fresh air to breathe.

I steeled myself to dive back out into the main part of the stable, into the flames. It was so counterintuitive that all of my alarms jangled. But they'd have been jangling anyway. Fire. Dragon on the rampage. Gloom and doom and ...

With a huge crack, an overhead beam split and half came down right in front of me. "Lyssa!" I shouted, only it came out as a cough. My lungs were singed and tarred, every breath painful and ineffective.

"Here," she said weakly.

I duck-walked blindly toward the sound of her voice, trying to stay low, hoping for more air, but there wasn't any to be found. My sense of danger pointed me toward the stall where she'd ducked, nearly engulfed by flames. Her eyes were bleeding pools of mania.

"You're going to have to—" she began.

I pushed up from the legs, sailing at her with a blow aimed

at her head. I hit right where I'd targeted and she fell like the other half of the downed beam, straight for the ground. If she'd been mortal I'd have worried I'd struck her hard enough to rattle her brains, but as it was, all I could feel was relief at the knockout. The blow had felt good ... more and more necessary the more closely I approached. She was a menace. In her transferred mania, there'd been no allowing for half measures or pulling my punch. I was no longer so sure we'd been smart to keep her close, but I didn't see what choice we'd had. Then or now. I couldn't abandon her in a burning building. Which meant she was coming along.

Forgetting myself for a moment, I took a deep breath as I heaved her over my shoulder. The smoke instantly invaded my lungs on a search-and-destroy mission. The coughing doubled me over, flopping Lyssa roughly back to the ground and sending me to one knee, catching myself with one hand to keep from toppling the rest of the way. I tried to force the cough down, but the extra tension only made it worse. Relaxing was counterintuitive, but I tried. I was breathless from the coughing and the thickening smoke, sweating like a pig from the fire raging around us. Nearly blind for the same reason. Tears washed away whatever images the smoke revealed.

I had to feel around on the stable floor for Lyssa's unconscious body and then get somewhat intimate with her form to figure out where to grab her to hoist. But embarrassment was the last thing I had time for.

Apollo's feedback loop of fear was pounding at me now, and I knew he'd arrived, seen the fire, *not* seen me and done the math. Or maybe he'd just talked to Lau. For the first time ever, I wished our link were more intimate rather than less so that I could tell him to stay out.

Another great crack and suddenly another beam was falling down on us, bringing most of the roof with it. I dropped to both knees, ducking as if that would help, but something caught the falling beams, stopping them somewhere above my head. Apollo's voice yelled to me from the direction of the door. "Tori, this way!"

He had to be holding up the burning beams the way Atlas supposedly held the world on his shoulders. I didn't know whether to kiss him or kill him for placing himself in danger, but right then all I could do was leave it up to the Fates. If the fire didn't take him out, who was I to finish the job?

I fumbled blindly for Lyssa and found one of her arms, which I grabbed firmly. I hoped the floor wasn't too littered with debris, because hoisting her up was no longer an option. I was going to have to drag her out.

"A sec," I rasped out in a great whiskey-blues voice. "Got to get Lyssa."

Her body caught on something at that moment, and I yanked her harder. Something ripped and the tension released, but the ripping sound continued as I dragged her until it didn't anymore. If she was now indecent, well, she'd be too sooty for anyone to notice or care. Except maybe Hermes, and bless us if we got that far.

"Hurry," Apollo said, voice full of the strain I could feel through our link.

A downed beam was right in front of me and suddenly the length of the stable seemed endless and the distance insurmountable. I put my shoulder to the burning beam, trying to rush it like the football player I'd never been. It shifted, but from the creaking, cracking, sliding sounds, it wouldn't move on its own and I didn't know what it might be holding off us at that very moment.

I had to grab Lyssa into a new position, one in which I could maneuver her around the beam. I hoped she was up to date on her tetanus shots or that it didn't matter with Maniai, because I couldn't see all the debris in our path ... or much of anything else. I headed toward Apollo's voice, but not quickly enough.

Lyssa's added weight and my useless lungs were costing me. Anchors seemed to be dragging at my feet with every step.

When arms wrapped around me, I cried out. The added weight just too much. I started to sink. And then Lyssa was gone. Just gone. The superheated air that rushed to take her place felt like a cool breeze as it hit my sweat-drenched back.

Another set of arms caught me as I started to pitch forward, at the end of my strength, and then *I* was being dragged away from the inferno. And dragged. And dragged. Waves of pain—from my wings, back, chest, throat, eyes—competed to overwhelm me, but finally it was Apollo's voice that did it. "Tori, you're okay."

I wondered at his definition of *okay*, but took that as my cue to pass out.

12

―――

I woke coughing up a lung. Trying to, anyway. The troublesome organ seemed contrarily determined to stay right where it was. But it was the roar of an engine that had me bolting upright.

I blinked into the front grille of an oncoming canary yellow Hummer. I blamed my recent unconsciousness for trying to fend it off by throwing my arms up in front of my face. I waited for impact, but the next thing I heard was squealing and screeching. Then a high, fluting voice shouted, "What are you waiting for? Jump in. Whoa, *that's* not going to fit."

My eyes flew open and I looked up from the grille to the girl —wide Julia Roberts-type mouth opened in awe, high black ponytail shining in the sun, face pale, emphasizing puffy, dark eyes. Mel's roommate?

"Cori, that's Eu-meh. Eu-meh, Cori," Hermes said quickly. "I thought I told you to stay home."

"Like that was going to happen. I couldn't just leave Mel out here. Or Apollo. You, on the other hand ..."

Even through puffy eyes, her glare was pretty effective.

I coughed again, raising some kind of clumped ugliness this

time. I tried to wave away all the gazes on me, telling them with hand gestures to go about their business as I turned away to hack up my tremendous loogie. There was no other choice. It wasn't as if I could or would swallow it down.

My eyes watered and my chest nearly seized trying to force the lump all the way out. I rolled onto my side to keep from choking on it and finally forced it out, expelling it into a thick, awful lump on the ground.

Everyone looked away, not only from the grotesquery but to follow Cori's stare, which had skipped right over the novelty of a dragon and laser focused on her half-eaten friend. The worst part was that Mel seemed to be equally focused on *her* and on crawling her way over for a nosh.

"Oh, Mel," she said in a hush. "You'd love and hate this. So tragic."

I hadn't even thought of that. Melpomene, the muse of tragedy. The irony burned. "We've got to get her home," Cori said, heedless of the danger. "Maybe if we swaddle her or ... something. You've got to find a way to reverse this."

We all looked at each other, not even sure it was possible.

"First," Apollo said, taking charge, "we have to find a place big enough to hide a dragon. Any ideas?"

It was only then that her gaze swung to really take in Eumeh. Her ridiculously long-lashed eyes went anime-wide. "Holy shite. Is that ... Seriously? I thought they were a myth."

Coming from a Muse, that was quite a statement. If the ironies kept piling up, we'd have to build an armory to house them.

"Not a myth. Any ideas?"

"Large enough for a dragon? You do realize we're in the city, right? We can't take her to my place. She'd never even fit through the door. I'm not even sure she'd fit in the apartment." Chopper blades sounded off in the distance, and I wondered if they were coming to search for their out-of-contact colleagues. If so, it was too little, way too late, but I had no idea how thinly military forces might be spread. If not for their downed colleagues, they might be coming for us.

"We have to hurry," Apollo said, as if reading my mind. "Somewhere close by?"

Cori couldn't take her eyes off Eu-meh. "Well, there's the Sheep Meadow Cafe. It's not huge, and I don't know what the space inside is like, but it's close and closed for the season."

"Lead on," he said.

The chopper was getting closer. We all looked to the sky. "Quick, everyone in the truck. I'm going to have to get it out of sight. I assume the dragon will follow?"

She looked to Apollo for an answer, but it was Lau who said, "She will if I ask her to."

Cori's gaze caught her for a split second of awe. "Too cool. Get in."

We all crowded into the Hummer, which was *not* built for quick getaways. I thought of my cute little Camaro out in LA. It might not have handled off-roading in Central Park, but it was great for speed. Cori took off just as Hermes pulled Mel's still-straining body inside. I had Lyssa on my lap and for a moment had flashbacks to the circus, and especially the clown car, but there was nothing funny about this situation. There was no way a chopper would fail to catch a bright yellow Hummer in the midst of all the spring greenery of the park.

The Hummer drove like a tank, but Cori was right, the cafe was close by. Almost around a bend, we found a circular wooden building with a pitched roof that made it look like a planked-over big top tent. It was shuttered for the season, with segmented iron curtains pulled down and locked against intruders. There wasn't any kind of garage or awning for Cori to hide the Hummer under. The place was made for foot traffic, not vehicles, but there were enough spreading oaks and shade trees that Cori was able to get the Hummer out of sight from the air. As long as no one was using infrared tech, which would pick up the heat not only of all our bodies, but the engine as well, we ought to be safe ... for now.

Apollo was the first one out of the Hummer, and he ran to the largest of the iron screens, looked up at the angle of the sun, down to the massive padlock that held the screen in place and back to the sun. I made the mistake of following his gaze and burned my retinas, bright purple spots spreading like ink blots across my vision.

The ink blots hadn't cleared when there was a flash and the smell of overheated iron. When I blinked back the spots across my vision, I saw the padlock had melted to slag, Dali-esque and barely recognizable. Apollo risked burning his hand to grab the iron screen and yank it up.

We all held our breaths, hoping it wouldn't be a long glass snack counter or one-at-a-time entryway. We were well beyond due a break and, miraculously, we got one. Behind the metal screen there was a bistro/bakery type place with not just a door, but an entire wall that slid open to form a large entry. Wide enough, I thought, to fit Eu-meh with minimal scraping of her sides. If she ducked. Definitely it wasn't high enough to admit her at full height.

Lau checked it out first, waiting for Apollo to melt the wall lock as well before she slid it open and slipped inside. The center of the place was cleared of displays, tables or anything else, all stowed away for the season. It was perfect, but ...

Lau looked back at Apollo. "This will work, but how are we going to keep the slagged lock from being discovered?"

Apollo looked sheepish. Appropriate, given where we were.

"We'll just have to get a new one," I said, "weather it a little and put it back in place. With a zombie apocalypse going on, who's worried about snack shacks with no visible damage?"

Lau went out to Eu-meh, who had followed us. Her head hung now in exhaustion or regret for having attacked Lau. Could dragons feel regret? Given Eu-meh's hangdog expression, I expected so.

With her head hung, it came just about level with Lau's, and as she reached out to stroke Eu-meh's neck, the dragon rested her chin on Lau's shoulder. It had to be heavy, but Lau didn't bend, just put her cheek to Eu-meh's and spoke to her in a musical language I didn't understand. The dragon's eyes closed as a cat's might at being petted beneath the chin, and we all stood in wonder, but also anxiety, at the moment. We had to go. But we had to do it right. Poor Eu-meh deserved some under-standing.

Lau said a few final words and pulled back. Eu-meh raised her head reluctantly and blew into Lau's face, ruffling her already disheveled hair. Then she plodded into the open cafe, belly scraping the ground, her wings pulled in tight. When she got to the center, she turned slowly so that she'd be facing the way she'd come and settled into a ball, tail curled around herself and tucked up under her chin. She watched Lau through barely open eyes, clearly ready for sleep.

Lau touched her fingers to her lips and held the hand out to Eu-meh, as if giving her a goodnight kiss. "I'll be back," she promised, in English this time. "I'll bring you something nice." She repeated it in that musical language.

When she turned to the rest of us, her eyes were moist, but none of us commented. The wonder of seeing the mutual feeling between the two was humbling. If every scrap of mois-ture in my body hadn't burned up in the fire, I might have had a tear in my eye.

Apollo left the glass wall open to let air through, but pulled the metal screen back down over the cafe. The slagged lock stayed where it was, just fine if no one gave it a second glance. Lau could bring the replacement when she came back for Eu-meh.

For now ... The chopper sound was close. Close and slowing, as though it had landed and momentum was all that was keeping the blades going. At a guess, they'd found the other copter....

No one said a word as we piled back in the Hummer and Cori took off, going slowly enough to keep the revving engine noise to a minimum but fast enough to keep us from a crawl. She ended up driving us along a footpath never meant to accommodate a tank, until we came to a set of stairs, and then we were off-roading it down a steep hill, sticks and stones thrown up into the air to catch in her undercarriage. The Hummer ate them for breakfast.

By the time we bounced out onto an actual road, my insides felt like they'd been scrambled, but we were mercifully alive and I wasn't about to take that for granted.

I BREATHED a painful and far-too-shallow sigh of relief when Cori stopped at the parking garage of a high-rise building and punched in a code to get us in. Hermes hadn't been kidding when he'd said she and Mel lived close to the park. The gate opened and I tensed, waiting for something to come at us, but, miraculously, nothing staggered out to swarm us. The normalcy of an actual garage, a residential building, actual electricity gave me a misleading sense of safety. We weren't home free. But danger was temporarily on pause.

"Come on, everyone," Cori said. "Let's get Mel home and then you *will* explain to me what's going on and how I can help."

She led us to an unremarkable elevator in the corner with

unremarkable steel gray doors ... until those doors opened onto an interior that was an art deco dream. The decor couldn't possibly be authentic, not descending down into a cement parking garage, but it certainly had the old-time glamour of curving yet geometric bronze cutouts backed by glass. We were underdressed in our battle-worn clothes. Something cocktail-esque would have been more appropriate—gowns, glitter, furs, sky-high heels, champagne. Not really my scene. The wrap I had over my shoulder was a living, breathing demoness. So chic.

The building had twenty-one floors, missing unlucky thirteen. Cori pressed the button for number ten. Not the penthouse then. Still, I was impressed. A place on the Upper West Side *with* parking couldn't come cheap. I was even *more* impressed when she opened the door on a Central Park view.

I tried not to gawk like a country bumpkin. I'd seen this kind of luxury ... on television. Apollo's condo in LA was well appointed, of course, but it was more Mediterranean inspired, oceanfront. Homey. This was ... Hollywood. Or, anyway, *Broadway*. Cori was right that Eu-meh never would have fit, but because of the doors and the clutter, not because of the size of the space. A grand piano sat front and center. Sofas and chairs, divans, music stands, instruments of all sorts were scattered about the room, as if she and Mel entertained regularly. One whole wall was taken up with floor-to-ceiling bookshelves filled with thin volumes that looked like scripts, musical scores, playbills and a few substantial photo albums. Faced out here and there were pictures of Cori or Mel—at least, I guessed it was Mel; she wasn't looking quite the same these days—clearly in the midst of some performance or hugging someone or other. I vaguely recognized a few and was blown away by others there was no mistaking.

The walls, where we could see the walls, were taken up with

play posters, almost all with multiple signatures scrawled across.

"Nice place," I said, almost in awe.

"Thanks," she answered, but there was no pride in her voice, and when I turned, she was looking at Mel. "Let's get her to her room."

"Lead the way," Hermes said. He held Mel carefully, tightly so that she couldn't bite him the way she so desperately wanted to.

"While you're at it, is there somewhere I can put this one?" I asked, nodding toward Lyssa. My back and chest and everything else were still protesting, but I hadn't felt that I could hand her over to Apollo or Lau. After that blow I'd given her, I needed to feel her still breathing.

Cori looked at the demoness, blood tears smeared across her face making track marks through snot and soot from the fire. "The bathtub, I guess," she said. "Follow me."

I did, and she pointed me toward a closed door with a framed Moulin Rouge poster affixed. I entered to find a small bathroom with a shower curtain pulled back around a white clawfoot tub. It was deep, and every muscle in me protested as I lowered Lyssa into it. There was a basket near the sink with sage green towels and washcloths, and I grabbed one of the latter, wetting it in the sink and lathering it up with green tea and ginger hand soap. I gently swiped it over Lyssa's face a few times, using the less soapy end to rinse. Lyssa looked like a fallen angel sleeping there. I wondered what torment it was to inspire only insanity in others. What a lonely existence.

But there wasn't time to dwell.

I closed the door behind me when I left and went back out to meet the others. The five of us stared at each other for a second, taking in the incongruity between our surroundings and our situation. "Can I offer you anything?" Cori asked, like she couldn't help herself, she was so used to hosting.

"Scotch?" Hermes asked. "Bourbon? Absinthe? I'm not picky at this moment."

Lau gave him a sour look. "At a time like this? Don't you think it's best to have your wits about you?"

"My dear Dragon Lady," he answered, "my wits are strongly tied to my spirits. Restore one and the other will follow."

I snorted. I'd called Lau Dragon Lady before I knew how literally I'd had her pegged. "Fine, scotch," Cori said. "Anyone else?"

"Yes," Apollo and I chorused. I was sure it was five o'clock somewhere, and, anyway, it was apocalypse now.

"Tea for me," Lau said. But it didn't take her long to add, "And it could probably do with a splash of whiskey."

Hermes patted her on the back, and I thought she was going to remove his hand ... or his head. It was a toss-up. I'd have paid money to see it, either way, but she settled for a glare.

I checked for my phone, hoping I hadn't lost it in all the action. Or that it hadn't melted to slag. I still had it on me, but it was deader than my hopes of a normal life.

"Does anyone have a phone?" I asked. "I need to call Nick's sister and see what's going on at the hospital, see how he's doing. Make sure—" *they're still alive*. I thought it but couldn't say it.

No one else had battery power, but Cori called from the kitchen. "There's a landline. You're welcome to use it. Or I can give you my cell."

"Charger?" I asked.

Now that my brain was starting to engage, I realized that without my phone, I didn't know Nick's number. Not in these days of voice dialing and all.

"In the kitchen." She nodded the way.

There was a charging cord right there on the counter, already plugged in and, luckily, compatible with my phone. I attached it to my phone to get the charge started, but the sense of urgency wouldn't leave me. Downtime was seriously bad. It gave me time to think and worry and KNOW that I should be doing something. I just didn't know what. And now that we'd lost the sword. That *I lost us the sword* ...

I collapsed onto a divan, my forgotten wings bumping the back. Agony ripped through them from their earlier abuse that hadn't had time to heal, but I ignored it and dropped my head into my hands, raising it only when Cori appeared with the scotch. As much as I wanted to, I couldn't bring myself to down it in one shot, not after the first taste. It deserved sipping, enjoying ... it deserved better than me.

I felt Apollo's gaze on me, felt his concern. "You okay?" he asked.

"Next question."

"Do you think your phone has enough charge now to turn on and grab that number? I know you. You're not going to be okay until you've checked in."

It did have enough charge and I made the call, praying it would connect. During the first rush of the hysteria there'd been so many calls into the city they'd jammed up the system. Now ... it depended on how bad things had gotten. How many people were still taking calls rather than trying to eat each other's faces off?

The call went right to voicemail, and even though I knew there might be a perfectly logical reason behind it, I started to panic.

I called 4-1-1 to find the number for the hospital and paid the extra fee to be connected directly, but the phone just rang and rang at the switchboard. My sense of something wrong ramped up to an eleven. Even if no actual person was available to answer, the automated system should still have been in place.

I got quickly back to the others, only to be stopped in my tracks by the scene of devastation on the television someone had turned to a news channel. Behind the newscaster, probably projected on a green screen, was something straight out of a disaster film or the LA Riots. In fact, it looked like the LA Riots all over again. Looting, running, people loaded down with stolen goods, other people lying behind them on the ground, damaged or dead ... In another clip, people spray painting cameras, tossed off fiery cocktails, which exploded into smoke and fire, destroying evidence left behind ...

"So the problem isn't limited to New York then," I said stupidly. Every time the footage shifted, it was a different city or borough mentioned at the bottom in the teletype.

"This isn't just about the plague," Lau said, something frighteningly ... suspended about her voice, as if she didn't dare let herself feel. "You missed the footage on the huge tsunami headed for LA. We're talking disaster on the level of Japan and the Philippines. Everywhere people are looting and panicked, sane people turning into doomsday preppers."

"What the hell is going on?" I asked.

"More than we know," she said in the same deadpan voice. "More than we can handle."

"Plagues, an overflowing underworld, Hecate gone rogue, now riots and natural disasters ..." I couldn't even put the full scope of the horror into words.

"Wait, Hecate gone rogue?" Cori asked, her voice going from high-pitched to shrill. "You'd better start talking. Tell me everything."

We owed her that much. I started with the Grey Sisters and went on through Hecate's betrayal, finishing with, "She said something about controlling the outcome. She's perfectly fine with the world devolving into rot and ruin as long as she's the one to pick up the pieces."

"Do you think she's under Hades's orders?" Apollo asked.

"I think she's done taking orders. She wants to be the top dog. And she's recruiting. She tried to get me to join up."

"Skip to the important stuff," Lau cut in. "Did you get through to Nick?"

The look I turned on her was empty-eyed. My insides felt like a great void, a vacuum that could only be filled by my deepest, darkest fears, and I couldn't invite them in. I'd collapse under their weight.

"No. I couldn't get through to the hospital or his phone. No one's answering."

Everyone shared a look, and I knew what they weren't saying—that the hospital was overrun. The dead outnumbered the living. I refused to believe it. I'd seen *The Walking Dead*— wounded cop survives the zombie apocalypse, comatose in his room. Nick was at least as tough as Rick Grimes, who was certainly no slouch. I looked to Hermes, struck with a sudden idea that had pushed its way into the void. "You can get me in," I said. "How many times have you tuned in to me, teasing me with information or just invading my privacy? The spa, my laptop ... You open a window or whatever it is you do. Let me talk to Nick."

Lau's head swiveled to look at him too. Oh, it was on now. No way was he going to refuse to do *her* bidding. Not and live to tell about it. And she was nearly as concerned about Nick as I was. "Do it," she said. Having a target to focus on brought some scary intense life to her eyes.

"Who are you to tell me—" he started, but Apollo cut him off.

"Cut the crap, Hermes. This isn't about your ego. We've got bigger fish to fry. Get it done, so we can move on."

Bigger fish ... The fact that Apollo was right, that we had a whole world to save and not just one man, didn't make me feel any warmer and fuzzier toward him at that moment. He had never liked Nick ... or had never acknowledged it anyway. Too busy trying to come between us. But was he being brusque to move Hermes along or because he was insensitive to the situation? It would help to know how much to hate him at that moment. My emotions were in turmoil.

Hermes looked away from Apollo as if he'd ceased to exist and turned to us women. "Just acknowledge how much you need me and I'll be happy to help."

"Truly, madly, deeply," I said. "There, is that better? Can we do this now?"

"*Agape*, you know I would do anything for you." He shot a glare Apollo's way and I was suddenly so tired of male posturing I could scream. "For you, I will try," Hermes continued, "but your Detective Armani, being merely mortal, does not have the signature that you do, and I haven't studied him nearly so intently. He will not be as easy to find."

"Do you need—" What? My sense of him? To follow whatever bond we might still have? I needed to know that Nick was okay more than I needed to keep Hermes out of my head.

"It would help," he agreed, somehow knowing what I'd left unsaid.

I gritted my teeth and reached out a hand to him, realizing I hadn't yet had time to wash it clean of Hecate's blood. The sight of it brought back the memory of the strange rush I'd had when tasting it and the sense—I thrust that out of my head quickly, before Hermes could get ahold of it. Instead, I tried to focus on Nick. First, as I'd last seen him—burned, fragile, hospitalized and horrified by all that had happened. So horrified he'd had to break from me. But that wasn't the true sense of him. Nick was ... duty-bound, dedicated, brave, ready to face things he couldn't possibly understand or defeat because it was the right thing to do. Tears streamed down my eyes as I focused on his essence. Not what he might look like with or without new skin grafts or still-raw burn wounds surrounded by a surgically sterile tent. But on *who he was* beyond all that.

"Tori?" a voice asked, barely recognizable as Nick's.

It was low, cracked, dry as the desert. I opened my eyes to

see Nick's bandaged face. He looked something like *The Phantom of the Opera*, his bandages forming a half mask, his eyes bloodshot, and his character lines deeper than ever, as if etched by the pain. His lips were as dry and cracked as his voice.

"Nick," I answered. There were worlds of things unspoken in that one word. So many things they created a logjam and none could get past the lump in my throat. "I'm so sorry." That was the one thing that came out.

Nick closed his eyes, took a moment to breathe down some pain, physical or emotional, and met my gaze again. "Where are you?" he asked. "Are you coming? There's been ... trouble here. Have you seen Amanda?"

"She's not there with you?" The bad feeling in the pit of my stomach was growing like a weed.

He started to shake his head, but his whole face convulsed in pain and he stopped immediately, moving only his lips. "Went out. Yesterday? This morning? Haven't seen her since. Not anyone."

"No one's come to check on you?" That bad feeling grew fangs and claws and took on a life of its own. Nick was in no condition to care for himself. If no one was looking in on him ... things were seriously wrong at that hospital. And his sister ...

"Nick, we're coming. Just ... hold tight. Try to rally. We'll be there as soon as we can." But what to do first—save the man or stop the apocalypse? I wanted to do both. Track down Hecate, recover the sword, find Namtar and his minions, take them down, save the day ... but all with Nick safe. Did he have that kind of time? A man could go without food for weeks, but without water for mere days. If one had already passed ... And what about antibiotics, pain meds and all the rest?

"I'm coming," Lau said, stepping right up beside me, her chin practically on my shoulder so that we looked two-headed. "Just hold on."

"But, you can't go alone, and we need—"

She spoke right over my protest. "I won't be alone." She turned her no-nonsense gaze on Hermes. "Trickster God Guy, from what I've gathered, you got us into all this with whatever you transported. You can get us out. Starting with Nick."

I looked to Hermes for his reaction, and he gave me an *are you effing kidding me?* look back. "You remind me of someone," he told Lau. "Let me think. Could it be ... Hera? Yes, that's it. Queen Bee-atch of the gods. So, if I go on this rescue mission, what's in it for me?"

"I let you live," she said, glaring daggers.

"*Aaaanh,*" he answered, voice going off like a buzzer. "God, remember? Try again."

Her glare could superheat stone. "What do you want?" she asked through clenched teeth.

"Dragon scales, nail clippings, baby teeth, whatever you've got that your dragon can spare."

I thought Lau's eyes were going to fall out of her head. *"WHAT?"*

"Huge on the black market. People think dragon parts cure all kinds of ills. Doesn't matter if they work, but I pride myself on authenticity."

"You would sell her for parts?" She was spitting mad now. If she were Hecate, she'd be building hellfire.

"Relax, I'm not out slaying dragons, am I? I'm happy with leavings. Hmm, I wonder if there's a market for *those*. Maybe if I wait for them to fossilize. Coprolites, I think they're called ..."

We were all staring at him now. But this was Hermes. On the scale of one to weird, this hardly tweaked the needle.

Nick coughed, and as weak as it was, it brought our attention immediately back to him. "I'm okay," he said, unconvincingly. "Just find Amanda."

"Fine," Lau spat at Hermes out of the corner of her mouth. "You have a deal. Just help me get to Nick."

My stomach twisted itself in knots. *Are you coming?* he'd asked. Did he even remember that he'd dumped me back in Greece? A note left with our hotel concierge, no less. Had that been the pain meds talking? Was it pain and dehydration talking now? If he didn't remember ... I couldn't even look at Apollo right then. What if our whole ... whatever we had started ... was a betrayal. What if ...?

"Nick, we're coming," Lau said. "Hang tight."

It should be me, I kept repeating over and over in my head. It *should* be me. I owed him. For so, so much. He was lying in that bed because of me. I should be the one to get him out. At the same time, my precog was screaming. I had to get that sword back. I had to stop the onrushing apocalypse. And I had to do it now.

The lights flickered in the apartment, then went absolutely dark before coming back at about half light. The television winked out and returned with some kind of rebooting screen.

Hermes's window into the hospital snapped shut along with it, as if he'd been drawing from the electricity for his illusion.

"This happen often?" Hermes asked, looking to Cori, who'd been watching and listening to everything with wide eyes. She was the muse of choral music and comedy. This had to be way the hell out of her comfort zone. Although, there were black comedies ... *Pulp Fiction, Kiss Kiss Bang Bang, Shaun of the Dead* ...

"We have roving blackouts sometimes in the summer, but this ... We lost power for hours yesterday. I was shocked when it was restored. If it goes out again, I'm not sure it's coming back."

"Crap on a cracker," I said, hearing Hecate in my head about my way with words. "Lau, I promise we'll get in there to save Nick, but we need all kinds of intel first. And it has to be now. While we still have power ... and cell towers. Who knows how long that's going to last." Because when I thought tsunamis, I thought Poseidon, especially when it came to threatening LA. He'd already conspired with Zeus and Hephaestus once to set off the San Andreas Fault and drop LA and its surroundings into the ocean to announce their second coming. Apollo, Nick, and I had foiled that and they'd never forgiven us. But, last I knew, Poseidon was in Greece ... and a federal fugitive. If he weren't a god with all the arrogance that entailed, I couldn't imagine him coming back to the States, but ...

I turned back for the kitchen to check in with Yiayia. I needed to make sure she and the rest of the family were okay anyway. Getting the *Goddities* hot sheet would be a bonus. She answered before the first ring had even died away. "Tori?" she answered, voice telegraphing her panic. "Tori, tell me this is you and not that *trelós* god Apollo calling to tell me that something has happened to you. I will snuff him like a candle. I will get ten-ton Trina to squash his head like a grape and pour libations from his blood. I will—"

"Whoa, Yiayia, it's me, Tori. I'm fine." Well, relatively speaking.

"*Fine?*" she asked, her voice rising to a ludicrous level. I winced and held the phone slightly away from my ear. "Fine? I have left you forty-two million messages, which you haven't returned, and you tell me you are *fine*? I expected you to be dead. Dying at the very least, possibly in some ditch somewhere. For you to be *fine* and not call your *yiayia*, it is as sure a sign of the apocalypse as I've seen."

"Like what?" I cut in.

"What, what?"

"You said 'as sure a sign of the apocalypse as I've seen.' What signs have you seen?"

"Tori, Fergus has boils. *Boils.* Turn on the news. There have been plagues of locusts, reports of winged demons, the dead rising, even one of the Horsemen of the Christian apocalypse. Lenny had to fly back to deal with a problem with the circus animals. Mad cow disease or something, but jumping species. The whole world's gone mad. What are you doing to stop it?"

Now I held the phone out to stare at it like I could see right into her insanity and face it down. Stop it? I could barely comprehend it.

"All I can," I said finally. Which was little enough. The odds seemed overwhelming, and I didn't even know the full scope of the problem. Or who all the players were and where to go now that I'd lost Perseus's sword. "I need some information. Where are Poseidon and Zeus?"

"Still here, for all I know," she said. "The CIA caught up with them after the big battle. I guess they tracked them down because of their hospital stay. They're in Greek custody, fighting extradition back to the US."

"So they're not, say, out in the Pacific stirring up deadly storms?"

"I thought you were in New York," she said.

"*I am in New York,*" I answered, impatiently. "Just answer the question."

"No, they're here."

That's what I'd been afraid of. "Yiayia, could you shoot me any contact information you have or any known whereabouts for every single god on your watch? We're going to need reinforcements. And we need to know who we're facing. Hecate's gone rogue."

"You were *working* with Hecate?" Her voice rose. "*Egona*, you have to tell me these things. I could have warned you."

"Warned me of what?"

"There have been rumblings of unrest. Rumor has it Hades is worried about a coup. I told you she was untrustworthy."

In deference to present company, I didn't tell her that it hardly needed to be said when it came to the Olympians, who all seemed to have their own agendas and considered them more important than the greater good.

As far as the rumored coup, I could well believe it. Hades had previously suggested to us that he expected something of the sort. Knowing what I knew now, it seemed more than likely that he'd sent Hecate to work with us on the demon situation just to get her out of his hair and out of his kingdom while it was in turmoil. We had to let him know that his plan had failed dismally and that she was now on the loose with a legendary weapon, possibly headed his way. Unfortunately, we didn't have access to her hell phone and I doubted Hermes's windows would penetrate into Hades's realm. He was hyperparanoid about infiltration and had his kingdom well warded against other gods.

"Does Hecate have any particular allies that you know about? Anyone we can flip?"

"They are gods, not houses," she scolded. "But you'd asked about Poseidon. Have you considered Amphitrite?"

"Amphitrite?"

"His *queen*. Estranged, of course. He's as bad as his brother about chasing every piece of tail ... Anyway, she's got powers of her own and is, of course, mother to Triton, so there's no question of a divorce. Can you even imagine trying to divide *those* assets?"

"Okay, Amphitrite. Any word where she is now?"

"Based on your killer storm, I'd have to say off the coast of California, but ... I'll see what I can find out. And also whether I can connect her to Hecate."

"Thank you, Yiayia, you're a lifesaver. Would you send whatever you find as quickly as possible? Our power is going a little mad."

"Aren't we all?"

I didn't answer on the grounds that it might incriminate me.

"Also, if there's anyone or anything else you can think of. There's so much going on up here, I don't know what's tied together and what isn't. Who's allied and who's in it for themselves. We've got gods from the underworld and the waters running amok, plague demons, looters, and loonies. Is someone taking advantage of the chaos or masterminding it?"

"These are rhetorical questions?"

"Unless you have answers. What about Hera?" I asked. She'd mentioned how like his brother Poseidon was. Were the wives similarly disillusioned and taking advantage of the power void created by their husbands' capture?

"Hera?" Yiayia asked. "I don't think so."

"Why? What is she up to these days?"

"I can't tell you. It would compromise the integrity of—"

"*Yiayia,*" I said sharply, "I wouldn't ask if it wasn't important."

I could practically feel her internal struggle through the phone, though I didn't understand it.

"She's not involved," Yiayia said. She sighed, knowing I'd want more. "Okay, she's a lawyer. On the surface, she does a lot of women's advocacy—divorce cases, child custody. She makes sure women get what's coming to them. Does a lot of *pro bono* work. Beneath the surface ... she runs an underground railroad for abuse victims."

"She hardly sounds like she has time to take over the world."

"Time, no. However, if she thought the world had gone too far wrong, possibly I could see her pulling a Great Flood or something to wipe the slate clean, but ... No, she would hurt too many of those she's tried to help."

My brain raced. I didn't know what it said about me that *I* could imagine it. Noelle's Ark. No men allowed but those chosen to carry on the human race? Hera had always been a vengeful goddess. I was surprised to hear she was now a women's advocate after throwing so many of Zeus's mistresses to the wolves way back in the ancient days. Like his seductions and dalliances were all *their* fault. Of course, people *could* change. It sounded like maybe Hera was a prime example. But I'd prefer to see for myself.

"Where is she now?" I asked.

"Wait a second," she said. It was more like ten. I counted doomsday scenarios as I waited, getting more and more spooked with every second that passed. We were going to need help. Big help. Monstrous help. Not just to fight Namtar and Hecate and whatever allies they'd amassed, together or separately, but to put the world back to rights afterward.

Yiayia finally came back on the line, but it was her sudden wet, hacking cough I heard first, followed by a massive blowing of the nose.

"Are you all right?" I asked her, worry rushing me like a pro defensive lineman.

"Nothing some vitamin C and some of that horrible zinc stuff won't take care of. But, Tori, I don't know if you're going to want to hear this. Hera is right now based in Brooklyn. Isn't that—"

"Just outside of Manhattan? Yes, it is."

With the city on lockdown, it might as well be a continent away, but somehow I was going to have to find a way to question her. Because even if Hera wasn't part of the problem, it seemed unlikely she knew nothing of the goings-on in her own backyard. Hell, Hecate had tried to recruit *me*. A disgruntled goddess with *real* power seemed a no-brainer.

Yiayia promised to send me the address ASAP, along with all other godly current whereabouts, and we signed off. I felt Apollo in the kitchen with me even before I turned to see him there ... which I almost didn't. I wasn't ready to deal with him. I didn't know what to think or feel or do. I didn't want to face him while I tried to figure it out. But avoidance wasn't an option.

"What?" I said when I turned. It came out as belligerent. Challenging. I hadn't meant it that way.

"You're beating yourself up for this. For Nick," he answered, meeting my gaze and not flinching away from the heat. He was the sun god. He could take it.

"Yeah, I am. But there's enough upset to go around. You might want to step out of my line of fire."

"No," he answered.

"No?" I was incredulous. What was the other option? Either he got out of my face or ... what? I made him? We had a knock-down, drag-out fight right here in Cori's apartment, mid-apocalypse?

"I'm putting an end to the pity party."

My glare rivaled Lau's. It rivaled the sun surge Apollo had called down on the attacking zombies in Central Park. He didn't even flinch.

"Really?" I asked dangerously.

"You're not responsible for Nick or his condition." He mowed over the protest that sprang immediately to my lips. "Stop feeling and *think*. When all this began, way back at the beginning when you realized the gods were real, what would have happened if you'd bowed out of the battle and decided not to fight Zeus and Poseidon? Would Nick have been safe? Would *any* of your friends have been better off?"

One of Zeus's thunderbolts couldn't have struck with more force. I didn't answer him, because the answer was *no*. If I hadn't stopped their plot, if Nick and I hadn't foiled them, Poseidon, Zeus, and Hephaestus would have set off the quake to end all quakes ... or to end LA and the San Fernando Valley anyway. It would have been destroyed, shaken apart, split from the coastline, the ocean rising up to swallow it whole. Nick and everyone else I knew, myself included, would have been history.

But it didn't feel right to let myself off the hook.

"And what did you do in Delphi? How was it your fault that Rhea rose or that she woke the Titans?"

"It was my fault Nick was *in* Delphi," I yelled, thrilled to have a clear-cut answer.

"And it was my blood Zeus's priests used to raise Rhea. So is all of this *my* fault? Should I be castigating myself? Should I be cutting you out of my life to keep you safe?"

"Do it and die," I raged, my glare ratcheting up.

"Exactly." Apollo's eyes blazed back, but in triumph, not anger. I could feel it through our link, and it set me off-balance.

"Exactly *what*?" I challenged.

"Nick would have given you the same response if you'd shoved him away to 'protect' him."

I took a step back, bumping my spine against Cori's kitchen counter.

"If you had tried to keep him safe, as a mere mortal or as your lover or whatever, you'd only have pissed him off," Apollo pounded away at me. "He would not have seen danger and left you to face it alone. Rival or not, I give him that much credit. Did he ever once try to hold you back? To forbid you from facing down danger?"

I couldn't answer.

"No, he had too much respect for you. Or for your wrath if he'd ever even suggested such a thing. You owe him that respect in return. Your Detective Armani is no milquetoast. He didn't blindly follow you into trouble. He made his own decisions for the good of all. To protect and serve. That's his job. *His* decision. You didn't bribe or blackmail or browbeat him into joining you. If we hadn't stopped Rhea's return and the Titans' rising, the whole world would be in trouble."

"You mean, like it is now?" I asked, the heat starting to ebb away, leaving me empty.

"Like it is now. And again we must fight. We don't have time for self-flagellation."

I could feel his sincerity through our link, but also an inexplicable flare of anger. "In other words, this is war, there are casualties. Just get over it?" I asked. "Would you 'just get over it' if I was the one who fell in battle?"

Apollo stepped up to me, invading my personal space, but the counter was already at my back and I had nowhere to go. "I would make it count. I would make people pay. And then I would mourn you for the rest of my years."

It took my breath away, the intensity. And then he was quite literally stealing my breath, his mouth on mine, breathing in my release of pent-up feelings ... rage and frustration, love and fear and blame. I tasted his fear that I would do the same with Nick—mourn and blame myself for the rest of my life, never let myself forgive or forget. Never be his. He'd waited, and even though he'd lived forever, he'd never learned patience. It was not one of his virtues. I felt it all and it overwhelmed me.

I had to break off. I pushed at his chest, but he didn't let me go, not at first. I was tempted to bite his lip, step on his foot, but it would be a rejection I didn't want him to bear. Not when he'd given me so much. He'd given me perspective, which was priceless. But also the realization that my blame was selfish, maybe even gratuitous.

Finally, I broke off by the simple expedient of dropping my chin so that his lips met only forehead.

"Thank you," I whispered, even though I wasn't entirely grateful just yet.

"You're welcome," he said, kissing my forehead. "You ready to rejoin the others?"

"Give me a minute." I needed more than that, but it was all I would allow myself. Time to clean off Hecate's blood and hope the dregs of my emotional overload followed it down the drain.

13
———

By the time I'd put myself back together, I had a text message from Yiayia with two addresses and two phone numbers for Hera, one at a law office and the other for a women's advocacy group.

No one but a machine answered at the first number. My heart started to pound as I dialed the second, as if my precog had grown stronger and I could sense trouble right through the line. No one picked up. It just rang and rang.

Wrong and wrong, my inner alarms insisted. But why? How? And what was I supposed to do from here?

I ripped my phone off the charger and carried it with me into the living room. "Hermes, you need to open a portal to Hera."

He was staring at the television, where some kind of kraken, a multi-tentacled monster of mottled blue-green, was trying to take down a ship. My first thought was that he'd switched over to some movie on the Syfy channel, but then I saw the network news logo ... At my entrance, he stared at me instead, "Huh, what?"

"Hera. She's in some kind of danger. Or causing some kind of danger. Hurry. There's no time for your little games."

"I feel it too," Apollo said, rising to stand beside me in support. "Do it."

Hermes looked from one of us to the other. "I don't know if I can. I need a person or place to center on, and I haven't seen Hera in a god's age."

"What about an address?" I asked.

"I can only try. Hera doesn't exactly keep up with the trends. If she hasn't changed too much, maybe ... But you realize it's only like a window, right. You can talk through it, but that's it."

"What about your little disappearing trick. I've seen you pop from one place to another."

"That I can *see*. And just me. Okay, and smallish objects just to mess with people's heads, but I'm no kind of troop transport."

"Do your best," I ordered.

Ordering Hermes was a dangerous business. I was sure to pay for it at some point, but right then my alarm klaxons were drowning out my common sense. Something about what was happening was not only urgent, but important and NOW.

Hermes rolled his shoulders, cocked his head from one side to another, cracking his neck. He linked his fingers together and did the same with them. Just as I was ready to throttle him for the delay, he went still, his gaze centering on a spot just above Cori's coffee table and going unfocused. The air rippled and popped, a pinpoint of space expanded rapidly. There was a nose, then a cheekbone, an eye, pretty soon a whole face and then another right beside it, sweat sheening both as they added their weight to the barricade they'd set up in what appeared to have been a classroom, based on the desks and chairs piled up in the barricade.

Cori gasped, and the second woman in the window screamed as she turned and saw all our faces staring in at her.

"Holy Hand Grenade of Antioch," Cori said nonsensically. "Hera!"

The woman whose nose and cheekbones had first been revealed looked up in response to her name. It was a wonder Hermes had been able to home in on her. She didn't look like the perfect and unapproachable mother goddess pictured on urns and ancient statuary. She didn't appear aloof or pissed off or poised or any of her usual expressions. She looked frantic and overwrought. Her hair was escaping what looked to have once been a tight updo, to straggle over her face and cling wetly to the sweat there. She wore just a silk shell for a shirt and every muscle, tendon and blood vessel stood in high relief as she pushed with all her might at the barrier between her and whatever was trying to get in. Pounding, snarling, kicking. There were no words. No "come out or I'll kill you," using totally the wrong conjunction, which led me to believe that whatever was beyond the barricade wasn't human ... or not fully. Not any longer.

Something hit the barricade especially hard, and a desk at head level to Hera started to topple. She deflected it from braining her with an upraised hand, but it was one less item between her and danger, and I could see the incremental backslide of the barricade. It wasn't going to hold much longer.

"Terpsichore?" Hera asked, staring straight at Cori. "How are you here? Never mind. However you're here it isn't safe. It isn't safe anywhere. Find shelter. Top of Olympus ... some-where. Just go!"

"Get us through!" I yelled to Hermes. The enemy of my enemy was my friend, right? Even if I could stand to watch Hera and her associate mobbed by whatever was after them, we couldn't afford to lose potential allies.

"I told you it's just a window," Hermes growled at me.

"And I told you to try!" I yelled. "Apollo, it's daylight. Can't you ... amplify him in some way? There's got to be something we can do!"

Apollo didn't waste his breath telling me he'd try. He rounded behind Hermes and put his hands to his shoulders, staring fixedly out Cori's beautiful windows and drawing power from the sunlight streaking through. There was a flare and momentarily everything was intensely bright. I had to look away, through the window into Hera's world, where more desks were toppling now, like an avalanche. There was a huge blow to the barrier, and the rest of the desks exploded outward. One hit our portal and punctured right through with a metal leg.

It was working! I didn't wait to see what else might come flying through, but knocked the desk aside and dove in face first, ducking and rolling to come up into a fighter's stance as the first nearly skinless hand pushed its way through the wreckage of the barricade.

Hera put her assistant, or whoever the other woman was, behind her and grabbed up one of the tumbled chairs, holding it like she was a lion tamer. As if on cue, the once-human creature coming in snarled and snapped at her and then lurched for the women. Others pushed in from behind, knocking the first one through off-balance and trampling right over her as she fell. Most grotesquely of all, the zombie now in the forefront was hugely pregnant, like seven or eight months. My attention was all on her stomach, waiting to see if the mass of it moved or if ... I couldn't even contemplate. Either way was too horrible to dwell on.

Then a clawlike hand grabbed me and whipped me around, blessedly diverting my attention, even as it slavered in my face. Human jaws weren't meant for ripping into things, but zombies didn't have enough going on upstairs to realize it. *See, want, eat* was about as far as they got, so while the thing held me in her grip and snapped uselessly toward my neck, I pulled back a fist and cracked it in an uppercut to her jaw as hard as I could. Her teeth snapped hard together and something flopped to the ground. A piece of tongue? I couldn't look. I followed the blow with a move I'd learned in self-defense to get loose of an attacker, and knocked the hands away. Others reached in to replace them. I quickly grabbed up a fallen chair and swung it around like a caber I was going to toss. But I didn't even make a whole circle round. Heads cracked, stopping my momentum, and a pair of hands ripped the chair away.

Another set reached for my back, ripping into my wings, and I felt a piercing pain. Then something exploded outward behind me, knocking me to the ground. Immediately the weight rolled off, and I turned my head to see Apollo.

But I didn't have time or breath to curse him. He had a massive sword in his hands—something he'd no doubt gotten from Cori. I hoped it wasn't just a stage prop or museum replica. He thrust upward with it as he burst to his feet, driving it straight through the zombie's back. So, no prop then. At least not cheaply made.

He ripped it from the zombie's stomach, but it only made her lurch for him. "Aim for the head," I called. I'd seen enough zombie films to know. And Hollywood was bound to be at least as accurate as Wikipedia.

Apollo cleaned the sword off on his pant leg and yelled, "Catch!"

I did as he said, catching the sword by the hilt as it arced toward me and immediately stabbing it over my shoulder at the zombie trying to tear my wings off and climb my back. Out of the corner of my eye, I saw Apollo pull something else out of his belt, one of the flip knives I'd grabbed off the Central Park zombies, but I couldn't spare the attention to watch him wield it like a pro. The thrust of my sword miraculously hit my target, zombies not having the self-preservation instinct to dodge. My blade bit into his skull ... but only by a couple of inches. And it stuck. I pushed back on the sword with all my might, trying to pry the zombie away and yank the sword free.

"Do it!" someone yelled, a shrill female voice raised in panic. "They're not people anymore, they're—"

I don't know what she was going to say, because the zombie on the other end of my sword suddenly threw himself forward, heedless of the blade, which sank in another inch, bringing the creature in just close enough to grab me by the collar and try to pull me in. He wasn't the only one now. We were surrounded, and my wings were a disadvantage in the close quarters. Already, two more were grabbing and pulling at me like I was a wishbone.

I met sword zombie's eyes and yelled, *"Freeze,"* but it didn't do anything to the ones behind me, pulling me away.

Beside me a voice raised rhythmically, sounding a lot like Hecate mid-chant. I turned my head to see Hera, surrounded by a nimbus of light. Apollo was fending zombies off her with the flip knife, buying her time.

"Duck!" she yelled suddenly, dropping to the floor to show us how it was done. Such a flash burst out from her that I was blinded. So painfully bright it took me a second to realize that the other pain and pressure—the attackers pulling me apart from behind—had stopped cold. When the brilliant flare died down, I blinked at the suddenly still room, all the zombies fallen like someone had cut their strings. I didn't know if zombie chests would rise and fall, but these weren't. They were dead. True dead, I thought. But I was no expert.

I stared into Hera's eyes. She met my stunned, horrified gaze with a pain-filled one of her own. Whatever she'd just done, she hadn't done it lightly.

"I'm not exactly the alpha and the omega," she said, "but I can give life and I can take it away."

"Why didn't you just do that to start with?" Apollo asked.

I stared at them both in horror. These poor people hadn't

done anything short of become infected. Any of us could be in the same boat at any moment.

"I just couldn't," Hera said, not looking at him. "It's not a precise thing—draining to the point of unconsciousness but not to death. And I've never ... I just don't know ... given their state. How much is too much? Are they already halfway to dead? More? Tracy's baby ..."

She couldn't finish the thought, and I couldn't blame her. I couldn't even bare to look again at the stillness. Meanwhile, the woman who'd been with her dropped to the ground beside the woman I supposed to be Tracy and put her hand cautiously to the still belly. She held it there for a moment before hanging her head and reaching up for the zombie woman's face to close the lids over the empty, filmed-over eyes.

"This wasn't the way things were supposed to go," Hera said, watching her. "We were supposed to be safe."

I latched on to that instantly and pinned her down with my stare. "How exactly *were* things supposed to go down?" I asked, trying and failing to keep my voice neutral.

Hera looked up from the corpse, devastation behind her eyes. "I'll tell you, but ... not here. I can't ... I can't take this."

The woman squatting on the ground rose, tears spilling down her face as she glanced at Hera and immediately away. "There are going to be arrangements to make, people to notify."

"The world's gone crazy," I told her as gently as I could. "We have to see what we can do to protect the living before we worry about burying the dead."

"This is my assistant, Michelle," Hera told us. She gestured our way. "Michelle, meet Apollo ... Demas?" she asked, as though to confirm that was the name he was currently going with. He nodded. "And, if I'm not mistaken, Tori Karacis, PI to the pantheon."

PI to the pantheon. That was interesting on many levels— that my reputation preceded me, for better or worse, and that

Michelle *knew* about the pantheon. I didn't know what to make of that. *Any* of it, but standing in a room surrounded by sorrow and death didn't seem the time to figure it out.

"Can we get out of here?" Michelle asked, barely acknowledging the introductions. I understood entirely.

I looked through the portal back to Cori's apartment, which had shrunk to a mere pinprick. "Hermes!" I called. "Hermes, let us back through."

When nothing happened, I met Apollo's gaze, only just realizing that he'd amplified Hermes's powers to open the window ... and he was now on our side of it.

His realization came at the same time. Or maybe we were so linked that mine fed his. Or vice versa. Hera looked at us both and then at the pinprick in the center of the room. "Your portal?" she asked.

I nodded, and she poked a finger into it, probing. Then she stuck a second into it, one from each hand. She closed her eyes and began pulling her fingers in opposite directions. The portal magically opened for her, expanding until it was a circle the size of a large Hula-Hoop.

"After you," she said, holding it open now with one hand and stepping to the side.

Michelle's eyes were huge, but she didn't say a word. I didn't know just how much she knew or had seen before now. Clearly enough to be awed, but not shocked or amazed. She looked at Hera, took a deep breath, held on to both sides of the circle like it was a window frame and stepped on through. Her hands were the last things to go.

Apollo gestured that I should go next. Such a gentleman. Either that, or he just wanted to watch my butt. Such as it was. If he could even think of such things after what we'd seen, more power to him. I looked back when I got through to see a half smile on his face, like he'd read my mind. I gave him a shaky smile back and stepped away from the portal so that he could follow me through, which he did.

Hera brought up the rear, letting the portal slam shut behind her, still standing on Cori's coffee table looking down on the rest of us.

"Well," Cori said, breaking the sudden awkward silence, "that coffee ought to be about ready. Why don't I bring the whole pot and you can tell us what the HELL is going on. Also, if you can give life and you can take it, maybe you can do something about Melpomene." She sounded like there should be an "or else" at the end of that sentence, but I wasn't sure she was in any position to make good on that.

Hera might not be the literal goddess of vengeance, but she was certainly well known for it, and Cori, being one of the Muses—Zeus's supposed love children with the Titaness Mnemosyne—probably already had one strike against her. On the other hand, Hera'd had eons to get over it, and it was hardly the kids' fault.

Hera drew herself up to her full haughty height and reached a hand down to Apollo to allow him to help her off the coffee table. She'd just set foot on the floor and turned her steely stare on Cori when all hell broke loose from the back of the apartment.

14

The snarling and cursing could only come from a full set of vocal cords and unmitigated rage. *Lyssa* was awake.

The door to the bathroom blew open on its hinges, taking part of the doorjamb with it, and Lyssa appeared like an apparition, feet not even touching the floor, hair flying out around her, crackling with power that couldn't be contained. Her torn dress and exposed limbs were streaked with dirt and blood.

She looked like a pissed-off Fury, and she was laser focused on Hera. "You!" she howled.

Hera's face went white when she saw Lyssa, and she immediately stammered, "I promise, I don't do that anymore. Since I split from Zeus, I'm a whole lot more centered. I help women now. I'm making amends!"

Michelle stepped in front of her, like Hera had done back at their office, but her wispy figure barely hid the goddess's statuesque form. "It's true."

Regardless, Lyssa's eyes had begun to bleed, and I could feel her rage reaching out, sweeping the room, raising my blood pressure and my bile. Rage bubbled up inside me, boiling, percolating, threatening to make me blow my top off—and not in the fun way Hermes would probably appreciate. I took a step toward Hera, half ready to rip her limb from limb myself.

Cori leapt first, but Michelle saw her coming and jumped to protect Hera. Cori's body hit hers, sending her crashing to the coffee table. If this had been a Hollywood set, the table would have been glass, and the impact would have shattered it, sending blood and shards flying, but it wasn't. The sharp thud of the bodies hitting barely impacted my brain. What did register was that I now had a clear shot at Hera.

My wings whipped out instinctively to help propel me, their abject failure and the pain that shot through me at the attempt didn't stop me. Neither did Apollo's arm, which lashed out to intercept. I thrust it aside, whirling to dodge as he tried to turn it from a block to a grab.

"Tori!" he yelled.

I didn't hesitate, but sent myself at Hera in a flying tackle. I didn't know why Apollo could even think to stop me. Myths had it that Hera had chased Apollo's very own mother Leto (pregnant with Zeus's twins) out of Olympus and made it so no place would accept her for fear of incurring Hera's wrath. She'd had to deliver her twins all alone on a deserted island and could very well have died in childbirth, which was no doubt the intention. I couldn't believe there was enough therapy in the world to get over something like that.

The second I should have crashed into Hera with the weight of Tornado Tori, the world glitched, flickered—

—and suddenly I was stumbling, full momentum and nothing to take the impact but a wall that was a lot closer than it should have been. I crashed into it, knocking the bottom of the framed play poster askew so that it swung dangerously, threatening to come down on me.

I turned, lightning fast, only to find I'd somehow been transported across the room and Hera wasn't even within range. I glared toward Hermes and Apollo, who looked fully prepared to port me again if necessary.

"Everyone just stop," Apollo commanded. "Lyssa, I know you have more control than this."

I doubted that. Her overflowing anger, her consuming madness made me feel as though my flesh would boil off my bones if I didn't act to relieve the pressure.

"I ... can't ..." Lyssa gritted out. She was going to break her teeth if she clamped them together any harder.

"You can," Hermes insisted. "Just remember Megaera and the kids. You don't want to go through all that again."

It was the wrong thing to say.

Lyssa let out an animalistic wail—pure pain. She was weeping blood again, and in the blink of an eye, flying across the room toward Hera, hands outspread, fingers like talons, as though she'd rip her to shreds, like the zombies or Dionysus's blood-frenzied followers.

Everyone was focused on Lyssa. I saw my moment and took it.

One step, two, and I'd built the momentum to spread my damaged wings to at least carry me over the back of the sofa that now stood between me and the action. I landed hard on Hera's back, knocking her to the ground and intercepting Lyssa. It was all I could do to lock with her instead of my intended target, meeting her madness for madness.

"No," I managed. "I mean yes. Maybe. Later. For now, we need answers."

I spat the words, every one a struggle. I had an opponent within my grasp. I wanted to grip, tear, rend. But in the back of my mind—the very back—I heard Apollo. His recognition that this was all *wrong*. His prayer for peace and sanity. He was thinking it *at* me, almost an attack by itself, meeting and grappling with my bloodlust and insanity. Cold water dashed on the bubbling cauldron of my rage, threatening to sublimate me into steam. I was going to be lost in the crossfire. Unless I took some control. Unless I *directed* the force.

I used that force to hold Lyssa in place, tried to transmit some of that sanity and calm Apollo was radiating to her, but she didn't have our connection, and—

Lyssa's bowstring-taut body started to slacken in my grip. I didn't trust it, sure it was a trick to get me to let go, but when I looked into her eyes, the blood was once again pulling back, draining away. I was getting through.

"Okay," she said. "You can let me go now."

I checked within myself first. If I let her go, would I lunge for a new target? But the sharpness of my mania had drained away as well, and I now felt like I needed a good sleep—like for a year and a day. I was wrung out.

I let her go and collapsed onto a nearby chair. I fixed Hera with a look powered by any leftover aggression and said, "Talk. And you'd better make it worth our while. Because I *felt* what being in your service did to Lyssa all those years ago, and if I had a hit list, you'd be on it."

Hera looked at me, and for an instant I saw the haughty queen bee she'd once been, and then it ebbed away. "I'm sorry," she said to Lyssa, to the room at large. "I'm not that person anymore."

"Prove it," Hermes challenged.

"I'm willing to tell you everything, but I'm afraid you're going to be disappointed. I don't know nearly as much as you think."

Lyssa growled.

From the floor, Michelle gasped as Cori let her up and the blood flow returned painfully to parts of her body. I ignored them both, riveted on Hera, impatient to get at the truth or, if she was recalcitrant, to beat it out of her. My inner hothead demanded it.

"Amphitrite came to me ..." Hera began, but then she stopped herself and turned to Cori. "About that coffee?"

It was Cori's turn to growl now, but she did go to the kitchen and come back with a tray laden with a coffeepot, cups, a sugar bowl, and little loose packets of various sugar substitutes, along with a variety of fancy creamers.

"All out of milk," she said, as she set the tray on her remarkably still-standing coffee table. "You'll just have to make do with crème brûlée creamer or whatever."

Ah, the deprivations of a zombie apocalypse.

"Still like your coffee like you like your heart?" Lyssa asked Hera. "Black?"

"As a matter of fact," Hera said, "I do." She poured herself a white porcelain cup of coffee and sat on the edge of the couch to down half the cup before she said another word. It would have taken a master carver to cut the tension in the room. When Hera made as if to set the cup on the table, Michelle took it from her and topped it off.

"Anytime now," Hermes growled.

Hera fixed him with a stare. "Sorry, I needed a minute. I've just seen women I've helped and grown to care for turned into mindless eating machines, with me and my assistant on the menu. I've had to cut their strings and escape through a portal, only to be attacked by a demon and her friends. I needed a jolt."

"I'll give you a jolt," Lyssa said. I concurred.

In fact, I took the seat on the couch beside Hera before Michelle could snap it up. Unless she was made of stone, she'd feel the menace coming off me in waves. If she had any sense of self-preservation, it would hurry her along.

"Amphitrite came to me," she said again, picking up her coffee cup and staring into it rather than at any of us. "She and the others had a proposition for me. They didn't start the apocalypse, but they were going to take advantage of the chaos to retake the world."

"What others?" Apollo asked.

"Amphitrite and the Oceanids, Hecate. She didn't say who else. She said the gods had tried and failed to rule the world. Zeus and Poseidon tried and failed to take it back. But now ... with trouble and turmoil everywhere, now was OUR chance. Amphitrite could take the oceans, the seas, everything else. She'd already begun seizing the reins while Poseidon was away in prison. Hecate could take the underworld. She practically ruled it already." I wondered if Hades would agree. "And if I helped them, I could have the heavens and earth ... as long as I was willing to share.

"I was tempted. Men have done a crappy job of things so far. Glass ceilings, abuses, slavery, sweatshops, legislation to control our bodies and who we can and can't love. Crappy. But it's not as if women are any better. Look at Michele Bachmann or what's-her-face ... the one with the big hair and the 'drill, baby, drill.' And, anyway, Amphitrite and Hecate don't have to deal with the real world. Souls, sure. Shipping lines, okay. But it's not the same. Here on Earth the lunatics are running the asylum and no shrink in the world, no matter how amazing, is going to restore sanity. I know. I deal with the craziness on a daily basis. I'm trying to help the victims of abuse and the best I can do is triage."

"But if you ran things ..." Lau began, and the rest of us whipped our heads around to stare. Whose side was she on?

"That's what they said—'but if you ran things.' It's a great theory, but one woman can't do it all. Not even two," she said, finally glancing up from her cup to meet Michelle's eyes. "Not even if one is a goddess." Michelle didn't even blink at that, confirming my initial impression that she was in the know. "It's too big a job. Even if I rule with an iron fist and micromanage everything, I will need minions, and they will take things too far, abuse their power or divert funds or approve black ops or other insanity. They'll decide I don't need to know because I'm too busy to be bothered. It will be the same thing all over again. There is no perfection."

"But the apocalypse ... Who started it? What made Namtar rise again? Did they say? Do they know?"

"I can only assume it's someone who's given up on the world and wants to wipe the slate clean. *Tabula rasa.*"

"The end then?" I said, the horror truly sinking in. "Really the end?"

"You sound like you sympathize," Apollo said, narrowing his eyes at Hera.

"I sympathize with the temptation to try. The world is a painful place. Famine, disease, sociopathy. Bad things happen to good people every day. Innocents ... or as close as this world produces. But there's a lot of good too. Progress is slow, but it comes if we just keep fighting. But if Amphitrite and Hecate have their way, they will take over the world and remake it in their owned flawed image."

I hadn't met Amphitrite, but I already knew I didn't want to play in Hecate's sandbox. "There's no remaking me in their image," Hermes said. "I'm too attached to my man parts."

"Aren't you all?" Hera said dryly.

Lyssa still stared at Hera with the intensity of a thousand suns, which had been growing hotter by the second. I kept watch out of the corner of my eye, ready to knock her out again if she risked starting another riot. "So, you didn't become part of the problem," she spat at Hera, "but you aren't part of the solution. You haven't done anything to stop them!"

Hera appealed to Apollo and to me, afraid, it seemed, to look at Lyssa, "What could I do? I'm already up to my eyeballs helping people who *want* to be helped. I'm out of the god game."

Lyssa studied her. "Well, that's convenient."

"Not as it turned out," she said.

"Look, this is all very interesting, and maybe later you can buy Lyssa a few thousand drinks or lattes or yachts or whatever you crazy kids do to make up, but right now we have people to save and asses to kick," Lau cut in testily. "So, spill. Where can we find the conspirators? They must have given you a contact number or *something* in case you changed your mind and decided to join up."

Hera's eyes widened. "They did. Just as you said. You don't suppose ..." she trailed off, but our minds jumped ahead of her. Or mine did, anyway.

Michelle gasped. "You think they infected our people and sent them after us?"

Hera looked like she was trying hard *not* to think that. "It's possible. What better way to sucker me into joining than to imperil the women I'm protecting and then take them out of the equation? No one left to save, only to avenge. I'm not exactly known for my restraint ... historically. If I thought someone was behind this plague, I'd go to the ends of the earth to stop them."

"But they didn't convince you," I pointed out.

"They might have. If you hadn't shown up. If we'd been overrun, if I'd lost Michelle ... there's no telling what I would have done."

"Or still might do," Lyssa cut in.

But it gave me an idea. "Call them. Convince them you've changed your mind. Set up a meeting." I could track Hecate, I was fairly sure of it, but this way maybe we could meet the rest of the cabal.

Angry energy was rolling off Lyssa again in waves now. The red was starting to bleed back into her eyes. "Send Hera straight to them? How do you know that isn't what she wants? We only have her word about whose side she's on."

"She won't be going alone," I answered. "I'll be going with her."

My skin was starting to feel hot and itchy, my eyeballs like there was a kind of pressure building behind them. My muscles twitched, wanting to go for something, and the sword Apollo had lobbed at me was still to hand. I fought it, knowing it wasn't my fury. I looked up to see Cori quivering as well, and Lau biting her lip, every muscle taut like she was fighting herself. Hermes, Apollo, and Hera, maybe by virtue of their age or power, seemed immune. "Enough," I snapped. "Lyssa, if you're not part of the solution, you're part of the problem. If you're really scarred by the bloodlust you've inspired in the past, you've got to get your nature under control. Or channel it. Namtar's nearness is driving you nuts." *Try saying* that *five times fast*, my brain taunted me. "Store it up. Once we find Namtar, you unleash the fury. But not until then."

"Can't. Help. It," she said, her eyes now totally consumed by the blood, her body vibrating with the need to fly into a frenzy.

"*Freeze!*" I told her forcefully. The vibrations halted immediately, and she stood like a statue, nothing stirring but a single blood tear that had reached critical mass and started the slow, thick descent down her cheek.

"Make the call," I told Hera. "Do it now. Hermes, you're the trickster god. You can arrange it to be somehow untraceable, right? Route it through computers and whatnot?"

"Who needs computers when you have magic? What is it they say—any sufficiently advanced geek-speak is indistinguishable from arcane mumbo jumbo?"

"I don't think they say that," Cori responded.

"I might be paraphrasing. Anyway, it's true. Do you have a phone you won't mind losing?" he asked her.

"Well, I *am* due for an upgrade." She pulled a phone from her hip pocket and offered it to Hermes, who gripped it, looked at it, front, back and sides, held it upside down and let it dangle there as he used some of that arcane mumbo jumbo on the device. It glowed a faint red, then strobed into purple, which died down into nothing.

"Here," he said, handing it over to Hera, "try it now."

She looked at Michelle, who recited the number right off of the top of her head. I eyed her suspiciously, like she too might be a goddess in hiding, maybe Mnemosyne, but then I remembered that M was a Titan (with whom Zeus had once had an affair), so it was beyond unlikely the two would have formed an attachment.

"Eidetic memory," Michelle said, seeing my look. "If I hear it, it's locked inside."

"Blessing and a curse," Hera said. "Great for party tricks. Great for an assistant, but if what she hears is wrong, that's locked away too, and good luck overwriting that file."

"You don't like it, don't be wrong," Michelle answered, but there was no bite to it, as though the conversation had been replayed a time or two.

Hera hit Send and looked over at all of us watching like this was a spectator sport.

Olympic cell signaling. "Here it goes."

The call itself was anticlimactic. Hermes amplified the sound coming out so that we could all clearly hear a mechanized voice inviting us to leave a message. Hera looked at us, at a loss, and then thought fast when it came to the beep. "You know who this is. This apocalypse thing has hit too close to home. I'm not saying I'm fully in your camp … yet. But if you're against this thing, then we're on the same side. I don't know where I'll be; I'm moving around, but you can try me at this number." She looked at Hermes, signing something in the air, and he quickly mouthed numbers at her, which she repeated into the phone. "Call me." She hung up. "Now what?"

"Now, we go to the hospital," I said. "We grab Nick, find his sister, get any intel we can and get out again. Maybe by then, we'll have a return phone call."

She looked around at the rest of us. "That's all you've got? A couple of gods, a muse, a gorgon girl, a *human*, and no discernible plan?"

"It's worked for us so far," I said defensively.

"Great," she responded. "Michelle, take a memo. We need to call in Athena. She's the sultana of strategy."

I grabbed Michelle as she reached for the phone Hera held out to her. "You can't," I said, intercepting it. "For all we know, she's part of the girl power clique. If you call her and she's on their side, you'll blow the whole thing."

"So we're just going to wing it?" Hera asked dubiously.

"It's called improv and it works for comedy," Cori said. "But, honey, this is war."

15

———————

W hat do you mean you can't just open a portal? You opened one just a little while ago."

Hermes gave me the hairy eyeball. "Yes, but you're talking about opening a portal into an overrun hospital. There's nothing to keep someone from walking through as the portal opens. Or lurching through. Do you really want to occupy the same space as one of the walking undead? I don't know what that'll do to you, but there's a certain scene from *Galaxy Quest* that comes to mind."

I looked to Apollo in appeal.

"He's got a point," Apollo said. "We can open a portal, but we have to weigh the risks." Hermes looked sour, and I realized what all the protest was about.

"You're scared," I said. It popped out of my mouth before I could think about it, finesse it. If he were Hecate his glare might actually have incinerated me on contact.

"I'm not scared. But like any trickster god, hell, like any sane person, I have a healthy sense of self-preservation. A field trip to ground zero of a full-on crisis seems like insanity."

"Who was it who said, 'There's a fine line between genius and insanity'?"

"I don't know, but I'm fairly sure he hadn't met you."

"Children!" Lau snapped. "Let's pull it together. Between breaking into a plague hospital and porting in, the safer choice seems fairly obvious."

Go figure, the two of us on the same side for once.

"Fine," Hermes said, "but if things go wrong, don't blame the messenger."

"What about any of this is *right*?" Cori asked.

"Point taken," Hermes said. "Okay, everyone, grab whatever weapons you want to go in with and give me silence while I work."

Cori went to the kitchen and rummaged around while Hermes linked his fingers together and twisted his hands outward to crack his knuckles. He put on a show of rolling his shoulders, stretching his neck, and generally limbering up. Cori came back a minute later with a serving tray filled with an array of knives, a cleaver, surgical masks and rubber gloves. She saw me looking.

"I'm not a germaphobe or anything," she said quickly. "I just like cleanliness and hate the smell of bleach. Anyway, I thought they'd come in handy in a plague zone."

It was smart thinking. If I'd had the time to give it any thought, I'd have expected the muse of comedy and choral performances to be a lot more ... I don't know ... giddy, maybe. Less practical. It was unfair, I realized. Comedy was hard work and heartbreaking in its own way, with humor being so subjective and everyone a critic.

Lyssa was coming out of her frozen state now, glaring around. Cori took several steps back, keeping the weapons tray out of reach.

"You stay," Hera ordered Michelle, eying Lyssa. "Keep an eye on things here."

"Who's going to keep an eye on *you*?" Lyssa asked. I felt the backlash of her hatred. "Perhaps I'd better come along as well."

Hera's struggle showed on her face. On the one hand, she clearly didn't trust Lyssa at our side. On the other hand, leaving Lyssa behind meant cooping her assistant up with the demon's barely leashed madness or taking her into a different kind of danger.

"If we could guarantee we were the only people you might whip into a murderous rage …" Hera began. "Wait, that came out wrong. We don't want *anyone* whipped into a homicidal rage, least of all our enemies, and we've already established that you have no control."

"I haven't killed you yet," Lyssa countered.

But it was a close thing. I could feel it. To her point, maybe Lyssa *did* have more control than we knew, but still. The rage was starting to boil my blood … again.

"Just go," Lyssa snapped. Her first clenched. Her body taut as a drawn bow. The control was costing her and she was truly going to snap at any moment.

"But—" Michelle said.

"GO!" Lyssa roared, her eyes flaring red again.

I reached for the tray, grabbed the biggest knife there and handed it to Michelle. "Just in case," I said.

She looked terrified.

"I'm staying too," Cori said to Michelle, "don't worry." When Apollo's eyes blazed her way, she said, "I'm not leaving Mel. You find a way to save her or, heavens help me, I will kick your fine ass from here to eternity."

"What about my ass?" Hermes asked.

"You want me to kick that too?" Cori asked.

"You could show a little appreciation."

"Enough!" Hera thundered. "Open the portal."

Hermes grinned as though he was thrilled to finally get a

rise out of someone—which probably he was—and turned to Apollo. "Shall we?"

Apollo growled and reached out to take Hermes's hand in a man shake. The latter closed his eyes and once again focused on the space above the coffee table. As before, the air rippled and churned, but this time it refused to fix on anything.

"Something's interfering," Hermes said. "I can't get a read on your detective."

"He's not *her* detective," Apollo growled, like *that* was the important part.

"You don't think—" I began, but I couldn't finish the thought. "Hell with that. I'm going in." I tested my wings. Stiff, but they'd do. Whatever had awakened in me, I was glad the superhealing was part of the package. "I can carry one person with me."

Because the only way I could think to get into a quarantined and barricaded building was via the roof. I doubted there were any handy-dandy subterranean tunnels leading to secret entrances into the facility, and I didn't have the leisure to go looking.

"Me," Lau said, unsurprisingly. "You're taking me."

"Hera," I said. My tone didn't invite argument, but Lau had never in her life waited to be invited. I cut her off before she could begin her rant. "She's got that kickin' I-can-give-life-and-I-can-take-it-away power. If Nick and his sister are in trouble, she can give them the strength to hold on. Right?" I asked her. I'd need Hera's strength, but, more than that, it was a test. Her history didn't exactly inspire trust, and if she was going to turn on us, better that I be the only one in the line of fire.

Hera nodded. "Good."

Apollo stepped up—ready, I could tell, to insist on joining up somehow. "I need you and Hermes here. If we get into trouble, you'll sense it through our link. If Hermes can't zero in on me, I know *you* can, and if we need you to open a portal so we can make our escape ..."

He looked down into my eyes, and I pleaded with him through our connection to just let it go. Let me go. I tried to reinforce how much I was determined to return. That much I could be sure of. The "to him" part that should have followed ... *that* was churning my gut. Faced with Nick in need ... I couldn't make that call.

I tried to push that confusion way down where Apollo couldn't sense it, to hide it behind the force of my determination. Anyway, it had no place right now when there was no guarantee any of us would live long enough for it to matter.

"Do your windows open?" I asked Cori. She nodded.

"Then let's go," I said to Hera.

How to carry her was the awkward thing. As weird as it was to have her arms wrapped around my neck and her body pressed against mine, it turned out to be the easiest way. My wings had to be free to flap, so there was no throwing her over my shoulder like a sack of potatoes.

We were on the Upper East Side, and the hospital was on the Upper West. Not far, as the crow—or gorgon—flies, but not close enough for my comfort. The fact that Hermes couldn't get a read on Nick had my panic kicked into high gear. My heart pounded in my chest, making it hard to catch the breath I needed.

I hoped and prayed I'd recognize the hospital from the sky. The upside: That turned out not to be a problem. The downside: Things were worse than I thought.

The barricades were easily seen from the sky ... as was the fact that they'd been abandoned. When we'd seen them on the news, they'd been manned by police officers in riot gear. Now ... most of the barricades were down, like they'd been overrun. Only two bodies had been left behind that I could see ... bodies too badly damaged to rise again, even if they were raging with the zombie plague.

Worse, a small white-and-brown dog stood over one of those bodies, muzzle buried deep. My stomach lurched, and Hera snapped, "Don't you dare," before I could lose my lunch.

I was terrified of what we'd find inside. My precog kicked my gut, as if to say that I was right to fear. I focused on the rooftop we were headed for. There was a copter sitting there all by itself. I waited for a challenge, the sight of soldiers with weaponry trained on us, but there was nothing. Silence. Eerie and unnatural.

Or … not nothing. There was smear. And then chunks among the smear. And then … My stomach rebelled and I wobbled in our flight. I had to get us down onto that roof before I blew chunks … Oh, bad thinking. Bad, bad thinking.

I aimed hurriedly for a slick-free spot on the roof, but in my eye-watering attempt to hold my nausea in, I overshot by the merest bit and we went sliding in the … stuff. The red slick of once human. Or animal. I couldn't know for sure.

But I could, because that was an ear and … and maybe a piece of scalp with blood-matted hair still clinging to it. Hera's feet came down to the ground and tried to dig in to stop our slide, but the sudden jolt only overbalanced us, and we went skidding and rolling through the bloody remains. My natural instinct was to throw out my hands and scrabble at the concrete roof, make myself as non-aerodynamic as possible. The blood slicked my hands, getting in under my nails, filling my nasal passages, sickening my stomach. At the end of the slide, I managed to twist just enough to avoid getting most of the sickness on myself when my stomach violently reversed peristalsis.

How Hera held in her coffee was beyond me, but when I twisted my head and groaned, there she was, coming up to her hands and knees and quickly backing away from the filth, slicking her hands down her marginally less mucky suit in the attempt to clean them off.

"What the hells happened here?" she asked. Like I would know.

I got shakily to my feet, holding my hands out before me, unwilling to rub the slime on my clothes and keep the smell with me forever. Hoping desperately for a sink and soapy water hot enough to take off at least one layer of skin. But I wasn't going to find it up here.

"Zombies?" I suggested hopefully. Better the devil you know.

"Are they usually so ... thorough?" she asked.

We both knew they weren't. Diseases existed to propagate themselves. It didn't do any good to infect someone who was in no condition to go around infecting others. We'd all seen ample shambling evidence of the way the plague usually worked. This was something else.

"Let's get inside," I said, avoiding the question.

She nodded, and we both headed for a door clearly visible from where we stood. It had a man-sized dent in it and a still-wet smear of blood across it. There was nothing to do but reach for the handle with my bloody hands. It turned easily, but the banged-up door scraped along as I pushed it out of the way, making stealth impossible. I listened for a minute, but the eerie quiet continued inside. Nothing came for us.

Not a creature was stirring. Not even a mouse, my brain supplied. I told it to shut the hell up. Nick was alive, somewhere. I'd know if he was dead.

But would I? I asked myself. Would I really? I wanted to think yes, but in truth ... There was nowhere to go but down. I was relieved to see that the carnage had stopped at the door, but also horrified because it meant that no one from the roof had made it this far. I touched the clinically bare walls, rubbing my hands against them, doing my best to leave the filth behind, careful to smear enough that there'd be no attainable prints. I didn't feel any better afterward. The horror had sunk in and found a home.

Hera was silent on the stairs behind me. I had to turn twice to make sure she was still there. At the first floor we came to, I pushed against the door to the hallway, and it opened easily. Too easily. Whatever had done the damage on the roof hadn't brought the devastation inside. Was it too big to enter, like Eu-meh? Or uninvited like the vampires I still didn't know actually existed. Or ... wait, this was a public building, so I didn't think the invitation thing was an issue. So not a vamp then. Maybe something patrolling the perimeter. Not so concerned with what was inside the building as what might get in for rescue or out for escape? But given the state of the barricades below, *something* had certainly gotten out.

This top floor seemed to be made up of offices ... empty, silent offices. I wanted to raid them for information, but my precog was like a dog in a disaster film, tugging desperately at my mind to tell me that Timmy had fallen down the well or the aliens were at our door. It was telling me we had to go down. But we had to pass the offices, and in one someone had left a smartphone out on a desktop. I grabbed it, hoping maybe it would reveal something later on. I tucked it in a pocket and continued on, Hera right at my heels.

We paused at the elevators. There were only two that came up to this level, and I hesitated before pressing the call button. The plague victims weren't exactly reasoning beings, but they might still have a Pavlovian response to the sound of the elevator if they'd previously discovered fresh meat at the ding of the bell. There was an inset sign by the call button, listing what could be found on which floors, which I committed to memory. Then I pushed the button. I wasn't sure we should risk the elevator, but if it turned out to be stuck anywhere, that would be a good indication of trouble. It might give us a place to start.

Hera and I stood in silence, watching the display at the top of each car to see which would come and from where.

Car one said it was currently on the second floor, which didn't change in the face of our summons. Car two started to rise up from the basement.

The second floor then. I hoped the elevator there wasn't blocked by a body. My precog rewarded me with a bolt to the heart at the very thought, and I knew that as much as I wanted it to be otherwise, I was dead-on. Emphasis on the dead.

We hit the stairs, but didn't clatter down them as I wanted to. We went quietly, listening at each level to make sure that we weren't wrong, that the fighting hadn't moved on. The silence was truly eerie until we hit the third floor, the one above the stalled elevator.

Hera and I listened at the door to the hallway, criminally close ... at least in some states. Our eyes met when we heard the growl. It wasn't human. Not even remotely, not even from a zombie that no longer fit that description.

It sounded like a large dog. A *pissed-off* large dog. Or maybe one that had been frightened or backed into a corner. Definitely a canine that was about to lash out in a big way. I remembered the dog down at the barricades, eating the face off a downed officer, and wondered whether we'd had some kind of cross-species contagion. Or ... was this something different? Yiayia had mentioned Fergus and boils. Who knew what else might be out there. If Namtar was the god of plagues and his followers were legion, all stirred up by his rising, we could be facing as many epidemic outbreaks as there were diseases. Not all of which could be cured.

There was a crash, like something throwing itself against a barrier, and a girl's high-pitched scream.

Hera and I burst out of the stairwell onto a scene of

carnage. Before us lay a nurse, her cheerful SpongeBob scrubs torn to shreds and blood blackened. Her stomach had been torn open. Her intestines ... I had to look away, beyond the body, listening for the direction of the battering.

The lights of the hallway flickered and returned at half-light, but none of it slowed me down as I headed where the noise and my precog led. My feet slid in something I didn't try to identify, and my heart nearly fell out of my chest at the sight of a little boy in a hospital gown slumped against the nurses' station, his legs and throat ... No, I couldn't look, couldn't catalog his hurts. The scrubs ... the child ... this was the pediatric wing. Dammit, if there was something still alive down here ...

The beating continued. Hera and I threw ourselves through an open doorway and drew up short at the sight of the snarling, howling, and slavering beast that continuously hurled its body full-force against a closed door at the outskirts of the room. It was—or had been—a yellow Lab. Man's best friend ... a breed often chosen as service dogs because of their great dispositions. This one's fur was matted with gore and bristled to where the beast looked twice its size. Its chest worked like a bellows, and it looked displaced inside this cheery room, walls strung with nursery rhyme figures—the cow jumping over the moon, the dish running away with the spoon, a little dog laughing. This dog was far from laughing. So were the bodies it had left littered about.

I hit the doorframe behind me to draw its attention—sure there had to be something ... someone or ones behind that other door that it was trying to get to—trying to give it a more immediate target. My blood chilled as it worked and the beast turned on us with eyes that burned hot with hatred and blood-flecked spittle frothing over its muzzle.

16

R abies.

It explained so much. Like the two adults in jeans and peppy purple T-shirts who lay practically at our feet. One was torn to shreds, beyond recognition, but the other, a woman, was still alive, trying feebly to crawl toward the mad hound, using just her arms and elbows. Her legs weren't working. It looked like a nerve cluster at the base of her spine had been laid open, but still she was ... not even inching, but centimetering toward the dog, cooing to it, as if it weren't beyond her reach, mentally and physically. Tears poured from her eyes. On the back of her shirt, above the bloody mass, were the words, *Cuddles for Kiddies*. It broke my heart. At a guess, she'd loved that dog. Still loved. And wasn't giving up.

There was no way she and her compatriot had brought diseased animals in to interact with sick children. I was shocked they'd been let in at all. So whatever had come over the animals must have come hard and fast. No rabies then ... or not the normal kind. That had an incubation period. There were signs....

The beast started to advance on us.

I stared it right in the eyes and yelled *"Freeze!"* at the top of my lungs. I didn't know if it would work through the madness. If this was rabies or a form of it, the beast's brain might be Swiss cheese right now.

The beast froze for a second, and for that second I thought something was actually going to go our way. But then it shook its head slowly from side to side. In another instant, it was going to come back to itself, and I couldn't let that happen.

I leapt into the air, letting my wings carry me across the distance between us, raising Cori's sword for a massive slice. Old Yeller tossed off the last of its paralysis and reared to meet me, its deadly jaws snapping at me. I let my blade fall toward its vulnerable neck, hating myself as I did it, knowing the beast wasn't in its right mind. My blade cut and caught, but so did Yeller's teeth. The pain as it latched on to my arm was nothing to the surprise of it whipping me around like trapped prey, trying to snap my neck. The caught blade acted like the harness on a bucking bronco, keeping us linked and me from flying off.

The door the beast had been attacking suddenly blew open, and a figure staggered out, slamming the door shut again and demanding that someone lock it behind him. I was shocked to hear the staggering figure speak, sure at first that it would be a zombie, another attacker, but ... I knew that voice.

I couldn't focus. My vision doubled and tripled as my brain bashed against one and then the other side of my skull as the beast shook me. Then, suddenly, my blade slid free of the beast's neck, having made no impression on it whatsoever, and my head hit the floor hard enough to knock stars across my field of vision. But he still had my arm in his jaws, and I could practically feel the poison in his bite racing through my blood.

Something struck at the dog. I knew because it opened its jaws to go for the new threat and I had enough presence of mind to rip myself away, draw my legs into myself and scuttle back on butt and hands. My sword had fallen and my head swam, but I closed my eyes and counted to two, all the time I could spare, before opening them again, hoping my vision had returned. I had to find that sword. Had to help Hera and whoever had come out of that room, because he'd sounded like ...

Nick.

Nick had apparently struck the dog with a metal chair to take its attention from me and now stood fending it off with his one good hand, wielding the chair like a pointy shield. Bandages still covered half of his face and more than that of his chest. He wore only drawstring pants and his fury. All three of him, occasionally resolving into only two. My vision was still a mess, and my thinking was just as fuzzy.

"Hold his attention," Hera told him unnecessarily. "If I can just get close enough!"

I reached for my fallen sword and caught it somewhere along the blade, which sliced roughly into my hand. I drew back with a hiss and carefully felt around for the hilt, keeping my eyes on the fight, waiting for the figures to resolve so that I'd know where to aim my blows.

I hit the hilt, wrapped my hand around it and gave a great "Hi-yah!" that nearly split my head open as the beasts finally resolved into one and I aimed right for it.

Hera spun out of my way, leaving the beast directly in my path. My blade hit home and cut deep. The beast howled in pain, its hate-filled gaze swinging up to meet mine, gathering itself to lunge and then ... it froze, stock-still. A strange gray patina swept over the beast and its eyes deadened to ... stone.

In an instant, the monster was nothing but a statue, frozen in place. No longer alive. I stared at it, unable to take it in. Too stunned to believe ...

Until Hera looked at me in something like awe and Nick—amazing, glorious, *alive* Nick—said, "Tori, you're bleeding."

I looked down at my arm, thinking he was talking about the dog's bite, considering rabies and how quickly it might set in. Then the blood dripped from the hilt of my blade onto my foot and I realized he was talking about where I'd cut my palm on the blade ... the same one that had turned Old Yeller to stone. Had my blood done that? Gorgon blood from one wound or the other? I couldn't see any other explanation.

My legs nearly gave out, and Nick was suddenly there to catch me, but I didn't give in to it, not with the burns over a good part of his body and him barely standing as it was. Collapsing into him was not an option. I locked my legs and caught myself with a hand to his good shoulder. We looked into each other's eyes—*eye*, in his case—and seemed frozen there.

A knock at the door Nick had shut behind him broke the spell, and he ran to it, giving some kind of counterknock. It opened just a crack, and a tiny elfin face appeared, peering out with one brown eye.

Nick squatted at eye level. "It's okay," he told her. "It's—"

She flung the door open and threw herself into his arms, and he caught her, heedless of what it would do to him. I heard him grunt, but that was all the indication he gave of the pain. Then there were other arms around him, and it was like a puppy pile, only without the frothing at the mouth.

One older boy hung back, looking from Hera to the frozen dog to me, gaze catching and holding on my wings. "Who're you?" he asked. And then, "*What* are you?" At least, I thought that was what he said. The words were tight and hard to hear through his wired jaw. He looked like he'd been in some kind of terrible accident.

"We're friends, and we're here to help," I said. He just snorted.

I looked to Nick, who was turned away from me, still wrapped in his embraces. He finally stood, arms loaded with the little elfin girl, hair done in a dozen little braids, with colorful beads on every end and dark bangs falling across her even darker eyes. She had a death grip on Nick's neck. I could see what it cost him to let her hang on so tightly, but he didn't say a word. My heart broke at the sight. At the completely selfish and unbidden thought of what our children might have looked like if ...

"Did you find Amanda?" he asked.

"No," I answered, looking away, trying to pretend my voice hadn't just cracked. "There may be other pockets like this one, people holed up safely, but the place seems mostly deserted. What happened here?"

"I couldn't take it anymore and went looking for Amanda myself, and I heard the snarls and screams—"

"He saved us!" the elfin girl piped up.

"Lacy, this is Tori. Tori, Lacy. She was bashing the bad doggie with her crutches when I got here. And winning, weren't you, sweetheart?"

That was when I noticed the full leg cast she was wearing, all the way up the thigh. "I'm a warrior princess," she announced, hugging him. The pain he was in must have been excruciating, but it only flashed across his face before he got it under control.

"So brave," I said, infusing my voice with all of the warmth I could muster when my heart was breaking. "Can we talk for a second?" I asked Nick.

Hera huffed. "We don't have time for a 'talk.' We don't know how many more of these things might be out there or what else we're facing."

I shot her a look. That was exactly what I'd wanted to talk about ... without impressionable young ears listening in.

Nick looked around—for Lacy's crutches? For someone to

pass her off to? No way could she walk on her own with that cast.

The teen boy with the wired jaw saw what was going on and recovered a crutch from the floor. I saw the other, but it was under the body of one of the *Cuddles for Kiddies* volunteers, and I left it alone.

Nick set Lacy down gently with her one crutch and asked the boy if he'd take care of the others for a minute and make sure no one was hurt. He nodded, but not like he didn't know he and the others were being sent away.

"I don't know," Nick said, his voice lowered. "When I pulled my IV and made it to the hallway, the hospital was already in chaos. People and dogs blew past me. I'm sure there were cats as well. There usually are. We've been in there for what seems like hours with that dog beating tirelessly at the door. I don't know what set the animals off."

"Or what possessed people to have a visit during all this. I thought the place was quarantined," Hera said.

"That's what's so terrible about all of this—Jeff says they thought the kids needed the comfort now more than ever, especially with some of their parents ..." he trailed off, looking toward the door where the children waited. "I guess they got special permission. And then ..."

"And then this," I finished for him. "But what are we going to do with them? I don't know what happened while you were locked away, but it really is a ghost town, except maybe—"

"The second floor," Hera cut in. "There's an elevator locked down on that floor, which means something's blocking it. It doesn't necessarily mean survivors, but ..."

"We have to check it out," I finished.

He looked from me, to Hera, to the kids. "We can't just leave them. If something's really gone wrong, there's no one here to care for them."

"Delegate," Hera ordered. "Put the boy in charge until we can see what we're dealing with and come back for them."

The unbandaged side of Nick's face went through contortions. It went against everything in him to leave them behind, I thought. If anything happened to them while he was away, it would destroy him. Far more than the fiery serpent he'd fought in Greece. But taking them into danger was even more counter-intuitive. He gave one single nod and turned back to the kids, drawing the older boy—Jeff?—aside for a minute.

Lacy must have heard, though, because she stumbled toward Nick with a wail of "But I want to go with you!"

Nick hugged her to his good side and chucked her chin with his finger. "I'll be back, princess, I promise. You just keep this handy." He gave a nod toward her single crutch. "I might need you to protect the others. But you keep this door locked and you should be just fine until I get back. Jeff is great, but I'm going to need you to keep the others calm, okay?"

She couldn't have been more than seven or a very tiny eight, but she nodded with a seriousness that belied her years, the beads on the ends of her braids clicking with the movement. Nick gave her a quick kiss on the forehead and told her again, "I'll be back."

She grabbed his ears and held him there for a moment, staring him dead in the eyes. "You'd better," she told him. Then she let him go and turned away before he could see her lip quiver. So strong. I wondered if I'd been half that at her age.

Nick was barely out the door when Jeff closed and locked it behind him. It felt weird to have Nick back at my side. Nostalgic and yet not ... not given the circumstances.

"Onward?" he said.

"You sure you're up for it?" I asked belatedly.

He gave me a dirty look out of his single eye and picked up the metal chair he'd wielded like a champ. "You gonna stop me?" he challenged.

"No," I said, turning for the stairwell.

It hurt less to turn my back on him. Maybe that's how he'd felt about me when he'd left the breakup note with the hotel concierge in Delphi.

I crashed down on that thought. Now that the third floor was quiet, I could hear the banging coming from below us. And banging. And banging.

At the stairwell I paused to listen, but it didn't sound like the pounding was coming from the stairwell itself. When I pushed the door open and stepped out into it, it was even clearer that it was coming from the second floor. It wasn't exactly rhythmic ... every time the pause would go on too long. I'd strain, waiting to hear, and then give a mini jump when it would come again. My precog wasn't in full-on alarm mode, but it was goosing up my adrenaline and directing my attention, as if to say, *"Hey, you may want to watch that."*

Hera and Nick followed me into the stairwell. The closer we came to the second floor, the more the pounding seemed to go right through me and my heart wanted to unsync with it.

When we hit the door to the second floor hall, we could see it bow in with each bang, but there was no window, no peephole to the other side to give us an indication of what we were facing. But it didn't sound like multiple bodies. If it was just one ...

Without thought, I put the sword to my healing hand and swept it along the cut again, slicking the blade in my blood. It scared me that I was becoming more gorgon, less and less human. Later, if we saved the world, I'd get back with the Grey Sisters and see what could be done. For now, I didn't have any choice but to go with it.

I looked back at the others. "Do I try the door or do we just leave it? Go back for the kids and get everybody out?" I asked.

"Out where?" Hera asked back. "They're safe for now. Can we say the same anywhere else?"

"Besides, Amanda is still missing," Nick reminded me.

That was good. Not that Amanda was still missing, of course. That was terrible. But that they didn't want to just take off. Adrenaline was still flooding my veins. The last battle had gone too easily. I was spoiling for more. It wasn't just Lyssa setting me off. She wasn't here, which meant Namtar was riling up more than just demons ... or that I had demon blood, as Apollo had speculated. I didn't want to think about it.

I reached for the door, only to find it locked. At the sound of the handle being jiggled, the body on the other side of the door threw itself against it even harder. The door bucked in its frame but didn't give. But behind that, there were more sounds, like attention had been drawn by the renewed effort.

"Let me," Hera said, and I stepped back against the wall to give her access to the door.

She touched the handle and muttered something beneath her breath. I thought I caught the old word for *rot* or maybe *decay*, which struck me oddly, as in my mind they went along with things more organic. But she signaled me and Nick to be alert and reached for the handle. It turned as she twisted, and I raised my sword up, ready to burst into the hallway and take down whatever awaited.

Hera yanked the door open and a figure fell into the stairwell with us. It wasn't Amanda, which was a good thing, as this woman had clearly seen better days. *Living days* where her dressy dress had probably been meant for a party and not her funeral shroud. One arm and shoulder hung limply, possibly from repeated pounding against the door, possibly from whatever had killed her. Her eyes were filmed over. Her paper white skin had gone gray, one cheekbone was shattered.

I didn't have time to catalog the rest of her damage before she was lurching for Nick and I had to cut her down, braining her with the flat of my blade. I didn't know if it was kinder than the alternative, but she fell at Nick's feet, completely out, at least for the moment.

But the commotion I'd heard behind her was that of others, an army of them, drawn by the new noise.

They didn't all shuffle. Only those without two working legs. The others ... they weren't exactly speed demons. More like kids in a rush to get to the ice cream truck but knowing that it would wait. It was a bad analogy. These things were beyond reason. But I didn't have the leisure to stand around thinking of something better.

I jumped into the hall, meeting them head on with my sword. I beat them off with the flat of the blade where I could and when I couldn't, the sword bit and held, releasing only with effort and finishing with solid, stonelike thunks to the floor. Hera and Nick were a mere flurry out of the corner of my eye.

I was desperately trying to yank my blade from a behemoth of a man whose mouth frothed with red, something like the rabid dog, when another zombie rushed me, latching on to my half-turned back and sinking jagged teeth into my shoulder. Instinctively, I flung my head back to slam my thick cranium into his to make him release. The pain was terrible, but the zombie clung, despite my abuse, becoming dead weight. Heavy and overbalancing. The bite was to the shoulder of my good arm, and I felt my strength ebbing quickly away.

Before it could drain entirely, I forced myself to rip my blade free and turn, but the zombie, still locked on to my shoulder, turned as I turned, and I couldn't get a decent angle to knock it loose. I realized then that it had become dead weight because that's exactly what it was ... dead. True dead. Petrified by my blood.

Others caught my moment of realization, using my distraction to leap for me en masse. Instinct kicked in, and I launched myself back into the fight, swinging madly with the sword, trying to take out as many as I could before they could bring me down or before the venom in the bite I'd sustained made me one of them. I didn't know what my blood might do to the virus. Or what it would do to me. Only that I'd now been twice bitten—the rabid dog and the zombie guy. My future was not looking bright.

"Nick!" I cried, thinking that his name might be the last on my lips.

I caught sight of him in that moment, pinned down against a wall. Hera had put him behind her, it appeared, but she'd been drawn out, leaving him unprotected. He was holding the zombies off with the chair he'd brought with him from the third floor, but as I watched, it was ripped from his hands.

"Freeze!" I yelled at the top of my lungs.

The mass around me went still, but the others, bent on biting and paying me no attention whatsoever, were attacking.

I shook off those who'd latched on to me and grabbed for the petrified leech on my back, flapping frantically with my wings, trying to dislodge him. He came off with a ripping of flesh, taking some of my shoulder with him, but I didn't have time even to feel it.

Hera was mumbling something else under her breath and the mob before her fell. I vaulted them to get to the group around Nick, some of whom were going down as well. The rest I lit into with the flat of my blade, sending them stumbling as they knocked into each other. When they turned on me, I yelled out another *"Freeze!"* feeling the power go out of me, leaving me shaky from blood loss or adrenaline overload or shock from all of my wounds.

They froze, and I hit the wall, literally, letting it hold me up as I turned painfully, my half-there shoulder smearing the once-white paint.

Nick caught me as the pain finally registered and I threatened to fall onto my face. "Tori, you've been bit," he said into my hair. I didn't have the energy to raise my head.

"Yeah," I mumbled. "Sucks."

He didn't laugh. I hadn't really expected him to.

"You okay to go on?" Hera asked. "Do you feel ... um ... Are we looking tasty to you?"

"In your dreams," I told her.

She gave a humorless laugh. "So not a zombie yet. Unfortunately, we don't know how long the incubation period is with this. We'll have to watch you."

"We still have to find Amanda," I said, much more comfortable *not* thinking about becoming a mindless eating machine, especially given what was on the menu.

"Already found her," Nick said, and the tone of his voice was ... desolate.

I jerked my head up to catch the look on his face. And then to follow his gaze to one of the fallen. One of the group he'd been holding off with his chair. I couldn't see her face—not well—but the woman he was watching wore blood-spattered jeans, an emerald-green sweater, and blood-matted hair. Dark like Nick's.

"Oh, Nick," I said, reaching for him.

"Don't," he snapped. "Don't. If you do, I'll break down, and I don't know if I'll pull myself back together. She was here because of *me*."

There was nothing I could say to that. I knew the feeling. I understood that blame game. He hadn't let me off the hook for getting him into trouble back in Delphi. He wasn't going to let himself off the hook any easier. It was a burden he'd have to bear.

"At least she's only frozen. If we can find a cure for this—" I tried.

"Yeah," he answered. But not like he believed it could happen.

"Sweep the rest of the hospital then?" Hera asked. "See about any other survivors, grab the kids and get out?"

I nodded. "A survivor might be able to tell us what happened here. We only talked to Nick a few hours ago and everything was fine then. Or ... not fine, but seemingly stable, and all of a sudden ... all this—overrun by zombies and rabid animals. Whatever swept through here, it happened fast."

"We'll figure it out," Hera said. She'd definitely had experience reassuring people in the face of mad odds, because she almost sounded convincing.

I didn't suggest that we split up. Neither did anyone else.

17

———

We started our search with the floor we were already on—quickly, before anyone could unfreeze or ... It only then occurred to me to wonder if the turning-to-stone thing was permanent or if it was just temporary, like the results of my gorgon glare. Sure, the sword itself had done damage to those I'd petrified, and maybe that would be enough, but ... damn this transformation. Why couldn't it come with a handy-dandy set of rules, like the *Gremlins*. "Don't feed after midnight" and all that jazz. But, oh no, I had to learn as I went. For all I knew, I was one bean burrito away from paralyzing an entire taco joint with a gas cloud.

My brain did its little digression dance as I tried not to see the bodies and parts the zombie army had left behind ... a hand here, an ear or gristle or something absolutely unidentifiable there. Down the hall there was a zombie left behind, trying to pull enough of itself together to lunge at us. It was half in and half out of the elevator. That's what had kept it from closing and coming when called. The zombie's back had been crushed by an overhead light that had been pulled down on top of it. It was a pitiful sight—trapped, broken, bloody, but still trying to rise. One that made me wonder whether it was kinder to put the thing out of its misery. Not that it probably knew misery. Or much of anything else but its urges. Fight, bite, spread the disease.

***

THERE WERE NO SURVIVORS, but neither were there as many dead as I expected to see.

Some must have gotten away.

The frozen ones were starting to stir, but not those I'd petrified as we gave up on the second floor and retreated back to the stairwell. But Hera had rotted the lock; we couldn't just seal it behind us and expect it to hold. Or so I thought, but she tapped the handle and muttered some kind of counterspell as voices and clanking rose from the first floor below us. Body armor, it sounded like. And orders.

Military orders. The cavalry had arrived.

The three of us looked at each other. My first thought was relief. Soldiers could do the sweep, take charge of the children ... But thoughts and feelings were two different things. Inside, my stomach churned. If they caught us, no doubt we'd be frisked, decontaminated, debriefed. I only had wings for one passenger. And the kids ... would they truly be better off with the soldiers? What if ...

My gut cramped with the signal my precog was sending me, and then I heard the flap of wings not my own. My precog and my every instinct turned my gaze toward the tiny stairwell window, where I caught just the end of a whipcord tail edged with spikes. Immediately, I flashed on the images from the roof, and I knew why the children wouldn't be better off. No one was making it out of here alive.

Not with that thing outside.

"Get to the children," I told Nick and Hera. "Protect them. I'll be back."

Nick grabbed me with his good hand as I turned to bolt toward the roof, hoping to hone in on the thing from there. "Are you crazy?" he asked. "You're not going alone."

As to the crazy, I'd have thought that truth to be self-evident.

"Do you have wings?" I asked harshly, knowing that I had to get him gone. "Right now you're more a hindrance than a help, and I've done enough to you already. The children trust you. Go to them. That's where you'll do the most good."

"You haven't done anything to me," he said, good eye meeting mine, breaking my heart even as my precog was kicking at my innards, screaming at me to go, go, GO! "I made my own decisions."

It was a complete reversal of what he'd said in Delphi. Maybe he'd had time to think, to come to a kind of epiphany, but ... everything was different now. Maybe. Possibly. Or not. Now was not the time.

I yanked my arm out of his grasp. "If we survive this, we'll talk. For now, you've got to let me go."

He did, and I was off in a shot, before I could see any potential pain on his face. He'd hurt me. I'd hurt him. Sometimes I thought that's what caring was all about. People hurt each other until they couldn't take it anymore and then moved on to the next, full of hope and the pretense that it wouldn't happen again. Just look at the pattern of Apollo's life. All those millennia and still alone. Did I really think it would be different with me? That he'd only been waiting all those lifetimes for some mythical concept of true love? Did it matter? Could I help myself? Or was it all part of the pattern woven by the Fates, who were way too fond of their daytime programming? Did anyone ever live happily ever after in the soaps?

Wrong time, wrong place. Maybe even wrong genre. This

wasn't a serial, this was an action flick, where the guy always got the girl in the end … right? The question was, which guy?

Gah! Battle now. Love, lust, confusion, whatever later.

My gorgon blood was boiling as I raced for the roof. I let it go, let the battle frenzy build.

By the time I crashed through the door onto the roof and slid in the blood congealing on the other side, I was ready to tear the plague demon I'd spotted limb from limb with my bare hands. The sword I held said I didn't have to. I wiped the zombie blood off onto my pants and nicked my hand again before the horror of the comingling bodily fluids could stop me. I'd already been bitten. If I was going to go zombie, it was already too late for me.

My precog snapped my head around to the right, where a beast waited in what shadows there were on the roof. Realizing it had been sighted, it let out the growl that had no doubt been building silently, and every hair on my body stood up in primal fear.

It was the sound of every imagination-amplified beast hiding in every bush on every dark, lonely walk home. I couldn't see its full shape. I knew that it was serpentine from the back, but from the front, it was somewhere between hyena and grizzly. Its back arched upward so that it appeared to be hulking. Its muzzle was long and powerful. I couldn't get a look at its teeth through the blood-flecked froth of its mouth, but I knew them to be all predator. Its legs stuck out from its body, lizardlike.

The monster lunged before my brain could even latch on to any nonsensical digression about Puff the Magic Demon or anything like that. I leapt into the air, rising above the rush and angling my sword so that when I dropped to its neck I could stab straight downward. In sci-fi flicks, they always showed the blade being driven right through the skull, as if that weren't the hardest, thickest bone in the body, as if remotely human strength could pull that off. I wasn't remotely human—not anymore—but I hadn't tested myself, and, anyway, severing the spine ought to do just as well.

But as I brought my wings in to drop, the whipcord tail knocked into me from the side. My wings belled out to catch myself, but only opened in time to take the brunt of the impact as I crashed onto the concrete of the roof. Pain and panic ripped through me simultaneously and my chest refused to rise, the wind knocked out of me and the muscles or whatever it took to gather new breath were stunned or paralyzed or …

The demon was on me before I could finish that thought. Its weight crushing, its clawed front paws digging into my shoulders and holding me flat to the ground, unable to lift my sword even if I could move.

It dripped stinking saliva onto my face, and it was all I could do to get my mouth to close so that at least I wouldn't have to taste it. For some reason, that was my most primal terror. Death seemed inevitable, but demon drool was right out.

Gunfire broke out from the stairwell and the beast howled in shocked pain, whirling on top of me and using my body as a springboard to pounce at the soldiers. The pain, as much as the weight, was crushing.

"Don't!" I tried to yell, thinking of the soldiers that had come before, but my chest wouldn't rise. No air was getting anywhere. Not to my lungs, vocal cords or brain. I felt things getting hazy. That superhuman healing that'd come with my transformation wasn't kicking in fast enough. Definitely not fast enough to save the soldiers. Maybe not fast enough to save me from whatever was broken inside.

I couldn't move, but I could still think and feel and scream internally, reaching out for the connection I had with Apollo. I hoped and prayed that whatever interference Hermes had encountered searching for Nick didn't extend to me, here on the roof. I tried to be loud and desperate. It wasn't exactly a stretch. I hoped it wasn't my imagination that I felt a frisson of fear come back at me.

A millisecond later I saw it, the air rippling practically right above me. And then Hermes and Apollo tearing through, stumbling over my legs, armed with Cori's largest kitchen knives.

"Tori!" Apollo said, ready to drop to my side.

I couldn't answer him. Couldn't tell him about the danger, but Hermes grabbed his shoulder and spun Apollo around to face the back of the plague demon and the rapid fire from the soldiers.

A bullet pinged off a stone near my hip, but I couldn't so much as flinch, still couldn't speak. I could only watch in horror as Apollo jerked to the side suddenly, blood blooming from his shoulder where the bullet had grazed him.

Knives against guns and a rabid beast. What had I brought them into? If my mind hadn't been numbed by pain, I'd have thought more clearly, kept them out of danger.

I focused on healing, as if I could speed it through sheer force of will. I strained with every ounce of my being to force words through my lips.

"Take ... sword," I managed. It wasn't more than a whisper, but Hermes heard me.

He glanced quickly from Apollo to me. "Hell with that, we're getting you out of here," he said.

The portal had closed to a pinprick above me. It was so tempting. They could reopen it ... we could be gone. But if people could get through, so could bullets. And there were still the children, Nick, Hera.

"No," I croaked. "Children."

He looked at me like I'd gone mental, but before he could say a word, the beast suddenly roared and leapt back, its spiked tail lashing and hitting Hermes upside the head, much as I'd wanted to do for ages now. I felt terrible for that thought as he landed hard beside me, bouncing on the concrete. He instantly rolled toward me, turning not entirely focused eyes toward the sword. He reached for it twice before wrapping a hand around the hilt and rising unsteadily to his feet. He couldn't even see straight after that blow to the head, but before I could protest, he was running toward the beast, sword upraised.

Apollo was there already, hanging on to the tail just above the spikes, climbing toward more sensitive spots, and keeping his head low to avoid flying bullets. As I watched helplessly, the beast roared and shook its head violently, and a soldier went flying like spittle from its mouth. His body as limp as a rag doll. He slid toward the edge of the roof and then ... over and gone.

I tested my arms, but they wouldn't move yet. I thought I could feel my fingers twitch, but wasn't sure it wasn't phantom sensation. I was breathing easier, though. Which meant I'd probably heal. Given time.

Time I didn't have.

Hermes leapt into the air and stabbed at the beast as high as he could on its flank, taking its attention away from a second soldier it had crushed beneath its front feet before it could take the bite it was contemplating. There was only one soldier still flailing that I could see, and that one was rolled on his side, reloading.

The demon howled and lashed out with the leg attached to his bleeding flank, sending Hermes flying ... but then the leg stuck, freezing in that position like the mother of all charley horses had taken hold. The beast panicked, letting out horrified squeal-grunts as it spun on its good legs, trying to see why the one wasn't working. But I knew what had happened. My blood, still on the sword, had begun its paralysis. The demon was much larger than the zombies I'd fought below—too big for my blood to petrify the whole monster with a single slice, but it was something.

The soldier's reload clicked into place and there was another burst of fire, center of mass on the demon. It squealed again and went for the last soldier standing, lifting him in over-sized claws and slamming him down again so that bones cracked sickeningly against the concrete and he went eerily limp.

I strained again to twitch my muscles and finally got some reaction out of them, enough to rock myself back and forth until I could roll onto my stomach. It hurt like hell, but I'd experienced the real thing and didn't have time for the nostalgia.

I forced myself to move again. Painfully, like a free climber at the end of a monumental ascent, muscles shaking and weak, threatening to give out, I belly crawled toward Hermes, where he'd fallen with the sword. Blood was flowing from a head wound where he'd hit and he wasn't moving. He was one of the Olympians. He'd heal. I had to believe that. But I didn't know if he'd heal in time. Or whether I would, but one of us had to finish off the demon.

I fell on the sword and whirled with it in time to see Apollo, now riding the demon's head, try the trick I'd discounted earlier on—jamming his giant butcher knife straight through the beast's skull. To my shock, it sank in, buried to the handle, but it only seemed to piss the monster off. The creature swept its tail toward its head, aiming straight for Apollo. I managed to push off the ground and go running for the beast. My legs felt as sturdy as paper and seemed to accordion on me as I ran, but as Apollo rolled off the beast's back and down its side, I leapt for it. My wings extended just enough to raise me to above the lower spine. I dropped onto the beast's back and thrust the sword into its nerve bundle at the base. Its back legs gave out as the stoning process began, paralyzing it from there on down. But it didn't stop the head, which the beast swung around, looking for the problem and ready to end it with razor sharp teeth. I twisted the sword as I yanked it out of the beast's back, going for maximum damage, and braced myself, trying to keep from being thrown off and seeking leverage for my next strike. My strength wasn't going to last much longer.

That massive maw came for me, dripping bloody foam. I quickly wiped the sword as clean as I could of the beast's blood and cut myself with it to refresh my own blood on the blade, then I timed my last lift of the sword and ...

Now!

I thrust upward as the terrible teeth closed around me, driving the blade straight up through the roof of the monster's mouth and into its brain. It stiffened immediately in shock ... and then didn't unfreeze. Beneath and around me, I could feel the body growing cold as stone, the breath going from fetid inferno to echoing stillness.

Yet I was trapped, teeth holding me in like a cage, and me too weak to pry open the stone jaws. Even if I had that kind of strength. I collapsed onto the nearest teeth, unable to do a thing when the sharp serrated edges bit into my back and sides. My eyes started to close when I realized that someone was calling my name.

"Here," I said feebly. "Go on without me. Save the children."

Something hammered away at the stone around me, pinging painfully. The sound like I was in a bell and my head was the ringer.

"Stop," I begged.

But it didn't stop, and when the stone teeth shattered around me, I fell off my perch, straight into Apollo's arms.

"We have to stop meeting like this," he said, gazing down at me like I was the most beautiful thing he'd ever seen, which was just ridiculous.

"Why?" I asked.

"Good question." He didn't put me down, though, but held me close to him. I looked to see that he'd shattered the beast's lower jaw to get to me, but that, otherwise, it looked like a life-like stone gargoyle, caught in mid-action. It was horrendous and amazing in its detail. It looked like it could breathe again at any instant. Which maybe it could.

"We have to get out of here," I told him. "We found Nick holed up with some kids. I sent them away to hide when this thing appeared, but we've got to get them out of here. It's not safe."

"We're taking in kids now?" he asked.

"Temporarily and yes."

I went to Hermes first and his eyes fluttered open at the sight of me. "Is it over?" he asked.

I looked back at the petrified plague demon. "For now."

Hermes tried to sit, but got dizzy instantly and lay back down. Apollo and I had to help him to his feet. "You okay?" I asked.

"How many fingers?" Hermes asked, holding his entire hand up.

"I think that's supposed to be our line."

"Well, you missed your cue," he scolded. "Mel would be so disappointed." The words came out slurred, but he was talking and he was walking. At the moment, it was all we could ask.

We led him around the downed officer, careful not to slip in blood or ... anything else.

We were just about to hit the door inside when Hermes said, "I can't sense him." I froze, my hand out to the door. "Who?"

"Your ... Nick. You said you found him, but it's like before when I tried to search him out. Something's blocking me. Interference or something."

The demon? Even in petrified form? "What about Hera?" I asked.

"Her too. I checked."

I wanted to think that Hermes was just off his game because of the blow to his head, but since it had happened before ...

I nearly ripped the door off its hinges, all the power and

strength that had been crushed out of me by the demon suddenly flooding back in fear. There was no way to walk three abreast in the stairs. Apollo and I clattered down, going for speed rather than stealth, leaving Hermes to grip the railing and follow behind as best he could. I hit that third-floor landing with a bone jarring impact that sent me falling toward the door, but I opened it before I could crash. Instead, I burst through, running for the room where I'd sent Nick, Hera and the kids.

18

"I half want to kill you and I'm on your side."
—Detective Helen Lau to Tori Karacis

Nick!" I yelled before I even got to the door. "Hera, it's Tori. If you're in there, open up! Nick!"

"It's okay. It's safe," Apollo said from right behind me, probably afraid the panicked tone of my voice might convey otherwise.

The door opened as I reached it, and, expecting Nick, I hurled myself forward … into Hera's arms. She stumbled back, surprised, and I disengaged instantly to look around. The kids and Nick—clutched tightly in little Lacy's arms—were all safe. No cause for alarm.

"Oh thank gods," I said.

"You're welcome," Hera answered wryly. "What happened out there?"

"Rabid plague demon or maybe the demon of rabies or bizarre animal diseases or … whatever. I'm not up on my demonology. He's stone now. Let's get out of here before it wears off."

"Does it?" Hera asked.

"Damned if I know. This is all new to me. Hermes, can you get us home?" I turned toward the door I'd burst through to see him leaning hard against it.

"Got it," he said, breathing hard from the run down the stairs. "I can sense home just fine. That's so strange."

Before our eyes, he began to open his window, starting with the usual wavery air. The kids gasped, and I heard a "cool!" escape from under someone's breath. Apollo stepped forward to add his power to the portal, and it grew and solidified until we could see Cori's living room and even the whites of her eyes and Michelle's as they watched us, relief dawning over them.

"What is that?" a boy asked, torn between awe and fear.

"It's what's going to get us out of here," I told him. "We just step through and we're somewhere else."

"Like Oz?" asked Lacy hopefully.

"No, but somewhere almost as good."

I stepped through first so that they could see me come out the other end, safe and sound. "Come on," I said, beckoning them through.

Cori leaned in to whisper in my ear. "We've got kids now?"

"We couldn't just leave them in the deserted hospital to fend for themselves."

"Deserted?" she gasped.

"We'll fill you in."

The first kid was stepping through now—the boy with the wired jaw, no doubt, as the oldest, determined to show the others the way. He immediately crouched down to welcome the others with open arms. Next was a wiry boy who could have been anywhere from seven to a small-for-his-age eleven. It was hard to tell with those sorrowful eyes that looked like they housed an old soul. Then a girl, probably pre- to early teen, who played with the tie string of the second hospital gown she wore like a coat over the first. She met Cori's eyes quickly, then Michelle's, taking them in, and immediately went to sit on the one recliner Cori had, tucking her feet up underneath her and curling in on herself. Nick came through next with Lacy held in one arm and his other hand clutching that of a little boy, dark like Lacy, but with his hair trimmed close to better showcase his widow's peak and deep, handsome eyes. He was in jammies of his own that someone must have brought him from home— bright blue with lighter blue splotches of Sully and green globs of Mike Wazowski from *Monsters, Inc.* The Olympians brought up the rear and Hermes closed the portal behind us. We stood in Cori's living room, blinking awkwardly at each other, except for the wiry boy, who was staring in awe at all of the pictures and posters. The sadness in his eyes seeped away in the light of excitement and he turned on Cori, sensing it was her place, I guess, from our body language or some other tell. Pretty impressive.

"Are you someone famous?" he asked. "Like an actress? You have to be to have a place this size."

Ah, kids.

Cori's face went from stunned at the latest invasion of her home to charmed. "I *am* someone famous," she said, pleased. "But I'm usually more behind the scenes."

"No," he said, studying her seriously. "That's not it. I've seen you before. I know I have."

She gave Apollo a raised eyebrow, amused and, I think, delighted. "Well, I did get a group together for a special show that went around to various schools to get kids excited about the arts. We called it *Greasy, Grimy Gopher Guts*, after the song. Maybe you saw it."

The boy's eyes lit up like a candle. "You were the good fairy!" he exclaimed. "When you did 'Little Bunny Foo Foo.' And you did other stuff too ..."

"That was me," she admitted.

"I was one of the field mice," he said proudly. "You picked me out of the audience."

I was no expert, but I suspected her plan to encourage kids in the arts had met with at least one success.

Cori held out her hand and introduced herself. The boy looked impressed with that and took her hand with his. "Blake Reinhart," he answered, even going so far as to bow over her hand.

"Pleased to meet you, Blake," she said. "Do you like hot chocolate?"

As far as I was concerned, it was a silly question. What child didn't like hot chocolate?

Oh, except maybe for the lactose intolerant and ... Okay, not so silly after all then.

He nodded deeply. "I think we all do," he answered, impressing me.

"Well then, you go sit with the others and I'll have some right out to you."

We were going to go through her whole allotment of mugs if we stayed here much longer.

The adults all collected in the kitchen. It was big by Manhattan standards ... tiny by the standard of more than two adults trying to fit into it at one time. So we were all up close and personal when the phone Cori had given Hera rang in her pocket.

We all looked at each other.

"Answer it," Hermes said, like no one would have thought of that.

Hera gave him a dirty look and did what she was planning to do anyway. She hit the button to accept the call and held the phone to her ear. "Hello."

"Pick Your Poison pub. One hour. Come alone," said the voice on the other line. We were all close enough to hear.

"But wait, I don't know where—"

"Google it," the voice responded and then hung up. Hera looked at us all.

"You heard her."

"Hell with that," I said, "I'm coming with you. They don't *really* expect you to come alone."

Nick and Apollo both started to protest at once, but I was ready for them. "Besides, girl power and all that. If I get caught, I can talk myself out of it."

They eyed me dubiously.

"What?" I asked. "You *know* I can talk."

"I've seen your mouth get you *into* plenty of trouble," Nick answered. "But never out of it."

Point taken. "Well, there's a first time for everything."

Hera was busy on her borrowed phone. "One hour. It's going to take us that long to get there."

She turned the phone toward us, the screen displayed an address and a map of the city, pinpointing the pub with a red bubble. Pick Your Poison was way down in Greenwich Village. We were way up on the Upper West Side. If everyone was listening to the reporters, which *never* happened, the streets would be deserted. People would be inside after stocking up on necessities. What doors still stood after looters got through with them would be barricaded against invasion and contagion. Which would leave only demons and plague victims between us and the pub.

Even if we knew who and what to fix on, we couldn't just open a portal. It would be a big red flag that Hera had help and that she wasn't approaching Hecate on her own. I couldn't fly her in for the same reason. At least, not all the way. There was no telling how far along the route they might have lookouts.

"You can't just take off," Apollo protested. "You need a plan."

"Fine, we women go out and save the day while you stay

home and take care of the kids." I blamed low blood sugar for that actually coming out of my mouth. It was my only excuse.

Apollo looked like he would like to throttle me, but I was used to that by now.

"Seriously," I said, trying to actually put on my serious face. "We'll call if we need you. You and Hermes and whoever can port in at a moment's notice."

"Unless they've got the place warded, which they will if they have any sense. Or unless there's something else interfering with our finding you."

"Well sure, unless that. Maybe you can work on that while we're gone." Which reminded me of something else. I grabbed the phone I'd found in the administrative offices of the hospital and handed it over to Hermes. "Oh, and this too. It was laying on a desk at the hospital, abandoned. I thought maybe you could hack into the email or ... something. See if there are any clues to the origin of the viruses or any potential cures."

Hermes took it, looking grim. "I don't like this," Lau said.

"Nobody has to like it," I answered. "It just has to be done."

"But it's a trap," she protested. "With no public transportation, she knows there's no way Hera can get down there in an hour. Not without help or some super-secret ability she has yet to reveal."

We all looked at Hera, who was shaking her head.

"I'd offer my car," Cori said, "but word is that midtown is a snarl. Accidents, cars abandoned. Nothing moving."

"That's it then," I said. "Wings it is. Our official story is that you couldn't shake me. I wanted in."

"But—"

"No buts," I said, sure about this and getting surer by the moment. It's amazing the clarity that comes from lack of other options. "They might not trust me, but I don't think they'll kill me. At least ... not right away."

"Very comforting," Lau said. "I half want to kill you and I'm on your side."

"Right, shall we go?" I asked Hera.

"Armed?" she asked.

"Better not. First thing they'd do is take our weapons. Might as well leave them at home in a show of good faith."

"Plan just keeps getting better and better," she mumbled.

"Wait," Nick and Apollo both said, as I went to open the window in preparation for flying out of it with Hera in tow.

This was going to get awkward. I'd been hoping to avoid it.

I turned slowly, not ready to face the music, but, hey, where better than in the lair of the muse of such.

The men were looking from one another to me, waiting. I debated grabbing Hera and going, but the truths would come out whether I was there or not. I doubted it would devolve into fisticuffs, but I couldn't risk it. Nick was in no condition.

"Can we talk first?" Nick asked, "Just for a second. There's something I have to say."

I glanced from Nick to Apollo. Torn. My heart aching. Back in Delphi, I'd have given anything to hear what Nick had to say. For "I'm sorry" not to be the last words I heard from him ... and in a folded up note written in someone else's hand on top of it. Now ... well, "it's complicated" seemed the understatement of the year.

"Later," I said gently. "When all this is over. I have things to say to you too."

I tried to avoid looking at Apollo, but my gaze just slid that way. Nick noticed. How could he not, when he was staring at me so intently, trying to read my reaction, all those little micro-expressions cops were trained to read in an interrogation.

"I see," he said.

I was very afraid that he did. I didn't know how to feel about that. We were over. He'd said so, and I was with Apollo now, but somehow ...

I was too confused to say anything but "later." I looked to Hera and added, "Let's go."

My gaze, I was sure, said something like *save me*.

Hera's lips thinned and hardened in disapproval. With all Zeus had put her through, I didn't wonder. This might look like cheating or leading both men on or gods knew what else, but that wasn't it. Maybe I could explain to her on the way. Maybe talking it through would even help me clarify things for myself.

But she had the good sense to focus on the problem at hand rather than on the undercurrents in the room.

"WHAT DO you think we'll face at the pub?" Hera asked as soon as we were up, up and away. The two men closest to my heart were back at the apartment and here I was, holding the goddess of marital love, fidelity, and making people pay. It seemed a cruel joke.

"I guess we'll find out soon enough. Just be ready for anything."

"Wow, I hadn't thought of that. Thanks."

I'd swapped sarcasm with the queen of the gods—one pantheon's anyway—battled Titans, Olympians and other things that went bump in the night. I was becoming one of them. Hells, my life was just about complete.

I didn't know the city, so Hera had to guide us with the GPS on her phone. The streets below were crowded with vehicles, as Cori had suggested they would be. But everything was abandoned. Signs of life were rare but not entirely absent.

More than once, I saw a bicycle tearing down the street with someone on it pedaling for dear life, one using a full-sized umbrella, point out, as a sort of lance to clear away anything that shambled too close. I wondered if these were thrill seekers or people dedicated enough to important jobs that they'd risk life and limb to make it in to work. I even saw two rollerbladers traveling together as if there were safety in that number. I watched them as far as I could, holding my breath when a massive dog leapt out of hiding, but we couldn't stop. I had only an hour to get Hera to her meeting, and I wanted time to scope the place out. It wouldn't help us to walk into an ambush.

As it turned out, though, the pub was located in a part of the Village far from optimum for surveillance. The streets were narrow. Some only seemed to go for a block before dead-ending—more alleyway than road. Some of the claustrophobic streets were even cobbled. Buildings in the area were mostly brick and only two to four stories high. I had to land us somewhere, and chose a building that rose slightly above the others.

We took the fire escape down to the ground floor, ignoring the apartments we passed until I heard an exclamation and a word I thought was *angel* in Spanish as someone caught sight of my wings. My batlike wings might have said *devil* more than *angel*, but maybe that was because I knew better about myself. If it gave someone hope to think of me as angelic, well, who was I to quibble?

Still, if I'd thought it through, I would have brought something to cover my wings when I wasn't using them. As it was, I was going to be far too conspicuous. The streets might be mostly empty, but I doubted the woman in the window was the only one looking out. And cameras ... I groaned as I thought about cameras. Traffic cameras, police surveillance, ATMs. Hopefully, Hera and I had flown high enough to avoid most of them, but *all* ... that was probably pushing it.

We hadn't been able to see the Pick Your Poison Pub from the rooftop of the building we'd landed on, and we couldn't see it from the street. Hera's GPS directed us around a corner, onto one of those streets that did nothing but connect two others that were meeting at an angle, forming a triangle in the middle. The pub was at the apex of the triangle. I didn't know my magical theory. Hells, all I knew of magic was that some had it and some didn't and that mine had rules that were changing by the day. But I suspected that being at a confluence might be important somehow.

I pulled Hera into a garbage alcove for one of the buildings nearby as we studied the pub. She nearly gagged at the smell wafting in from somewhere nearby. It was ... fertile ... as if entire civilizations of microorganisms had risen and fallen in the area, leaving their dead to rot.

The pub was shaped something like a church, with a rounded peak at the top like a bishop's hat, but inset with stained and painted glass panels representing various bottles, all looking old and some more apothecarian (if that was even a word) than spiritual (in the alcoholic sense of the word). Rather than brick like so many of the buildings around, it was made of irregularly shaped blocks of a lighter stone mortared together. The few windows were narrow and had wrought iron bars over them which matched the iron bands vertically marching up the door. It looked vaguely medieval, making me expect trestle tables and benches inside, ale served in tankards and drunken renditions of ... whatever men sang drunkenly while grabbing for tavern wenches back in the olden days.

"After you," I said to Hera.

We'd already decided not to play it coy. I wasn't going to skulk around and peek in on the meeting and risk getting caught, totally blowing any potential trust before it could be built. We were going in together. Two for the price of one. After all, Hecate *had* invited me. I couldn't see the wards on the pub like I'd seen the barrier to Tartarus in Hades's realm just before it blew, unleashing the Titans. But I could certainly feel them, even from the stoop outside. They tingled on my skin, vaguely threatening. And that was new. If I'd encountered wards before, I'd certainly never known about them. Maybe it wasn't the wards themselves pricking me like I was bathing in Pop Rocks.

Maybe it was my ever-strengthening precog letting me know they were there.

Either way, I was very aware and more than a little nervous as Hera reached for the door, even though we were invited and I didn't see what they had to gain by doing her damage before hearing her out.

Nothing happened. Or rather, the door handle turned as she twisted it and the door opened and no lightning or hellfire or demon shot out of anywhere to prevent our entrance. Hera stepped over the threshold, all of her parts still in place. She held the door open, inviting me to take it from her and do the same.

I'd come this far. I took the fatal step across the threshold and lived to tell about it. Inside there was none of my imagined drunken revelry. There was hardly anyone at all.

Only a few tables were occupied, and those entirely by women, all of whom watched us as we entered. Another seemed to come out of nowhere to fly toward Hera, though not literally as I would have done.

She was stunning—straight, gleaming golden hair, an ice-blue dress with a modern, above-the-knee cut but with belled sleeves that hearkened back to another time. And silver gladiatorial sandals that complemented her silver filigree necklace set with the most amazing moonstones.

"Sigyn?" Hera asked, stopping dead so that I nearly crashed into her. She sounded stunned, nearly breathless.

Sigyn? As in Hermes/Loki's wife ... well, one of them anyway. Could it be? Just how big was this cabal?

"Hera!" Sigyn gushed, grabbing her right up in the hug of old friends too long apart. "Hecate said you'd come, but I couldn't believe ..."

As they were embracing, I noticed that the pub's patrons were no longer seated, but had risen and begun to close around us. One even moved toward the door and lowered a bar across it, cutting us off from the outside world. I eyed them nervously, but didn't make a move. I was here to join their band of merry (wo)men. Freezing or turning them to stone would probably start me off on the wrong foot.

Hera finally put Sigyn away from her, but Sigyn wouldn't quite let go. "Let me look at you," Hera said. "You haven't changed in eons."

"Neither have you." Sigyn's gaze swept her, eyes lighting with amusement when she noticed the suit. "Well, maybe you've gotten a little stodgier." She turned toward her minions surrounding us. "Search them."

Those talons she was holding on to Hera with—long, sharp and silver to match her accessories—only let go when two of the women moved up behind Hera and began the pat-down.

Hera looked like she could chew nails. "I may have gotten stodgier, but you've gotten a helluva lot more paranoid. Is this how you're treating friends these days? Maybe you noticed, but I came under my own steam."

"You brought a plus one. You were told to come alone."

Hera looked at me. "You try getting rid of her. I promise you, it's harder than you think. Besides, Hecate invited her."

I was being searched. Thoroughly, but not any more intrusively than any standard pat-down. I was glad I'd suggested leaving weapons behind. In any case, I still had my gorgon glare and my biting wit. Of course, having weathered Hermes for longer than any sane person should, Sigyn was probably immune to all that.

The problem was that when the pat-down was done, two of the women still held me. One on each arm. Under normal circumstances and if these had been normal women, I'd have broken the hold, no problem. Especially with my wings to help. But these women were like crazy bodybuilder types—not a one of them under five ten or eleven. Their arms were like steel girders. Their hair was all slicked down or braided back or barely there. Nothing to grab hold of in a fight. Sigyn's shield maidens? Was I off on my mythology? Norse wasn't quite my thing.

"So is this how it's going to be?" Hera asked.

Sigyn stepped up to her, licked her finger and traced something on her forehead. A rune? A saliva rune? Gross.

Hera glared at her the whole time.

My precog was kicking and screaming and demanding that I not let Sigyn anywhere near me. I wished it could be a little more helpful. A little guidance on exactly what would happen if I allowed it would have been great. For instance, was I worried about cooties or full-scale bending toward Sigyn's will, which was a whole lot more terrifying.

I flinched back when she got to me. I couldn't help it. My wings flashed out, striking the women on either side of me, who had to take steps back, but they didn't let go. My arms ached from the way they were holding me, stretching me between them like a wishbone. My feet started to rise up off the ground.

I could use that. The thought flashed as quickly as action, which I took, using my arms like pivot points, like I was the front line in a foosball game, my legs kicking outward, catching Sigyn in the chest. She staggered backward, and while I was off my feet with no leverage, the two who held me took me down to the ground. I slammed hard onto my wings and immediately started to thrash, determined that they wouldn't hold me or that if they did, I wouldn't be still enough for any runes to be laid on me.

But a third woman dropped beside my head and grabbed it in a viselike grip, holding me still as Sigyn recovered. She glared down at me and then dropped to my chest, knees to either side of my neck, making it hard for me to breathe. The urge to fight revved up stronger than ever. Yet she had me completely immobilized and gasping for air.

Sigyn licked her finger and drew the rune on my forehead just as she'd done with Hera, and I couldn't do anything to stop her. When she was finished, she stood and got quickly out of the way of any thrashing feet.

The woman holding my head stood as well, and slowly those holding my arms released me too.

Was I harmless now? Powerless?

Hecate already knew about my gorgon glare. I had nothing to lose by trying it out. I started with the first of the women to meet my eye, the one who'd held my head.

"*Freeze,*" I told her fiercely.

She did, going so still she could have been a statue. I turned on Sigyn, who looked on me with amusement rather than anger. I hated that. "*Freeze!*" I said more forcefully.

She laughed.

Laughed.

"Don't worry, I didn't make you toothless. How would that serve our cause? But you can't act upon me. Or Hecate. Or ... anyone else to whom you'll answer."

"*Answer?* I don't answer to anyone. Look, I came here—"

"For reasons all your own. Don't try to convince me otherwise. We're none of us altruists. We've seen enough to know there's no such thing as selflessness in this world. Well, maybe once in a generation we get a Mother Teresa, but even she had her detractors. And now I don't have to worry about turning my back."

She looked at me, still sitting on the floor glaring up at her while I caught my breath. "You can get up now."

I snarled at further evidence that I was subject to anyone's will. I hadn't expected things to go easily, but neither had I expected to get my forehead spit shined with a rune to prevent rebellion.

"Great," I said, rising and brushing myself off, waiting for my dignity to return. And waiting ...

"So what now?"

"Now we talk about why you really came here and how we can help each other."

We settled at one of the long tables, which were just as I'd expected them to be. She didn't offer us refreshment. We weren't breaking bread, which might have conferred on us some kind of guest status and accompanying obligations. We weren't guests. For now, we were prisoners.

"I can't speak for her," Hera said, nodding my way, "but I'm here because this can't continue. This plague hit even the women and children I vowed to protect. I thought they were safe; I thought I could keep them that way. I was wrong. If you have a way to stop all this, I want to be part of it. Whatever it takes."

Sigyn eyed her before turning to me. "And you?"

"My motives are a lot less noble. Someone I lo—care for is seriously hurt. I can't heal him. At least not in any way he'd thank me for." It came easily because it was true. Ambrosia was always an option, but it was addictive as hell and it changed a person. Without any old blood running through his veins, Nick might not even survive the transformation it wreaked upon a person. And if he did … he'd never forgive me getting him hooked on it. Never. I could live with that if I had to, but the fact that he'd hate himself, or at least what he'd become … an addict … *that* I couldn't do. But I could sacrifice myself. I could join these women if that's what it would take. I could even convince myself enough to convince them. But I couldn't leave the world in their hands. Not ultimately. Absolute power corrupts absolutely, and I didn't think any of the conspirators were blameless to begin with.

"That's it? You're doing this *for a guy*?" The sneer in Sigyn's voice was nearly absurd. Like I'd just dropped to the level of gum on her shoe. Good. Maybe she'd underestimate me at some point. It could be useful.

"Not just any guy," I protested, knowing it wasn't going to help my case.

"Of course not," she said.

I remembered the ... myth? story? ... about Loki/Hermes being tied up in a cave somewhere for something horrible and Sigyn thanklessly catching the poison from a venomous snake in a bowl before it could drip onto his head, every once in a while having to desert him to empty the bowl. It had to have been a horrid existence for both of them, and, unlike Loki, she'd never done anything to earn it.

"You heard?" Sigyn asked suddenly, looking past me, past Hera, back toward what I assumed was the kitchen area, right now unlit and lost in shadows.

Hecate formed out of those shadows, or maybe just stepped forth from them. "I did."

"What do you think?"

"That she'll be very useful to us ... as a hostage."

19

Some say the world will end in fire,
   Some say in ice.
   From what I've tasted of desire
   I hold with those who favor fire.
   —"Fire and Ice" by Robert Frost

I tried to turn, and the sigil on my head flared, making me feel like my forehead was on fire. I ignored the pain, fighting to move through it, but it was too much, like the pain signals were disrupting everything else and no messages were getting to my arms and legs. I gave it up—momentarily anyway—to think of a better way. As soon as I did, the pain stopped and my body wanted to slip into bonelessness at the relief. Drying sweat soon cooled me down, maybe even too much. I sat there with the chills, glaring at Hecate.

"How could you think for a second that I'd make a better hostage than an ally? I want to end this more than anyone. I may not like you," I said, knowing she could sense my complete sincerity on that score, "but I've worked with mortal enemies in the past to get things done. You know that. Zeus, Poseidon, Hades—"

"And what do they have to show for it?" she asked.

"Not being under Rhea's thumb," I bit back.

"So you woke the Titan and you put her back to sleep. And no one's thrown you a ticker-tape parade? I can hardly believe it. Sigyn, call the mayor!"

If I thought my gorgon glare would get through, Hecate would be as stiff as a bathroom brush.

"I stand by what I've said. You've seen me fight. You need me."

The Grey Sisters had said as much. Hadn't they? I thought back. They'd said I needed to get Perseus's sword and defeat Namtar before they'd help me with my wings. They never actually said I *would* defeat him. Or that I was the only one who could.

Hecate was completely unmoved. "Fighters I have. I'm not worried about fighting our demons. What I need is a cure for any lingering effects."

She reached into her wicked leather jacket and I tensed, thinking she was going for a weapon, even though my precog didn't send out any warning signals. What she came up with was a cell phone, which she handed to me. I looked at her blankly.

She wiggled it in my face, indicating that I should take it. "Call him," she ordered.

I took the phone, still unenlightened. "Call who?"

"Apollo. If anyone knows the whereabouts of his grand-daughter ... if anyone can get her here, it's him."

"Panacea?"

A million thoughts raced through my mind, from *but he doesn't know* to *does she seriously think if he did, he wouldn't have called her in by now.* But Hecate looked deadly serious. I couldn't say any of it. I didn't know what Hecate would do if she thought she had no more use for me. Plus, she wasn't wrong about our needing Panacea. Maybe Yiayia had found some leads. Or maybe there was something on that smartphone we'd taken from the hospital … At worst, at least Apollo would know the situation.

I dialed his number and didn't have to wait long for him to pick up. "Hecate, what the hell?" he asked. I could imagine steam coming out his ears. "What do you mean by running off, taking the sword, betraying us all—"

"It's Tori."

His tirade cut off midsentence. "Tori? What's going on there?"

"I'm—"

Hecate grabbed the phone out of my hand and pushed her wild hair back so she could hear. "Hello, Sunshine."

"Hecate, what the hell?"

"That's right, darling. Hell on earth. Not exactly the way I would have done it, but … there it is. Yes, I have the sword and, yes, I heard that. You were talking practically loud enough to wake the dead. People always seem to do that with cell phones, don't you find? Anyway, the sword isn't all I have, as you may have surmised."

She let the cursing and threatening go on for about half a minute and then cut him off. "Well, she said she wanted to help. I assume you do too. I've seen the way you look at each other, and I'm willing to make a trade. Panacea for the gorgon girl. All for the greater good. The countries of the world all get their cures … for a price … the people get their health back. Me and mine get all the power and money we could want. Everybody wins."

"Don't—" *do it*, I tried to yell, but at the first word out of my mouth, Sigyn snapped her fingers and my jaw locked. I couldn't plead with him not to listen. I'd be damned if I'd be used as a pawn, but I couldn't tell him. And we were too far apart for our strange empathy to work.

I lost what Apollo said next in my fight to be heard, but then Hecate jumped in again. "Time? Of course, darling. We're looking for Panacea as well, you understand, and if we find her first, your gorgon girl will be of no use to us. So you take all the time you think you can afford. We'll be waiting."

Hecate hung up the phone and gave me an evil smile. "Take her to the freezer," she ordered the brawny babes. They rose and grabbed for me when Hera finally spoke up.

"Are you sure you want to do that? I saw her defeat a demon almost single-handedly. Her blood ..."

I glared and she shut up, but not before it was obvious to all that there was more to that sentence. I wondered what Hera was up to. Had she slipped up and given me away? She seemed too smart for that. There had to be some bigger game she was playing, but which side was she playing for? Did she want me to believe she just *oops*ed so I wouldn't know her true loyalties, or did she think she was helping me by making me too useful to throw away?

Hecate raised a hand that apparently the others understood to mean halt. "Her blood what?" she asked Hera. Her dark eyes piercing and completely no-nonsense.

"Her blood can turn things to stone. She's not as strong as a full gorgon, but she's not wrong that you want her fighting by your side."

"Why didn't I know this?" she asked me suspiciously.

The sigil insisted that I answer. "Why didn't I know you were a stone-cold bitch?" I asked in return.

Hera looked like she completely despaired of me, but I already knew whatever she was up to wouldn't work and I had to get my licks in while I could.

"Take her away," Hecate ordered. "And then bathe your blades in her blood."

If I hadn't already been chilled, that would have done it. I didn't think she meant for them to kill me, but becoming a human pincushion didn't sound like fun either. And what if they nicked an artery?

As they were dragging me out kicking and flapping, Hecate got a call. I stopped fighting entirely when the light of triumph flared in her eyes, the better to listen in. I wasn't the only one waiting to hear. The women dragging me away had slowed almost to a stop, anticipating what would come. Hecate ended the call and looked at us with a feral smile, one that would frighten little children.

"Make it quick," she said. "We've found him. We're going in."

Him? Him who? Could it be Namtar? Were they going to do half my work for me and defeat the lord of all plague demons? Surely, he wouldn't be alone, not if Lyssa was right about hearing a call to his side, a call to action. And not if the demon I'd fought on the hospital roof was any indication. Were Hecate and her cadre ready for a war?

The dragging resumed, now at double speed. "What about me?" Hera asked behind us.

"You're going to have to prove yourself sooner or later. Now is as good a time as any."

Then my guards and I were through a doorway, through the kitchen faster than I could locate, let alone grab, any knives and into ... oh hell to the no ...

We were headed straight to the kind of thick, reinforced metal, pull-handle door that screamed meat locker. If it was subzero—and weren't they all?—I was in for a massive amount of trouble. Was it ironic that I froze people with my gorgon glare and that I was about to have my ass quite literally frozen off? No, I didn't think so. Not at all. Alanis Morissette might have other thoughts on the matter.

I started to struggle again as if my life depended on it,

which it very well might. They tried to thrust me in. I couldn't reach out with my captive arms, but my wings belled out to make me too big for the doorway. Twin blows to my knees buckled me, and a powerful kick to my back tested the strength of those wings, which screamed as they hyperextended, but I didn't give. Unfortunately, half on the ground as I was with my back bowed, I didn't have the leverage to fight, and I was facing the wrong way to freeze the shield maidens in their tracks.

The warrior women each grabbed a wing and twisted painfully. "Give up or we rip them off," one threatened.

I had a moment of indecision. Could I really get rid of them that easily? But the wings had come in handy more than once, and ...

Piercing pain blanked out all rational thought as something slid sharply into my back, scraping a vertebra. My wings sagged with the pain and a second slicing sensation went through me.

"She did say to wet our blades," one of the women said, her voice dripping malice. Nothing registered but the pain. There were more knife thrusts or sword thrusts or ...

My vision started to swim and my strength failed. I fell on my face, just enough awareness left to turn my head so I wouldn't mash my nose when I crashed onto the concrete. My cheekbone took the brunt of it. Broken maybe. Definitely bruised. Not important in the grand scheme of things. I lay there freezing and bleeding, internally screaming in pain until darkness set in.

I fought it back. As tempting as it was to fade out and let unconsciousness take away the pain ... or at least my awareness of it ... I was afraid that if I passed out in the frigid freezer I might not wake up again. My body would go into hibernation mode to conserve energy, and if no one came for me soon enough, I might never wake up. I'd die in my sleep.

I was so tired, though. So drained. My teeth didn't even have it in them to chatter. It was all I could do to open my eyes every time they wanted to close, to blink away the unformed dark-ness, especially when all that did was reveal blurry shades of gray.

At least the cold would slow my bleeding, maybe enough so that my crazy healing could kick in. But I couldn't wait for that. I didn't know how the battle would go, whether anyone would be coming back or what they'd do when they did—wet more blades or make the poor trade to Apollo for his long-lost grand-daughter.

Even if he could find her, would he turn her over?

He wouldn't. *Couldn't.* The fate of the world depended on it. If he gave Panacea up to the cabal, they'd use her up, sell her miracle cure at a cost. Anyone or any country unable to afford the treatment would be out of luck. Whole countries might die out. The void created—the battle over boundaries and resources—would cause no end of chaos.

To avert that horrible future, all Apollo had to do was sacri-fice me. I knew he *could* do it, but would he? Whatever his faults —and I was having more and more trouble seeing them—he'd never once left me behind or not come when I called. I wondered if my *"Don't—"* had gotten through and if he'd take that much to heart. Most of me wanted to believe he would. The rest of me wanted to want to believe, but was secretly terri-fied of dying this way.

The cold hadn't been too bad at first. It had barely even registered over my pain. But now it crept in and took root. I could practically feel myself dying by centimeters, as though ice were replacing the water in my veins. I had to get up and get moving. I had to keep the blood flowing. But my body didn't want to react to my call to action. I wondered if one of the shield maidens' blades had severed my spinal column.

If I couldn't move, at least maybe I could blush, get my blood pumping that way. I tried to summon up the view of Apollo in our last quiet moment—naked, sated, smoothly stroking his hands over my stomach and breasts, so warm and wonderful ... Visions of Nick crept in unsummoned—showering, soaping, just as I'd jumped him in that hotel in Delphi, before ...

My two men. The two loves of my life....

Crap. Now? *Really?* Lying prone on an icy-cold slab waiting for death to overtake me and *now* the L-word comes out? And indecisively at that. Loves. Plural. Life didn't work like that. Apparently, death thought it got its own set of rules. If all went well ... if Apollo did what he should ... I'd never have to choose. They could go on for the rest of their lives mourning me as a tragic, heroic figure and I didn't have to break any hearts.

I wallowed in that for a time. There was no telling how long. Cold had meaning. And pain. Time, not so much. But the thought of me as a tragic figure, maybe something from Shakespeare—Ophelia or Juliet or ...

Hell with that. Two critically lovesick women without the experience to realize that "it gets better" was more than a mantra. I was *not* going out that way.

I gathered up my strength, trying to pull my arms in, to get them under me so they could push me up to a seated position, so that the minimum amount of flesh was pressing the cold, cold ground. My hands twitched, but that was about all. My body wouldn't obey. Well, I didn't listen to anyone else. Why should the contrary stop at my own mental doorstep?

I was about to try again when the air in front of me whirled and my stomach threatened to rebel. A cyclone of icy air and then a stillness in its midst and a pinprick of light, which irised out until I could see an eye and a nose, and then an entire face. *Hermes.*

"Hermes," I said brilliantly, thrilled to hear my voice again. I was afraid Sigyn had stolen it for good.

"Tori, oh thank gods."

"You were worried about me?" I asked, wasting what little

breath I could catch in the frigid air on that bit of wonder. Hermes and I had fought on the same side, but usually it was because we had no choice ... or because I'd blackmailed or bribed him.

He smirked. "*Agape*, the world would be so much less intriguing without you in it. As the God of Chaos, I approve this message."

I knew my eyes could still roll when they did that very thing. "Can you get me out of here?" I asked.

He looked around, as much as he could through his little window. "Freezer, huh? She wasn't always such a cold bitch."

"Hecate?" I asked, confused.

"Sigyn. This is her handiwork, right? I feel her touch all over you." He was Hermes enough to waggle his brows at that, like there might be another meaning that would involve nudity and perhaps Jell-O. Or maybe pudding. "Her wards are strong. She always was a rune master. Or mistress, I suppose you'd say." Again, the brow waggle. "But no. I learned ages ago to get around her runes so that I could sneak out and—well, never mind all that. But getting out myself is one thing. Getting in or tinkering remotely ... I'm trying, but I can't make any promises. I just wanted to see if you were okay. Apollo had a bad feeling ..."

"I'm not doing well, but I'm alive. For now. Tell Apollo not to give in. Tell him to find Panacea, but not turn her over. Save the world. I'll take care of myself."

"He's already looking. We found something on that phone you filched from the hospital. Something about a miracle healer in Uganda. Whoever's phone it was didn't believe it, but the hospital admins were grasping at straws, willing to try anything. And your grandmother sent a message, about a Doctors Without Borders group that had encountered the same thing. We're trying to trace the leads."

Hermes hesitated before saying more, and my heart sank.

"One more thing you ought to know. Just before I opened this window, something happened. Some kind of call went out or something. Suddenly Lyssa went insane. I mean really insane. Insane even for her." Okay, I got it. "Her eyes went all-over red and she fought like a Fury."

"And?" I said.

"Lyssa escaped. Your friend Lau wanted to get her dragon and go after her. Nick told her no. Even he can sense it. There's a war coming. We need to stick together and not spread our troops too thin."

"You think Namtar put out an APB, like *Calling All Demons*."

"Something like that."

"It makes sense. Hecate, Sigyn, and their minions are on the warpath. If they've gone after Namtar, he may be calling in reinforcements." My teeth were starting to chatter now, which made it seriously hard to talk. It was a good and bad sign—good that my body had the energy, bad that it needed to expend it so uselessly. I was losing heat faster than I could generate it.

"What are the chances the two sides will wipe each other out?" I asked.

Hermes eyed me, and not, per usual, like a piece of meat. "You're blue," he said. "Are you sure you're okay? You've got to get moving, get your blood pumping until I can find a way around these wards and get you out."

"I'll keep that in mind," I said wryly. No point telling him what he couldn't do anything about, like the fact that I was effectively paralyzed and that my blood was pooling rather than pumping. I couldn't tell him anything he might pass along to Apollo that would distract him from what needed to be done. "Tell Apollo ... and Nick ... Hell, just save the world, okay. I'll tell them myself when we come out the other end of things."

"Tell them what?" he asked, eyebrows raised, leaning forward in anticipation.

"Tell them to play nice," I hedged.

"Is that all?" Nick asked, suddenly in-frame, pushing Hermes out of the way.

"No," I said, "but you'll have to wait on the rest."

Coward, I called myself. But I'd either have to live with that or I wouldn't.

The portal started to contract suddenly, and I called out, "What's happening?"

"The wards are shutting me down," Hermes said, only his lips visible in the window now. It was disconcerting. "More soon ... I hope."

And with that, the window popped out of existence, and I was left alone in my meat locker of doom.

The shivering got bad then. Crazy bad. My arms, my legs, even my stomach seemed to jitter with the attempt to stay warm. I tried again to move, and this time my hands clenched, but that was as far as I got.

I lay there bemoaning the loss of my ambrosia. I'd have done anything to kick the addiction back when it had its hooks into me, but now that I'd unnaturally been "cured" by whatever was making me into the winged wonder and turning my blood to magic, I was no longer susceptible to its more amazing properties, like the miraculous healing. My body could heal itself now. I only wished it were quicker about it. But maybe coming back from paralysis and near death took a little time.

The trembling became absurd, its own exquisite torture. I wasn't thinking about the guys anymore. Or escape. Or anything but surviving the cold. I had to shut my eyes to protect them from freezing, hold in what warmth I could. Already they felt like mere marbles—dry, glassy, and going on useless. My hands were so cold they burned, and I hugged them tightly into myself, feeling a moment of elation when I *could* do that, realizing that movement was coming back. I curled into a fetal position. Just long enough to get my core temperature up, I told myself. Just to get warm enough to make myself sit.

But with my eyes closed and myself all curled up on the floor, I was in danger of falling asleep, going out like a light that might never be relit.

Cranky about it, I forced myself to uncurl. It felt like the hardest thing in the world. I hissed in pain as my fiery-cold left hand hit the concrete to push myself into sitting, and I had to work every muscle to help myself along. Every single one of them screamed. Along with the popping and realignment of several vertebrae that had gotten nicked by the blades, I was my own one-woman horror show.

What was the scientific principle? Something about an object at rest tending to stay at rest. I wanted to be that object and at the same time I knew it for a death sentence.

And sitting, as monumental as it felt, was only the first step. I knew I had to stand, to move, to keep myself awake and the blood pumping, like Hermes said. But it was going to have to wait. I was still breathing through the pain. With things snapping back into place, the nerves seemed to be reknitting or newly able to get their messages through, and they mostly seemed to consist of profanity and pain signals.

I tried the in-through-the-nose and out-through-the-mouth thing, my breath coming out like I was Puff, the Magic Dragon. The cold seemed to crystallize any moisture in my nose until I could picture little icicle stalactites dripping down from the top of it, cutting off airflow.

Enough! I could live or I could die, but I was not throwing myself a pity party on the way out.

I got my legs under me and tried to rise, but they were having none of it. I was going to have to alligator crawl to a shelf and pull myself up, which meant bare skin touching subzero metal and likely losing that very skin.

I tried one more time to get myself to stand on my own steam. Two deep breaths, trying through force of will to send strength and energy to my lower extremities. Okay, two more breaths. And then ...

I forced myself up in a rush and miraculously I rose, but not steadily. I stumbled into the door, catching myself on my hands and pulling them back with a hiss when they freeze-burned on the frozen door. I blinked several times, trying to wet my eyes enough to see in more than blurs. It would work for a fraction of a second and then my eyes would cloud over again like a frosty windshield.

I couldn't see whether my hands were chapped red or growing dangerously white, but I had a sense. I prayed my super-healing would keep them from frostbite. I didn't want to lose my hands. My wings, maybe, but not my hands. Or my feet. Or ...

I pushed all of that out of my mind and reached half-blindly for the door, running my hands over it for a protrusion of any kind. Surely there was some kind of fail-safe for anyone who might get locked in. My hands were so frozen I couldn't feel what was beneath them, but I would know if they bumped into something like a knob or a handle.

Which they did. I could hardly believe it was anything so simple. A push bar. A freakin' push bar, like a school or a library might have to allow people to get out in a hurry, say in the case of fire. My heart leapt, suddenly upping my blood flow and giving me hope.

I pushed into the bar with everything I had, just in case the freezing temperature made it stick, and ... nothing. It barely even compressed. It certainly didn't spill open the door, releasing me into the pub and escape.

Locked. Well duh. Had I really thought it would be that easy? Had brain freeze set in already?

My legs wanted to give out and slide me back to the floor, but I wouldn't let them. I pushed myself back from the door before my hands became permanently attached and stood, alone and chattering in the center of the freezer, wondering what next.

I pulled my sleeves down over my hands and then chafed my upper arms and shoulders as best I could with them as I shuffle-paced the small space.

I don't know how long I chafed and froze and paced, growing slower with every turn until I was hardly moving at all. A snail could have run circles around me. It seemed like an eternity. It could have been an hour or two or five ... when my internal alarms started going off. Like I didn't know I was in danger.

Then suddenly something slammed into the door with enough force to shake my foundations and I realized danger of another kind had come to my door.

20

It came again, something huge knocking into the freezer hard enough to, I imagined, dent the outer door. But inside, nothing changed.

My hands were frozen into claws without any feeling left, but I bumped them up against the push bar, trying to budge it. Again nothing.

Outside, a battle raged. Maybe the cabal had retreated and Namtar had followed them back to base, ready to eradicate. I was torn about that. The bad guys came out on top, no matter which side won. And I was in no position to stop it. But where was Hera in all of this? And whose team was she playing for?

That question was answered a minute later when the meat locker door opened and she stood there staring in.

"Quick," she said. "The fighting has moved into the main room, but ..." She grabbed my arm and propelled me out of the freezer, chafing my arms quickly to try to warm me. I'm sure it would have hurt if I could still feel. "Tori, they're not winning. Even with the arrival of Hušbišag and her army, there are too many demons. And your blood was only good for the first three or four. They need you."

Wait, Hušbišag, the skeleton queen? Last I knew, she and Hecate were trying to kill each other over Perseus's grave. Had that all been pageantry to allow Hecate to gain our trust and learn our secrets? Or had Hušbišag been recruited later? Gah, so many questions, so little time.

I could hear the crashing and fighting and cursing coming from the main part of the pub, but I couldn't move yet, certainly not fast enough to save myself from any onrushing danger.

"You said *they* need me," I pointed out, working it through for myself more than for her.

Presumably, *she* already knew which side she was on. "Yes, will you come?" she asked.

There was a massive crash and a chunk of wall blew out between the kitchen and pub area. A beast came hurtling through it that I couldn't make any sense of at first. There were fledgling feathers and a beak of sorts, but also a reptilian sort of tail with a sailfin at the back. Not quite archaeopteryx or pterodactyl or winged serpent, but something of all of these. About the size of a goat. It flapped furiously, fighting its trajectory and getting itself straightened out. As soon as it did, it spotted us with eyes that were primeval and filled with malice. It snapped its beak menacingly at the sight.

"Weapon?" I asked Hera.

She held up the handle she'd apparently ripped off the freezer door to liberate me. "Great," I said. I looked the beast straight in those evil eyes and ordered, *"Freeze!"* through still-chattering teeth.

It faltered for a second in the air before plummeting toward the ground, but the paralysis wore off just shy of a crash landing, and it pulled up at the last second into a glide, gaining momentum in the short space. It quickly turned the glide into a strafing run and swooped up toward our heads.

"Get down!" I told Hera, throwing her to the floor to be sure she obeyed.

I ducked with her, and the beast sailed over our heads, but wheeled in the air like a remote controlled copter to come for us again.

Down was apparently the wrong decision. It made us sitting ducks. I realized it the moment I twisted to see the beast incoming, beak out like a lance.

I jumped up into its path, shielding Hera, and reached out my frozen-claw hands. If it pierced me—and there was little chance that it wouldn't—maybe I could bleed all over it and affect something that way.

Already coming in low, the beast couldn't correct quickly enough and crashed into me at thigh level.

I was still frozen enough to numb the pain, but not stop it entirely. I caught the beast's body in both my hands before it could veer off for another run at us. The thing thrashed and struggled so that I could hardly hold it in my frostbitten hands, but I managed to hang on and launch toward one of the food-prep stations. Stainless steel. Sturdy as they come.

The demon craned its neck and bit down on one hand holding it, catching the fleshy part between my thumb and fingers. It ripped away nerves, tendons, muscle. My grip started to slip but I held on long enough to slam the body down on the prep table like I was cracking open a coconut.

The beast's body stiffened suddenly, and I realized my blood was taking effect. Within seconds, it had turned to stone in my hands.

One fight was over, but others were ongoing. Quickly, I pulled open drawers, looking for a knife or, better yet, a bazooka. But all I found was a set of kabob skewers. They would do. I was already bleeding, so I rolled two around in the freely flowing blood, sucking air in between my teeth to keep in the howl of pain and focusing hard to keep my grip on them with my frozen fingers.

Hera was up now, peeking through the busted wall into the main part of the pub. I joined her there, in time to see a monstrous thing, nearly the size of Eu-meh, looking half man, half winged demon. Like something out of Revelations.

There was no doubt about the half man, because he wasn't wearing a stitch of clothing, but was almost hairy enough not to need it ... almost. He had several sets of bony protrusions, something like horns, across his head, poking up out of the mane that, coupled with his somewhat feline mouth, made him look leonine ... though one done up in the colors of night and shadow. The hair covered his body, thinner over the extremities and thickest in the ruff over his shoulders and down his chest. His legs were back-bent like a lion's as well—or like the typical conception of a goat-legged demon. A tail thrashed, but there was nothing leonine about that. It was a scorpion's tail. Segmented, sinister, and with a gleaming poisoned tip that made me quake just looking at it.

As we watched, that tail struck at a woman on the floor before him with her arm raised as if it could protect her. I hadn't even noticed her before in my shocked awe over the creature, and with her back to us. I wouldn't have recognized her now, but for that dress. Sigyn.

Without thought, I hurdled through the hole in the wall, wings flapping as soon as they were through, desperate to save her from a nightmare. All thoughts that maybe they'd destroy each other gone from my head. I couldn't watch it happen.

But I was too late. The stinger bit deeply into her side before I could reach her. She convulsed around it, practically hugging the spike to herself momentarily, before her whole body went slack, and she seemed to melt into the floor.

I hit the beast with a bloody skewer in each hand, aiming for the heart, but those eyes—odd rectangular irises gleaming like twin forges—burned into me, branding me with scorn for my puny little effort. He batted me away like I was nothing, and I went flying, straight into ... Lyssa.

I didn't register that at first, only that I'd hit a woman rather than a demon ... or so I thought. Then her arms clamped around me, and I could feel the madness bleed into me. A red haze overtook my vision, and my heart began to race—too fast, like it might burst out of my chest. But it was the violence that most wanted to explode out of me. I wanted to kill. I didn't much care what. Everything in my path seemed a place to start.

I'd left the skewers behind in the monster's chest. I was unarmed, facing away so that I couldn't hit Lyssa with my glare.

Someone else hit her for me.

Hera called Lyssa's name, and when she looked, caught her with a blow to the jaw, which made her loosen her grip on me just enough that my wings flared and busted me free. Lyssa whirled, snarling at Hera, who was chanting something under her breath. I thought I caught the word *wither*, and then Lyssa seemed to dry out almost before our eyes, shrinking in on herself.

Talons sunk into my shoulders before I could see if she fought it back, and I reached up to claw at them, to try to get them loose. Hera grabbed for them as well, repeating her spell with even more force this time, but the talons didn't let loose. The demon uttered a trilling cry that seemed almost of triumph or mockery.

"The Maniai was one thing, but the plague demons aren't susceptible to my magic," she said.

The thing that had hold of me was already lifting me off the floor, my wings crushed to its chest so that I couldn't fly off on my own. No wings, no footing meant no leverage. Squirming alone wasn't getting me anywhere.

"See if you can find the Sword of Perseus among the fallen," I called down to Hera. "Or anything else that will help."

The winged wickedness trilled again, and I gripped its taloned feet to use as I would trapeze rings in my family's acrobatic act—as something to hold on to while I swung the rest of my body upward to plow my feet into it full force.

Namtar rolled with the blow, taking me with him. I heaved myself up again, using all of my newly thawed core muscles to kick myself up and over. It would have brought me onto the creature's back if my muscles hadn't chosen that moment to fail. I lost my grip, crashing toward the ground, heading for it at a bad angle. I got my wings working just in time to avoid crash landing, and as I soared just shy of the floor, I noted the bodies everywhere, mostly human-esque. The demons were finishing up their opponents ... or snacking on them.

Namtar's gaze fixed on me again, and his tail whipped my way. "Tori!" Hera called.

Out of the corner of my eye I spotted something sailing for me. A sword! I hoped it was *the one* and reached out to catch it, but Namtar's tail got there first, thrashing it out of the air and then swinging his tail back for me. I dove under it, going for the sword, skimming bodies as I flew. Claws closed on my hair, pulling me up short. The sword was within reach. I could brush it with my fingertips, but I couldn't grasp it.

Those claws started reeling me in. I couldn't let it happen. For the first time in my life, I wished for one more gorgon trait —serpents for hair. Poisonous serpents that might take exception to being manhandled.

But I had to work with what I had. With a monumental yell to cover my inevitable scream, I wrenched my head out of his grip, leaving half of my hair and some of my scalp behind. I fell on top of a woman with a half-eaten face and fought down rising bile as I crawled over her to get at the sword.

As soon as my hand closed on it, I rolled so that anything coming for me would get the point. I prayed that Medusa's blood would still be strong on the sword, a thousand times more powerful than mine. When Namtar's tail came for me again, I slashed for all I was worth, slicing into that hard, venomous tip. The sword went right through as though it were butter, and the howl that went up was deafening. It shook the walls of the pub and reverberated right through my rib cage, bruising my heart ... or so it felt.

Suddenly, Namtar whirled, hitting me with his hardening tail, and took off back toward the kitchen and the wall that had been busted down when they chased the cabal back to base. He sent out another cry and all the other plague demons took off after him, screaming threats or promises as they went. I could be wrong, but I thought they promised vengeance. I looked around for Hera and found her on her knees, swaying like she might fall over.

Her eyes were glazed. One hand was clutched to her chest, trying to staunch blood that came from a wound too big to cover. Like something had tried to rip out her heart. Her other hand was held just slightly out, as though to catch herself if she fell. I didn't think it was going to do the job.

I caught her before she could collapse, and lowered her gently to the floor. I whipped off my shirt, not really caring about the nudity, especially with no one around to see, and peeled her hand away from her chest to press the shirt into place and then return the hand.

"Hold this tight," I ordered.

Frantically, I searched for Hecate among the wreckage, but while I saw Sigyn, downed shield maidens or whatever they were and Hušbišag's skeletal warriors, the other ringleaders were missing.

I went back for Hera and airlifted her as carefully as possible. I'd get her back to Cori's. She was one of the old ones. Goddess of home and hearth and all that. She couldn't die. Prometheus had had his liver ripped out again and again in punishment for delivering fire to mankind and *he* hadn't died. That didn't mean he hadn't suffered. I didn't like leaving Sigyn behind. Or Lyssa. Or any of the others who might awake and still be enemies at our backs. But there was only room for one on Gorgon Air, and Hera was it.

21

I hefted her over my shoulder just as the air did that ripply thing in front of me and suddenly Apollo's voice was coming through it, before the window was even big enough to see.

"Tori! Are you okay?"

"Apollo," I called, so relieved I could collapse. Super-healing be damned, I'd been through a lot today and wasn't sure I could make it the whole way back to Cori's place with a plus one. "Can you open a portal?"

"Hermes?" I heard him say over his shoulder. There was a discussion that didn't make it through the window, and then the window grew from a pinprick into a mailbox into the size of a large doggy door and Hermes's face appeared. It wouldn't have been my first choice, but no one had asked me.

"Sigyn ... is she gone?" Hermes asked. "Her wards have fallen. It's the only reason we were able to get through to you."

"She's down," I told him. "If that's a full-blown portal, can we talk about this when I'm on the other side?"

"I'm coming through," he answered.

The protest hadn't even formed on my lips when a leg was

pushing through with an arm to help it on its way like he was climbing in a window. His head and torso were next.

He was looking around as he came—not frantically, but not casually by any means.

They might be exes, but the thought of Sigyn down clearly had him worried.

His gaze seemed to snag on Sigyn almost immediately, as if there was still a connection after all these years. He ignored me and my passenger to head straight for her.

I didn't know what to do. Would the portal work with his attention elsewhere or would it snap closed on us if we tried to step through?

"Hermes?" I started.

He held up a hand to silence me and crouched beside Sigyn, gently turning her over and brushing away the hair that had fallen over her face. The demon's sting had swollen her up to the size of a carcass that had been floating for days in the water, and her skin was gray, her veins starting to blacken as if the blood was clotting inside them. It was the most horrific thing I'd ever seen, next to Nick with burns over a third of his body. Hermes cradled her to him and glanced at me with such a look of seriousness and desolation in his eyes that I wouldn't have recognized him if I'd met him on the street.

"She's coming with us," he said.

It was his portal. I wasn't in any position to disagree, and yet: "She's got some kind of rune on me. She's too powerful and she can't be trusted."

"I'm not leaving her like this," he said. He wasn't asking. He was telling me.

With Sigyn in his arms, he rose and walked to the portal, which had telescoped down to almost nothing. A dime-sized oddity floating in midair. He adjusted Sigyn so that he could reach a hand out to it, and at his touch it expanded. More like a door now.

"Go," he ordered. "I can't hold it like this for long."

I went, carefully tucking myself and Hera through. I stumbled as I came down on the other side, but arms caught me, and slid Hera away from me as a second set reached out to make sure I wouldn't fall on my face.

Apollo held Hera. Lau held me.

Lacy still had Nick in a death grip. But he rose with her at the sight of Hera's limp body and let Apollo have the couch to lay her out on.

I got my balance and stepped quickly out of the way so that Hermes could come through. "Incoming," I told them. Unless they'd heard through the portal, it was all the warning they were going to get because Hermes was already coming through, Sigyn clutched to his chest.

Cori looked from Hera and the blood soaking no doubt irrevocably into her couch to Hermes and Sigyn. "I don't know where you're going to put her."

"Bathroom," I said. "In the tub. I know we have to help her, but we've also got to chain her up. She's too dangerous to let loose."

"Not in her current state," Hermes said. I couldn't argue that.

"There's only one bathroom," Cori said. "It's going to make things ... interesting."

"We'll make do," I told her. "No showers until all this is done, and we'll just draw the curtain across the tub. Anyone with a shy bladder is out of luck."

Apollo was studying Hera as Hermes carried Sigyn off. I watched him, waiting for the verdict.

"I could cauterize the wounds to stop the bleeding," he said, "but that would really just trap any poison in with her and slow the healing. It's going to take some time, and she'll probably be in a coma in the meantime, but she'll come out of it."

That was all I needed to hear. There were no chairs or couches left, so I collapsed down onto the coffee table.

Nick tried to put Lacy down and come to me, but she clung like one of those puppets whose arms and legs Velcroed around you. He finally gave up and said, "Your hands."

I looked down at them. The formerly frozen skin, dead now, was starting to slough off. I'd been frostbitten, most definitely. It was as though my body was self-amputating. Nick should never have drawn it to my attention. Now I'd want to pick at it like a scab, and I knew that the skin underneath would be pink and new and hypersensitive.

"They'll heal too," I said.

"What's happened to you?" he asked. He wasn't just talking about the eerie healing. It was the wings he was looking at now, as if seeing them for the first time.

"I don't know," I answered. "I think I'm becoming ... other." I looked away. I didn't know if I was finished changing or where it would stop. I knew I didn't want it, and at the same time, I did. I wanted the power. Needed it to fight what we faced. I was tired of being the human with the lame power in the face of overwhelming odds.

That stopped me. Was that how Nick had felt, especially after the burns? And he'd never had even the lame power. Just his heroism and a badge that didn't get him anywhere with the horrors he faced. "Let's talk about something we have answers to," I suggested. "Where are we with Panacea?"

Apollo pushed back from Hera and rose to his feet. "Your *yiayia* sent a message while you were gone. Coupled with the information we got off of that phone, we've been able to trace her down to a village. If Hermes is able to open a portal to her, I can have her here by dinner ... if she'll come."

"Why wouldn't she?"

"It's not like she isn't dealing with an epidemic there. And if the plague demons hit Uganda as well, there's no telling how crazy things might be."

"But—" Dammit, I didn't want to say it. Didn't want to even think it, but it was too late to cram the thought genie back in the bottle. "But if she's been unable to stop that epidemic, why did Hecate seem so convinced that she can stop these plagues? She's only one woman and you said it yourself, she needs to be hands-on to heal. One person at a time. But plagues spread faster than that, exponentially."

"Hecate must have some kind of ace up her sleeve. She must have some plan," Apollo said.

I hardly dared hope. "Okay, so we find Panacea. We find Hecate and we force her to spill the beans. I'll go with you."

It was Lau who spoke up at that. "You can't just walk into a village—any village—with your bat wings and steal away their healer."

"We'll return her," I protested.

"Even so."

I looked at Apollo in appeal. With everything at stake, my wings seemed the least of our issues.

"I'll take Nick," Apollo responded, shocking the bejeebers out of me. Him too, it looked like. "He's wounded. Panacea won't be able to resist helping him and it will give us a chance to talk."

"Why wouldn't she talk to you?" Lau asked suspiciously.

"She's never forgiven me for not being able to save her father. Or the rest of the Olympians for condemning him to death."

"What did he do?" Lau asked.

Apollo paused before answering, a look of *eureka!* crossing his face. "Asclepius was bringing the dead back to life. Hades was worried it would stop the flow of souls into his realm. Zeus was pissed at him for usurping the power of the Olympians. He killed him with a lightning bolt to the heart."

"So he would have died and gone to Hades ... where Hecate would have access to him," I said.

"Well, the legend is that he was made into a constellation, but that's just an old wives' tale."

"Holy shit," Hermes said. "Why didn't I think of that? Asclepius found a way to bring the dead back to life. If he's escaped the underworld, or if Hecate's smuggled him out ... there's no telling what he might do."

"But not without Panacea," Apollo said, picking up where Hermes left off. "Clearly they need her ... her healing, anyway. Maybe Asclepius is working on some way to disseminate the miracle cure."

"Hecate did mention controlling the cure," I added. It all made horrible sense. Mankind had been searching for the elixir of life for as long as there'd been death.

"I'll go along," Nick said suddenly, stepping up. "Anything to help."

I didn't protest that he was in no condition to go. The protest wouldn't have worked if our situations were reversed. I knew it wouldn't work on him. And if he was able to bring Panacea back, there was every chance she could make him whole again.

"Great," Apollo said. "Now, Hermes, can you open us a portal?"

Hermes rolled his shoulders and stretched his neck from side to side, like he was getting ready for some heavy lifting. "I can try. Come here," he said to Apollo. "I haven't seen Panacea in a lifetime or ten. I'll need to draw on your memories."

I didn't think Apollo had seen her any too recently either, but if I remembered my mythology, he was Panacea's grandfather. Maybe blood made all the difference.

Apollo offered his hand to Hermes, who took it. Cori snorted, and when I looked at her sidelong, she said quietly, so as not to break anyone's concentration. "Sorry, they're just so cute. My friend Ben would eat them up with a spoon."

I didn't say a word. The air was going wavery again, and in a moment we had a view of dirt. It expanded on more dirt. And pebbles. And then ... it looked like maybe the outer ring of a well.

"Come on," I said gently to Lacy, holding my arms out to take her from Nick. "I'll take care of you."

She shook her head vehemently and tightened her grip around Nick's neck until he choked. It had to hurt—not just because of the fierceness, but with all the burned flesh. It had to be excruciating, but only a fraction of it reached his face.

"Lacy, honey," he said in a strangled voice. "I'll be right back. Go to the nice lady."

He tried to pry her off and I reached for her at the same time, putting my hands to her sides.

"No!" she yelled, and I was blasted off my feet. I came crashing down on the coffee table, reducing it to firewood. For a moment, pain overwhelmed all thought and hijacked every signal going through my body. I couldn't move. I could only stare dumbfounded.

Everyone was dumbfounded, and stared at Lacy like she'd grown a second head. But she had just the one and right now it was buried in Nick's shoulder.

"I'm sorry. I'm so sorry. I'm sorry," she kept repeating breathlessly, sobs in between. "I didn't mean to."

Nick recovered first. "Lacy, it's okay, honey. You were scared. We know you didn't mean to ... What did you do?"

"I have a feeling I know what messed with me opening a window to Nick back at the hospital," Hermes said in a hush. He had the tone of one who doesn't want to disturb and set off a wild animal.

"Don't know," Lacy said, raising her huge Precious Moments eyes to look at Nick. There were tears in them, which made them seem almost luminous. "It's just something that happens sometimes ... when I'm scared. Mommy says I'm not 'sposed to tell."

"It's like a force field, isn't it?" Hermes asked. "Like a shield."

"Don't know," she repeated. "Mommy—"

"Where is your mommy?" I asked gently.

She turned those eyes toward me, and my heart nearly broke at the look in them. So vulnerable and devastated. "She's ... one of them."

We'd already thrown the word zombie about or I might have softened things. It hadn't occurred to us in the midst of everything that some of these kids might have lost families. "One of the zombies?" I asked.

She nodded and hugged Nick even tighter. He winced and I thought I saw his knees start to buckle.

"We're trying to help," Nick said. "We want to bring her back to you. But for that, you need to let me go."

She pulled back to look at him, studying his face to be sure, as if to be *absolutely sure* this was the way it had to be before she relented. Finally, she loosened her legs from around his waist and allowed him to slide her to the ground. She hugged herself rather than me or anyone else.

"Do you like cartoons?" Cori asked. "I have some Looney Tunes."

Of course the goddess of comedy would have some good, old-fashioned Bugs Bunny.

It only stood to reason.

"Can't hold this portal much longer," Hermes said, strain in his voice.

Nick bent and gave Lacy a kiss to her forehead, so quickly she didn't have time to change her mind and grab him again. Then he was through the portal with Apollo. It closed so quickly after them that I worried it would cut them off.

Hermes's shoulders slumped, and he looked a little ragged

around the edges. He wasn't used to creating portals, and even with Apollo's help they must be taking a lot out of him.

"How will you know when it's time to bring them back?" I asked.

"I'll open a window to check as often as I can. They have no way to signal me from there. I can't keep the portal open, especially not where we're going."

"Where are we going?" I asked.

Cori was settling the kids in front of the television, sitting cross-legged on the area rug in front of the broken coffee table, which was in front of the long couch on which Hera rested, blood still seeping from her chest.

"We're going to see a man about an artifact," he said. "Remember I told you about Javier, the rich collector who'd hired me to transport Namtar in the first place?"

"Yeah."

"I still haven't heard back from him, but I think I've uncovered his location, thanks to your *yiayia*."

"You have?"

"I could be wrong, but I think he's one of us."

"Us?"

"An Olympian. Reclusive millionaire with the largest collection of doomsday artifacts ever, well, collected. He lives in a penthouse on the Upper West Side."

"Don't keep us in suspense," Lau snapped. "Who is it?"

He held the suspense out for another few seconds while Lau made a fist. Finally, he sighed, like we were ruining all his fun. "Janus. Two-faced god of beginnings, endings, doorways, crossroads ... in short, change."

"Sounds like your kind of guy."

Hermes shuddered. "He's always creeped me out. No one likes a guy who can see right through you, least of all a trickster god."

"You think he'll help us?"

"I think that if importing Namtar was his way of bringing about the end of the world, then he's the mastermind behind all this and we're screwed."

"But Namtar woke before he was in Janus's custody. That has to mean something."

"Only one way to find out. It could even be that Janus's left side doesn't know what his right side is doing. Anyway, if he can't or won't help us, maybe we can find something in his collection that will do the trick."

"Fine," said Lau, as if she had the last word on the subject. "You go see a god about a whoziwhatsis. I've got to go check on Eu-meh. And bring her some food."

"Can she talk to others of her kind over long distances? Telepathy or anything like that?" I asked.

Lau gave me a look. Startled. Suspicious. "Why?"

"We might need backup against the plague demons. We're tough, but they're tougher. One bite or one sting and we're like Hera here. We can't fight them on our own."

"And you expect the dragons to risk their lives for *our* survival?"

"This is their fight too. The plagues aren't just affecting people. Exhibit A—the rabid animals back at the hospital. I don't know if any of the plagues specifically target dragons, but if all of their food sources become infected ..."

Lau chewed on that for a minute. "I'll talk to her, but that's all I can do."

"That's all we can ask. But you're going to have to wait. You can't go in alone, and right now there's no one to go with you."

Lau gave me the evil eye. It was weird that I'd sort of missed that. No one did it better. Not even Hades with his furnace flare. "Who's going to stop me? I saw a motorcycle down in Cori's parking garage. It'll be a lot faster and more maneuverable than a car and safer than going on foot. I have weapons. I'll be fine."

I boggled at her. "*You're* going to steal a motorcycle?"

Lau was as by-the-book as they came. "I'm going to *comman-deer* a motorcycle ... without the owner's knowledge. I plan on returning it. I'm sure you'd agree that in the event of an apoca-lypse, standard rules don't apply."

"*I* agree. I just never thought to hear *you* say it. If I can't convince you not to go, I hope you'll promise at least to be safe."

"I will if you will," she said.

22

"In the country of the blind, the two-faced god is king."
—Tori Karacis

We had Javier/Janus's address, my wings, and Perseus's sword. But only two out of the three were any good to us right then.

I was exhausted. Being stabbed, frozen half to death and forced into a beastly brawl took a lot out of a girl. I asked for protein bars, about a gallon of water and ten minutes to get myself together. It was a matter of survival. If I'd tried to fly us there in my current condition, we'd be splattered all over the pavement in no time.

I ate the first protein bar down in three bites on my way to the bathroom. The curtain had been drawn over Sigyn, but even so I was very aware of her as I did my business and then grabbed a washcloth out of the cabinet, wet it down with water as hot as I could get it and went liberal with the suds.

I started on my face, scrubbing and scrubbing at the rune

Sigyn had put there. I didn't know if it did any good, but I felt a little better for it. At the very least, I'd scrubbed the saliva away, if not any supernatural residue. I took off my shirt and scrubbed everything underneath, cringing like a girl when I had to put the shirt back on, blood, filth and all. I wasn't even going to try to detangle my wild hair. That alone could take an hour, especially without salon grade conditioner. I left it as it was. I'd probably have to cut it out of its ponytail holder later on, but for now it was out of my face and that was good enough.

I didn't exactly feel like a new person, but the protein bar had helped with some of the shakes and the gallon of water was calling my name. I went back to the kitchen, downed half, ate another protein bar, scarfed a banana and went through a one-serving bag of chips. I was still hungry, but I knew I had to let it all hit, and I didn't want to weigh myself down. I suspected now that I'd live and that Hermes would be safe enough with me ... probably.

"LET'S GO," I said.

"How do you want to do this?" he asked.

"Sadly, I have to hold on to you. You have to hold me back. You cop a feel, I drop you. You harass me in any way, I drop you. Are we clear?"

His smirk was practically harassment enough. "Yup."

"Why don't I believe you?" I asked.

He didn't answer that, and I didn't push. We had places to go and a two-faced god to interview. I had to admit I was intrigued.

We spotted Janus's penthouse while still a few blocks away. It was the one with the windows blasted out and smoke rising. I flapped faster. My muscles protested and groaned, but I could hardly hear them over the blood rushing through my ears.

We hit the edge of the roof—not only a penthouse, but a garden apartment ... or at least it had been. The place now looked like a jungle that had been trampled flat by invaders. Hanging baskets had been knocked to the ground. Leaves, dirt, palm fronds, and flower petals were scattered across the roof. Inside was worse.O. Or at least more deadly. Shards of glass, some dagger-sized, some bloody, lay strewn about the floor.

Then, even as we stepped inside, the broken glass began to shake and shift, beginning to slide to the center of the room ... and then to fly through the air, whipping and biting at us as it gathered into a small tornado. The thin membrane of my wings took it hard.

Between my arms, which were up, shielding my face, I could just make out the tableau in the center of the room.

Hecate was directing the tornado—or so I gathered from the fact that she had one arm wrapped around her waist, as if she'd been wounded, and the other lashed out toward one of the strangest figures I'd ever seen. The man at the center of her cyclone, standing as if impervious to it all, had one head but two faces. As I was trying to decide whether to intervene, and on which side, Janus—because who else could it be?—raised a fist and made an abrupt explosion with it, like after a hearty fist bump, and the glass and debris swirling around him burst outward. Hermes and I dove to the floor, and Hecate let out such a scream I immediately knew she'd been directly in the blast zone.

I landed badly. Half on Hermes and half on a jagged piece of glass that punctured my knee as I went down and sliced deeply. I pulled it out mercilessly, before I could heal around it and make it a permanent part of me, and looked toward the terrible twosome in the center of the room.

Hecate was on the ground now, but there was hellfire in her eyes, and I could see it gathering in the hand still clenched to her stomach, the one not currently pushing her up from the floor into a hunched over position. I didn't think Janus could see the hellfire from his angle, even with two sets of eyes. One watched us steadily, while the other seemed riveted on Hecate. It was eerie.

"Hit me with your best shot," he taunted her. "It won't matter. Not as long as I wear the Stasis Stone."

I looked him up and down for a honkin' huge stone … or even a teeny-tiny gem … something that I could rip off or smash to smithereens if need be, but he had to be keeping it close to the vest. Maybe literally. His clothing was from another era. Victorian, maybe. It hearkened to the time of ballrooms and the *beau monde*. A brocade vest, a flowy shirt, tight pants he probably called breeches. Even an ascot.

"Recall them," Hecate ordered, the glow from her hand becoming more obvious by the second.

"I wouldn't, even if I could. They've dispersed to all the ends of the earth."

"You're going to destroy the world," Hecate spat.

Hermes grabbed me by the ear and whispered into it, "You get Janus; I'll take Hecate." Of course, he'd leave me the hard one.

"Give me a sec," I whispered back. "I want to hear."

"That *is* the general idea," Janus responded to Hecate. "A new world will rise from the ashes. It is well past time for a change. Haven't you been paying attention? Movies are the new myth. They've predicted our future. Mankind will destroy this planet and its resources. We'll be forced to the level of barbarians or abandon this world for the stars, to exploit another planet where we will be nothing. The gods forgotten. Left behind on a dying world. This one *will* end, but it will end my way. Begin again *my* way. Where I am king."

"He's crazy," I whispered to Hermes.

"If you had two faces on one head, you might be crazy too," he whispered back.

"I heard that," said the closest face.

Hecate lashed out with her fireball at just that moment, maybe figuring Janus's attention was on us. I was in motion before it could even hit, my wings propelling me into the air, sword raised and ready to come down hard, aiming for the sweet spot between shoulder and head, otherwise known as the neck. Even if I couldn't hurt *him*, maybe I could sever his fine threads and get to whatever talisman lay beneath.

But the fireball flattened and dissipated against his chest, and my sword bounced right off, numbing my hand as it quivered and reverbed. I couldn't touch him. I didn't think the gorgon glare was going to faze him either. But I tried it, looking him in the closest set of eyes and yelling, *"Freeze!"*

He just laughed, and it was like he came with his own laugh track. Laughter in duplicate. I wanted to hurt him. Badly. Maybe Lyssa was somehow still affecting me, because I didn't just want to knock him out and make the laughter stop. I wanted to thrust my sword down his throat. Or cut off both sets of lips. Or ...

For a moment I thought I had an idea, inspired by the hell I wanted to unleash on him. We might not be able to hurt him. But entrap him ... that was a whole other matter. Porting wouldn't actually harm a hair on his head. If Hermes could send him to Tartarus or into the belly of a whale at least we could be rid of him. But then I remembered that it was the combination of Apollo's power with Hermes's that did the trick, and Apollo wasn't here.

When I went for Janus, Hermes had gone for Hecate, taking her down in a flying tackle. She now lay squashed beneath him, the fight gone out of her, but not the fervor. That burned from her eyes as she glared at Janus and at me and would have glared at Hermes if he weren't right on top of her.

"You've sealed your fate," she said, mostly to Janus. "I'm not stupid. I knew failure was an option. I arranged with

Amphitrite that if she didn't hear from me or Sigyn within an hour, she should unleash everything at her disposal on the city. Hurricanes. Tsunamis. She's got Poseidon's trident, and she's not afraid to use it."

Hermes and I locked eyes. Last we'd seen on the news Amphitrite was on the other side of the country, threatening LA with the storm to end all storms. I hoped that Hecate had called her to this coast in time to save LA from total destruction.

And now she was here. Somehow, in the midst of stopping the plague demons and saving the world, we were going to have to pencil in saving New York City. Go us.

"You've got to call it off," I told Hecate.

"If he calls off his demons and grants me control I'll call off the destruction of New York," she said, her glare now all for Janus.

"Not *my* demons," he said. "And never going to happen."

"Then let it rain," she responded.

I stared at her, unable to believe that she'd be so casual about the destruction of an entire city full of people. Hermes, still seated on top of her, gave her a blow to the back of the head, knocking her out. Before she could do any *more* harm.

I turned on Janus. "Aren't you going to do anything?" I asked.

"She is only hastening what I have begun," he said with such supreme unconcern that I wanted to give him something serious to fear.

"Gah, they deserve each other," I told Hermes. "Let's go. We have a city to save."

"What about her?" he asked.

"Take her with us. Between her and Sigyn, we might be able to get one to call off the destruction."

"You think so?" he asked.

I didn't know what to think. Right now all my mental

powers were focused on the fact that there were two of them and one of me. *Take her with us*, I'd said. But *how*?

I scanned the trashed penthouse for inspiration. The windows and floors had been wrecked, of course, but the walls had been largely untouched, and there was a device that instantly caught my eye. It was made of wood, sinew, and hide, and looked like something da Vinci would have devised.

Janus saw me see it—with two sets of eyes, it was inevitable. The closest set fixed on me with a gleam of gamesmanship. "Don't even think about it," he said.

I didn't dignify that with an answer, but leapt for the wall, my torn wings nonetheless displacing enough air to propel me faster than the two-faced god could move. I grabbed the device off the wall. It was unwieldy, spread open as it was for display, but I closed it up, yelled Hermes's name and threw it as hard as I could, sending it like a javelin flying over Janus's head.

He reached for it, but the Stasis Stone only made him invincible. It didn't turn him into an action hero. He caught an edge, blowing its trajectory, but Hermes, the trickster god, was skilled at games like Keep-Away and launched himself into the air for a two-handed catch. Janus turned on Hermes with a bi-voiced growl, and I leapt at him from behind. The field of the Stasis Stone kept me from connecting and doing anything useful like slamming him with my sword. Instead, I threw the blade around him like an extra arm, catching at the flat of the blade with the hand not on the hilt and holding it like a bar around him to prevent movement, at least long enough to give Hermes a chance to escape. "Use it!" I yelled to Hermes. "I'll take care of Hecate. Go. Open portals, spread the word. Get everyone out you can. Just go!"

Hermes didn't need to be told twice. If he felt any qualms about leaving me, they certainly didn't show as he latched the device's armbands around himself and quickly tested out the workings.

Janus, unconcerned about my blade, pushed against it, rushing to get to Hermes. I tangled my legs up with his to trip him, entwining far more intimately around him than I was comfortable with. I ended up cheek to cheek with his second face. The side that had faced Hecate had been intense, very in the moment. Determined, resolute, terrifying in its ferocity. The one that faced me was sloe-eyed with a distant look. The face of a dreamer only half-awake.

The dreamer blinked at me sorrowfully as Janus's hands pushed against the flat of the blade to free himself. But while I'd never joined my family's acrobatics act because of my fear of heights, I was an expert at death grips. I *would not* let go, even as the blade started to bite into my hand. Janus had slowed to a near stop, and Hermes was now in the air, flapping the wood-and-hide wings like a giant bird.

"Go!" I shouted again.

Hermes headed for the nearest window, and I had a second to marvel in amazement before Janus decided that if he couldn't dislodge me, he could at least fall backward and smash me into the glass-spattered floor.

I felt the intention, but wasn't able to disengage in time to stop it. I hit the broken glass and pain lanced through me as shards pierced my back and further shredded my wings. My hands flew wide as I struck a nerve, and the blade went flying toward the broken windows, slipping over the edge of one, lost.

I howled at the loss and tried to go for it, but Janus was up first. He kicked me to keep me down and sprinted for another wall, this one full of shelves holding artifacts and gadgetry that looked like a steampunk's dream.

I didn't know what he was going for, but with his reputation for collecting doomsday devices, I wasn't waiting to find out. Whole body screaming in pain, I lunged for Hecate, grabbed her awkwardly to my chest and ran for the window through which the sword had vanished. Before I leapt, I tested my trashed wings. They were willing to give me a little lift, but I wouldn't know until I jumped out the window whether it would be enough, particularly with two bodies to support.

I couldn't resist a glance at Janus to see how close he was to firing off whatever weapon he'd grabbed, in case I'd have to dodge it. The device he pointed at me looked like an antique flare gun—a big muzzle that flashed in that moment.

Frantic, I dove for the window, launching myself and Hecate into the air before I even hit the ledge. There was an explosion behind me that threw me forward, blasting us away from the building, all uncontrolled. I beat my wings desperately to compensate, but they weren't working properly. Gravity, however, was working just fine, sucking at me and trying to pull me down.

Hecate and I hung momentarily in the air, like Wile E. Coyote when he didn't realize the cliff had dropped out from under him, and then we started to plummet, the wind whistling through the rents in my wings. I beat harder and faster, and when that didn't work, I tried to bell my wings like a parachute to slow our fall. It worked, but not well enough. The ground was rushing up to meet us far too fast. My heart was beating harder than my wings ever had, and I was sure we were going to dent the pavement and break every bone in our bodies when we hit.

In my panic, it took Hermes's call two or three times to get through to me. I only realized he was there when he swooped past me, close enough to add temporary wind to my sails. He made another run at us and flapped in front of me, doing his best to match my descent without precipitating his own.

"You're going to have to let her go," he said.

I was too panicked even to glare. I'd thought a million times about dropping Hecate on her head—Hermes too, for that matter—but I didn't think I could actually do it.

"Can't!" I called.

"Do it!" he insisted.

The ground was right there. So close. Two stories? One.

A blast from above hit me then and took the decision—and Hecate—out of my hands. Lightning or a blast from Janus's weapon had struck me, and I was on fire. Every muscle locked up—hands, back, neck, shoulders, wings—and I plummeted to the ground on fire.

Hecate broke my fall, and not at all willingly. We rolled together in a way that under other circumstances would have made Hermes grab a video camera and consider selling the footage on pay-per-view. A crash stopped our tumble, and we smacked up against the back of a white panel van.

My brains were still scrambled when the impact woke Hecate. Her head bobbled like a dashboard Elvis, still disoriented from the blast, but she froze momentarily as though something had caught her attention. I willed my head to stop spinning so that I could follow her gaze, but it hadn't complied before she suddenly lunged for something and came up with a sword and held it aloft.

The Sword of Perseus. The very one I'd dropped. Back in enemy hands.

That got me moving. I lunged for her, my vision still unfocused, but I was too slow. She sidestepped easily and swung the sword for my head like a baseball bat, aiming with the flat of the blade.

"You saved me. Now we're even," she said, as the blade hit me like a ton of bricks. I blacked out with her words still ringing in my ears.

I came to fighting, only there was nothing left to fight. Hecate was gone, and the sword with her.

A growl from between two nearby buildings got me moving.

Rabid or hungry street animal, I didn't care. At this point, a pissed-off kitten could probably do me in. Woozy, I rose to my feet, using my good hand pressed to the van's side to keep myself from falling over. I tried my wings, but they were a no-go. Singed, torn, battered, and possibly broken. I was going to have to walk ... or, better yet, drive, assuming I could teach myself to hot-wire a van. I'd done it once with a car, back in my wild youth when I'd borrowed Pappous' boat-like Crown Vic to run off and see the outsider boyfriend my family disapproved of. But that had been long ago and far away.

I staggered around to the driver's side of the van as the body behind the growl slunk out toward me. It was wild, all right, but no animal. A girl, early teen years, it looked like. At first glance, one might assume she'd been eating cherry Popsicles and gotten the goop all over her face and clothes. At a second glance, it was nothing so innocent.

I ripped at the driver's side door as she began running at me, barely favoring the leg turning brokenly beneath her, throwing off her gait. Mercifully the door was unlocked. I swung the door open and myself up into the seat, slamming the door shut between me and the zombie girl before I had to fight her. I ... I couldn't. Not unless it became life or death. Frantically, I looked around for keys, checking visors, cubbies, glove compartments. But regardless of the movies, it was never that easy. I *did* find a screwdriver in the glove box and used it to get loose the wires I'd need.

The girl slammed into the van as I tried to finagle the wires, clawing at my door. When the van roared to life, it was more dumb luck than skill. I jammed the van into Reverse, wincing as the girl's nails screamed painfully along the siding. The second I was clear of her, I shifted gears and roared away, leaving her in the dust, racing toward Cori's apartment, using sidewalks where the streets were blocked by abandoned vehicles or, worse yet, bodies. Sigyn's shield maidens or whoever they were had confiscated my phone and I'd never gotten it back. I had no way to call ahead to Cori for the garage code or any way to reach anyone inside. When I got to her garage, I pressed the intercom button there, probably for people who'd forgotten their codes or clickers or whatever, but no one answered. Or at least, no one answered within the time I dared wait. From around the corner shambled a zombie with his face half-eaten away and an arm mangled beyond use. He wasn't alone.

I gunned the engine and sped around the front of the building, blowing past the zombies gathered toward the front entrance. Pulling up before it, I saw two things immediately—that the zombie gang had already turned, tracking the sound of the engine and the possibility of fresh meat, and that the entrance was too narrow to drive through, even if that wouldn't leave the whole building exposed to invasion. The entryway was a single glass door that would allow people in one at a time or possibly two by two if the pair was holding hands. And it was probably reinforced glass. Maybe even bulletproof given what the apartments within must cost. The only way in was to get buzzed in. I hoped the electricity was still working in the building. A brown or blackout might be the end of me.

There was no time for indecision. The zombies were in bad shape, but they hadn't been around long enough to decompose to the point of falling apart.

I pulled a three-point turn, caving in the side of a car unfortunate enough to be directly across from me on the other side of the street and aimed the van for the oncoming zombies. Then I put the car temporarily into Park, kicked off my shoes, positioned them so that one jammed up under part of the lower dashboard and down into the other shoe, which pressed down on the gas. Then I climbed out of the car and reached back in to put it into Drive. I withdrew with an impressive speed, spurred on by adrenaline, and still got smacked in my shoulder by the door to the car as it started to move forward.

Then I ran toward the entrance, listening for the impact of the car with the zombies ... or the side of the building. It would either take out some zombies or drop some wall on top of them —or so I hoped. At the very least, it would provide an obstacle for them to climb around or over, buying me some time.

I hit the entrance without slowing, but with both hands out in front to catch me. The keypad was immediately to the right of the door. I didn't know Cori's number, so I pressed all of the buttons frantically, muttering, *"Comeon comeon comeon,"* under my breath.

A voice came over the intercom. "Jason. Ohmygod, is that you?"

"No, but I'm being chased by zombies. You've got to let me in!" I infused as much fear as I could into my voice, which wasn't hard, because while the van had crashed sickeningly into one zombie, crushing him between it and the side of the building, the rest were now climbing up, over, under and around.

"How do I know you're not infected?" the girl asked. I didn't have time to convince her.

Luckily, another voice came over the intercom as she waited for me to answer. "Who is it?"

The voice sounded familiar. "Cori, please tell me that's you!"

"Tori?"

"Let me in!"

The closest zombie was still steps away when the buzzer sounded, but as if it understood the significance of the sound somewhere in the depths of its being, it sped up suddenly.

I grabbed the door, dashed in and tried to slam it behind me, but it was one of those spring doors that couldn't be slammed, probably a liability thing, and the closest zombie managed to get a hand in the door. I was out of bladed weapons or even blunt objects to beat down inconvenient limbs.

"Freeze!" I yelled through the door, catching its gaze.

The zombie froze, arm still reaching through, but I slapped it down hard. As the arm started to clear the doorway, I jump-kicked, landing a blow to its stomach, sending it falling back into its fellow zombies. Then I yanked the door as hard as I could, managing to speed the latching by possibly a mere millisecond. But it was closed. And auto-locked. The zombies left standing slammed into the glass as they tried to push in, to break in to get to me. The door bucked in its frame, but held ... for now.

I ran toward the elevators, which thank the gods already had one car on the ground floor that opened the second I pressed the button. I dashed inside and hit the floor I remembered Cori had brought us to from the garage. As soon as the doors closed behind me, I breathed a huge sigh of relief.

There were only two apartments on Cori's floor, and I turned in the direction I thought we'd taken. At my knock, I heard, "Who's there?"

"Tori."

"Tori who?"

Least fun knock-knock joke ever.

"Tori who's going to huff and puff and blow your door down if you don't let me in this instant."

The door swung open and Hermes's face appeared in the gap. "Sorry, I had to be sure it was you and that you hadn't become a slavering beast."

"Yet," I said, "but you keep this up ..."

He stepped aside and let me in. I looked around the apartment as he closed the door behind me and met Nick's one good eye.

"See," a childlike voice said, and I looked down to see Lacy on his lap, staring earnestly into his face. "I tol' you she'd be okay. I had a vision."

Wait, if Nick was back, that meant ... I swept my gaze around the room and spotted Apollo in the back hallway, the one with the bathroom where Sigyn lay fighting for her life against the poison from the plague demon. A cool blue glow emanated from that area as well.

I was drawn to it, and when I reached Apollo's side, I stopped at the sight of a young woman bent over the tub, hand out, resting on Sigyn's chest. Panacea, I presumed, somewhat awed. Neither Apollo nor I spoke a word as we watched.

After what seemed only moments, the glow dimmed and died. The woman rose from her crouched position, and I looked beyond her toward Sigyn, whose color looked a lot better. She was still swollen, but no longer several times her size.

"She's going to be fine," Panacea said, looking to Apollo, "but she'll need rest. I've broken down the poisons, but she'll need lots and lots of fluids to flush the remains out of her system."

She looked so much like Apollo—a *female* version of Apollo, of course—that there was no mistaking that she was of his bloodline. While the hair escaping from under her colorful headcloth was as dark as night, her eyes were the same amazing turquoise. But where Apollo's lit with life and the potential for trouble, hers were clouded with sadness from all the pain and suffering she'd seen. Her face was deeply tanned and weathered from time spent out in the sun.

But I didn't have time to marvel and Sigyn didn't have time to rest. "She's going to have to sleep when she's dead," I said, deciding just to rip the Band-Aid off. We had no time for gentle. "Which is what we're all going to be if she doesn't get up and call off the hit."

"The hit on who?" Apollo asked.

Lacy gasped loudly, and I started immediately back for the living room to find her standing like a statue, her eyes huge. Her gaze was far, far away, as if she could look through buildings, maybe even time and space. "The city," she said, in a voice deeper than her own, hollow and somehow ancient.

"City swept away by sea.

Buildings not for rent but rust,

The ruins bones and beams and blood.

The refuse washed away by flood.

The people ne'er mourned too long.

Ocean casts a siren song,

And some deny while others flee.

But this world will no longer be."

No one said a word as her pronouncement died away. Prophecy. There was no doubt about it. Lacy had to be an Oracle.

An Oracle ... proclaiming the end of the world.

No time. I couldn't process. Process and I might accept.

"She's right," I said, "at least about part of it. Amphitrite is set to destroy the city on Hecate's orders. Anytime now. We have to fight it. We have to stop this."

Lacy fell forward into Nick's arms, as if the foreseeing had taken everything out of her. I strode forward to shake her awake and demand to know what she meant by it all, though it seemed terrifyingly clear for an Oracle. Apollo got between us.

"Don't," he said. "She won't be able to tell you what she means. But you, start talking."

So I did. I told them everything I knew and concluded with, "So Sigyn doesn't have the time to rest. Either we find a way to call this off or this whole city will be underwater."

"I always thought it would be LA," Nick said. "New York ... it just doesn't seem possible."

"Well, it is," I said. There was no time for mercy. No time for smelling salts or waking Sigyn with a gentle shake. I strode back to Sigyn and heard Panacea gasp as I slapped her face. Hard.

Sigyn rocked with the blow and her eyelids fluttered, but that was about all. "Monster," Panacea gasped. "She's out. As she should be. Let me, if you must."

She stepped forward and I tried to feel terrible about slapping Sigyn, but all I managed was a minor torment that I'd made a crappy impression on a goddess—demigoddess?—who amounted to the Mother Teresa of the ancient world. Sigyn had already mind-controlled me and left me for dead. A single witch-slap seemed the least I could do.

Panacea put a hand to Sigyn's forehead and closed her eyes as she mouthed ancient words that seemed to mean "open sesame," since Sigyn's eyes fluttered open in response. They went from dazed to alarmed in literally the blink of an eye, and she tried to push herself upward on her elbows, but Panacea held her down. "Best not yet," she said, and Sigyn tore her gaze away from me to stare up at Panacea.

"What's happened?" she asked.

"Plague poisoning," I said, cutting straight to the point. There was no time for sugarcoating. Outside, the sky had grown dark, the clouds sitting right over rooftops like the ceiling of the world was coming down on us. They were thick and angry-gray, and there was a grumbling sort of sound rolling back and forth between them. Not thunder. Not yet. More like the building disgruntlement of a crowd before full-on riot. The storm was coming. "You've been out for a while, so here's how things stand," I continued. "You fought the demons and lost. Hecate fought Janus and lost. I understand that if things didn't go your way, the cabal had arranged for Amphitrite to swamp the city, but here's the deal—the plague demons have flown the coop, off to the ends of the earth. If you were hoping to gain control of them through battle or threats of death and destruction, you've failed. Only one part of Hecate's plan has come to fruition—Panacea is here. But a fat lot of good that's going to do if Amphitrite kills her when she wipes Manhattan off the map. If Panacea goes down and the plague demons continue unchecked, life as we know it will end. Oh, there *might* be some survivors for you to lord over, at least to start, but with so many diseases running rampant, no one can possibly be immune to them all. Maybe not even the gods."

As if to punctuate my statement, the thunder that had been threatening suddenly crashed with enough force to rattle windows. Outside, the wind rushed loudly enough to drown out the television and then a flash of lightning lit the sky, forking spectacularly over a building not so far away. Kids cried out, the lights and television snapped off, possibly even in that order.

"Crap, is she—" Sigyn began.

"She is," Apollo said, holding out a cell phone. "Call her. Call it off."

Sigyn was shaking her head. "Not that way. Underwater. She can't—" She seemed incapable of finishing a sentence.

"What then?" I asked in frustration. "There has to be some way to reach Amphitrite."

"Shell phone," she said, and I was about to get really angry, thinking she was making a joke at a time like this.

"No, really," she continued, spotting the thunderclouds gathering on my face. She touched her hand to the chain at her neck, and I noticed that there was a little shell dangling from it. And a skeleton. And a key. Direct dials for major players in the cabal?

Sigyn tapped the little shell and muttered a single word under her breath, and then called loudly, "Amphitrite, can you hear me? You've got to stop this. We've got Panacea. She's here in the city. You've got to call this off. Amphitrite?"

She waited for an answer. We *all* waited. And waited. "If you're playing games ..." Apollo threatened.

"I'm not," Sigyn swore, looking frightened enough at the lack of response that I believed her. I didn't think she'd like the picture I'd painted. Or the idea that the high-rise she was in might come down around her ears. "She's not answering. Too caught up in battle plans, maybe."

"Or maybe Hecate got to her first," I said. "Damn, we've got to do this the old-fashioned way then. We've got to go right to the source. Where is she?" I asked.

She looked away. Apollo loomed as if to command answers, but Hermes pushed him out of the way.

"Sigyn." He squatted down beside the tub where she rested so that they were practically chest to chest, faces close. She turned to him and their gazes locked. "You don't want to die. You don't want *me* to die unless you get to kill me yourself. You won't get that chance if we don't stop this."

Oddly enough, that made her lips crack upward in a half smile. "You're right there. But she could be anywhere. I just don't know—"

The rain hit us then, not starting gently and working its way up to impressive, but with a sudden wet sheet slapping against the windows, making us all jump. Between the wind and the torrent, the glass rattled in its frame, threatening to shatter and let the outside in. The others had joined us now, everyone standing in the hallway, listening in. Lacy plastered herself once more against Nick, and the littlest boy was pressed against his other side, the damaged one. Nick winced, but wrapped an arm around him just the same. It was about the sweetest thing I'd ever seen, and ... I had to look away.

"We have to call Helen," Nick said, bringing my gaze reluctantly back to him. "Make sure she's okay and see if Eu-meh's been able to reach out to other dragons."

I recovered my cell phone, but found a *No Signal* warning before I could even attempt to dial. "Damn, it looks like relays are down. Can anyone get a signal?"

The rain sloshed again at the windows and the wind rattled them so hard in their frames that if they were teeth they'd have fallen out by now. It didn't bode well.

"I have a landline," Cori said.

"Try it," I answered, as though she needed to hear it from me. She was already headed back for the kitchen and the phone mounted there.

Wall mounted, I thought stunned. *Still with cord.* I barely knew those kinds of phones still existed.

"Dead," she said. "I guess with the power out ..."

"Hermes?" Apollo asked, "Will you do the honors?"

Hermes was holding Sigyn now, and I wondered what that meant for his relationship with my best friend, Christie. I wouldn't exactly be crushed if they ended it, but Christie might feel differently. She deserved happiness. I just didn't think the trickster god was the one to supply it.

"Fine, whatever," he said, waving a free hand at the air and opening a tiny pinprick of a window that grew into a view of Lau stroking Eu-meh's neck, her cheek to the dragon's muzzle. It was the second sweetest thing I'd seen today, ranking nearly up there with Lacy's attachment to Nick.

I had a pang, my second of the day, for the easy adoration, the domesticity. When things died down, I wanted that for myself. Maybe not forever. I wasn't a cuddly, casserole and dishes-doing kind of girl, but for an evening or more—curled up on the couch with a warm, wonderful man. Fuzzy socks. A blanket. A good movie on the television or in front of a roaring fire ... I thought I could trick my brain into supplying which man would be there with me, but the fantasy flickered from Nick to Apollo.

Apollo ... there was no way that we'd make it to the end of the movie with clothes still in place. Nick ... right now all I could think of was his wounds and how I was partly responsible for them. I wanted to nurse him back to health. I wanted to care for him and protect him and, yes, curl up on the couch with him. But Apollo—

I realized that my gaze had strayed to him and I had to look away. He couldn't read my mind, but my emotions were another thing, and that fantasy had mutated into something else altogether. Something he could probably sense and which was completely inappropriate while we still had to face down death and destruction. Afterward, if we survived ...

I wondered if that meant I'd made my decision. Apollo and I shared a connection that Nick could never be part of, which was completely unfair to him. Maybe it was time to let him go like he'd let me go back in Delphi.

I focused on Lau. It was easier. She'd spotted me—us, anyway—and was staring back through the window. Sound was coming through, and I could hear the wind in Central Park whipping all around them, whistling through a piece of loose siding. Lau shivered.

"What's going on with this storm?" Lau asked, the first to speak.

"Long story short—You know that cabal we've talked about? They had a kill switch. In other words, if a few major players don't check in, Amphitrite, Queen of the Seas, tears the city apart."

I expected horror, concern, something, but Lau was made of sterner stuff. She just nodded. "That jibes with what Eu-meh's learned. The sea dragons and other creatures are amassing at the South Street Seaport."

I wondered how Eu-meh communicated. Were her kind telepathic? I didn't imagine cell phone or shell phones or whatever came into play, but there were more pressing questions.

"Can she get the sea dragons to hold off?"

"This is far bigger than them."

"But can they help? Not just bow out, but stop the others?"

"Turn on Amphitrite? She controls the seas, the oceans. *Where they live.*"

"Save her from herself," I protested. "Save their waters. They must feel it—the taint. With the plagues that have already been unleashed, things will wash into the ocean, poisoning it. Gas from cars and plants, sewage, decaying batteries, diseases ... Sure, the waters are huge. Things will be diluted, but eventually, with enough death and destruction ..."

"I'll try to communicate that," Lau promised. "But in the meantime, we've got to get down there. We've got to stop this."

I didn't know that we had anything in our arsenal that *could* stop it, but we weren't left with any choice but to save the day or die trying. I just hoped it was the former and not the latter. Assuming I went to the afterlife of my gorgon ancestors ... well, I'd been there, done that and not bothered to buy the T-shirt, so a one-way ticket held no appeal.

"We'll meet you there," I said.

The portal snapped shut on my final word. I looked to Hermes, and he looked wiped, as though one more portal today would knock him straight out. He rested his head on Sigyn's chest, and she allowed it to stay, even bringing a hand up to rest on his temple. She stopped short of stroking his hair back, but it looked like it took effort.

"How do we stop her?" I asked Sigyn.

Her gaze met mine. "I don't know. The trident, I guess. Go for the trident." Why hadn't I thought of that?

"We heal Hera first, take her with us. You think she has access to Zeus's bag of tricks?" I asked Apollo.

"If not, she has tricks all her own," he answered. "As for the healing, Panacea took care of that while you were out fighting Janus."

"Did someone call my name?" Hera asked, standing in the hallway, leaning against the wall, still clearly weak.

"You're not sleeping," Panacea gasped. "Who could sleep

with all this noise?"

"Good, how do you feel about helping us save the city?" I asked.

"My city? Damn right I will."

"I'm going too," Nick said.

"Nooooo!" Lacy moaned, gripping him tighter, until the pain finally broke him and he moaned out loud. She immediately loosened her grip. "I hurt you," she said. "I'm so sorry. I didn't mean it." She kissed her first two fingers and then held them out to him. "Where did I hurt?"

Panacea, watching the whole thing, looked from Lacy's kissed fingers to Nick and spoke up before he could, taking Lacy's hand and guiding it to his burned shoulder. "Right here," she said, gently applying it along with her own hand.

Nick's eyes got really big and then rolled up into his head as a blue glow rolled off Panacea's fingers and the healing began. Lacy whispered an awed "oooh" but we couldn't see the results, hidden as they were beneath the bandages. But it was clear when the lines of his face relaxed and his shoulders slumped and his whole body went slack at the relief of what must have been horrible and constant pain that he'd been hiding heroically. Apollo caught Nick as he started to fall, and Panacea grabbed Lacy out of his arms before he could take her with him. I grabbed Nick's legs to help carry him to the newly vacated couch.

"What was that?" Lacy asked, awed.

"Healing. Your friend is going to be okay, but he needs some sleep and no hugging for a little while."

I was so stunned and amazed at the thought that Nick would be whole again, and in such a way that he couldn't protest, that when the first tear fell, I thought the ceiling was leaking. Then I realized it was me.

"Let's go," I said gruffly to the others. "Before the storm gets worse."

23
____

We got down to the garage—only five of us—me, Apollo, Hermes, Hera and Sigyn, the only ones with any sort of battle skills. Five of us against an angry sea goddess and her legions. Or four, if you didn't count Sigyn, and given what I'd been through with her so far, I didn't trust her any farther than I could throw her. But if Amphitrite was going to listen to any of us, it would be Sigyn, and we had to take any advantage we could get.

Cori's happy yellow Hummer waited for us in the garage like vehicular irony.

"I'm driving," Apollo said. "You and Hermes keep an eye on Sigyn. Hera, up front with me."

I instantly wanted to argue, not because he was wrong, but because I didn't like anyone else calling the shots, but it was petty and I let it go, except for a "sir, yes, sir" and a mock salute. Hermes gave him a similar salute, only it involved a single finger, right in the middle of his hand. If we didn't have smart-assery in times like these, what did we have?

I climbed into the back on one side of Sigyn while Hermes bookended her on the other side.

"Try Amphitrite again," I told her.

She pressed her hand to the shell pendant and muttered the trigger word, cocking her head as if to listen, but once again nothing happened.

"Not answering," she said.

I sighed. "Fasten your seat belt, it's going to be a bumpy ride."

And that was *before* I saw who was waiting there when the garage door went up ... Namtar, larger than life, seething with fury and dripping wet. I didn't know how he'd tracked us. I didn't even know how he'd survived not being paralyzed by Medusa's blood on Perseus's sword. The last I'd seen him, his tail was already starting to petrify from the blow I'd dealt him.

Then his tail came up as if in reflex, and I noticed the stinger no longer attached. In fact, it was half what it used to be. Namtar or one of his minions had cut it off before the stoning could spread. Somehow, the sacrifice made him more terrifying, not less.

Apollo apparently felt the same. He hit the gas hard. The Hummer lurched forward, grinding as if the parking brake was still on. Apollo quickly jammed it down, and the truck roared like the beast it was, headed straight for Namtar. The lord of all plague demons leapt into the air, coming down hard on the hood of the Hummer, denting it. He broke off the windshield wipers scrabbling for a handhold on the truck, but as soon as we were out in the storm, the force of it bore down on him, and Apollo torqued the wheel to one side to throw him off.

Namtar stared death at us, fisted one giant hand, and punched it straight through the windshield at Apollo, who swerved again trying to avoid it. The Hummer, even as massive as it was, lost traction on the ground and for a breathless moment, we were sliding down the street with no control whatsoever, the truck fishtailing into another car.

The impact set us straight again, and Apollo took back

control of the Hummer while Namtar continued to grab for him, his arm elbow deep in broken glass with a busted-out center where his fist had gone through and cracks radiating out from that. The window hadn't shattered, but between the cracks, the loss of the wipers and the storm, I couldn't see a thing, and I couldn't imagine Apollo could either, unless he had X-ray vision he'd been keeping from me.

Namtar shrieked something at us, but I couldn't understand the words, just the fury behind them. Likewise, Hera sat beside Apollo, a chant gaining volume as she went, but not enough to make out the details over the raging storm outside. And not from where I sat helpless in the backseat.

I undid my seat belt, ready to catch Namtar with the gorgon glare, but Hera got in my way, leaning forward and grabbing his wrist in her hand. Her fingers barely closed around it, but the contact was apparently what mattered, because immediately Namtar's wrist started going gray, lifeless ... limp ... Namtar's gaze shot to Hera's.

He gave her the scariest smile I'd ever seen, and then turned his wrist in her hand so that his fingers could latch on to hers, his nails digging into her skin, the sickness he carried with him transferring like germs in a public restroom. Hera turned green. I saw her hand begin to slacken before she realized it herself and reinforced her grip.

It was a battle of death versus disease. She was trying to steal his life, and he was fighting to do the same to her. But she'd already said back at the pub how little affect her power had on the demons of disease. Their powers over life and death were too compatible. It was a losing battle.

Apollo pulled another crazy maneuver to dislodge Namtar, but it was no good. His lower body flopped about, but his upper was riveted by his hold on Hera and hers on him. "Namtar!" I yelled at the top of my lungs, but he was totally focused on

Hera. He didn't so much as turn to look at me. I had to do something.

Cursing fluently, I rolled down my window and climbed out. The wind threatened to whip me away, and there was nothing to grab on to that wasn't slick with moisture and icy with cold. I did my best, beating my broken wings and trying to ignore the pain from the wind reopening the rents. Apollo slammed on the brakes at the realization that I was gone. Namtar nearly went flying, bringing Hera with him so that her head hit the dashboard.

I slammed into the Hummer as it stopped and grabbed on, pulling myself over the roof to get to Namtar. When he looked up, I bit my tongue and spit in his eyes. It was the lowest kind of fighting, but my bladed weapon hadn't made it out the window, and if my blood did what it was supposed to do ...

He howled and let go of Hera's hand to claw at his eyes as they began to petrify in his face. As soon as he let go, Apollo whipped the Hummer into Reverse. It squealed and spun its wheels on the wet asphalt until they caught and the truck flew backward. Namtar went crashing and rolling to the ground.

Apollo threw the Hummer into Drive again, and sped forward, straight into Namtar, who was raising himself up on his front arms. It hit him hard, caving Cori's grille. The sound was terrible, and I wondered if everyone cringed as I did. Apollo backed up again and then accelerated as quickly as he could in a short space to drive again right over the plague demon with a sickening thump that I felt from my toes to my temples and all the way through my gut, particularly since I was holding flat to the roof, trying to stay on myself.

As soon as we were at a safe distance, Apollo stopped and I climbed back in through my window, soaked and chilled to the bone. Sigyn scooched as close as she could to Hermes and as far as she could get from me.

"Are you okay?" I asked Hera.

She held her arm out for me to see. It was green-black. The flesh looked eaten away, even down to the muscle. And it stunk to high heaven.

"Can you—" I started.

"Brace yourself!" Apollo cut in with an urgency that had us all paying attention.

I fastened my seat belt again without a question and the next thing I knew, we were crashing into more things, but from the sound and feel of it, these were vehicular. Apollo was clearing road obstructions by simply barreling through.

"Can you even see?" I asked him.

He didn't answer. In the rearview mirror the concentration on his face was clear. He didn't have any attention to spare.

"No," he said finally, when we were through the worst … or at least carrying a good part of it along with us, based on the perpetual scraping and grinding noises from below. "We're going to have to bail at some point. Or find new wheels. I can barely see out of the windshield, and signs are a no-go."

"That way," Sigyn said, pointing to her right. In the opposite direction I would have guessed for the seaport, but what did I know? With no landmarks or sun to steer by, I was utterly at a loss.

"How do you know?" I asked suspiciously.

"I just do. Directions. Winds, weather. I could always tell."

"She—" Hermes began, then ducked instinctively at a shadow swooping toward us, despite the fact that he was within the Hummer with a roof over his head. "What was that?"

The Hummer rattled at the air displacement overhead as the huge shadow blew over us, and we all looked to see the distinctive shape of a dragon, gold against the angry-gray clouds.

"Eu-meh," Apollo said. "I guess you're right about the direction."

He turned the Hummer to follow the dragon and Sigyn's

directions, though we quickly lost the former. She was traveling too fast for us to follow. I had a pang for Lau, dragonback in the midst of this storm. I hoped she had some kind of weather flap or, I don't know, ancient dragon storm-repelling stone to keep her out of the elements and safely on board. I didn't envy her … or particularly want to face her mood after traveling in this madness. Amphitrite had better watch herself.

We'd gone as far as Wall Street, which even I knew to be on the southern tip of the island, which meant we were nearing the seaport when all the bells and whistles of my precog went off at once. They'd been at wakeup alarm level ever since the storm started, low enough that I could tune them out and do what needed to be done, but something had changed. Now they were going off like air raid sirens, and I wanted to clamp my hands over my ears … or my stomach, which was roiling like the clouds overhead.

"Hurry!" I told Apollo, even though it was probably too dangerous to go any faster, with the wet roads and obstacles.

"Something's wrong," Apollo echoed.

And then the roar of the storm kicked up several decibels and gained direction. Not just all around, over and above, but … right in front of us. Something big was coming.

"What do we do?" I asked him.

We were all searching the horizon, which didn't extend far in the close-in city clutter. Down this far to the southern tip, buildings closed in claustrophobically. Streets were narrow and cluttered with cars parked where they shouldn't be. We pushed them aside with the Hummer's sheer brute force. The clouds were so low—

As we watched, something punched through the clouds to the buildings, bursting them at the seams. Glass shattered all around us, raining down like razor-edged hail. The grandpappy of all tidal waves came towering toward shore, and we were right in its path. No time to dodge, even if something so massive *could* be dodged. I wanted Lacy and her force field more than I'd ever wanted anything in my life.

I reached up to clutch Apollo's shoulder, trying to convey with a touch everything I didn't have time to say.

Sigyn and Hermes grabbed on to each other. Hera looked out of her mind with terror.

The wave crested and crashed down, loaded with debris it had swept along with it. We all screamed as the force smashed down on the roof of the Hummer, crushing it down on top of us, cracking door seals and windows and practically our heads. Water came pouring in through the cracked windows, quickly filling up what little space we still had for air. The whole Hummer itself lifted off the ground, swept by the tidal wave, which churned all around us. We were now part of the debris.

The Hummer was a death trap. Blasting our way out, even if it were possible, would let the torrent in, sweeping us apart and probably drowning us even faster. How could we fight something so mindless and primal?

"Can you port us?" I asked Hermes desperately, fighting to speak with my knees compressed into my chest and my lungs nearly crushed.

"I'm wrung out," Hermes said. "Even if I could ... where? Where is safe? Back to the apartment to wait out the end of the world?"

But I had an answer ready. "To Lau. Focus on her. And Eumeh. We have to end this."

"But I need Apollo's power, and he's cut off from the sun—"

Water choked off the end of his sentence, but I got the gist of it. My hand still on Apollo, I could feel his struggle. The front of the car was almost completely filled with water now, and it was all he could do to keep his nose free and hold Hera there as well.

You can do this, I thought at him. I knew he couldn't pick up the words, but the sentiment ... I felt panic reach back for me, quickly pushed away by reassurance. In the midst of everything, he was trying to calm *me*.

The car bucked suddenly, canting the Hummer so that the rising water pooled to the back of the car. Water and debris swamped my mouth and nose. My heart kicked against my chest in panic that I knew Apollo picked up on through our link. I didn't let go of him. Instead, I reached across Sigyn to grab Hermes, hoping that I could be the bridge between him and Apollo, adding whatever power I had to give. I willed it to flow, even as the car shifted again and the last of the air was forced out of the Hummer. We were all underwater now. Seconds to live.

I channeled the panic, and the adrenaline and whatever cocktail of fight-or-flight hormones I had in my system. I used it all, sending it Hermes's way. I thought I felt something, a tingle throughout, but it was hard to tell over my blaring danger alarms—like I couldn't figure out on my own that I was screwed. Maybe the tingle was just my body going numb. Soon I'd gasp for air, despite my best efforts, and swallow water, starting the terrifying process of drowning. My worst fear come to life.

My lungs started to feel as though they would burst, and it was all I could do to keep my energy flowing to Hermes when all I wanted to do was claw my way out of the death trap. My vision started to waver, little spots appearing ... And then I realized that one of the spots was different from the others. A silly little Sesame Street song from my childhood ran through my head as the window expanded, right there in the center of the Hummer, above the central console. It was a tease. I could look in on a world that while storm lashed, wasn't wall-to-wall water.

Hermes opened his mouth and bubbles came out, but Apollo, looking back at him, seemed to make some kind of sense of it. He grabbed Hera from her seat and pushed at the portal Hermes had opened, through which storm water was now streaming. But as quickly as it flowed out through the portal, it was flowing in again through our busted windows.

My lungs burst as Hera disappeared through the portal, and air began escaping. Against my will, my mouth opened to release some of the pressure building up inside me. I choked on the storm instead and it now raged on inside me as I gagged and coughed and swallowed even more.

Apollo motioned back for Sigyn, and Hermes guided her forward with his free hand, trying to tell her with his eyes to go. She seemed reluctant to leave him, but Apollo took over, grabbing her and pushing her through before she could hold things up.

I was next. Apollo and Hermes were the portal movers and shakers. I let go of both their hands, praying they'd be able to keep it together, and swam for the portal, pushing feebly off the backseat with my feet. I fell through onto storm-sloshed streets, coming down hard on my hands and chest, too out of control to duck and roll.

Hera yanked me out of the way of whoever was coming through next, which was a good thing because for my part all I could do was double over coughing, my throat a raw mess and my lungs bleeding for air. I staggered on my feet, the footing treacherous with water up around our ankles and an undertow that wanted to rip them out from under us. The winds were whipped into a frenzy, playing "Blow the Man Down."

Sigyn ... I looked around for Sigyn, and realized that we were on the docks. Or one particular dock anyway, this one not so much meant for big ships, but for shopping. The glass-fronted mall area had already been reduced to iron beams, all of the glass blown out and lashing around our ankles with the swirling waters like stinging nettles. Eu-meh was perched atop the infrastructure, roaring defiantly but musically into the storm.

Sigyn stood apart from us, frantically tapping her shell pendant and yelling at the storm. "Stop!" she called, choking on the water the storm threw at her, breathing droplets as she should have been breathing air, then coughing spasmodically, even as she continued to try to communicate. "Amphitrite, you have to stop! You'll kill us all!"

The storm whipped away her words. There was no way Amphitrite could hear or understand her.

Apollo and Hermes came tumbling through the portal together, falling into the churning water. Hermes came up first, spitting and bleeding. He'd landed badly on a piece of glass, and his shoulder was covered in blood. It was hard to tell how much or how serious it was with the water sloshing it all over. No time to worry about it now anyway. We ended this or it was over for all of us.

"What's she doing?" Hera asked, looking toward the dragon in awe.

Calling, I thought. Maybe she was trying to reach her sea sisters. Or ... I didn't know. I only knew that I usually had some kind of plan, however tentative, but in this ... Water wasn't my element. I was lost.

"One way to find out," I said. "I have to get to her." Maybe with a bird's-eye view, I could come up with something. I looked at Apollo, who was pushing himself up, his chest working like a bellows, coughing and choking and looking like something a wildcat had dragged in. Water was no more his element than mine. "I don't know how much you two have left in you, but see if you can find the center of the storm. Even if you can't port Amphitrite somewhere else, like an active volcano, maybe you can get the trident away from her. Sigyn, you keep trying to reach her. Hera, stay with Sigyn. Watch her."

Hera was holding her gangrenous arm in her other hand. She looked like she was half in shock, but she nodded. Made of sterner stuff and not about to give in. I respected that. If the battle could be won on will alone, we had it in the bag.

I tested my war-torn wings, and while they were shivery and only half-healed, it was as much as I was going to get. I launched myself into the air. The wind instantly tried to blow me back, but I thrust hard with my wings and then pressed them to my body, did it again. It was a herky-jerky movement, but I did my best, beating hard against the wind and then making myself as small a target of resistance as possible.

But I was flying into the wind, and it was all I could do to go forward rather than get blown back. My hair whipped my face, and I had to let it, no effort to spare for pushing it aside, especially when it would only whip back. I fought until I was exhausted, my lungs burning again, but I could see the top of the mall's iron infrastructure. I could see the bronze dragon atop it. I was almost there.

Almost ...

Eu-meh's tail lashed out, and I grabbed on to it, as I thought I was meant to. She brought me the rest of the way in, landing me on a beam beside her. Beside Lau, who crouched close against her body, sheltered from the wind and lashing rain.

From up there, I could see the goddess of the seas, rising above the tumult on a cone of sea spray. Her white-green hair flew all around her with the force of the storm, alternately covering and revealing her form, which didn't sport so much as a clamshell bikini, though she did wear strands of pearls and coral that dipped to her navel. And, yes, she held the trident aloft, directing the storm like a virtuoso. She'd grown, as I'd seen the other old ones do when full of their power, to three times her former size. The trident itself was easily my height or larger.

"What's she doing?" I asked Lau, cocking my head at Eu-meh.

"She can't reach the sea dragons," she said. "They can't hear her above the trident's call, but she has others like her looking out for the plague demons, rounding them up."

"Great," I said without the enthusiasm it probably deserved. Rounding up the plague demons was awesome. It still meant I had to get through sea dragons and other nastiness to get to the queen of the seas.

I looked out over the insane waters, churning and foaming, lashing at where we stood, and took a deep breath. "I'm going in."

Lau turned on me like I was insane, her foot slipping on the beams with her speed. She had to grab Eu-meh's side to recover her footing.

"You barely got *here* through the storm. How are you going to fly into the heart of it?"

"I don't have a choice. We've got to get that trident or we're lost."

Before she could stop me, I launched myself off the roof. No plan. No weapon. Probably no hope, but the very idea just made me ornery and want to prove that wrong.

The storm lashed at me, and for a second I went nowhere, hovering right where I'd started. Going *mano a mano* with the storm in an epic battle. My wings felt as substantial as tissue paper, the barely healed rents in them growing by the second.

Then Eu-meh's tail came up again, swinging into me this time, like it was the bat and I was the ball. I went flying through the sky, fighting for control, but at least moving in the right direction. I flapped furiously until I got my wings beating fast enough to keep up. I was moving like a rocket, straight for an angry, naked goddess bent on destruction.

She saw me. I knew she did, but she couldn't be bothered to acknowledge my flight with more than a flick of a finger, and suddenly the ocean burst upward in a confusion of tentacles. *Huge*, terrifying and angry-red, in contrast to the churning gray-blue color palette all around us. My brain noticed inconsequentials like that when it was trying not to gibber in abject terror and shut down all together.

I beat my wings harder, trying to rise above the tentacles. *Kraken?* I wondered. And a part of me thought, *How cool is that?* But I got my inner six-year-old under control. Unfortunately, my wings weren't as easy. I was running on empty, and the tentacles struck before I could rise, one knocking into me, sending me sideways, straight into another that started to curl around me, but too slowly. A third was more successful, wrapping around my waist and squeezing me tight. The constriction choked the last of my air out of me, so I knew that when I hit the ocean I wouldn't have any reserves left. It pulled me down, faster than I could escape.

The shock of the cold water hit me like a punch to the gut, and my mouth opened. I didn't have any breath left, and the icy, churning water that rushed in choked me instantly. I coughed and sucked more water, until it was a vicious cycle, and all along the tentacles were tightening, tightening. I thrashed, half a dozen ideas flashing through my head and discarded just as quickly.

I could bite down on the tentacle holding me, but that was no help unless my saliva had the same properties as my blood ... and if so, Apollo would already be one helluva handsome statue. So no help there. If I bit the creature, all I'd have to show was a mouthful of sushi. I thrashed around for other ideas. I could bite my tongue to draw blood and *then* bite the monster, but as tightly as it was wrapped around me, I might not be able to get free before it turned to stone and sank with me to the bottom of the ocean.

Being rescued by a SEAL team—unreliable and massively unrealistic.

Kicking, screaming, flailing, panicking, drowning—already doing all that. Incredibly sucky plan.

I had to hope that those on land were having more luck. Hera and Sigyn. Hermes and Apollo. Lau and Eu-meh.

The tentacles around me suddenly squeezed even more tightly, and I felt like they'd meet in the middle, snapping me in half. But it was a recoil. Instinctive. It loosened up a second later, and I didn't wait to see if it was a fluke, but pushed my hands down hard on the tentacles and propelled myself out of its grip, kicking as hard as I could once I was free and swimming frantically for the surface. My muscles were all oxygen deprived now, and swimming was harder than it should have been, but terror was very motivating.

I burst upward, gasping for air, coughing, and treading water for all I was worth. The tumultuous waves washed over me, swamping me once, twice, again. I flapped my wings hard against the water, but all that did was make me splash around like a wounded animal. Like prey, attracting any predators around. I stopped the wings instantly, swiped wet hair momentarily out of my face, and tried to get my bearings. I could see Amphitrite ahead. I was no judge of distances, and things looked closer across the water than they actually were, but I thought I could get to her if the kraken didn't grab me again.

I looked around for it, and it thrashed behind me, as if grappling with something. I didn't wait to find out what could take on a giant squid. Colossal squid? Supersized?

I swam flat out for Amphitrite, calling mentally to Apollo with everything I had. *Now. Grab the trident. Do it now!*

I hoped and prayed they'd be able to port the trident, but Amphitrite was thrusting her hands forward forcefully as if to lob some new threat. If they were too busy fighting for their lives, they'd never find the focus. I had to distract her.

"Yo, sea skank!" I yelled. It was probably unfair. She might be a very nice person when she wasn't playing on the homicidal side of the street. But none of it mattered, because she couldn't hear me over the raging storm. Or she just didn't care.

Around me, the ocean was still just as furious, the rain coming down in sheets rather than droplets.

My arms were beyond tired, and my legs felt like they had anchors tied around them. I was very afraid I was getting nowhere, when suddenly something burst out of the water nearly beneath me.

My fear-o-meter burst its casing, and I thought my heart was going to go with it. Something had me on its back, rising out of the water, rising up into the air. I grabbed for a hold and cut my hand on a scale.

A scale. I focused on what was beneath me. Bronze. Beautiful. More beautiful than anything I'd ever seen before in my life. Eu-meh had been the beast fighting the kraken, even though water was no more her element than mine. And it looked like she'd won. I wasn't much of a prize, but she'd come for me. I dropped my forehead to her back and reveled for a millisecond in breathing. The sheer joy of it.

"Can you understand me?" I asked. "A million times thank you. And I hate to ask one more thing, but we have to get that trident."

I didn't know if she understood or not, but she didn't immediately veer with me back toward the pier. Instead, we headed right for the sea witch. Goddess. Whatever.

We flew in, and I forced myself to grip Eu-meh with my legs, hanging on to her with only one hand, holding the other out as though I could outstretch a dragon's reach and get to the trident. It wasn't going to happen. Her wingspan alone ...

And as we swept in, Amphitrite took note, swinging the trident our way. Eu-meh was better at evasive maneuvers than I was. She turned herself at the last second, avoiding a direct blow from whatever blasted out of that trident, but nearly dumping me off, as I wasn't expecting to suddenly be perpendicular to the waters. I clung tightly, desperate to stay on, and then wondered why. I couldn't do any good from where I was.

Eu-meh flashed past the trident and wheeled in midair, ready to dive back in, this time aiming for the goddess herself. While Amphitrite could ignore little ole me, a dragon her size was a whole other matter. The trident swung around again, this time aiming a blast at the ocean itself.

Not half a second later, tentacles rose again out of the depths, and two gnarled heads poked up at us from the deep, one looking like an oversized sea dragon—head like a sea horse or kelpie crossed with a plesiosaur, long muzzle opening on dagger-sharp teeth—the other like one of the great armored fish of old, only with the body elongated like a stretch limo ... a stretch placoderm? The sea monsters came right for us, rising out of the depths.

Eu-meh made a sound that I translated as terror and flapped her wings hard to propel herself higher, out of reach of massive jaws or tentacles, and as she strafed the great goddess, I did the dumbest, bravest thing I'd ever done in my life ... I let go. I fell through the storm, reaching out to catch myself on Amphitrite's upper arms and struggling to keep hold of her rain-slicked skin. I had to wrap myself around her, my body nearly the full length of her arm, but it was her *trident* arm, and while I was hugged to it, she couldn't wield it properly. She shook me hard, and my eyes rattled in my head. My brain crashed against the sides of my skull, but I held on and began inching myself down her arm toward that trident.

Tentacles grabbed me around the waist again, tried to drag me down, but I was pulling Amphitrite's arm with me, and she barked an order that had the tentacles retreating. Instead, a spiky head bumped me hard. My back contracted at the pain of it. My nerves wanted to seize up, but I wouldn't let go. I kept shimmying down, down. I was going to get to that trident if it was the last thing I did ... which it might very well be.

I didn't count on Amphitrite being ambidextrous. She passed the trident off from one hand to another and immediately aimed the triple tines right for my battered body. She shouted something loudly enough that I could almost hear it over the crash of the ocean, and then let me have it.

There was a pop and a sizzle—a jolt went through me, quickly cut off, but not quickly enough that my nerves didn't melt down like plastic under a plasma rifle. I spasmed uncontrollably, everything contracting inward, and I lost my grip on Amphitrite. I fell toward the ocean, staring wide-eyed up at her, my last thought the awareness that her trident was gone.

It was satisfying. I could pass out now. The thought flashed across my mind, comforting.

A relief.

But then the frigid shock of the waters stole that away. My muscles were still seized. It hurt to move, but it hurt more not to. My stupid alarm bells were firing on all cylinders, even if my mind wasn't, and my feet started to kick. They were the first part of me to respond.

When something bumped against my feet, fear stopped my heart for a split second, then I went on kicking twice as fast. The adrenaline spike got my arms moving again too, but sluggishly. There was no way I could outswim any beastie in the water with me.

It bumped again, and this time rose with me on top of it. I panicked and thought to roll off, only to realize that on top it couldn't eat me. In the water …

I spread my hands out across its body, looking for a handhold and felt the bony plates of one of the water dragons. I found purchase as it breached, the sucking waters wanting to take me with them, unwilling to surrender me.

And then …

Nothing. The bony beast I was riding swam through the ocean and I risked opening my eyes against the icy sheets of rain to see that it was headed back toward the piers … to smash me into them? That was my first thought, but my alarm bells had gone quiet—as had the storm, except for the rain, wind, and still-churning ocean. Looking behind me, I could no longer see Amphitrite on her sea spray commanding the fray. And no trident aiming TASER-like blasts.

There was a sound behind me, almost a nickering—the sea dragon?—and then a set of oversized claws seized me by the shoulders and carried me off. I held on to the claws as they held to me, and looked up to see Eu-meh's bronze belly and outspread wings.

It was over then? Truly over? Had the stretch placoderm actually saved me now that Amphitrite no longer had the trident to command it?

Eu-meh swept over the ocean to the pier and bypassed that to get onto more sturdy footing, since a good portion of the pier had already been washed away. She dropped me from the height of a few feet into a jumble of soggy, battered-but-still-breathing heroes, one of whom—Oh great gods no—*Hermes* held the trident.

I watched in horror as he leveled it at the ocean and wondered *what now*? Would the trickster god decide it was time to remake the world in *his* image? I prepared to dive for the trident when a cool misty vapor started to issue from the end of it, flowing toward the crazily churning ocean, but Apollo sensed what I was about and grabbed me by the hand to keep me in check, apparently having a lot more faith in Hermes than I'd ever been able to muster. I watched as the vapor settled over the angry waves and they slowly seemed to become less angry, less violent, just *less*.

With the hand not holding me back, Apollo reached out to the sky, closed his eyes, and chanted something under his breath. I fed him my belief through our connection and reached out to Hera as well. She winced as I connected, and I remembered about her arm. We had to get her to help, but first—

The clouds directly overhead moved, blowing ever so slightly apart, and the thinnest halo of sun gilded them with gold. In the next instant, a pinprick of light reached us, and we all raised our faces to it. The rain still fell, but moderately now, and I had hope that it would soon become a sun shower. Complete, I hoped, with rainbows, puppies, and healing.

24

Eu-meh arrived then with Lau, whom she'd flown back for as soon as she'd dumped me off. Lau slid to the ground when Eu-meh landed, eying the sky and then each of us. "Nice teamwork," she said.

A compliment from Lau ... wonders might never cease. Oh sure, it wasn't personal, but then what had I really done but keep Amphitrite busy while others did the heavy lifting?

"We still have demons to round up," Apollo said. "And Hecate to hunt down."

"We've got the demons covered," Lau said with pride. "Namtar slipped through our net, but Eu-meh's network rounded up a good many." Of course, she didn't know we'd already taken care of Namtar.

"Network?" Hera asked.

"Sure, you didn't think she was the only dragon in North America, did you? She's not even the only one in the Northwest. Or New York, for that matter. Lots of mountains. They like that." Then Lau spotted Hera's arm. "I think we'd better get you some help."

The Hummer was trashed. Every other vehicle on the street

was in the same condition. They'd been lifted by the storm, dropped down again, slammed around, flooded ... I knew just how they felt ... or would have felt if cars could feel anything.

Hermes was barely able to hold himself and the trident upright. A portal was out of the question. Eu-meh could only take four people at a time, and it was a no-brainer to send the others on ahead. Apollo insisted on staying back with me, as I knew he would.

Anyway, we had to talk.

We watched the others fly away and then stood there in the rain like the end of some romantic movie. When they were a mere mote in the sky, Apollo turned to me and brushed soggy hair out of my face. It wouldn't stay. I knew that. He knew that. But even wrung out and feeling like a drowned rat, I felt the zing of his touch, and, of course, he felt me feel it.

"So," he said, his voice deep and full of churning emotion he was trying to keep out of it, pretending that we had any secrets between us. "What's it going to be?" he asked.

I knew what he was talking about. Him. Nick. Me. Love triangles always seemed like so much fun when you were reading about them or watching them on television, but when you were in one ... someone was getting hurt. And doing the hurting was every bit as painful as being the odd man out.

"You know," I said. He did, I had no doubt. But he needed to hear me say it.

He kept his gaze steadily on me, and my heart flip-flopped, my breathing went shallow, as if I were fighting for breath all over again. It was fear, pure and simple. Terror, actually. Plague demons, zombies, and killer goddesses had nothing on commitment.

"It's you," I said, breathlessly. "Okay?"

I couldn't believe that last word had slipped out, along with all of the vulnerability attached. I wanted to take it back. Or argue things logically—Nick was human and I was, very decidedly not. Not anymore. Where I would go, he couldn't follow. Not safely. And I cared too much ... It was all true, as far as it went, but it wasn't the whole story. I loved Nick. But I was inexorably drawn to Apollo in a way that would always preempt any other relationship. I'd gone from one addiction (ambrosia) to another (him). I knew it, and I was sunk. I didn't *want* to be in love. It felt a lot like a tornado or a whirlpool, something that caught me up and swept me away. Something I couldn't control.

I'd fought long and hard against it, but I'd lost that war. Apollo had finally defeated me.

Apollo stared, and I had the worst panic attack of my life waiting for him to say something. I hated this. *Hated it.*

And then he picked me up and whirled me around, screaming a *"whoo-hoo!"* at the sky. A *whoo-hoo*. Over me.

The look in his eyes was everything. Like I'd given him the world. It was so surreal, so impossible, that I laughed nervously, sounding very nearly hysterical ... until he shut me up with a kiss. Through our link, I felt that same terror, that same love, that same wonder over the whole thing, and it gave me back my equilibrium.

That was, of course, when a zombie pulled himself out from under one of the trashed vehicles and began crawling toward us. I stopped him in his tracks with the gorgon glare, but, still, the moment was gone. Apollo and I didn't dare get distracted again.

Instead, I tested out my wings, just in case they were back in business, but the remaining wind sheered right through them.

The sound of wings flapping—wings far larger than mine— riveted our gaze on the sky, to the coolest dragon I'd ever seen or even imagined. It was, quite literally, a dragon-fly—a blue-green iridescent lizardlike body but with a beak instead of a snout. It had a double set of wings, just like a dragonfly, gossamer and moving so quickly they blurred. It came in for a landing beside us and buzz-clicked something to us that I thought was language, even if it wasn't one I understood. Or maybe I did.

I was sure that Eu-meh had sent the dragon-fly and that it was there to take us to her. But there was no place to sit on *this* smaller dragon. The back was entirely taken up with the wings. We had to let ourselves be grabbed, one in each set of claws, front and back, and be carried aloft like prey. It was a little harrowing, but I was too exhausted to tense up over the whole thing. I even might have dropped off to sleep for a second or two, until my precog kicked me in the head and I heard Apollo curse in old Greek, something that I thought translated to "Zeus's flaming sack." I didn't really want to know.

I looked around wildly for the source of the danger. We were nearing Cori's apartment.

She must have been watching for us, because the window blew open …

Blew being the operative word. In its place was a whirlwind, and I could just make out two figures within it—one all in black leather, her dark, wild hair whipping around her like lashes, and another whose colorful headscarf was whipped away by the cyclonic winds, revealing short black curls. Hecate … with one arm wrapped around Panacea, the other holding the Sword of Perseus to her throat.

Holy hells.

"Follow that whirlwind," I yelled, hoping that our dragon-fly friend would hear and understand, but there was no change in our trajectory. We were still headed for the now-open window.

I squirmed like a worm on the end of a hook, trying desperately to get free of the dragon-fly's claws, and it must have gotten the message because it let out a questioning sort of trill and then opened one claw, the one holding my legs. Instead of kicking and screaming and panicking, I pushed against the other claw with my hands, trying to release my wings and squeeze my upper body out as well. That seemed to be all it needed to know. The second claw opened, and I started to plummet.

I flapped my wings crazy hard, fighting my exhaustion. The rents in them must have healed up somewhat, because in what seemed like an eternity but was probably only a few milliseconds, they caught the air. Not perfectly, but enough for me to soar toward that whirlwind, which was headed for the ground. Hecate couldn't keep it up forever, especially not with her concentration divided between the spell and her captive.

I dove as they landed, headed straight for Hecate … or the sword, I wasn't too particular at that moment, but she anticipated me, whirling so that Panacea was in front of her like a shield and pushing the sword point right up under her chin so that it dented the skin. Even a nick might be fatal, given that the blade was eternally coated in Medusa's blood. I stopped cold, except for the slow beat of my wings that kept me hovering without getting any closer. "Stay right there or she dies," Hecate said, as if the threat weren't clear enough. "The fate of the world dies with her. You might have stopped the demons, but the plagues have already been unleashed. More will die. Thousands. Billions. Unless you back the hells off and let me finish what I started."

"Selling life … at a price."

Hecate's face was a marble mask of unconcern. "Just like our entire health care industry. Just like doctors and nurses, hospitals and clinics."

"But in this case, you'll have a monopoly."

"You say that like it's a bad thing. Now, *back the hells off*."

I didn't for a second doubt that Hecate would do it—kill Panacea and seal the fate of the world. Maybe she thought her blood or body parts would be good enough. Maybe she just didn't care, but I beat down with my wings, rising up and up into the air, farther and farther away from Panacea and her rescue. I wasn't giving up, not by a long shot, but I couldn't risk a frontal assault. I had to catch Hecate by surprise.

"I'm going," I said to reinforce my actions. "Don't hurt her."

"That's up to you," she called back.

She waited until I was in Cori's window, looking down at her, before yanking Panacea away and disappearing. I didn't know if they'd vanished behind a vehicle or into one of the portals to hell, but they were gone.

Luckily, I knew I could track Hecate, given that taste I'd had of her blood. But I didn't know if I could defeat her alone, especially not with a hostage situation. I ducked back inside and asked before I could think to phrase it better, "What the hells happened?"

Lacy and the younger kids were sobbing. Nick and the oldest boy, Jeff, were trying to comfort them. Michelle, Hera's assistant, had rushed to her side in time to catch her as she collapsed onto the couch. Her arm was now almost entirely eaten away, the remainder putrid and stinking. It extended all the way up to her shoulder and by the way she was holding herself, might be starting to creep across her chest. And Sigyn ... Sigyn was a statue. Stone through and through. Hecate must have struck her with the sword.

It was Hermes who answered me, his voice sounding broken, and his gaze never leaving Sigyn. "She jumped in front of me. Just like she's always protected me. Even from that acid way back when, even when some of it ricocheted back out of the bowl, catching her, burning her hands."

Cori took it from there. "Hecate appeared with that sword of hers and threatened the kids to get Panacea to give herself up. Lacy did that force field thing, and protected everybody, but she was weakening. When Hermes and the others arrived, they fought Hecate, but, well, you can see how that turned out. Panacea gave herself up to prevent anyone else from meeting Sigyn's fate."

"And you let her?" I asked, stunned.

"She didn't give us the chance to stop her."

"We've got to go after them. I can track her, but I'm going to need backup."

"I'll go," Apollo said at once.

"And me," Hermes added. "I'm going to make her pay."

"So am I," Nick said, glaring at me, daring me to knock him out again.

I started to protest, and he cut me off. "You've got nothing to say about it and no time to argue. I don't know how much longer Hera can hold out." We all looked at her. The sickness creeping through her veins was turning her gray and green. It wasn't a good look for her. If the gangrene had progressed this quickly already, it wouldn't take long for the poison to reach her heart.

"And besides ... Lau."

I hadn't seen Lau, and it only now occurred to me. I'd assumed that she and Eu-meh had flown off, maybe before they realized trouble had arrived.

"What happened to Lau?"

He waved behind the couch, and I rounded it, dreading what I would see. I'd missed her because she'd fallen down behind it, arms up as though she'd been wrestling someone for something. Hecate for the sword, at a guess. From the defensive wounds, it looked like she'd caught part of the blade on her hands. One slash would have been enough to turn her to stone.

"Holy hell" escaped my mouth. "Eu-meh?"

"Lau waved her off."

I looked out the window to our dragon-fly friend, wondering ... One way to find out. "Can you call Eu-meh?" I asked. "Get her back here?"

The dragon-fly stared steadily at me, and it was disconcerting to see the compound eyes in the dragonesque face. Then it looked away, off, I thought, toward Central Park. A second later it looked back to me, bobbing its head in a way I hoped signaled the affirmative. I didn't know what kind of reward might be suitable for dragons, but if we lived through this, I was going to find out. And come through in a big way ... assuming it didn't take the kind of budget I didn't have.

I hoped I was right about the dragonspeak. And that Eu-meh hadn't gone far. While we waited, we had to let Hades know what was going on. Maybe he could even help. The more I wondered about my certainty that I could track Hecate from her blood, the more it started to make sense. My precog had started to get directional some time ago, and the changes happening inside me seemed awfully bound up with blood. But knowing which way to go didn't necessarily tell me how to get there. The tracking thing was new to me, but I suspected it wasn't any respecter of walls and other barriers, like the River Styx and its fearsome ferryman, assuming Hecate had fled back to the underworld.

But Hades could open doors and speed things along. The longer things took, the farther Hecate got away from us, and the more Hera struggled to survive.

There were no cell towers down below, which left us with just one choice. "Hermes, do you think you can reach Hades?"

I wasn't asking for a portal this time. I hoped he had enough left in him for this.

"I'll try," he said. No *what's in it for me* or *what'll you trade me for it*. All the mischief had been wrung out of him.

He closed his eyes and focused. We all watched the air as it rippled and then seemed to rip down the center, not a graceful pinprick irising open, but a tear that opened onto a scene of chaos. Hades faced an invisible barrier, behind which souls were howling, slamming through each other and into the wall, gnawing at their own incorporeal limbs, or trying for those of others. He'd told us of souls going mad, of the underworld overrun. It looked like he finally had things locked away ... or so I thought before I realized that several of his hellhounds had been caught behind the barrier and that not all of the souls were gnawing on the incorporeal. I could see at least three of the once sleek black bodies nearly hollow from having their insides torn out. Focusing in, the stark white of bones that had been ripped out of their bodies was a contrast to the translucent gray of the souls. There was no more meat, but the blood left behind coated the mouths of several lost souls.

Hades seemed to sense that he was being watched and whirled on us. I almost flinched from the fire of hatred burning in his eyes, safe though I was back in Cori's apartment. "What do you want? Why haven't you saved the world yet? What else do you have to do all day?"

I ignored the implication that we'd been at play while the world died around us. If only he knew ...

"We haven't saved it yet because *your* bitch goddess turned on us," Hermes said, beating me to the punch.

"*Hecate?*" The barrier trembled with the force of his anger, and the souls behind it grew even more agitated, many doing their best to dash their brains out to get to him. "I knew she wasn't to be trusted. Where is she?" he roared.

"We were going to ask you the same question," I joined in. "Wherever she is, we assume she's either got Asclepius or is coming for him. We think he's part of her plan."

"Plan?"

"Yeah, it's not just your world she wants to rule. Now, where is he? I assume when Zeus killed him he was sent to Tartarus for punishment?"

Hades looked aside, and I knew we wouldn't like whatever we were going to hear next. "I don't know where he is," Hades said, his voice low and angry. Someone was going to pay for the fact that he had to make the admission. "When the Titans broke out of Tartarus, they weren't the only ones who escaped. We rounded up many. Most. But ... he hasn't been seen since."

"Any chance Hecate helped him hide out?" Hermes asked.

"She's capable of anything. Do you think she's come back here?"

The others in Cori's living room all looked to me. I'd said I could track her. I closed my eyes and checked in with my inner compass. I expected her to be long gone and, yes, underground, but ... "No," I said, shocked. "She's actually not that far away. More toward midtown, but ..."

Hades's look was considering. "No portals in midtown. Closest you get is downtown, a place that used to be called The Vault. Track her," he said, like he was the boss of me. "When you get close enough to get an address, let me know. I'll send reinforcements."

It was the best we were going to do. I nodded, and Hermes closed the communication between us and Hades, then collapsed back against Sigyn's stone cold body. "Poseidon's prickly ... Never mind," he said, seeing the kids watching him, hanging on our every word. "I'm beat. When this is over, I'm going to sleep for a week."

A trill from outside Cori's window let us know that our ride had arrived. Eu-meh hovered right outside, doing her best to stay level.

I went to her, and she craned her neck, trying to see past me into the apartment ... to Lau, I was sure. My heart broke.

"She's okay, girl," I said, pretty certain at this point that she'd understand. "Or she will be. I *will* make it right. But we need your help."

She dipped her head and raised it again as I'd seen the other dragon do and then stretched out her neck for me to climb on.

My fear of heights tried to kick up again, but it had been through too much and was too exhausted to put up much of a fight. Still, climbing out the window onto the dragon's back was harder than it should have been, even with wings of my own to help me if I slipped. It went without a hitch, and I leaned back toward the window to help the others—Nick, Hermes, Apollo —all of us about done in, except maybe Nick, fresh from his healing.

I wondered what Cori's remaining neighbors might think if they happened to peer out their windows and catch sight of dragons right outside their building. Of course, they were New Yorkers. They might just take it in stride. By tomorrow, this whole thing could be written off as some movie promo or special effect gone wrong or ... Except for the dead they'd have to bury. No, maybe not. Even New Yorkers had limits.

She took off the second we were all on board, with me using the pressure of my hands and legs to indicate right or left and keep us headed toward our target.

I could feel Hecate as we got closer, her blood calling to me. I even wanted ... just a little ... I diverted that thought before it could hit full acknowledgment.

I wanted nothing so much as to defeat her. That was all.

I knew right when we hit the building housing her because it seemed to glow with a red haze. One quadrant, in particular, centered, I thought, a few floors up. It was the first time my directional sense had come with a bull's eye ... The color of blood, so I didn't think it was a coincidence.

The blinds there were all closed, the windows still intact. Even if I knew which office, we couldn't risk a frontal assault. Hecate could petrify Panacea and Asclepius, if she had him, with a single flick of the wrist.

This required stealth. And, perhaps, the trickster god doing what he did best.

I indicated for Eu-meh to take us down. She landed on the sidewalk down below, and we all slid off her back on touch-down. "Stay close?" She bobbed her head.

We were going in. We'd come to a boxy medical building. The sign on the front read *Caduceus Medical Associates*. The door to the foyer was locked, of course, and while there was a security desk, I couldn't see anyone behind it to let us in. But locked doors meant nothing to Hermes. The doors that wouldn't even budge for me opened wide for him. I took a look at the directory on the wall, focusing especially on the fifth floor. There was just one company there, a medical lab.

"Of course," I said. "Even working together, Panacea and Asclepius will probably have to test their cures or their dispersal methods. Hecate must have hijacked an office."

Not hard, I was sure, considering that all nonessential personnel had probably been kept home by the state of emergency. Or maybe there was more to it than that. Hecate was a healer herself when she wanted to be. For all I knew, she owned the place or a share in it.

"Okay, so we know where," Nick said beside me. "What about how?"

"I'm going to call her out," I answered, giving him the look that he'd given me earlier, the one that said I wouldn't be swayed.

"You can't," he said. "She'll slaughter you."

"Thanks for your vote of confidence," I said wryly.

"I mean—"

"I know what you mean. Right now, I look like something the cat dragged in. I feel like it too. She's going to think the same way. We've gone head-to-head several times already. In the shape I'm in, I suspect she'll be up for a final battle, winner take all."

"And if you don't win?" Apollo asked.

"You too?" I glared, but not with any real force. "It won't matter if I win or lose. While I've got her distracted, you all will be spiriting her hostages away."

"It matters to me," Apollo said, at the same time Hermes said, "Do you think she's dumb enough to fall for that?"

"I think she's arrogant. *And* I have absolute faith in my

ability to be annoying enough to get her to throw caution to the wind, especially if she already thinks she's won."

"She'll never be convinced you came alone," Nick said, leaving Apollo's comment behind.

"I've got it," Hermes said, snapping his fingers. "We've got a secret weapon. You." He was looking right at Nick, and I wasn't sure I liked the gleam in his eyes. "You're right. She'll suspect something. She'll assume Tori is a distraction. We'll give her exactly what she suspects. Apollo and I will sneak in to get Asclepius and Panacea out. *And we'll get caught.* Inevitably. She's expecting us, after all. When she or whatever minions she has are busy dealing with us, that's when you come into play. As long as she doesn't see you, she'll have no reason to expect you. You've been injured. Yes, healed, but you're *only human.* If she thinks of you at all, it won't be as a threat."

"You know, Hades's helmet of invisibility would help with this a whole helluva a lot," I said.

"Do you think he'd lend it out," Nick asked.

"Only one way to find out. Hermes, call him," I said, and he raised his brows at the order. "Give him the address. I'll go up now, though. Hera can't afford for us to wait. Follow me in five, with or without Hades and the helmet. I don't doubt that I can hold out at least that long."

Three men stared at me. I wanted to kiss them all good-bye ... just in case. Even Hermes, pain in my ass that he was. But ...

I went for the stairs. The elevator would ping and alert Hecate when I arrived, and while I wanted to challenge her, I didn't exactly want to alert her to any ambush potential.

I didn't run, knowing pounding steps would echo and be heard long before I hit the proper floor. But I didn't dawdle either. I went as quickly and as quietly as I could. On the landing, the door was going to make noise opening. It was unavoidable, but ... it opened onto the hallway outside of and across the hall from the lab's office door. No one was there to greet me. There were no windows onto the hallway from the lab so that I could see in and scope out the situation. Just blank industrial-white walls.

I tried the office door, but it wouldn't budge. I hadn't really expected it to. So I did the next best thing to opening the door myself ... I knocked and then pressed my ear to the door to see if I could hear anyone inside.

No one answered. I knocked again before I noticed a buzzer mounted on the wall beside the doorframe. I pressed the button. Waited. Pressed again.

"Hecate, I know you're in there. Don't make me huff and puff and blow this door down. You know we're just going to keep after you. How 'bout we settle this, here and now?" There was no answer, but I could feel her inside. We'd come to the right place.

She wasn't opening the door, even after I'd asked so nicely. I wouldn't have either, of course, but there's one thing I *would* have done. Only one visible way in, arrayed against a trickster god for whom locks were child's play ... I would have rigged the door.

I tested this against my precog, cursing that I had to even ask for it to tell, but right now the door was a passive threat. No doubt if I'd begun to open it, the alarms would have deafened me, but by then it would have been too late. The thought of bursting through the door set all of my nerves on fire and those alarm bells to ringing. Sure enough.

I retraced my steps, back to the lobby, where I met Apollo, Nick, and Hermes on their way up. I stopped them on the first-floor stairway. "There's no going through that front door. She's got it rigged to blow. We're going to have to go in through the windows."

Nick looked at me in alarm. "Are you sure they're not booby-trapped too?"

I tested that out in my head ... smashing through the windows like commandos on a mission ... My heart beat double-time, but it didn't threaten to burst.

"No," I said out loud. "She didn't get the windows. Change in plan. Nick, you head for the door. Rattle it, yell, make a fuss, but whatever you do, don't open it. It's locked anyway. I want her focused on that door, waiting for the explosion. If we're lucky, it'll take a second when the windows burst for her to realize it's not the explosion she was waiting for."

"Who's going to get everyone out?" Nick asked.

"We'll improvise."

BACK OUT ON the street I stuck my fingers in my mouth and gave a whistle, hoping Eu-meh would recognize it as a call. This would be so much easier if I spoke dragon. I expected her to come from the air, but she was already on the ground, just a block away, waiting. She was not nearly as graceful on land as in the air, but a beast that size doesn't have to take too many steps to get where she's going, and she was with us in no time.

The fifth floor, I tried to convey and mimed breaking in the windows. She looked at me steadily, blinked once and then sank down to the ground for us to climb aboard. I didn't know if she understood, but she'd gone where I guided her before. The smashing was going to be the tricky part.

We climbed onto her back and held each other. I gripped Eu-meh tightly as she sprang into the air. She circled away from the building first, to get momentum and height, and then aimed right where I directed her at the fifth-floor windows. She hit them head on. Even though I suspected they were hurricane glass, given their survival in the face of the storm that had passed, they shattered, tinted glass flying everywhere. She flapped and lowered her neck toward the floor for us to slide down.

I'd just hit the floor and looked around for something to use as a weapon when Hecate and two minions came running into the reception/office area we'd blown into. I recognized one of them, Thanatos, the god of death, whom I would have called Hades's right hand. But one of Sigyn's sigils glowed on his forehead, and I didn't think his heart and soul belonged to Hades at that moment. He looked a little less like the Grim Reaper this time, since his hood was pushed back and you could actually see his face with its prominent brow and even more prominent nose.

The other I didn't recognize—a woman, dark hair tightly coiled all around her head, wearing an outfit that looked like something out of Mad Max, all futuristic road warrior with spikes and leather, buckles and zippers going every which way, part of the badass-biker collection.

We were in an office. The closest thing I could find to a weapon was a letter opener that looked like a small bronze dagger. I grabbed it from the nearest desk, flicked it hard against my palm and drew blood. I was as ready as I was going to be. It was three on three. Except *her* three were armed.

"Eris, Thanatos, take them," Hecate ordered. "But the girl is mine."

Eris? As in the goddess of discord? Just what we needed.

Thanatos, of course, had his trademark huge honkin' sword. Eris swung something that looked like a nunchuk with a chain and spiky ball on the end. A mace? Truly?

They advanced on Apollo and Hermes and I wanted to jump in to save them, but I had problems of my own. Hecate was whirling the Sword of Perseus in front of me like I might be impressed. If I were Indiana Jones I'd have pulled out my gun and shot her in that moment. But all I had was my little letter opener. If I handled it right, that was all I needed. But with the size of her sword, she had reach on me, not to mention an actual honed blade. Even if Medusa's blood wouldn't have the desired effect on me, the weapon itself was enough to kill me dead.

I thrust my tiny dagger at her, hoping to catch her while she was showboating, but she was ready for me and parried without an effort. The impact of her blade with mine reverberated up my arms, but I didn't stop to appreciate the pain. I instantly dropped, tried to sweep a leg out from under her. She swung the blade down for me, but I'd whirled away and wasn't where she expected me to be. In fact, I was behind her, stomping down hard on the back of her knee to buckle it. She turned her forward fall into a roll. I thrashed down with the dagger again, but it only glanced off the leather of her jacket. Damned blunt piece of crap.

She pivoted as she came up, thrusting upward with her sword, and I had to jump to the side to avoid being skewered. It sliced through me anyway, just above my hip, missing anything major. Adrenaline flushed the pain away until I had time for it, and I fought the temptation to throw my dagger at her. It wasn't sharp enough to pierce without my force behind it, and if I lost it, I could kiss my ass goodbye. I had to maintain hold.

I feinted left, then went right as she raised her sword to block. It got me in under her reach and I sliced through the jacket right under her armpit. I struck flesh, but I didn't know if I drew blood before she dropped her arms down, knocking mine away, and then struck me in the collarbone hard with the hilt of her sword. I felt something crack, and this time the pain wouldn't be denied. It rippled through me with the force of one of Amphitrite's tsunamis and my arm holding the dagger-opener went numb.

I waited for Hecate to follow up with a killing blow and spun to face it, only to find her struggling, her skin taking on the grayish tint of stone. One side of her body had succumbed to the cut from my blood-tainted letter opener. The other half was still flesh, and she swung for me with the sword, but couldn't move properly. It was easy enough to dodge and to sink my little dagger into her other arm, grabbing for Perseus's sword before her hand could petrify around it.

Better armed now, I turned to help the others ... in time to see Hermes kick Eris out the window toward Eu-meh, who caught her in her claws and held her in place while she thrashed and struggled, her mace lost. Apollo had jumped out of Thanatos's way and thrust a chair into his gut. Thanatos, still under the spell of Sigyn's rune, didn't even seem to notice. He kept coming, something like the Terminator. I swung the sword once, getting the hang of it before I flew at Thanatos's back. He sensed me just before I hit and turned with his own sword, catching mine in midair and sending it back at me. I instantly changed the trajectory, sweeping for his leg, realizing as I swung that he was going for my neck and I wasn't going to be able to bring my blade up in time.

But angling in through the window, the sun suddenly flared, blaring hot, bright enough to burn out his eyes, and Thanatos hissed like a vampire in sunlight, recoiling from the pain, sword arm over his eyes as if it could belatedly protect him. My swing connected with his leg, and unlike with the dagger coated with my own blood, the full-on gorgon blood coating Perseus's sword stoned him on contact. It took an effort to yank the blade out again, he petrified so quickly. I felt like King Arthur, pulling the sword from the stone.

I looked around, unable to believe that it was over.

"What's going on?" a voice yelled from the doorway. "Let me in!"

It was Nick. Poor Nick, who'd missed all the action. Thank gods. He'd seen enough of it in Delphi and it had nearly killed him.

Hermes went to the door to check out the rigging and to

undo the booby trap and let Nick in. He spotted Eu-meh with her claws full of Eris, the three of us, not much the worse for wear, and the two new stone statues, and a huge smile broke out across his face. "Score one for the good guys."

"Panacea!" Apollo called. "Asclepius!"

A voice came scratchy over an intercom. "Hecate or whoever, come quick. This is amazing."

We followed Panacea's voice down a hallway, past several rooms and into a viewing area outside a sterile room reachable only by first going through a chemical shower, followed by a staging area and air locks. We opted to stay where we were, looking in through the thick glass.

Panacea held a vial aloft. It was filled with a pale yellow liquid that from her reaction I took to be as good as gold.

"Is that—" I asked in awe.

As I watched, she walked it over to one of a few gurneys in the room, this one holding a man with his arms strapped closely to his sides. His face was half-gone, and he was missing both his legs, stumps rough as if he'd been torn, literally limb from limb. Still, he was straining at his bonds, trying to get at Panacea, hunger in his eyes. It was grotesque and horrible, but none of us looked away as Panacea sucked some of the liquid into a tiny dropper and sprinkled it over the zombie-man.

He convulsed once, everything stiffening so that his back lifted straight off the gurney, and he collapsed back again, his whole body falling into a completely boneless state. Then, as we watched, his face seemed to ... regrow. His skin took back some of its vitality. And then ... and then the ragged stubs of his legs started to throb and ... I had to look away for fear that I'd be sick, even as I knew that this was a good thing. Very good. Asclepius was avidly watching the transformation, his face full of wonder and a kind of hunger.

A booming voice came from behind us, "I see you started without me."

I hushed Hades and pointed through the glass at the miracle going on inside. "Ah, Asclepius is up to his old tricks. Raising the dead."

I turned on Hades, meeting his hard gaze dead-on. "Healing the living," I said instead. "With Panacea's help. Healing the world. And unless you want the underworld truly overflowing with psycho zombie spirits, you're going to let him."

And for the second miracle of the day, Hades didn't have anything to say to that.

25

P anacea and Asclepius hadn't yet figured out a way to restore those who'd been turned to stone, but they were working on it. In the meantime, their miracle cure was a huge success. Asclepius knew how to raise the dead and Panacea knew how to heal them so that they were more than just the walking wounded. What she didn't know was how to do any of that en masse and at a distance. Alone she'd been strictly one touch/one healing. Together, they were dynamite. As in, all the gods were going to want to control or kill them. Add in Hera, who could take life as soon as give it, and Janus's Stasis Stone and ... well, if *that* cabal ever formed it would truly be the end of the world.

It had taken time and some of Nick's contacts in LA—which had mercifully survived Amphitrite's killer tidal wave, which had worn itself out before it got to shore when she turned her attention to New York—but we'd managed to locate next of kin for all of the kids from the hospital. The hardest part had been extricating a tearful Lacy from Nick, accomplished only after he pinky swore to keep in touch.

Nick reunited with his sister, who thanks to the miracle

cure had come back to herself with most of the horror forgotten. The time between leaving Nick's room at the hospital and regaining her humanity was lost to her. Probably for the best.

And then it was time for that talk I'd promised Nick when things settled down. They were as settled as they were going to be for a good while, while the world itself tried to heal and make sense of the absurd. Even with the miracle cure, not everyone made it back to the land of the living. There was death, destruction, families torn apart ...

I now stood with Nick in a room in the hotel we'd all retreated to in order to give Cori back her space. We'd already given her back her roommate. Melpomene had been one of those we'd been able to save.

We stared at each other across the bed, which stood between us like a wall. His eyes seemed tired and infinitely sad.

"Tori," he said finally, and I nearly sobbed hearing my name on his lips, knowing we were at goodbye.

"Hold on a minute," I answered.

I stepped around the bed, right into his personal space and gave him a hug. It was something I had to do, and I didn't know if he'd let me afterward. I hadn't meant to, but his warmth and the memory of ... everything that had been between us ... had me melting into him. Our bodies had always fit so well together. Now was no exception. He held me too, his arms wrapped tightly around me, his face buried in my hair. I breathed in the familiar tangy, spicy scent of his neck and tried not to want to kiss it. It would only confuse the issue and it wouldn't be fair to anyone involved.

I could have stayed there forever, but I had to step back and meet his gaze. Nick studied me back.

"Tori," he started again, "when I said ... those things ... I was in pain and on meds and not in my right mind."

"I know." I had to look away for an instant, but it was a cop-out and I didn't let it last. "But they were all true. I think that with your usual ornery-self suppressed, you were able to get to what's real. I love you," I said truthfully, "and I know you love me. And I think if we lived on a deserted island somewhere with no gods and grief, we could make it work ... until one of us went insane from the lack of adventure. But here, in the real world ... you're right. We live in different worlds. It's not that mine is too dangerous for you"—*though it is*, I thought—"it's that it's not yours."

There, I'd said it. The words had actually come and not gotten all garbled up between my head and my lips.

I waited with held breath to see what he'd say. I *did* love him. But I knew this was right. Even though I'd chosen Apollo, which had possibly always been a foregone conclusion, part of me was afraid that Nick would find just the right words to make things different. Or maybe I hoped it. Life with Armani would be trading one set of fears for another—the fear of losing him over the fear of losing myself. But love wasn't about fears or rationality or ... Well hell, if it were just about love, we could just make a threesome and be done with it. Well, okay, maybe not.

Finally, Nick let out the breath I'd been holding. That's what it felt like anyway. On the exhale he said, so quietly that I barely caught it, "I know. But it hurts. Should the right thing be this hard? Doesn't that mean it's the wrong thing? Shouldn't love conquer all and crap like that?"

We looked into each other's eyes, and Nick cracked a smile first. It was tainted with sadness, but still.

"Did you really just ask me about love conquering all?" I asked.

"Yeah. I did. Don't mention it around the station, would you?"

Because Nick would be going back to LA, back to work as a police detective, and I ... guessed I'd be going back as well. Sooner or later. Not right away. I needed to go back to the Grey

Sisters, learn what to do with my wings. I needed time and distance. Nick probably needed that as well. Because our paths *were* going to cross. As the Fates would say, our weave was too intricately linked for things to be otherwise.

"Promise," I answered.

"One last kiss?" he asked.

I knew it was a bad idea. Knew it with every fiber of my being. And not a one of those fibers gave a damn. We'd never truly had our breakup ... until now. We hadn't had the chance to do that awkward dance. The will-we/won't-we of getting back together. We still weren't going to get that. Not with Apollo in the picture. It would be cleaner. Easier. Yeah, easier.

I nodded, and when he stepped toward me, I tilted my head up to meet him. Instead of wrapping me in his arms and pulling me in for some film kiss meant to drive home how the hell we shouldn't be breaking up in the first place, he cupped my chin in his hands and brought his lips down to meet mine. It was so sweet and so ... not enough. Not after all we'd been through.

Regardless of Apollo waiting in the wings, it all came flooding back. Our flirtation, Nick showing up at my door with pizza, fighting alongside me at the La Brea Tar Pits and at Dionysus's compound in Napa and ... It swamped me, dragged me under. I fought back to the surface just as he was pulling away.

There was a determined tapping at the door. "Everything all right in there?" Apollo called through it. He could sense my every mood through that link of ours, and right now I cursed it. At least he hadn't burst in. I suppose that was restraint.

"Go to hell," Nick said. "You get her—" he stumbled over the next part, "—when I'm gone. But for now, this is our time."

I could feel Apollo outside the door. Fear and love and something like hatred warring right then. It was dangerous. The myths and legends were full of what happened when someone flouted Apollo's will. And yet, this was what I was getting myself into, trusting he'd changed. In a way, this was a test.

He walked away from the door. I didn't exactly give a sigh of relief—if I hadn't trusted in his restraint, I wouldn't be sticking around—but maybe I did breathe a little easier.

"But why did it have to be *him*?" Nick asked. So he knew. It wasn't like I'd been trying to keep it from him, but Apollo and I hadn't exactly flaunted anything either, respecting that I had to wait for the right time to tell him.

"I don't know," I said. "It just does."

"You know I'm always here for you," he said.

My heart felt like it was breaking. He was such an incredible person. Why couldn't it be *him*?

"I know," I answered.

"I lied," he said, sweeping in for one last kiss.

HE WAS GONE before my lips stopped tingling, and Apollo stood in the doorway, puffed up like a cat whose fur someone had rubbed the wrong way.

"Is it over?" he asked, not setting foot inside the room while he waited for my answer. I knew he didn't just mean our farewell.

"It is," I said, sadly. "Are you okay?"

I looked into Apollo's eyes, fell into them. We had the all-clear now. Nothing between us.

IT WAS SCARY AS HELL.

I nodded and added, "Just hold me for a while?"

The door to the hallway opened and closed. Nick was gone.

Apollo took a deep breath as though it were his first in a while and came to me, taking my hand and leading me over to the bed, where he lay me down and tucked me against him. He held me, and I readjusted to the feel of his arms around me, his heat reaching out, the beat of his heart against my hand resting on his chest. *See*, I thought to myself, *we can be domestic.* It was nice. Comfortable. Amazing, after all we'd been through.

And after a while, Apollo's hand that had only been soothing, stroking my hair, stroked lower, and I rolled to give him access to other areas and nice could no longer begin to describe it.

Magical. Amazing ... Addictive.

ABOUT THE AUTHOR

Lucienne Diver does not actually come from circus folk, though you'd never know it to meet her family. She is, however, in no particular order, a wife, mother, literary agent, book addict, sun-worshipper, mythology enthusiast, travel-junkie and crazy person. In addition to the *Latter-Day Olympians* series, she writes the *Vamped* young adult novels (*Vamped, Revamped, Fangtastic, Fangtabulous* and *Fangdemonium*) as well as YA suspense. Her short stories have appeared in the *Strip-Mauled* and *Fangs for the Mammaries* anthologies edited by Esther Friesner (Baen Books) and *Kicking It* edited by Faith Hunter and Kalayna Price (Roc). Her essay "Abuse" is included in the anthology *Dear Bully: Seventy Authors Tell Their Stories* (HarperTeen).

More information can be found on her website at www.luciennediver.com. You can also follow her on Twitter @luciennediver.

IF YOU LIKED …

IF YOU LIKED BATTLE FOR THE BLOOD, YOU MIGHT
ALSO ENJOY:

Blood Hunt
by Lucienne Diver

Taste Like Chicken
by Kevin J. Anderson

The Love-Haight Case files
by Jean Rate and Donald J. Bingle

OTHER WORDFIRE PRESS TITLES BY LUCIENNE DIVER

Bad Blood

Crazy in the Blood

Rise of the Blood

Blood Hunt

Our list of other WordFire Press authors and titles is always growing. To find out more and to see our selection of titles, visit us at:
wordfirepress.com